ALSO BY
BRIANA McDONALD

Pepper's Rules for Secret Sleuthing

THE SECR
STONE

THE SECRETS OF STONE CREEK

BRIANA McDONALD

SIMON & SCHUSTER BOOKS FOR YOUNG READERS
New York London Toronto Sydney New Delhi

To Melissa, my greatest adventure yet

SIMON & SCHUSTER BOOKS FOR YOUNG READERS
An imprint of Simon & Schuster Children's Publishing Division
1230 Avenue of the Americas, New York, New York 10020

This book is a work of fiction. Any references to historical events, real people, or real places are used fictitiously. Other names, characters, places, and events are products of the author's imagination, and any resemblance to actual events or places or persons, living or dead, is entirely coincidental.

Interior design by Tom Daly
The text for this book was set in Adobe Caslon Pro.
Manufactured in China
0722 SCP
First Edition
2 4 6 8 10 9 7 5 3 1
Library of Congress Cataloging-in-Publication Data
Names: McDonald, Briana, author.
Title: The secrets of Stone Creek / Briana McDonald.
Description: New York : Simon & Schuster Books for Young Readers, [2022] | Audience: Ages 8–12 | Audience: Grades 4–6 | Summary: After losing her best friend and feeling overlooked by family members, Finley decides to prove herself by finding a missing woman in the remote tourist town of Stone Creek, but after convincing her brothers to help her, Finley discovers she may be in over her head.
Identifiers: LCCN 2022002384 | ISBN 9781534498266 (hardcover) | ISBN 9781534498280 (ebook)
Subjects: CYAC: Adventure and adventurers—Fiction. | Missing persons—Fiction. | Brothers and sisters—Fiction. | Friendship—Fiction. | LCGFT: Novels.
Classification: LCC PZ7.1.M434353 Se 2022 | DDC [Fic]—dc23
LC record available at https://lccn.loc.gov/2022002384

GREATEST FEMALE ADVENTURER NUMBER ONE: JUNKO TABEI, WHO NOT ONLY WAS THE FIRST WOMAN TO REACH THE SUMMIT OF MOUNT EVEREST, BUT THE FIRST WOMAN TO CLIMB THE HIGHEST PEAKS OF ALL SEVEN CONTINENTS.

Mom pulls the car over, wheel bumping against the curb. For the first time in over three hours, she cuts the engine. "We're here."

I watched the trees fly by as we drove, waiting for the moment the forest broke to reveal the small but lively town I envisioned Stone Creek to be. But the winding route the GPS led us down has consisted of small auto shops, rickety and abandoned buildings, apartments with broken shutters, and a whole lot of nothing else. I kept searching for the perfect photo op, the perfect image to send Sophie to make her wish she'd decided to spend April break here with me, like we'd originally planned. But every picture I took was nothing but a blur of green trees, and it wasn't like she'd bothered texting me anyway.

With the car finally stopped, I stir like I'm waking from a dream. Maybe, somehow, this little patch of civilization in the middle of the woods will be infinitely more interesting than the last hundred miles proved to be. I lean over my eight-year-old brother, Griffin, despite his whines and protests, and press my nose against the car window. Beyond the fog of my breath is a small, weather-beaten wooden building. The red paint of its front door is chipped, and a rusty sign swings overhead: MEGGIE'S CUP.

"Who's Meggie?" I ask. "His long-lost lover? Estranged wife?"

Mom shoots me a glare through the rearview mirror. "Be nice. Jeff is being very kind by letting you stay with him while I'm at the conference."

"Yeah," Oliver, my thirteen-year-old brother, grumbles from where he's slumped in the front seat. "Too kind."

Mom sighs, eyes flickering back toward me. All I can offer her is a shrug because, for once, my older brother isn't overreacting. "It is pretty weird."

"It's not weird," Mom snaps, pushing her car door open. "It's what family does: help each other out in times of need."

I'd never thought of Mom's cousin Jeff as family. He's never been more than another Christmas card on the mantel. And not the nice kind with glitter, pop-up snowmen, and long scribbled notes about how their year went. His always had some Hallmark one-liner like "Season's Greetings," followed by his name—printed, not signed.

I'm also not so sure about the whole "helping family

in need" thing. I glance at Griffin, who's chugging the last of the soda I begged Mom to buy me at the last rest stop. Then Oliver, who's still pretending to listen to Spotify even though we lost service over thirty minutes ago.

I noticed we lost service right away. I was refreshing Sophie's feed over and over again for photos of her April break. At the top, with over fifty likes, was the photo of her posing outside of Busch Gardens with our seventh-grade classmates Veronica and Chloe, wearing matching heart-shaped glasses. Her nose was already burning, a red splotch over her giant grin. When we hang out—used to hang out—I was always the one to remember sunscreen. Veronica and Chloe don't burn like we do, so by the end of her trip, she's going to be a giant, neon-red raisin.

Not that I care. Because I don't. Because my vacation is going to be better. No matter how quiet and remote and weird and mosquito-infested the town oh-so-cleverly titled "Stone Creek" turns out to be, I'm going to make sure Sophie wishes she'd chosen to spend break here, with me, rather than with those other girls on a trip only one of us was invited to.

The future of the Walsh-Higgins Adventure Agency depends on it. Sophie Higgins is half the agency, after all. Always has been since we first cofounded our adventure duo back in first grade, when we found our first copy of *100 of the World's Greatest Female Adventurers* at the elementary school library. We decided we'd be adventurers One Hundred One and One Hundred Two: so brave and daring and courageous that no matter what happened—from my parents' divorce in first grade, to her mother's chemo in fourth—the world could never forget us. We searched for adventures in our suburban town in Massachusetts, and when they ran out, we'd make up adventures of our own—always moving, always exploring, always in brave pursuit of the truth.

Long before Veronica and Chloe came along and invited her to join them on their fancy April break trip. Back when it was just us.

I climb over Griffin to get out of the car, ignoring his shouts of protest as I wedge myself past him and onto the sidewalk. Mom is either too tired to deal with us or doesn't notice, head bent into the trunk as she reaches for our luggage. I stretch in front of the café, muscles aching from the three-hour drive from Massachusetts to Vermont. As I look up and down the deserted street, everything looks the same: old, weather-worn buildings with musty windows and overgrown lawns, with no more than two cars parked out front.

Oliver appears beside me, back leaning against the car. "Who would ever choose to live out here?"

He doesn't look at me as he asks, as if the question was for the humid air around us. I resist the urge to stomp hard on his foot to get him to acknowledge me. I've considered it a few times at school, when he passes in the hall with his eighth-grade friends and ducks his blond head as though I'm just another laminated poster on the wall.

But I always grit my teeth and steady my heel against the tiles, because no matter what Oliver thinks about me now—that I'm annoying, or embarrassing, or whatever he's made up as an excuse to ignore me—he'll have to take me seriously once Sophie and I are world-renowned adventurers. She may not be here now, but I'll make sure our stay in Stone Creek is chock-full of history-making escapades. Otherwise, she'll have been right in choosing Veronica and Chloe and Busch Gardens over me. And Oliver will keep turning up his nose each time he sees me—until I achieve something great and finally prove him wrong.

"We'll make it fun," I say with determination.

Step one: survey the area. Being a great adventurer means knowing where to look. Sophie and I learned that early, since our suburban town doesn't exactly lend itself to adventure naturally. We have to create our own missions, just like the women from *100 of the World's Greatest Female Adventurers*. No one invited Bessie Coleman to be the first-ever African American pilot. She had to move all the way to France to learn how to fly, and it's that kind of stubborn determination and love for adventure that makes history.

I squint against the afternoon sun, toward the half-lit store signs and splintery signposts down the road. I scan the shop names, reading them aloud under my breath. "'Meggie's 24/7-ish Diner' . . . 'Meggie's Food 'N' Fuel' . . ." Then Stone Creek Library, which seems normal enough. Until it's followed by Meggie's Realty.

I cup my hand over my eyes. There's no way I'm reading

these right. And yet there they are—all worn down, their walls speckled with graffiti and parking lots cratering with potholes. I almost take out my phone to snap a photo, but it's too soon to text Sophie, and I don't have service anyway.

"I guess Meggie was everyone's long-lost lover," I joke.

But whoever Meggie is, she must have been pretty incredible to get all these shops named after her. I don't recognize her name from my book, but a flare of excitement rises in my chest at the thought of discovering who she is.

Oliver rolls his eyes. "There's no way everyone was in love with the same girl. Some people don't even . . ."

His voice trails off, and he kicks a piece of gravel loose with the toe of his sneaker.

I continue to study the signs, straining to read the name of what looks like a pet shop at the end of the street. "Don't even what?"

Oliver shakes his head and stands upright. "She probably helped found this town, like, a million years ago. It's not that interesting."

I think it is, but arguing that won't convince him. I'm just glad I brought the Walsh-Higgins Adventure Agency business cards when I packed. Even if Sophie's not with me for this week's adventure, if I can show her what she's missing out on, we can work together on the next one. And all the ones after that.

"Come on," Mom calls, standing by the trunk surrounded by our suitcases. "Help me wheel these inside."

We grab our respective suitcases and drag them across

the uneven sidewalk. "Are we staying in Jeff's café?" I ask.

Now, that would be an adventure.

"No, we're just leaving your things here until Jeff closes shop and can take you to his place." My chest falls. "We're interrupting his workday, but he's being very understanding so I don't miss my flight to Chicago."

As though summoned by her words, the bell hanging from the café door jingles and a man climbs down to the front step. He wears a faded flannel shirt rolled up to his elbows, thick jeans worn white at the knees, and a baseball cap pulled a bit too far over his forehead, its off-white bill pointing out toward the street. Mom mentioned he was about her age, but with speckles of gray in his stubble and a few tired lines beneath his eyes, he looks older than her. And older than Dad looked the last time I saw him, when he dropped off presents on Christmas before he headed back to his apartment in New York.

Jeff's skin looks dry from one too many sunburns, and though he stands tall in the doorway, his shoulders are angled at an uncertain slump and his eyes flicker quickly between us, like he's not sure where to look, or what he's looking at.

Mom makes the first move, stepping forward with her arms extended. "Jeff, it's so good to see you!" She gathers him in a stiff embrace, not fully touching as they softly pat each other's backs. "It's been too long."

Long enough for me to barely remember the last time I saw her cousin Jeff. We used to travel up to Maine and

Vermont to visit Mom's family, back when Griffin was in diapers and Oliver wasn't too cool to be my playmate. I never thought much about why we stopped visiting, or what happened to Mom's cousins and uncles and aunts and their kids.

It didn't start until a few years after Dad left. It was like Mom was running on overdrive for the first years after the divorce, determined to ensure our family still felt complete, as if Dad had never been there in the first place. The way he left—packing all his things neatly in a duffel bag, agreeing to a few weekends with us a month before kissing us goodbye at the bus station—it really did feel like it had been just the four of us all along. Mom, working overtime and weekends. Me, distracting Griffin with games and playing the role of homework police. Oliver, keeping tabs to make sure I followed Mom's laundry list of rules and didn't fall out of line. But eventually, it was as if her fuel ran out, and suddenly she was running on fumes. Relying on Oliver more to manage us. Exhausted by the smallest things I'd do, like trekking sand into the house after an adventure with Sophie on the beach. That's when she started to spend more time on Facebook, hunting down relatives like Jeff and reminiscing over Messenger into the late hours of the evening.

I wondered why we ever stopped talking to them, expecting some deep family secret, some dramatic explanation that could fuel my next adventure with Sophie. "I just got so busy with you kids," Mom would say when I asked, and I'd feel that pang again, because without knowing it, I'd done something wrong. Taken her attention, her time, her energy. Consumed the world around her until there was nothing by the time Dad moved on to his next life, leaving her trapped in a bubble with us.

With me. And so far, I haven't accomplished anything great enough for the me part of it to be good enough to make up for everything else Mom's gone through.

Mom releases Jeff and steps aside so we're standing, staring at him, in plain view.

He clears his throat, loud and clanky like a garbage disposal.

"Hey, kids," he says, words slow. "I'm Jeff. And this is Malt." He crooks his neck toward the shop. "Hey, Malt! Come here."

A tiny white dog scampers past his boots, wagging his stubby tail in response to the call. Griffin kneels down and scratches behind his floppy ears. A pink tongue dangles happily from the dog's mouth.

Oliver's upper lip curls. "Malt . . . the Maltese?"

Jeff nods matter-of-factly. "Yep."

A giant grin sweeps across my face. "I love it."

"Of course you do," Oliver mumbles, and I jab him quickly with my elbow.

Jeff wiggles the doorknob back and forth in his hand. We all stand, looking at one another as though waiting for a sign of what to say next.

Jeff inhales a steading breath. “Well, no use hovering by the stairs. Let’s get you and your things inside.”

Mom leads the way up to the door and we follow, suitcase wheels smacking against the stone steps. Malt scampers through between my legs, and I’m greeted by thick, humid air and the overwhelming smell of burnt coffee. Sweat immediately beads at the back of my neck, and I imagine that Sophie is about to board a water ride. My stomach does an angry somersault and I shake the thought away, taking in my new surroundings.

I haven’t been to many coffee shops—Mom doesn’t even give me tea without supervision—but there’s a café in our town where Sophie and I would go sometimes after soccer practice for smoothies and almond croissants. The walls were decorated with antique clocks and splatter paintings, and there was a shelf in the back dedicated to a take-a-book-leave-a-book program.

But Jeff’s café is unlike anything I’ve seen before. It’s small—almost too small for all five of us and Jeff’s dog to stand comfortably between the mismatched tables and chairs. But, more important, every inch of the three walls facing the front counter is decorated with nothing but framed newspaper clippings. All sizes, black and white or color. Front page all the way down to a clipping of just a few paragraphs by the edge of an ad. The headlines stare at me in big, bold print, as though calling to be read, desperate to be heard.

**TWENTY-THREE-YEAR-OLD MEGGIE RILEY
LAST SEEN IN STONE CREEK WOODS**

**FAMILY OFFERS $100,000 REWARD
FOR MISSING DAUGHTER**

**SUSPECT RELEASED IN CASE OF MISSING WOMAN
FAMOUS FOR DISCOVERING THE "STONE CREEK TREASURE"**

There are too many to read—at least this fast—but one name stands out in all of them: Meggie Riley.

As in the Meggie of Meggie's Cup, Meggie's 24/7-ish Diner, Meggie's Food 'N' Fuel, and probably every other business in Stone Creek.

Sophie and I once spent an entire sleepover watching terrible Bigfoot documentaries on her laptop, ducking under the covers each time we heard her parents come upstairs. We'd joke about towns built around old myths, wonder how many tourists really came each year that justified every motel and pizza joint being named after him. We'd laugh at how boring it would be for the Walsh-Higgins Adventure Agency to have only one local adventure to pursue.

Right now, as I'm surrounded by Meggie Riley, "boring" is the last word I'd use. I'm not sure what other word I would, so I just crane my neck and stare, jaw loose, at the articles plastering the room like a strange wallpaper. But something flutters in my chest, and I know right away that I need to find out.

Especially because of that third headline. "Discover" is a code word for adventuring. And when you're famous for making a discovery, that usually means you're a legend, like the women in my book. But I've never heard of Meggie Riley or the Stone Creek Treasure, which could mean the headline is misleading.

Or that I, too, am on the cusp of a great discovery.

"It's safe, I promise," Mom says, fast, like she was prepared for this moment. "This whole thing with the disappearance was almost twenty years ago, and there hasn't been any major crime since."

"Tell that to Anne Thornton," Jeff grumbles, as if we know who she is. "Woman's called the police every time I've had to raise my coffee prices."

"The family still lives in town," Mom says to us, low and serious like a confession, "but Jeff says they're very nice people, and they keep to themselves, and I hope you'll respect their privacy. They've gone through an enormous amount of pain over the years, and the way people sensationalize their tragedy surely hasn't helped."

Oliver and I exchange a silent glance. For some reason, he decides to voice our thoughts out loud. "Isn't this café sensationalizing it?"

Mom gapes like a fish about to blow a bubble. But Jeff looks indifferent, like he's gotten this question a million times before. "They love that we sensationalized it," he says with a wave of his hand. "They basically invented this"—he gestures to the decor—"themselves. They're the ones who advertised that insanely high reward and attracted every Nancy Drew and Hardy Boy in the Northeast to this town."

"Which I can understand," Mom says, fiddling with the strap of her purse. "They'd do anything to get back their little girl."

I scan the walls, studying the photos of Meggie. Most are photos of her as an adult, tight blond curls puffing around her head and a spattering of brown freckles over the bridge of her nose. In some she's posing with a graying man who must be her father, both wearing suits. My stomach sinks, thinking that whatever she discovered was probably just some boring old invention that made her family a ton of money.

That is, until I spot one article featuring an image of her as a girl. I can tell it's still Meggie from her tightly coiled blond hair and spattering of light-brown freckles. But in some ways, she looks like a totally different person. As a girl, she has a wide, sweeping grin, different from the stern, flat look she has in the business photos with her dad. Her shoulders are sunburned, her tank top stained with dirt and sand. Band-Aids cover scuffs on her elbows, similar to the ones I always have to slap on after collecting scratches on an adventure.

There are photos from after her disappearance too: a mother and father with thick bags under their eyes, speaking to a reporter. Heads bent down as they rush from the police station to a car. Tears lining her sisters' cheeks as they beg readers to come forward with any clues. I watch the years pass in the photos. Years of perseverance, of hope. All because they wanted her back so badly.

In the photos of her as a kid, she doesn't look too different from me—other than her chunky headband and the outdated jeans that flare below her knees, that is. But she has to have something special—be something special—for an entire town to care this deeply about rescuing her.

I wonder what it is. If, through these snapshots, I too could learn it. I stare at the frames and posters, eyes wide as gumballs. "What's the Stone Creek Treasure? And do they have any leads on where she went?" I ask, my voice getting louder with each word. "Do you have any theories?"

"Finley!"

Mom has a way of calling my name that makes me shut up fast. I've often wished it worked the same on Griffin.

"Just curious," I say, much quieter this time.

Jeff shrugs in response. "Folk around here all have their theories. I've heard everything and anything you could imagine over the years." The first hint of a smile appears at the corner of his mouth. "At this point, I'd welcome any new ones."

Mom shoots him a glare that's like the silent version of her "Finley."

Griffin doesn't seem to notice. "Aliens!"

Jeff shakes his head. "Heard it."

Griffin considers. "Aliens . . . in a flying pirate ship!"

I smile. This would have been perfect for the Walsh-Higgins Adventure Agency. My back pocket bulges with our business cards. I can almost feel them stirring, wanting to fly out and into Jeff's hands. He could tell me all the facts the locals and tourists collected over the years, and I'd develop a gutsy action plan to finally turn their investigation into a real rescue mission. I'd video Sophie and share my plan to confront the kidnapper and save Meggie from wherever they've been hiding her for nearly two decades. Sophie would convince her mom to drive her up here from Busch Gardens. Together, we'd be like Greatest Female Adventurer Number Forty-Six, Admiral Michelle Howard, who led a rescue mission for a captain captured by real-life pirates. We'd be local heroes, with our names printed right next to Meggie's on the store signs, and—in its next reprint—awarded the labels "Greatest Female Adventurers Numbers One Hundred One and One Hundred Two."

Everyone would have to take me seriously then.

"This is super creepy," Oliver says. His arms are crossed over his chest, and his eyebrows furrow as he studies the newspaper clippings.

My stomach drops. Who am I kidding? If I sent a photo of this place to Sophie, she'd probably react the same way. And even if she felt even the slightest pull in her chest, drawing her back to the adventure agency, the second she showed my message to Chloe or Veronica, they'd talk it right out of her.

My cheeks burn. It's as if I can hear them laughing at me, clear, as though they were standing here in the room. Clear, as though I was back in the cafeteria, barely fitting on the end of our bench as Chloe and Veronica swallowed the space around me. As Sophie forgot I was there.

Maybe I'd prefer she laughed at me. At least then I'd know she still noticed me at all.

Mom swats Oliver's arm. "Don't be rude. Jeff is being extremely generous by letting you stay here."

Jeff scratches the back of his head and glances to the side. Either he's regretting his generosity or he is bad at accepting thanks. Considering how empty his tip jar is, I hope it's the latter.

"Generous enough to let me raid the pastry case?" Griffin asks, eyes wide and hopeful.

Mom opens her mouth to object, but Jeff almost looks relieved. "Go ahead, kid." He nods his head so the bill of his cap points toward the case. "Half that crap is stale anyway."

Mom shoots him her classic Mom Glare. I've been on the receiving end of that one before and can't help a sympathetic shudder.

"Junk," he says as Griffin peels around the counter. "Half that junk is stale."

Griffin whips open the case and grabs two cinnamon buns in one greedy palm. Oliver rolls his eyes toward me. "Great, now he's going to be sugar high, too."

Mom and Jeff stand, awkwardly shifting and opening and closing their mouths like they're not sure what comes next. It reminds me of the first few times Dad called after he left. How I'd mentally beg Oliver to get off the phone, just to clam up once he finally gave me my turn.

"I've got it from here, Em," Jeff says, shoulders raised in a way that makes it look like he's definitely not got it. I know Oliver's thinking the same thing by the way he stares holes into Mom's back, as though begging her not to go.

I, on the other hand, am ready for what comes next. While she hovers in the center of the shop, eyes scanning the three of us one by one as though she's mentally herding us like sheep, I'm counting down the seconds until it's just us and Cousin Jeff. The fact that he's letting Griffin dig into his third cinnamon roll in sixty seconds means he has no idea what he's in for. Which means I can get away with anything once Mom's gone.

Like reopening the Walsh-Higgins Adventure Agency for its first solo mission.

Mom inhales a steadying breath, then extends her arms like wings. Her fingers bend back and forth, ushering us toward her. "Come here, kids."

Griffin barrels into her open arms, wrapping his sticky fingers around her skirt. Oliver lingers, eyes fixed on the frame behind Mom's head. I move toward her, pushing him into her arms with me.

We tangle together, Griffin's short hair scratching my cheek, Mom's chin digging into my scalp, and Oliver's arms pressed stiffly against my side. Just before I close my eyes, I catch Jeff watching us, eyes focused and lips parted. I can't imagine there's anything interesting about this awkward mess of a group hug, and can't help but wonder how—in a town as interesting as this—Jeff manages to bore himself into thinking we're the most interesting thing in this shop.

I'm ready to pull away as soon as I can, get on to my new adventure. But my fingers clasp around the fabric of her shirt and I huddle closer, taking in the lavender scent of her perfume.

"Okay, we get it, we'll miss you too," Oliver grumbles against Mom's shoulder. "But it's way too hot in here for long hugs."

Something furry brushes my ankle. "And I think Malt is getting jealous."

Mom kisses the tops of our heads, oldest to youngest so Oliver doesn't have time to object. "Okay. But promise me you won't give Jeff any trouble."

"If you don't want to cause him trouble, you'll take both of them with you," Oliver whispers, as though seriously hopeful she'll say yes.

I wrap my arms around Griffin's shoulders so he's standing snuggled in front of me. "You can go, Oliver. We're staying."

"Ollie can't go!" Griffin whines, stirring in my arms. "He's going to take me hiking in the woods! We're going to catch salamanders and build a tree fort."

He twists around, glancing up at me so his icing-glazed mouth comes into full, horrifying view. "And I guess you can come too, Finley."

I shove him away. "Thanks for the afterthought, Griffin."

Mom turns to Jeff, looking ready to thank him again.

He glances between her and the door, and she tightens her lips. She turns to go, and the air in the room shifts as though ready to settle into its next scene: Griffin running back around the counter, Jeff leaning down to scratch Malt behind the ears, me edging toward the wall, closer to the newspaper clippings. But just as she moves toward the door, car keys already in her hand, I see her turn and hear her murmur to Oliver: "Take care of them, okay?"

Oliver's arms go tense at his sides. But I know all Mom sees is his nod and smile. "I will."

With a jingle of the cowbell dangling from the shop door, she's gone.

Mom doesn't know that I overhear everything—that it's part of my job as cofounder of the Walsh-Higgins Adventure Agency. Always knowing what's going on—from which teacher is hiding a pop quiz we need to uncover like a missing treasure, to which classmate is willing to gamble their lunch money in a kickball match—is part of being Finley Walsh. But she always acts like I don't hear anything, don't see anything. Like I'm some kid who can't handle the truth. Can't even handle myself.

As if her saying "Your dad is just busy" will stop me from hearing their late-night arguments on the phone about canceled visits and missed holidays. As if saying "You don't need to worry" will mean I won't notice the way she flinches when the cashier rings up the cost for my new clothes. As if "You can do anything you set your mind to, honey" could ever be words I'll believe, when it's

Oliver she always goes to when she needs something real.

His eyes catch mine and I look away, staring hard at the newspaper clipping as though it's the most interesting thing I've seen in my life. Which, to be fair, it probably is.

MISSING WOMAN is the core phrase connecting all the clippings, but I'm drawn to the ones that talk about her as a girl, that version of her that seems so similar to me. Most of the articles use her younger photos next to the ones from when she disappeared as an adult, with just a vague mention of the "Stone Creek Treasure." But one of them—an older article, yellowed with age but well-preserved, with a frame—details the discovery of the Stone Creek Treasure, long before her disappearance.

12-YEAR-OLD MEGGIE RILEY UNCOVERS "STONE CREEK TREASURE"

Meggie Riley, the oldest of Robert and Maria Riley's three daughters, said she was "in search of adventure" when she set out into the Stone Creek Woods with four classmates last Saturday. As the weather worsened, fallen branches and rising water from the creek obstructed the children's paths. Meggie continued to lead her classmates forward, toward the northern end of the Stone Creek Woods.

This area, referred to by locals as a "dense no-man's-land," is one parents tell their children to avoid—including the Rileys. Whether afraid of consequences from their parents,

> the storm, or the woods itself, four of the children decided to turn back. Meggie, however, continued forward and made an independent discovery that would change her family forever.
>
> With the rain loosening the soil, Meggie was able to dig and uncover a series of high-value antiques that had been buried decades before. Despite the worsening weather, Meggie worked through the storm to retrieve the items, which would later be appraised and valued at tens of thousands of dollars.

I stop there, because Oliver's reading over my shoulder now, eyebrows pinched together so there's a small wrinkle over his nose. "So everyone's obsessed with her because she dug some trash out of a mud pile as a kid?"

I stomp on his foot and he lets out a quiet yelp. "You're reading it wrong on purpose," I say. Because how could that be what he gets out of the article? What I'm reading paints the image of a young adventurer, just like me and Sophie, but one who went on to make a real discovery. Who ran into the unforgiving wilderness and forged ahead even when all of her classmates turned back to safety.

"That trash was worth thousands," I say, gesturing to the article. "It's obvious her dad and her were super successful. I'm sure all that money helped. I bet her friends regret not following her into the woods. They could have been rich too."

Oliver would have been one of those four kids who turned back—if he came in the first place, that is. I want him to agree that those kids made a mistake by ignoring Meggie's call to adventure. That they should have followed her into the woods that day, just like Sophie should have chosen Stone Creek—chosen me—over Busch Gardens.

But, as usual, he barely looks at me and just shrugs. "She's just lucky a tree didn't fall on her, or she didn't end up sunk in the mud with all those antiques," he says. "And if everyone was angry enough that she got the money instead of them, it could have put a target on her back."

He gestures to one of the other headlines before walking away: **VALIDITY OF RUNAWAY NOTE ALLEGEDLY LEFT BY VICTIM BROUGHT INTO QUESTION**.

In the reflection in the glass, I see my mouth hang in awe. If Meggie left a runaway note, she may be missing because she doesn't want to be found. Looking at the photos of her as a kid compared to the one of her and her father in the office, I can see how much happier she was outside, on the brink of adventure. I imagine she escaped the dull day-to-day office life and ran off into the wilderness to go out in the world and experience it—scary and dangerous and risky and fun—just like I want to do someday.

If I found her, I'd be meeting a real-life adventurer, just like the women in my book, but even better—because she became great when she was my age. That means that if I found her, she could teach me how to be great, even as I am now.

But that's not all: as much as I love the idea of a restless Meggie escaping her white-collar life for one of adventure, there's the possibility the runaway note is fake, too. If it is a fake, that means her kidnapper could have forged it to distract the detectives.

If Meggie isn't a runaway, that means she was taken by someone and needs to be rescued. And if I found her, not only would I be able to meet a famous explorer, but I'd be a hero, too. Then Sophie would definitely want to rejoin the adventure agency—to be like Meggie, not like the kids who left her behind. And maybe Mom would take me more seriously too, the way Stone Creek looks up to Meggie.

I scan the headlines, hungrily searching for more information on this real-life adventurer who was here, in the same town I'm in now. One of the framed papers, hung back in the corner of the café, has a giant headline that consumes almost half the front page: **FOUL PLAY SUSPECTED OF FAMILY IN CASE OF MISSING WOMAN.**

I blink up at the headline, lips parting in shock. What family would put out an enormous, sensational reward for a missing girl they didn't want anyone to find? And how bonkers must this case be for even the parents to be suspects? Parents who still live here, in this town, searching for her to this day?

The buzzing questions in my head scatter when Jeff clears his throat and Malt releases a high-pitched bark in response. I whip around, so fast my ponytail slaps the frame and sends it swinging on its hook. I'm already sucking in a deep breath, ready to shout out a hundred excuses or say, "No, I wasn't reading that," when I realize he's not looking at me—or any of us, for that matter. His gaze is fixed on the ground, where his boots tap anxiously against the dusty floorboards.

"Sorry I can't bring you kids to the house to settle in quite yet," he says slowly, as though finding his words as he goes. "As soon as the shop closes up for the day, I'll take you over."

Now that Mom's gone, it suddenly seems quiet in here. Griffin stands, midbite, and Oliver's thumbs are frozen half an inch above his phone screen. I can hear the old building settling, as though it's holding its breath too. Jeff works his jaw, like he's begging the right words to find their way out.

I wonder how long he's been out here, alone. I wonder—if I can't fix things with Sophie—if I'll be alone long enough to lose my words too.

"But feel free to make yourself at home, or step outside if you want. I just need to unload some shipments in the back, but"—he taps the counter, gesturing toward a small bell by the cashier—"ring if you need me."

It comes out sounding more like a question than a statement. I exchange a glance with Oliver. He bites his lower lip.

"Um, thanks," he says.

Jeff nods, almost as though reassuring himself, then trudges around the counter and toward the back room.

The swinging door sways behind him like a waving hand.

Griffin leaps up onto the seat behind the counter and slaps his palms onto its wooden surface. “I run the shop now! Welcome to Café Le Griffin!”

Oliver rolls his eyes. “God help every customer in this town.”

A bickering match ensues between the two of them, Malt dashing across the empty space between them like a tennis ball being served back and forth over a net. I take my chance to turn back to the newspaper clipping, but with the sound of their rising voices, it’s hard to focus on the words. They’re scrambled, letters mixed in my vision like mismatched Scrabble pieces.

I blink hard, over and over, to regain focus. Instead, I just get bleary eyes.

Sophie wouldn’t get overwhelmed like this. She was always focused. Always attentive. While I decided on our missions and barreled in, full speed ahead, she was my brains. She was the thought behind it. She was half the job.

Without her, I’m not whole.

“It’s not a good business practice to eat all your product,” Oliver is saying.

Griffin lets out a dramatic scoff. “And it’s that kind of attitude that will drive away customers.”

“What customers?”

“Finley,” he calls, singsong, “will you be my first customer so I can prove a point to Ollie?”

That stirring feeling returns to my pocket. I reach in

and pull out the stack of business cards, crisp, glossy, and perfect, just like Sophie and I hoped for when her dad finally agreed to order them. I run my finger over the edges, the pointed ends flipping over the pad of my thumb.

A bad idea takes root in my mind. I turn around, already smiling despite myself.

Griffin's eyes light up. "Oh, I'm totally about to win this fight."

"Forget watching his coffee shop," I say slowly, to hide the rising excitement—and nerves—from my voice. "Forget stale pastries."

Griffin gasps. Even Malt stops, ears up at attention.

I swallow. I can't stop now. Adventurers never give up before the mission begins.

"I have a proposition."

Oliver shakes his head and turns back to his phone. "I'm out."

I gape at him, nostrils flaring. "You haven't even heard it yet!"

His head keeps swaying, blond locks shaking at his ears. "If it's your idea, I'm out."

I clamp my mouth shut to keep my jaw from trembling. He remains bent over his phone, though I can tell he's not scrolling by the way his eyes remain fixed ahead in one place. Like in the car, he's pretending not to listen while still totally listening. Which means I still have a chance to win him over.

I straighten up and stomp toward the counter.

"Maybe you'll consider it, then." I slap a business card onto the surface and slide it, facedown, toward Griffin, all official-like. He glances over his right, then left shoulder, then flips the corner like he's about to read a winning card during a game of blackjack.

"Our mission is to find the missing explorer," I say, spinning my finger to point to the café's three decorated walls. "And our prize is never-ending glory."

The kind even Sophie, Veronica, and Chloe can't ignore.

Griffin's eyes light up like little fires. "Oh, I'm in."

Oliver stomps toward us, so heavily that the frames tremble on the wall. "Okay, fine, what is this?" I toss a card his way, and he snatches it as it flutters toward the ground. His brow goes tight. "Walsh-Higgins Adventure Agency?"

I grab a pen from Jeff's jar by the cashier. "Cross it out. We're rebranding."

I scribble on one of my copies and hold it up for them to see.

Oliver's face remains flat. "Walsh-Walsh-Walsh? I can barely say that without getting tongue-tied."

"And don't forget Malt!" Griffin says, doodling a cartoon dog in the corner of the card.

Oliver's mouth is open, ready to muster some objection Mom's trained him to give. Some brilliant, oh-so-mature reason why we shouldn't have fun this break, why we should stay inside and help Jeff with the shop. A reason why I should keep still and quiet so I don't cause trouble. Don't bother anyone.

So no one has to notice me at all.

Griffin looks up at him, eager and hopeful. The second Oliver says no, he'll move on to the first chance at shenanigans that come next. But right now I have him on my side, for once. And if I use my supersonic-hearing powers for evil, just this one time, I can keep it that way.

"We're pursuing this, one way or another," I say. "You can either join us and make sure we don't get into too much trouble, or . . ."

I glance at the doorway, where Mom said her secret goodbye to him. His mouth falls shut; a quick surge of guilt floods my chest. But I'm not asking him to do a bad thing. I'm asking him to be brave—like Nellie Bly, who risked her safety and sanity to go undercover at the Blackwell's Island asylum to write her famous exposé. Part of what makes a great adventurer is having guts and a passion to uncover hidden truths—the kind everyone else is too afraid to pursue.

Besides, a mission with good intentions is a win for everyone. The fame and glory are a nice icing on the top—in Bly's case, her reputation after the exposé earned her the ability to be one of the first international female travelers.

And I never ask Oliver for anything, anyway. Not when I've waited outside alone while Sophie, Veronica, and Chloe huddle close so there's never quite enough room for a fourth. Not when I've got my head ducked, sniffling quietly in my locker, and I notice him walk by, know he sees me, even though he pretends he doesn't.

But my chest still feels hot and unsteady as I watch his guard fall and he nods in surrender. Maybe because I know how it can be when Mom expects too much—like when she makes me help Griffin scrub mud off his shoes after a hyper run through the rain, or makes me review his long division workbook when, really, I'm the last person on the planet who should ever be helping anyone with long division.

Mostly, though, I wish he'd just say yes to the adventure. Wish he wasn't another person I had to convince to come along.

"Okay," he says in defeat. I muster a grin, as though this is what winning should feel like. "I'll help. But only to make sure you two don't get yourselves killed."

I extend my hand for a shake. "Fair enough, sir."

He rolls his eyes but accepts my hand in his.

"So," Griffin says, running his hand over the round curve of his chin with melodramatic flair, "where do we start?"

Everyone's eyes are fixed on me. Even Malt is staring up at me, tail wagging in anticipation. The adventure agency is back. And I'm still its leader.

Future Greatest Female Adventurer One Hundred One, Finley Walsh, has just begun her greatest mission to date.

GREATEST FEMALE ADVENTURER NUMBER TWO:

ANNE BONNY,

ONE OF HISTORY'S ONLY FEMALE PIRATES, FAMOUS FOR HER BRAVELY DEFENDING HER SHIP AGAINST BRITISH PRIVATEERS.

Oliver's and Griffin's eyes are on me as my brothers wait for next steps. My heartbeat rises in my throat, and I'm sure the moment I open my lips, they'll hear it—how nervous I am. But for once, I have the room's full attention. Have their full attention. So I swallow down the fears bubbling and boiling in my chest and hold my posture high like I know what I'm doing.

"The first step when starting a new adventure is developing a plan," I declare. "That way, no matter what we discover along the way, we're prepared. Then we take action."

Usually, the Walsh-Higgins Adventure Agency's first step would be me suggesting immediate action, then Sophie arguing that we have to put a plan together first, followed by us finally taking action. But without Sophie here and without knowing how useful my brothers will actually be, I have to conjure a Sophie voice in my head like a quiet voice of reason.

"We can't let Jeff know we're looking into Meggie's disappearance. At least not yet," I say. "We still don't know if he'll rat us out to Mom, and she definitely wouldn't want us looking into it."

The way she talked about Meggie, it was as though it happened so long ago we shouldn't even think about it anymore. Probably because she doesn't want us doing anything to get in trouble while we're staying with Jeff. But it still sends a pang through my chest to think that there are so many people who have given up on the search for Meggie.

100 of the World's Greatest Female Adventurers highlights the successes of the hundred women included in the book. But some explorers do end up going missing. There's the famous case of Amelia Earhart or more recent disappearances of Kris Kremers and Lisanne Froon during a solo expedition in Panama. Sophie would text me every news article about missing Panama girls, but the news fizzles out over time for stories like this. To most people, tragedy is an expected risk of expeditions—something easy to explain away, so they can forget and move on.

Meggie was a great adventurer from a young age, and she still went missing. I wonder, if I follow in Meggie's footsteps, if instead of saving her, I'll share her fate. And if I did, would anyone look for me—someone who hasn't accomplished anything yet, like Meggie did, who hasn't proven why they're important, why they matter—like they did for a hero like her?

Either way, I have to at least try to find her. Staying in Jeff's café during our entire spring break isn't going to get me any closer to the glory I need to secure, so I might as well put my all into finding Meggie, even if there's a risk that I could fail. "Jeff said we could go outside, so I say we find a place to talk it over in private," I say.

Oliver leans against the counter and shrugs. "This town's so empty, that could be anywhere."

Griffin smiles, revealing the gap between his front teeth. "There was a diner across the street. We could go there!"

Oliver frowns. "You can't seriously still be hungry?"

"Griffin is right." I hold my hand up for a high five, which he eagerly accepts. Oliver rolls his eyes. "The diner is a perfect place to get some privacy while also getting a feel for the neighborhood and collect any discoveries the locals have made over time."

"Then that's that!" Griffin bangs the bell so it chimes loud enough to make Malt bark. "We're going out for a walk, Uncle Cousin Jeff! Bye!"

He charges around the counter, nearly tripping over the dog, and bursts through the front door. Oliver shoots me a dirty look.

I hold up my hands in surrender. "I won't let him order sugar, okay?"

Oliver huffs, but follows me out the door. Malt

remains behind, settled sleepily by the coat rack.

Outside, the humidity is rising. My hair starts to rise with it, and I tighten my ponytail to keep frizzy strands from puffing out. Across the empty intersection, at the edge of a thick cluster of trees, is Meggie's 24/7-ish Diner. It's got an old, classic vibe like a scene from *Grease*. Crossing the street with a quick glance both ways, I feel like I'm in fourth grade again, heading to the school musical with Sophie, matching poodle skirts swaying at our ankles.

Our *Grease* set somehow managed to be cuter than this place, though. The windows are fogged with age, sills cracked just enough to make a perfect ant highway inside. A neon sign advertising burgers and shakes is missing half its letters, and the remaining ones blink out of sequence like Morse code. I lead my brothers up the steps to the front door, sneakers stomping the weeds growing from the concrete. Inside is an empty hostess station, and beyond are empty booths with torn red cushions.

For everything to be Meggie themed, there must have been a huge number of people coming to town to take a shot at the mission before. But the foot traffic has died down, which means three things:

One: This mission may be harder to pull off than I thought. Maybe too hard for me, my idiot brothers, and a Maltese named Malt.

Two: If I can't pull it off, I'll lose my best shot yet at becoming a famous adventurer. And if I'm not successful, there's no reason for Sophie to reappoint me as her best friend. Or for Mom to trust me like she trusts Oliver. Or for Oliver to care enough to take me seriously for once.

Three: If I can't find Meggie, I'm just another person giving up on her.

The thought makes my stomach clench like a fist. No matter how many years go by, Meggie is still Meggie. She's still worth something. She's still someone. I hate the thought that time could change that. That with each year her being gone gets easier.

Easier for people to forget.

"Besides the morbid ambience," Oliver grumbles, scanning the decorations by the front wall, "the service in this town is the real problem."

While he pounds his palm against the hostess bell, I survey the wall. Beside a tall, lopsided plastic plant is a giant picture frame featuring a front-page newspaper article, like how Jeff decorates his café. An enormous, color photo of the diner—back in its prime—consumes the front page.

LOCAL DINER PRINTS CLUES ON RECEIPTS TO SUPPORT SEARCH FOR MISSING GIRL

I frown. "Why would they print clues on their receipts? They're not the police. And even if they did have real clues, shouldn't they be giving them to actual detectives? Not tourists?"

"No such thing as real or fake clues in this case," a gravelly voice responds. A lanky blond woman with a loose bun approaches the hostess station. She wears all black, except her white, coffee-stained apron—which seems a little backward, if you ask me. "There's a whole lot of questionable evidence and no crime scene, so anything we print on our receipts has as good a chance of being true as what you'll find down at the station."

Oliver turns toward me, head tilted in a way that very clearly asks, *Can we stop with this nonsense now?*

But as Great Female Adventurer Twenty-One Freya Stark once said, "Curiosity is the one thing invincible in nature." Keeping an open mind and hunger for the truth is what drives the best explorers and makes us stronger than anything the world can throw at us.

I answer by planting my hands on my hips and stepping up to the counter. "You wouldn't mind sharing all your clues with us, then, would you?"

She stares, eyes wide so the wrinkles cross her face smooth like an ironed shirt.

Then she bursts out laughing.

"You're gonna have to order a whole lot of pancakes for me to hand all those over, kid," she says, shaking her head in disbelief. My chin trembles, but I maintain my power stance—more for my sake than hers. "But you were right to start here. You could spend your entire life reading every article that's been written on this case, but they've all got some angle—some theory about what *really* happened. But here, we stick to the facts. Plain and simple." She draws three laminated menus from beneath the hostess station and waves them so their plastic edges flap. "Table for three?"

I hold up a finger. "One moment while I hold council with my associates."

I spin around and wave my brothers into a huddle. Oliver is the first to speak, a bit louder than the super-secret whisper I was anticipating. "It's a scam. A tacky scam. A woman is missing, and they're charging people to help look for her? That's messed up."

"Technically, we're charging for the food," the hostess calls. "Clues come at no extra cost."

I shoot Oliver a dirty look, pressing my fingers to my lips with a *shh*. He sucks in his cheeks and blows out a long breath.

"Look," I whisper. "I know Mom gave you a credit card for emergencies."

His face scrunches. "She's been missing for almost two decades. This isn't an emergency."

My fingers curl by my sides, nails pinching the soft skin of my palms. I try to keep my voice from trembling. "It is to her family. They still miss her. There shouldn't be an expiration date on that."

Isn't. I meant to say *isn't.* But the doubt creeps into my words.

My big mouth and telltale expressions. Sophie used to be the one to take over when I was about to blow a mission. Like the time I almost spilled to Ms. Green that the reason I wanted to check the school dance sound system wasn't because I was secretly a tech genius, but because I planned on swapping the playlist. Or when I barely convinced Mom I wanted to learn to fish when, really, Sophie and I were on a top-secret hunt for the Loch Ness Monster.

But everyone knows the Loch Ness Monster doesn't live in Massachusetts. Playing imaginary like that is why Sophie outgrew the Walsh-Higgins Adventure Agency. Even if she never officially quit. Or built up the nerve to tell me.

But this mission is real—something she'd have to take seriously. Something that—if I completed it—would force her and everyone else to take me seriously.

"Imagine it, Oliver. If we rescue Meggie, we'll be the heroes of this town. This'll be called the Walsh Diner, and every receipt will have our autographs on it."

Oliver opens his mouth to object, but Griffin cuts in. "And we'll have so much money from the reward," he says, voice still high and full of excitement, "that Mom won't have to leave us when she goes on her next work trip."

Oliver's mouth clamps back shut. His eyes flash to mine, almost too fast to notice, before he steps back up to the counter.

"We'll take that table," he says.

My eyes go wide, and I give Griffin's hand a hard squeeze.

The woman smirks. "Thought so."

We're led into the restaurant, past a semi-empty counter with red barstools and plastic cases displaying full, uncut pies. An old man sits at the end of the bar, hunched over a plate of eggs and sausage, and a younger man with a big brown hat sits a few seats away, nursing a cup of hot coffee. The hostess leads us to a booth, and Griffin dives onto the seat and slides up to the window. I settle in beside him, ripped plastic cushion digging into my thigh. Oliver slumps into place across from me.

The hostess drops the menus onto the table with a thump. I reach for the top one, its plastic sticky beneath my fingers. “Word to the wise: avoid the fries,” the hostess says. “They have the texture of bread pudding.” Oliver clamps a hand over his mouth. “Assume everything has touched gluten, and if you want a burger, go a temperature up to be safe.” She whips out a small notepad and golf pencil from her apron. “Name’s Sam, and I’ll be back for your orders in a minute.”

She turns to go. I clear my throat. “Excuse me, Sam?”

Her upper lip curls as she turns back to me in slow motion.

I imagine all the sugary sweetness Griffin has consumed today and pump it into my voice. “Can we borrow a paper and pencil?”

She rips a sheet unevenly, half of the right corner torn full off, and slaps it on top of the menus. The pencil rolls into place after it.

Sam leaves and Oliver glares at me across the table. “Are we passing notes or something? Because there’s no one to overhear.”

He gestures toward the far end of the diner, where the only other patrons sit quietly by their meals.

"First of all, trust no one." I write that down for good measure, with a few underlines for emphasis. "Second, we need to keep track of our clues."

Despite my B– in English, I know keeping records of what I discover is important. Most of the World's Greatest Female Adventurers went on to publish books or articles about what they found on expeditions, which is part of what keeps their legacies alive.

Griffin edges closer to me. "We have clues?"

"What I read at Jeff's café, at least."

"I didn't get to read them," Griffin says.

Oliver raises an eyebrow. "Because you were stealing Jeff's stuff?"

"Because Mom was there," he says with a slight shrug. "She'd freak out and say I was too young for it or something. But I read murder mysteries and watch spy shows all the time when she's not home. She just doesn't know about it."

Oliver and I exchange a glance. Maybe it isn't a good idea, getting Griffin involved in a mission like this.

That's my first thought, at least, and the one I know Oliver's having. But I never noticed what Griffin was reading or watching either on the nights Mom had to work late. I was usually just grateful he was focused on something else than begging me for another round of *Mario Kart*, or challenging me to a reenactment of

Obi-Wan and Anakin's last battle, where the living room floor is lava. I'd finish my homework, or text Sophie, or download the latest episode of *Riverdale* and pretend he wasn't there. That he wasn't my problem.

I wrap my arm around his small shoulders and squeeze him to my side. "Well, I'll tell you what the newspapers said. Or what I remember, at least." I release him and pick up the pencil. "So, obviously, Meggie has been missing for almost twenty years."

Oliver pulls a tight smile. "We got that part."

"What you two may not know is that she was last seen in the woods." My heart rate rises at the mention of Stone Creek Woods. Back home, Sophie and I never had any woods or mountains or wilderness to explore. But Meggie actually vanished out in the wilderness. And if her runaway note was real, that means she used the woods as her escape in pursuit of a new life full of adventure, like the one she completed when she was my age.

Nearly half the women in *100 of the World's Greatest Female Adventurers* made it into the book because of grand expeditions, or brave outdoor survival stories, or fearless treks into unknown lands in pursuit of new truths. If I follow Meggie's footsteps into Stone Creek Woods, I'll be closer to becoming Number One Hundred One than I've ever been before.

"I also learned that her own family is a suspect," I continue. "She left a runaway note that may have been forged, and I think one of the headlines I skimmed mentioned something about a phone discovered around where she vanished . . ." Their eyes begin to cloud over. I'm losing them. "Her family sounds rich . . ."

"So, basically, we have nothing."

"We have everything," I object. "But it was too much for me to read all at once, and even when we do get all the facts together, we need to sort through it all. We'll learn what we can here to develop our plan, then I say we head to the woods."

My brothers' eyes go wide, but for different reasons.

"Yes! That's a great idea!" Griffin cries. "Let's go now!"

I block him from crawling over my lap and out of the booth. "Easy there. We need to gather the facts first."

Adventurers never go into battle unprepared. That's why Greatest Female Adventurer Eighty-Seven, Anna McNuff, has an entire organization dedicated to prepping female explorers for surviving in the wild.

Oliver stares me down. "We need a map, better cell service, a bodyguard—"

Sam appears then, flipping a new sheet on her pad. "Doesn't sound like we're having any breakthroughs yet, so I'll take your orders."

Griffin swings his feet beneath the table, heels smashing the booth so it shakes to each beat. "I'll have the chocolate-chip pancakes please. Extra, extra syrup."

I tap his head with my menu. "No more sugar! I can't handle you if you have any more sugar."

Oliver turns to the waitress. "He'll have a glass of milk."

Griffin rolls up his menu and slaps mine away from his head. "Chocolate milk."

"Three of those," I say before Oliver can object. "And on separate checks, please."

The woman gives me a flat, dead stare. "Like we haven't heard that trick before."

I give her a big, toothy smile, trying to look as innocent as I can. She rolls her eyes but doesn't say no before walking away, which I take as a win.

"Three clues isn't a lot, but it's a start," I say. "From there, we can—"

"Go into the woods!" Griffin interjects. "To the place she was last seen."

I nod enthusiastically. "We'll retrace her steps, walking the dangerous and secluded paths she did before she vanished. After fearlessly uncovering evidence from the deadliest corners of the woods, we'll be the first people to ever uncover the truth."

Griffin pumps his fist in the air. "Then we'll fight her kidnappers!"

"Or meet the greatest adventurer in New England's history," I say. "But whatever we discover, the town will be amazed by our brilliance and perseverance. We'll become local heroes, just like Meggie was when she was our age."

Griffin bounces in his seat. "And get rich, and have bragging rights for life!"

Oliver remains typically quiet on the other side of the booth. Usually I wouldn't think anything of it, but his eyes keep drifting behind the main counter, toward a curly-haired busboy buffing silverware.

I plant my palms on our table's greasy surface and lean toward him. "Did you notice something?"

Oliver blinks and stammers, snapping back to focus. "What? No. I wasn't looking at anything. Zoning out."

I pat his hand with mine. "All theories are welcome here. It's basically the town motto, remember?"

He pulls his hand back. "I don't have any theories."

His eyes tell a different story, darting back toward the boy. I frown. "Then why do you keep staring at that boy?"

His ears go pink, shoulders rising to his ears. "I'm not staring at that boy! There's no reason I'd be staring at that boy!"

Griffin kicks Oliver under the table. "Are you hiding clues? Are you trying to solve the case without us?" He turns to me, eyes wide and desperate. "Finley, we have to team up: me, you, and Malt. We'll complete the mission by ourselves, before Ollie has the chance to steal all the glory."

"I don't want any glory!" Oliver snaps. "I barely want to do this! I'm just playing along because Finley . . ."

I lean back, cross my arms. "Because Finley what?"

"Because Finley's crazy ideas are going to get us all killed if I'm not here to keep her in check."

I squeeze my hands into fists under the table. Great adventurers don't become great while being micromanaged by their older brothers. But anytime Mom leaves me alone with Oliver, he's ready to throw cold water on my best plans.

"I don't need supervision," I say, voice unsteady. "And if you're going to keep your theories from me and Griffin, you might as well not join us at all."

Oliver's expression doesn't soften, and I look down at my shoes to hide the angry heat rising to my skin.

"Hey!"

We all snap to attention as the busboy with the curly hair approaches our table, full and furious speed ahead. He's tall and lanky as though puberty stretched him out like old bubble gum, apron tied loose around his too-slim waist. He stomps to the foot of our table, jaw squared.

He glares directly at Oliver. Which, I have to admit, feels pretty good right now. I lean back in my seat, letting the boy do all the Oliver-directed fuming for me.

"I saw you staring at me," he starts.

Oliver's voice is all muffled and weird, like he's got a mouthful of marbles. "I wasn't staring—"

"And I know why."

The boy takes in a heavy breath, chest rising and falling with the weight of it. Oliver's shoulders shrivel up like a wet straw wrapper.

"But my father is innocent, and I'm sick of tourists like you coming in and pointing fingers over something you know nothing about."

Oliver blinks, as though he was expecting something

else. I rise in my seat, plastic squeaking beneath me. "Why do people suspect your father?" I ask, trying double hard to keep the curiosity out of my voice.

"Because people are idiots," the boy snaps. Then, after a beat, "And because they were dating when she went missing."

Oof. No wonder this boy is so defensive. After the butler, the second-most-likely culprit is always the boyfriend. Sophie and I learned that when Miss Winters was absent for three weeks and we suspected foul play.

Turned out it was just mono, but still.

"They started dating in high school and were only together five years, so the relationship barely even counts at this point," the boy adds in a rush. "But it doesn't matter anyway, because my dad's not a killer."

Griffin leaps up onto his seat. "Aha! Who said Meggie was killed?"

Oliver reaches over and yanks him back down by the end of his T-shirt. "Sit down and shut up." Then, to the boy, "I'm sorry, he didn't mean that. It was the sugar talking." He bites his lower lip. "I'm Oliver. These idiots are Griffin and Finley."

I take the opportunity to whip out a business card and pass it the boy's way. "While it's too early for us to rule out any suspects, we appreciate your passion for finding the truth. Walsh-Walsh-Walsh"—Oliver was right, it's hard to say, but I carry on—"Adventure Agency is here to help."

He eyes the card before snatching it from my hands. "Jason Jeffords. I'd say nice to meet you, but the verdict is still out."

"Fair enough," Oliver says. When the boy looks back his way, he averts his gaze to a crack in the table.

Jason slips the card into his apron and walks off slowly, with a last glance over his shoulder. I pump a fist by my side. "Look at us, making allies with the local kids!" Oliver doesn't look back up, and I give his shoe a tap with mine under the table. "How did you know he'd have information, though?"

The pink returns to his ears like a light turning on. "I didn't," he grumbles.

I'm about to push when Sam reappears carrying a tray with three glasses of chocolate milk and three separate checks. "Here you go. Don't forget to tip."

We lunge forward before the tray is even down—Griffin for the milk, Oliver and me for the receipts.

I snatch mine and Griffin's and smooth out the plastic-y paper on my empty placemat. Below the (frankly overpriced) total for the chocolate milk, the clue is written in bold print.

> Despite photo evidence only showing Meggie with one other person, some locals believe that she encountered a second person in the woods, suggesting that there is more than one abductor involved in her disappearance.

The paper shakes in my fingers, wrinkles rewrinkling against my clammy skin. That theory would mean that we'd be taking on not just one, but two kidnappers. And if they're still here in Stone Creek, they could find us before we find them.

Which would make completing this mission twice as risky and, therefore, twice as glorious.

I hungrily turn to the next receipt, which shares more about the mysterious phone photos.

> When detectives found Meggie's phone in the Northern side of Stone Creek Woods, there were a series of blurry photos taken of her walking through the dark. There appears to be a boy with her in several of them, who detectives suspect to be her boyfriend at the time, Devon Jeffords.

"Wanna trade?" Oliver asks, edging his receipt toward me.

I hand him the first but not the second. His hand remains flat on the table, palm up.

"Come on, Finley. We're on the same side here."

A smile fights at the corner of my lips. I hand him the second receipt. "I just felt bad for our new friend. He works here, and they're still printing stuff about his dad on these."

Oliver's gaze rushes over the receipt, features knit with

concentration. A muscle in his jaw twitches, and he runs a hand over his chin as though he could conceal his reaction.

As though I don't already notice everything. Even if I don't always know what it means.

"I'm sure they have to be impartial," he says, voice low. "We should be too."

Oliver hunches over the receipt, body bent as though trying to vanish from my view. Maybe he does suspect something about the busboy and his dad, and that's why he's acting so weird. But if we're supposedly on the same side, he should feel comfortable telling me his theories. He should trust that I can handle it.

But going to Jeff's house for break and being forced to hang out together doesn't change the fact that Oliver probably wishes he were anywhere else but stuck here with me. If it were up to him, he wouldn't be sitting here with me now; he'd be across the diner, head turned as though I don't exist, just like it is at school.

"Look at mine," he says. "It takes 'impartial' to the next level."

I look down at his receipt. The clue reads:

> Police suspect that the professional rivalry between victim's father and other local businessman, Bryan Phillips, may have ties to the crime.

I blink. "And you know who Bryan Phillips is how?"

He points toward the front of the diner. Behind the

main counter, where a few rusted pots and pans hang below a chalkboard, is a plaque with a photo of an old, fat man with round glasses.

"He owns this diner," I say as I read the plaque, "and a bunch of other stuff in the area."

"The clue seems to suggest Meggie's dad did too." Oliver glances out the window, toward the empty street. "Not a town worth fighting over, let alone killing for."

Griffin perks up, milk mustache in full display. "Again, who said anything about murder?"

Oliver kicks him under the table. "I'm not a suspect, idiot. But literally anyone else in this town could be."

The thought sends a chill up my spine, like ice dropped down the back of my shirt. The first receipt suggested that there would be more than one kidnapper we're dealing with. Mom and Jeff don't seem to think anything has happened since Meggie's disappearance, but with so many theories and conflicting clues, it's hard to know what to trust.

Great adventurers don't back out when things get tough. If they did, Ada Blackjack never would have survived her time alone in the Arctic after an expedition gone wrong. But this early into the mission, being cautious doesn't hurt, so I glance over my shoulder to survey the two other patrons in the diner.

The old man is napping on today's newspaper. But the younger man—the one with the big hat—is staring right at me.

I jump and do the least subtle thing possible: immediately turn back around, head bent toward the table.

"What is wrong with you?"

"Is Finley dying?"

I hold the sides of my head as though this somehow makes me less conspicuous. "Don't look but also, please look and tell me if that man is coming over."

I'm answered by approaching footsteps, followed by the appearance of two black shoes at the edge of my table. Slowly, I lift my head to face the man with the hat.

He stands, thumbs looped through his empty belt straps, with an eager, open smile on his face. His age is hard to determine—although tired lines paint his pale face, blotches of black hair stick out from beneath his hat and throughout his stubbly beard. He wears a loose, long-sleeved button-up with tiny blue polka dots texturing the fabric.

"I saw you looking my way and figured you wanted to swap receipts," he says, holding his up. "In a town like this, tourists like us stand out like sore thumbs, huh?"

Oliver straightens up. "Who are you?" he asks, a bit too sharply. "I mean, um, why are you visiting this place?"

Not much better, but apparently his save worked well enough, because the man smiles.

"Richard Connors. I write long-form journalism on local crimes for an online newspaper." He reaches for his pocket. Oliver flinches, but all Richard pulls out is a business card that looks like mine and Sophie's—which,

I hate to admit, makes me edge forward eagerly in my seat. "It's called the *Burlington Biweekly*. My brother lives a few towns over, and he recommended I do a feature on the twentieth anniversary of her disappearance."

I take a giant gulp of my chocolate milk to hide my reaction. Mom mentioned the disappearance was almost twenty years ago, but I didn't know the anniversary itself was coming up. Or that it was a big deal.

Jeff hadn't mentioned it either, despite dedicating his entire café to Meggie. Seems like it would be a good opportunity for him to draw in new customers. I can't help but wonder why he isn't advertising it.

Richard continues. "I thought there might be a bigger crowd this close to the date, but I guess it's still three weeks out. So"—his fingers extend, drumming against the business card—"with you kids being the only other tourists I've run into so far, I'd love to pick your brains sometime."

I reach for the card, but Oliver snatches it up first. "Why would you want to interview a bunch of out-of-town kids for a missing person investigation?"

Despite the edge to his tone, Richard smiles. "Everyone here is pretty set in their theories about Meggie at this point. I'd actually find it a lot more interesting to hear your takes than any of the older locals around here."

A surge of confidence rushes through me, warm and steadying. Usually, I'm being told to stop pushing things, or that my ideas are too much or too dangerous. Having someone interested in my theories and ideas, as if they matter, makes me feel even more sure that I'm the one meant to find and rescue Meggie. "Well, my coffee's gonna get cold." Richard points his thumb toward his high-top counter stool. "You have my contact information if you come up with any fresh leads, ideas . . . or just opinions. I'm happy to listen."

With a friendly wave, he heads back to his seat. Once his back is turned, Oliver pinches both ends of the business card between his fingers and begins to twist. A tiny rip forms in the paper's center.

I dive across the table, nearly knocking over his chocolate milk. "Don't do that!"

"What? I thought you wanted to lead this mission? Unless we're about to become the Walsh-Walsh-Walsh-Connors Adventure Agency?"

The card wrinkles in my palm as I yank it from his grip. "No, but this goes both ways. If he's investigating with fresh eyes, just like us, he may notice things locals don't." I point to the receipts. "Like he said, people around here have been studying the same facts and theories over and over again. Jeff even said so! But this reporter might find something they overlooked. Something new he can share with us."

Oliver studies me, expression softening as he slowly but surely comes to my side. But Griffin, on the other hand, lets out a giant yawn.

"Can we go to the woods now?" he whines. "Sitting

and talking in a diner isn't exactly adventurous."

"I still think this is a bad idea," Oliver says.

I slide across my seat and out of the booth. "But it's our only idea, so we're going with it," I say, as if there's any universe in which my next step is not running directly into those perfectly mysterious woods. Griffin beams, eagerly following after me. "Once we pay, it's off to the scene of the crime!"

Oliver trudges to the front counter with Mom's card, and Griffin rushes to the door. I reach into my back pocket for my phone. For the first time since I lost service on the ride here, two full bars light up the corner of my screen.

Still, no messages. Not from Sophie. And not from Mom. Which means she's probably on her way to the airport, but for some reason, my chest sinks like an anchor.

"Let's get Malt first," Griffin calls from the door.

I muster a smile and slip my phone back into my pocket. It settles, heavy against the fabric.

GREATEST FEMALE ADVENTURER NUMBER THREE: AMELIA EARHART, THE FIRST FEMALE PILOT TO FLY SOLO ACROSS THE ATLANTIC OCEAN, AS WELL AS THE FIRST PERSON TO FLY OVER BOTH THE ATLANTIC AND PACIFIC.

We wait on the curb outside the diner while Griffin rushes across the street to grab Malt. An anxious flare rises in my chest at the thought of Jeff noticing what we're up to. But, like Mom, he's seemed too busy to notice, so even with his dog, we may still get away with our adventure yet.

I balance the heels of my sneakers on the curb, swaying my weight back and forth. On the other side of the diner, behind Meggie's Cup and its tiny parking lot, is the edge of the woods. The trees stand close together, growing in a thick huddle. Small, dark patches of space gape between their plump trunks, and even from here I can tell the summer sun doesn't break through the leaves well enough to provide real light.

Oliver reaches into his backpack and pulls out a folded sheet of paper. "The waitress-slash-hostess woman, Sam—she gave me this when I checked out."

I leap off the curb and peer over Oliver's shoulder. He stretches the wrinkled page in front of us, revealing a poorly drawn map on an old tourist brochure.

"She said they usually charge extra for the map, but didn't want our deaths on her hands. Or something theatrical and morbid like that." He shifts on his soles. "I'm sure she tells that to all the customers. As part of the act."

I swallow. The word "death" bounces in my head like a Ping-Pong ball. I hadn't considered this adventure could be that dangerous. Partly because I hadn't considered that Meggie was gone—that there was no Meggie left to save.

But I have to believe she's out there. If everyone believes the worst, that means everyone stops looking. Which is no different from being forgotten.

I brush my fingertips over the crinkled paper. "How do we know this isn't a red herring?"

Oliver tilts the brochure, angling it toward the sun. "Doesn't look red to me."

I straighten up. For once, I know something Oliver doesn't. "It's a saying. It means false clue," I explain. "It was strange that the diner included a clue that incriminated the owner on the receipts. But like you said, it made them seem impartial. Like they weren't trying to sway anyone one way or the other." I tap my finger against the map. "But maybe that's part of their plan. Include a real clue—one that makes them look bad—on the receipts. Then hand out maps that are written to guide tourists away from the truth. Away from what really happened to Meggie."

When I look up, Oliver's staring at me, not the map. I can't tell if he's not following my theory, or if he's wondering why he's following me at all.

Suddenly, the sun feels a bit too hot on my skin. "That's only if the diner's owner was the one who kidnapped her, of course," I say in a rush.

Griffin appears at the opposite side of the street, Malt nestled in his arms. Oliver maintains his hold on the map. "Either way, this map is our best shot at keeping on the trail. If anything happened to one of us out there, it's my head on Mom's chopping block." My fingers curl by my sides, a comeback poised on my tongue. Then he adds, "She's already checked in to make sure you're keeping out of trouble, and off Jeff's nerves. She's going to call at seven, once she's checked into the hotel."

I gape, feeling weightless, like the cracked sidewalk vanished beneath my feet. Mom texted Oliver, and not me. Probably not Griffin, either. Just Oliver, because he's the only one she trusts, the only one she notices, because Griffin and I are just nuisances that have to be handled.

I extend my hand, fingers waving. "Let me see her text."

Griffin skips up to my side, Malt panting happily in his arms. "Uncle Cousin Jeff thinks I'm taking him on a walk, so we have to be fast."

I glare at Oliver. He groans and reaches for his phone.

"I'm pulling up the text. Do not click on anything

else." He twists the phone toward me, revealing his thread with Mom.

Just arrived at the airport and wanted to check in. How are you guys doing? Is Jeff too overwhelmed yet?

I'm going to lose service soon but want to talk to you all at seven.

xoxo mom

The screen goes black. "See? Not that interesting."

Oliver's summary of her text was a lot harsher, which makes sense because, well, Oliver. But he wasn't all the way off. "What does she mean by 'too overwhelmed yet'? As if it's inevitable we're going to annoy Jeff?"

"It is inevitable," he snaps, gesturing toward the woods. "Look at the nonsense you've already dragged us into, and we've only been here what? An hour and a half?"

I cross my arms. Griffin edges toward the woods. "Speaking of Finley's nonsense . . . can we go on our adventure now?"

I give his foot a playful stomp and the tension lifts as we all turn, shoulder to shoulder, toward the woods. Standing here moping won't fix anything. But completing a worthwhile adventure—and through it proving that I, Finley Walsh, am capable—just might. I tighten my ponytail, brush my sideswept bangs from my eyes, and march forward, leading the way.

Oliver may have the map, but I've got the moxie.

I storm forward, straight through the opening to the woods. It's like entering another universe: the concrete and old-timey shop fronts disappear, replaced with a maze of tall trunks, mossy rocks, and clumps of fallen leaves. Within the first few steps I feel the relief of the sun leaving my back. Small pockets of light trickle in from the gaps in branches overhead, but the leaves are like a canopy, secluding me from the outside world. I press on, twigs snapping beneath my sneakers. I'm sure Meggie used to come out here often, going on self-directed adventures like mine, searching for a way to prove she was bigger than what the world saw in her. Walking where she must have years before, when she was my age, makes me feel closer to being a real, official adventurer than ever before.

If Sophie were here too, I know she'd be saying the same thing. She'd walk alongside me, thoughtful and quiet as I tromped forward. Then, pausing in the thick of the woods, she'd look up into the dark web of branches above and say, "Meggie really was just like us. Which means we can be just like her."

"Wait up!" Oliver calls. Griffin releases Malt, and the dog scurries forward in my tracks. I crane my neck, taking in the scenery above as I imagine Sophie would, then turn back toward my brothers.

As I do, something dark shifts ahead in the woods. I snap my head in its direction, but see nothing but trees, their branches dancing softly in the spring wind.

From the corner of my eye, I see Oliver shaking the map above his head. "So this is definitely not a map I'd want to bet my life on, but it looks like the last place

Meggie was seen is just a few yards northeast, which"—he lifts his other hand, which holds his phone—"thankfully I know is that way, because my phone's compass doesn't need Wi-Fi."

My gaze remains fixed on the distant tree where I'd seen the shadow. "Last seen by who?"

"Sam said it was an anonymous source," Oliver says, head bent toward the map as he approaches. "Not even the cops know their identity, apparently."

"Or they're covering for someone," I murmur, mostly to myself. I take a cautious step forward. Something moves again behind the trees, so fast it's just a blur. Goose bumps erupt across my skin and I know, in that instant, that we're being watched.

"Hey!"

I blink and the figure is gone. When I turn, Oliver is glaring holes into me.

"Listen to the guy with the compass," he says. "Let's at least pretend we know what we're doing."

I raise my arm, poised to point in the direction of the shadow. But when I look again, there's nothing there but old, rustling trees and anxious, scurrying squirrels.

If I say something and I'm wrong, Oliver will never trust me again. If I say something and I'm right, Oliver will never trust my adventures again. Either way, keeping quiet is my best bet if I want to make any progress on our adventure.

Besides, it'd be silly to assume we're the only people out on a woodsy walk on a warm April day like this. As long as nothing else weird happens, we're probably safe.

Reluctantly, I let Oliver and his map lead the way. Malt patters alongside us at Griffin's heel. We weave between thick trees, climbing over gritty rocks and dodging clumps of mud. Bugs swarm around my ears and birds flutter overhead.

I can't help but feel a little jealous that Meggie grew up somewhere like this. Sophie and I had to invent adventures in our small, suburban town. But out in the woods, surrounded by nature and uncertainty, anything is possible.

Maybe, somewhere like this, Sophie wouldn't have grown bored of the adventure agency—of me—so fast.

Griffin points toward a tree up ahead. Its trunk is thicker than the others, swollen with age. Thick, twisting branches jut from its sides like uneven slats on a ladder. "I want to climb that one!"

I nod—that tree is perfect for climbing. Which means if Meggie had been hiding from someone in these woods, or if someone was sneaking up on Meggie in these woods, they probably used this tree as a vantage point. From up there, we'd be able to scan the entire area where she was last seen. Maybe we'd spot something no one else has yet.

Griffin rushes up to the tree's trunk, patting his hand against its bark. I move to follow when he asks, "Ollie, will you show me how to climb? You promised, remember?"

My stomach drops. Beside me, Oliver shakes his head. "I don't remember promising anything. And we don't have service out here, so if anything happened—"

"What makes you think Oliver is the only one who can teach you to climb?" I ask. My brothers' attention snaps to me. "I used to climb trees with Sophie all the time! She was always afraid of losing her balance, but I"—I stomp up to the tree, nudge Griffin out of my way—"am not afraid of anything!"

I reach for the first two branches and wedge my shoe against the old bark. With a deep breath, I push off the trunk and hoist myself up.

"Well, you should be," Oliver calls from below. "Because if you fall, we're all dead, not just you."

His voice sounds a mile away as I reach for the next branch. I don't want to listen to Oliver right now. I don't want Griffin to either. None of this adventure has been Oliver's idea, so why does Griffin keep looking to him as if he's going to lead the way? As if he's the one brave enough to decide what comes next?

"Is it because Oliver's a boy? Do you think girls can't climb trees? Because I once climbed all the way up the old oak by Sycamore Park—" I pause to catch my breath, debating my next step. I'm already a quarter of the way up the tree, and the branches get thinner the closer I get to the top. I reach up and give the next branch a shake, gauging its strength before continuing up. "Sophie and I set a mission to find out what the strange noises were coming from Phil Morrison's backyard. His fences were so high, I had to climb to the top of the oak tree to see."

Sophie had waited below, holding the tree trunk

like it was the base of a ladder. My eyes remained focused ahead, up where the light broke through the top branches. But I could hear her calls below, rooting me on.

"Finley Walsh, super-special secret agent of the Walsh-Higgins Adventure Agency, is on the case!" she called. "With each branch, she's one step closer to the truth! Is Mr. Morrison building a battleship in his backyard? Is he digging a hidden underground bunker to survive an impending apocalypse? Or does he just need to replace his lawn mower? Thanks to the World's Greatest Female Adventurer Number One Hundred One, the answer is just moments away!"

Now it's silence below me as Oliver and Griffin watch, debating whatever rebuttal or objection they're going to hurl at me next. I wonder if Meggie climbed this tree, back before she disappeared, and if she had a friend there to cheer her on.

Last time I suggested Sophie and I climb on an adventure, she'd looked at her feet. But I still saw the way her nostrils flared, like the thought repulsed her.

"I don't like how the bark gets stuck under my nails," she'd said. "And last time I got sap on my sweatshirt. It took hours to scrub it out."

I'd gone home that afternoon swallowing down tears, yelling to Mom that Sophie had become boring. That Veronica and Chloe made her boring. Mom hadn't turned from the sink while she listened, other than to push a few strands of loose hair back each time she sighed, soapy suds caking her dirty-blond hair.

"I'm sure you can find something else to do together," she said, voice barely audible over the clank of dishes. "Something a little less messy, like . . ."

But I stopped listening there, because mess was our forte. It was adventure. It was us. That's why our names—just our names—were printed on our business cards. And that's why we did the things all the other kids were too chicken to do, like climb the Sycamore Park oak tree. Like spying on old, grumpy Mr. Morrison.

That's what made us important. What made us great.

A branch snaps beneath my sneaker and I slip. My heel scrapes against the bark, and I flail as I try to catch myself. I stumble down, arms stretched above me, before securing my foot on a lower branch.

"Finley, please!" Oliver calls below. "We don't need that view to find a clue."

I grit my teeth and pull myself to the next branch. A spider rushes over my knuckles, but I resist flinching. "I'm teaching Griffin, okay?"

"Teaching him how to fall?"

"When do I get to go?" Griffin whines. "I can't learn by watching. And I've been waiting years to try."

A few feet above me is a thick branch, conjoined at its base with another. The perfect spot to sit and look down on the world below. I lick a bead of sweat off my upper lip and reach for the next branch.

Down below, Oliver's voice is strained. "It hasn't been a year, Griffin. It's been less than two hours."

"Dad told me he was going to teach me ages ago," Griffin says. "But he's always too busy when we visit, so now I'm eight and still don't know how."

I settle onto the branch, testing my weight before lowering myself completely onto the spot where it meets the trunk. I maintain a hold on a nearby branch, the leaves trembling with each heavy breath I take. From up here, Oliver and Griffin look like little blond garden gnomes. I feel light, like nothing bad and muddled and messy can reach me.

Not that the thoughts don't try. I'm not surprised Dad promised Griffin he'd teach him something, then never followed up on it. Whenever he doesn't postpone our visit, he's got some project he's working on, something more important because everything is more important than the family he outgrew like an old pair of shoes. Somehow, it's worse than when Mom leaves Oliver in charge, armed with a set of rules. Her work keeps her busy too, but not in the same way; while Dad always seems to be dredging up projects to keep him distracted from us, Mom's always working for us. It's why I want to show her she can trust me and take me more seriously, so I'm less of a burden, and not just someone else she has to stretch herself thin to look after.

"You don't need Dad to teach you," I call to Griffin. "You can't teach someone how to climb. You just have to start. The important thing is having someone with you in case you fall. So they can catch you."

"She means so they can call an ambulance," Oliver says. "Which we can't do right now, because we don't have service, which makes this entire thing a deadly mistake."

The word "deadly" snaps me back into focus. I didn't just climb this tree to prove a point to my little brother—though that was definitely part of it. I squint, peering through the sea of branches ahead, taking in the woods from the same vantage point Meggie—or her kidnapper—may have twenty years ago. So far, it's nothing but a whole lot of green-and-brown nothingness, but I wouldn't be a semiprofessional adventurer if I took everything at face value. I learned that from Great Female Adventurer Number Fifteen, Louise Arner Boyd, who traveled beyond a seemingly endless row of glaciers to find the beautiful Arctic lands beyond their icy peaks.

I angle to the left to look around one of the thicker trees in my view. The branch wobbles beneath me, and I grasp at the trunk to steady myself. Its surface is jagged beneath my fingers. I turn toward the trunk and slide my fingers, ever so slightly, to reveal the carved wood beneath.

MR + PW

"Mr. Peewuh," I sound out. Nope, that's definitely not it. My fingers trace the letters and catch against tiny divots in between. They're initials—"M. R." as in "Meggie Riley."

I can't help but break into a giant grin. This means

she had been up here, once—just like I guessed. I'd made a discovery all by myself. And all while Oliver critiqued me from below, and while Griffin turned to him instead of me.

I press the pad of my thumb against her initials and imagine her here, balanced on this branch. Her blond hair pulled back, just like mine. And maybe she wasn't alone—maybe P. W. was her best friend. Her Sophie. Maybe she'd climbed this tree with them on a woodsy adventure. Maybe P. W. hadn't come one day. Maybe they decided they were too old for adventures, and that if Meggie wasn't going to grow out of adventuring, then they had to grow out of her.

Maybe that was the day Meggie was kidnapped: the one day everyone, at the same time, happened to look away.

Cautiously, I reach into my back pocket and pull out my phone. Up here, I have service bars for the first time since entering the woods, but still no new messages. Ignoring the pang in my gut, I snap a photo of my discovery.

As I move to return it to my pocket, I spot something move at the base of a distant tree. Behind the chitter of birds I hear the faintest echo of twigs snapping beneath someone's heel. Then, again, like a dark flash from the corner of my eye—a silhouette, just like the one I spotted when we arrived.

My heartbeat rises in my chest, thumping hard and loud until I hear it echoing like drums in my ears. If the café and diner were any indication, we're basically the only tourists here right now. So even if these woods used to be full of tourists looking to crack the case, it doesn't make sense for there to be anyone in the same area right now.

Unless they followed us from the diner.

The figure remains at the base of the tree, angled from my brothers' view. If they were trying to save Meggie too, why would they be quietly following and watching us, hidden? Maybe they want to steal our leads, see if we find anything first. Or maybe they want to make sure we don't find anything. Because they want the reward money.

Or because they know something about what happened to Meggie—something they don't want us to find.

I clench my jaw and inhale a steadying breath, because the top of a tree is not the place to panic. I can't warn my brothers from up here, or else the shadowy figure will hear. I need to get down fast so we can all get out of here safely.

"Nothing up here!" I call. I swing my legs over the branch and settle the toe of my foot on the one below. I climb down as safely yet quickly as I can. It takes all the focus I can not to check for the onlooker, but I keep my eyes on the branches and my hands.

At last, my sneakers meet firm ground. I step into the grass, my head feeling foggy from the exercise and my too-fast heartbeat. I try to keep my voice low. "Don't panic or react," I say, and Oliver's eyes go wide, "but I think we're being followed, and we need to leave. Now."

Oliver looks about ready to scream, but clenches

his jaw teeth-grindingly tight to keep quiet. He grabs Griffin's hand. "Let's go."

Malt stirs at his feet. I'm sure he's about to follow us when he darts off in the opposite direction, straight into the woods. I clasp a hand over my mouth to keep from shouting and immediately regret letting a dog into the adventure agency.

Griffin yanks his hand free from Oliver and bolts straight after him. "Malt! Stop!"

"Griffin!"

I race through the woods at his heels, fallen branches and old leaves crunching beneath my feet. Pebbles threaten to throw me off-balance as I dash after my brother. Malt continues to race ahead, a white blur darting between bushes and over rocks. He's gunning straight for the mysterious figure, which means that by following him, so is Griffin.

If anything happens to Griffin, it's my fault—but I know Oliver's right. That Mom will blame it on him.

I pump my arms by my sides, sweat slicking my shirt to my back. Malt vanishes from view, darting around a tree. Griffin is finally within arm's reach and I grasp his wrist, tugging him to a halt.

He pulls against my hand with all his might. His skin slides in my grip, but I just hold tighter. "We can't lose Malt!"

"We'll come back when it's safe," I say, pulling him to face me. "Right now, we're in danger, Griff."

"Then so is Malt." He turns, revealing the tears in his eyes. "Bad things happen to people in these woods. That's the whole reason we're out here. We can't let anything happen to Malt, because then he could vanish too! And people might not look for him like they do for Meggie." He sniffs, chin wobbling. "And he'll be gone, and Jeff will hate me, and Mom will trust me even less than she already does."

Oliver approaches from behind me. Griffin's voice goes quiet, gaze focused on me. "Please, Finley. We can't lose him. Please."

His eyes are wide and desperate, and I remember that this isn't just an adventure for Griffin, either. It's easy to forget that when he's buzzing from a sugar high, talking an octave too loud, stomping through the woods with the subtlety of a clumsy moose. But Griffin needs this too.

I slide my hand from his wrist to his fingers and give them a hard squeeze. "Okay," I say. "But you stay here. I'll get him."

I release his hand and run before Oliver can object. Dirt pounds beneath my feet and I dart forward, weaving through the trees in the direction Malt went. Anything—anyone—could be up ahead, but I don't slow down. Griffin is right—a great adventurer never leaves a friend behind. When the *MS Express Samina* sank, Great Female Adventurers Seventy-Eight and Seventy-Nine, Heidi Hart and Christine Shannon, not only stuck together to survive, but saved a few other passengers as well. If I ever want to be a world-renowned adventurer, I need to show up for my team like Hart and Shannon did for each other.

Someone should have been here for Meggie when she disappeared. Someone should have run toward the danger, not away, for her sake.

So I run, twenty years too late.

There's a flash of white up ahead. Whether it's Malt or a really pale raccoon, I charge in its direction. I spin and leap over a stump and spin around a fat tree, toward the blur of white.

Then something grabs my arm.

I twist, hard and fast, and the hand—it's definitely a human hand—loses its grip. I turn to run, but my heel catches on a twisted root and I fall face-first in the dirt. Soil cakes my face, clogging my nose and mouth. I feel a presence looming over me and turn onto my back to face my attacker.

"Calm down! It's just me."

Jeff hovers over me, hands up and fingers extended in surrender. Malt paces behind him, panting happily.

"Sam told me you'd taken one of her maps and headed out into the woods," he says. His expression seems to add, *like a bunch of idiots*, but as if Mom's still watching, he leaves that part out. "When I said you could go outside, I meant on the front steps, or to take Malt on a short walk. Not to go alone into Stone Creek Woods on a witch hunt!"

I remain on the ground, propped up by my elbows, chest heaving with uneven breaths. It's just Jeff. Of course it was just Jeff. That's why Malt ran off, and why it felt like we were being followed. Because he was looking for us. Looking after us.

But still, something sits funny at the base of my stomach. Maybe the milk Sam gave me was a bit spoiled. Or maybe it's just that this doesn't add up—Jeff finding us just as we discover a clue. Jeff watching, but not approaching, even after he'd found us.

But not just that. As he stands over me, hand extended and face tired and worn, I can't help but wish he hadn't chased us down. That, just like Mom, he turned away and told us to entertain ourselves, just to turn around and get mad at what we ended up doing when left alone.

I bite the inside of my cheek, draw the iron taste of blood to my tongue. I thought this break could be different—that staying with Jeff meant I could go on a real adventure, finally prove Sophie and Veronica and Chloe and everybody else wrong. But it's no different from Saturday mornings, when Mom tells me to play with Griffin while she finishes some work emails, then gets mad if the cartoons I put on for him are "too violent" or "too mature." No different from when she puts Oliver in charge of me being in charge of Griffin, so I get yelled at a second time by him, as if the one year he has on me makes him mature enough to be Mom's second-in-command.

It's no different, but I need it to be. Somehow, someway, I can't let taking Jeff's hand and leaving the woods be the end of this adventure.

"Come on, kid." He leans down and I slip my hand into his, let him hoist me up from my spot in the dirt. "Let's get out of here before coyote hour."

I brush dirt and leaves from my shorts and follow him and Malt back toward my brothers. They're closer than where I left them, Oliver following my tracks with Griffin behind him. Relief washes over Oliver's face when he sees Jeff, and Griffin rushes over to Malt.

While Griffin bends down to pet Malt, I fall in step with Oliver and await Jeff's lecture about the dangers of the woods and looking into Meggie's case. But he just shuffles forward, eyes ahead and mouth in a tight line. Perhaps because, once again, he doesn't quite know what to say. Doesn't have the practice Mom and Oliver have in scolding me.

Or maybe he's afraid that if he starts talking about Meggie, he'll say too much.

"I'm not used to cooking for more than one, so I have some pizzas coming from Stone Creek Slice," Jeff says as we trek back toward the street. "Hope you like pepperoni, because that's the only topping they get right."

Griffin and Malt walk up front with him while I trail behind with Oliver. I run my hands through my ponytail as I walk, shaking soil and pebbles from my tangled locks. I'll have to show the photo I took of the initials to Oliver and Griffin later, after Jeff thinks we're asleep. Watching Jeff trekking along ahead of me, broad shoulders slightly slumped and hands tucked into the pockets of his jeans,

I wonder what it means if he really does know something about Meggie's disappearance. What it means to stay with him for a whole week while we're investigating it.

What will happen if we find something he doesn't want us to find.

Something slips beneath my sneaker and I'm plummeting, once again, toward the ground. I catch myself at the last minute, arms flailing by my sides to catch my balance.

Oliver scoffs. "You're pretty clumsy for someone who carries around business cards with the title adventurer on them, you know that?"

"Being a professional adventurer is a journey, not a destination," I snap, leaning down to tie the guilty shoelace. Jeff and Griffin continue ahead. Oliver starts to follow and I tie quickly, double knotting just to be sure.

As I rise, something shifts in my peripheral vision. I spin around, fast, so my ponytail flaps against my neck. There, half a dozen yards back, is that same shadow—a figure, ducking quickly behind a tree. A tingle traces up my spine and I know, without a doubt, it's no raccoon or coyote.

We were being followed. And not just by Jeff.

This is the third time I've spotted someone, and I'm not sure which time was the stranger and which time was Jeff. So I keep my mouth shut as I catch up with him and my brothers, even as I feel a gaze digging into my back as I go. Regardless of who was who, one thing is certain: the only people who knew we went into these woods, searching for the truth about Meggie, were Jeff and the people in the diner:

Sam, the hostess and waitress who works for Bryan Phillips, the man police suspected because of his professional rivalry with Meggie's father.

Jason Jeffords, the busboy, whose father was Meggie's high school sweetheart and long-term boyfriend at the time of her disappearance.

Richard Connors, the visiting reporter from the *Burlington Biweekly*, and the only other tourist visiting before the official twenty-year anniversary of Meggie's disappearance.

And, of course, Jeff. Mom's estranged cousin who lives alone in the woods, isolated in a town obsessed with its darkest mystery.

As we step through the edge of the woods and into the empty diner parking lot, I realize we've officially got our suspect list. But I still feel like a ton of mortar is resting on my shoulders.

Whoever is involved with Meggie's disappearance, they know we're on the case. Which means this adventure just got a lot more complicated.

GREATEST FEMALE ADVENTURER NUMBER FOUR: ANN BANCROFT, HONORED IN THE NATIONAL WOMEN'S HALL OF FAME AND FIRST WOMAN TO CROSS BOTH POLAR ICE CAPS.

I'm hopeful Jeff will bring us back to the shop so I can snap quick photos of the clippings on the café's walls, but once we leave the woods, he leads us straight to his car. I can't help but wonder if—now that he knows we're on the mission—he's purposefully keeping us from the clues. But as he unlocks the car, I remember this means we're headed straight for his home—the perfect place to learn more about him and his connection to Meggie. I'll be an amateur adventurer in disguise as an innocent little girl, using dinner as an excuse to pull intel from him like I'm the Greatest Female Adventurer Number Thirty-Six—the first female detective, Isabella Goodwin—going undercover.

I also need to share the photo of the initials with my brothers and tell them about the second figure in the woods. Thinking about the shadow person makes me shiver with fear and excitement all at once—because the best discoveries come with the feeling of both, and the best adventurers are the ones skilled enough to survive and share the experience.

"Can I see that map now?" I ask Oliver, wiggling my fingers toward the front seat expectantly.

He groans, drawing the meticulously folded sheet from his pocket. "Don't get any ideas."

I snatch it from his hands. "Too late!"

I smooth out the crinkles on the map, flattening the paper against my lap. It's a bit cartoonish, with bright blue splotches marking the creek's path and boxes with triangles on top symbolizing the residential areas of Stone Creek. But water paths and rural homes aren't what matter here, anyway. Meggie is what matters—what makes Stone Creek special and unlike the sleepy suburbs in Massachusetts, or the fake thrills of Busch Gardens.

In the center of the map is a big circle marking where Meggie was last seen, where we just were on what the diner receipts refer to as the northern tip of Stone Creek Woods. The woods extend out farther, interrupted occasionally by the creek or a small farm. In the northeast corner of the woods is a note marking the location of Meggie's first adventure, the "no-man's-land" where she found the Stone Creek treasure. It's not far from the Riley residence, which is depicted with a house drawing three times the size of any other house on the map.

South from the Riley house is downtown Stone Creek,

tucked off the side and separated by the winding path of the creek. On the opposite side of the water is another patch of residences, and a street called Meggie Lane. Then, back west past where Meggie disappeared, and another cluster of trees, is nothing but more woods and houses—like the one we're headed to now.

Jeff glances back through the rearview mirror, and I quickly fold the map and shove it in my pocket. I'm not sure how I'm going to get all over Stone Creek before Mom picks us up in a few days, but I'm determined that by the end of the trip, I'll have explored every spot on this map, like a modern Gertrude Bell.

After a short drive down a winding, tree-lined road, the car stumbles over a cluster of potholes and takes an abrupt right onto a patch of yellow grass. Then the engine dies. "We're here," Jeff says, voice faltering at the end, as though unsure how he feels about "here."

We're parked on the patchy lawn of Jeff's worn-down ranch house. The shutters are wide open, the blinds inside tilted and snapped to reveal glimpses of the dark, empty house beyond. A flat wooden deck stretches across the front of the house, cluttered with tall boxes and mismatched junk, from chairs with three legs to stacks of tires and heavy bags of soil. Lonely vines stretch up the left side of the house, thin and curled as though unsure if they want to continue their pursuit of the roof.

As Oliver moves to help Jeff unload the trunk, I linger by the car door and take in my surroundings. I always wanted to live in a house. Somewhere with a yard that Sophie and I could run a metal detector over, or with a roof where we could watch the stars and exchange scary stories in the dark.

But Jeff's house is an afterthought. Which would make sense if he put his energy into his shop, but he barely showed any interest in Meggie's case. He's not even advertising the twenty-year anniversary, which could be a perfect opportunity to draw in caffeine-reliant tourists.

As Jeff hauls our suitcases from the trunk, his car groaning in relief, I wonder—if he's not at the café, and if he's not here—where the real Jeff is.

Malt bounds toward the deck and Griffin follows after him, just as bouncy and overeager as the puppy. Oliver scowls, struggling to drag the wheeled suitcases over the uneven yard. "Hey, a little help here?"

Griffin jiggles the front door as though expecting to find it unlocked. "Uncle Cousin Jeff, do you have an Xbox?"

Jeff tosses his keys at me. I sprint to catch them as he says, "I don't know what he's yammering about, but let that kid inside."

Oliver—tripping over two suitcases—starts to object, but I run to reach the porch and Griffin. I bump him from the door and insert Jeff's key. "Just so you know, I could totally break us into this if I was the one with the credit card," I gloat.

Griffin's eyes go wide, and my chest expands. But

then he asks, "Is that why Mom gave Ollie the card for emergencies?"

The front door swings open with a creak. I frown. "Oliver doesn't know how to do any of that stuff. I'm the semiprofessional adventurer, remember? I'm the one trained to deal with emergencies."

Griffin looks up at me eagerly. "So can you help if Jeff doesn't have an Xbox? Because that would be an emergency."

I huff and shove him inside. We stand in a living room, decorated with oversized brown furniture, a TV, and a worn-in dog bed that Malt steamrolls right into. But it's the walls that capture my attention: just like the café, they're crowded with so many frames that the wood paneling barely peeks through. Rather than newspaper clippings, though, these are filled with photos of people, some posing and smiling, others capturing snapshots of a scene, still smiling.

I feel like Mom when we're watching TV and she points at a guest star, stammering, "Oh, they're the person from . . ." and keeps mumbling to herself until, a commercial break later, she finally remembers the character or actor's name. The faces in the photos I'm looking at are all semifamiliar, a mixture of foggy childhood memories and a simple recognition that they are relatives: that man has our blond hair; that girl has Oliver's pointed nose.

"Whoa," Griffin murmurs, crawling onto Jeff's leather couch. He sits with his knees digging into the cushions, hands clasped on its back as he stares with his stubby nose inches from the photos. "Is this your suspect board?"

"My what?" Jeff barks as he stumbles inside, rolling my suitcase in after him. "No, these are your relatives, kid. Though I guess you'd be too young to remember—you were in diapers last time I saw you at one of these things."

"Ew!" Griffin shrieks, but despite the terrifying memory of a pre-potty-trained Griffin, I find myself smiling. This house is like the opposite of our apartment, which has blank walls interrupted only by the occasional watercolor painting Mom picked up in a yard sale on the way home from work. When we were little, the walls used to be covered in photographs just like this. But over the years, the photos were replaced with stock art, the same way trips to visit extended family were replaced with work trips and TV movies. It's like all the photos Mom tucked away by trying to forget our life before Dad left ended up here, jammed into Jeff's tiny living room, preserved in all their glory.

I even spot a six-year-old Oliver and five-year-old me in one of the photos that's hanging above a yellowing lampshade. We're dripping wet, my dress sticking to my knees and Oliver's white shirt almost see-through. I faintly remember that day: us leaping into the hotel fountain because we were sad there wasn't a pool. Mom and Dad were furious we'd wrecked our outfits for the family reunion, but all we could do was smile and laugh.

Sometimes I forget Oliver used to play with me. Back before he stopped being lectured at and joined Mom in being a lecturer.

Warmth floods my chest, and not only because Jeff's house has been baking inside its shut windows all afternoon. It's a feeling of relief, seeing all these people kept alive, seeing this monument to them even after I'd forgotten. They may not be famous adventurers. But Jeff, at least, saw something in them worth remembering.

Oliver appears beside me. "Kind of weird they're all so old, huh?" he whispers. "Why hasn't he seen anyone in the past whatever many years?"

"Maybe he just ran out of room for new photos," I say, weirdly defensive. But for once Oliver is right: I know why Mom got too busy to keep in touch with our extended family, but if they were so important to Jeff, why did he disconnect? Why did he opt to live here alone, in Stone Creek, his life and business dedicated to a cold case he shows little interest in solving?

The potential answer sends a chill up my spine.

"I cleaned out the upstairs for you kids," Jeff says, pointing to a narrow staircase at the edge of the hall. "Feel free to settle in and I'll keep an eye out for the pizza guy." He frowns. "Last time I didn't keep watch, he gave my dinner to Mr. Wilkins across the street. I'm still waiting on that refund."

Griffin leaps off the sofa and runs to Jeff, clasping his hands on Jeff's elbows. "Please keep guard for our pizza. We're counting on you," he says, low and serious, before turning and bolting toward the stairs. Jeff stands, blinking, as though Griffin moves and talks too fast for him to digest.

"Finley, you're helping this time," Oliver grumbles, nodding toward my suitcase. I take hold of its handle and follow him up the stairs, heaving the heavy bag behind.

At the top of the stairs we're greeted by musty air and a semifurnished attic space with a slanted, triangular ceiling. Griffin is already spread out on one of the three cots, shrieking, "Dibs!" while running the heels of his dirty sneakers over the argyle comforter. I settle my suitcase onto the one beside him, surprised not to hear the mattress springs groan under its weight. Tugging the comforter back, I see pristine white sheets underneath, crisp and new. Even the pillow is perfectly fluffy, not dented with years of age like the furniture downstairs.

I lift my hand, my palm leaving a puffy indent in the pillow. "It's all new. He bought it just for us."

The bed is soft, inviting. But thinking about earlier—the shadows in the woods, and that it could have been Jeff watching, but never approaching—makes me wonder about his intentions. I wish I could swat the thoughts away like gnats and just focus on the comfy bed and all the relatives I want to ask him about when I'm back downstairs.

"This must have cost him a lot, and considering the café isn't exactly the tourist hot spot it once was, he could be getting the money from somewhere else," I say. A thought shoots through my head like a bullet. "Like the Rileys, or Bryan Phillips! They're both rich, and would have reason to pay off an accomplice to keep them quiet over the years."

Oliver rolls his eyes. "Enough with your theories. You're never going to rescue Meggie if you keep making up stories, like the rest of the people in this town."

Something like a restless bear stirs in my chest, angry and ready for a fight. I glance at the attic entrance, the doorless space that leads to the stairs and Jeff below. I wasn't planning on showing the photo to my brothers until after Jeff was asleep, but a great adventurer is nothing without her instincts. And I'm going to go ahead and consider the urge to prove Oliver wrong to be a good instinct.

"You can doubt me after you make a discovery," I say, whipping out my phone. "Look what I found in the tree." As he steps around his cot toward mine, I add, "While you were down below, too scared to help." For good measure.

Griffin frog-leaps from his cot onto mine. Oliver leans over my shoulder. With their attention on me, I straighten my shoulders and swipe to zoom in on the initials.

"M. R. As in Meggie Riley," I say, low and serious like I'm reporting secret intel. Which I kind of am. "She was with someone with the initials P. W. Which means she probably used to climb that tree with a friend. They could know why Meggie was there alone that day, and who else could have known to find Meggie in the woods."

Oliver jabs at my screen, zooming in further. I roll my shoulders to get the weight of his arm off me. "I dunno. It looks like something a couple would carve, not friends."

My stomach drops, all the way through the attic, the living room, to the Earth's molten core.

"What?" I say, loud so Griffin leans back. "No way Meggie was climbing trees with boys. It had to have been a friend. Someone she didn't mind getting messy with."

Like Sophie, before sap on her sweatshirt was reason enough to cut me loose.

Oliver leans over me, nose scrunched and lips drawn in a cautious line. It's like he's just solved the universe's easiest long-division problem and feels so sad I couldn't figure it out that he doesn't even know how to start explaining it.

"She could have gone up in the tree to carve it with them," he says, "or she could have done it alone, too. Especially if the crush was a secret."

He talks slow, each syllable even and flat like I won't get it otherwise. Somehow, it's worse than the quick and giggly way Chloe and Veronica talk about boys, voices high and confident as they speak that new language Sophie somehow learned overnight, without me.

Oliver, Chloe, Veronica, Sophie—they all make me feel like I'm walking around with a plastic dome around my head, their words distorted and distant so I can't quite make them out, but hear enough to know that there's a big, complicated world beyond me that I'm too childish to notice—or want to notice.

No one made it into *100 of the World's Greatest Female Adventurers* because they were the best at talking about crushes. Even Jeanne Baret, who completed her greatest adventure alongside her boyfriend, made a name for herself on her ship, outside of her relationship. So how, if no one famous or great or magnificent is known for their crushes, can everyone act like I'm the immature and stupid one for not speaking Crush?

"Why did you know that?" I ask, raising a sharp eyebrow at Oliver.

His jaw dangles just enough for me to know I'm regaining the upper ground. "It's obvious! The real question is how you didn't know that."

I don't back down. "Since when are you the expert on love?" I ask, my smug grin creeping into my voice. "Do you like someone? Or someones?"

"Oooo!" Griffin sings. "Ollie's in looooooove!"

Oliver's ears turn beet red. "I am not!" He talks fast, words stumbling over each other in a very non-Oliver way. "It's common knowledge that couples will carve their names into trees or whatever. People do it in the bathroom stalls or on the lockers at school all the time, and—"

"And you know this because you've done it too," I tease, sitting up on my knees to face him, "because you're secretly a hopeless romantic, and harbor secret crushes just like Meggie Riley did!"

My tone's a bit sharp on that last part, tongue lashing like I want it to sting him. Because Meggie is supposed to be mine, an adventurer, survivor, maybe runaway who's too big for the tiny world she grew up in, just like me. I don't want Oliver to have her, to take her. I don't want this case to be just another thing that makes him great to the world, to Mom.

Greater than me.

"You don't know what you're talking about!" Oliver shouts, so loud it echoes off the angled ceiling and the thin, floral-printed walls. "You always talk, talk, talk, but you don't know anything. You act like if you say enough, some of it will make sense, but it never does! You're just loud, and annoying!"

He stops, mouth hanging open like I'd slapped him, even though I haven't moved or said a thing. I'm still, the folds of my comforter indenting my knees, my empty hands open, half-cupped, in front of me. Beside me, Griffin tugs quietly at a loose thread on the sheet, his eyes fixed on the ground.

Oliver gapes. "Finley, I'm—"

Someone clears their throat from the other side of the room. We spin in unison to see Jeff hovering awkwardly at the foot of the stairs, his eyes fixed past us and never meeting our gazes.

He probably thinks this is why Mom was gushing about how grateful she was when she dropped us off. And sure, we argue and fight and bump heads all the time. But this was something else, even for me and Oliver.

Which makes me wonder why he reacted that way. And makes me feel like he's even more distant than I thought—far off in another world I can't understand, just like Sophie and Veronica and Chloe. And just as unwilling to guide me there, to have me join.

"Um, pizza," Jeff says, grasping for words. "It, uh, was pretty hot when it arrived, so half the cheese slid off during delivery. But you get what you get in Stone Creek, and—"

"Pizza!" Griffin shrieks, leaping over the other side of the bed. Either because he's really that excited for dinner, or to escape me and Oliver.

As their footsteps retreat downstairs, I swing my legs over the cot. "The women who make history are always the ones stupid boys like you think are loud and annoying," I say, looking Oliver square in the eye, my gaze hard and unflinching as though it can make up for the way my chin wobbles.

He opens his mouth, probably for some classic-Oliver backtracking that's more excuse than apology, so I quickly add, "Besides, you're missing the most important point of this whole discovery."

His mouth clamps shut, swallowing back down whatever he was going to say. Then, after a moment, he asks in a softer voice, "And what's that?"

I hate that as much as I want to throw my pillow at him, I feel like I've won something when I get his attention. "If those were a lover's initials, that means Meggie liked—or was maybe even seeing someone—other than her boyfriend, Devon Jeffords. And that's a pretty good motive for hurting Meggie."

Oliver's face crumbles and I wonder, again, what it is

about Jason Jeffords that he's noticed and isn't sharing with me. Earlier, I thought I could trust him with the truth about the second figure in the woods. But it's obvious that he doesn't trust me—not my instincts about clues like the initials, and not even with himself: his real thoughts, his real theories. All the things he keeps from me when he averts his gaze in the halls at school, or slams his door at night just as I'm walking past.

If I'm going to solve Meggie's case, I'm going to have to keep some things to myself. Especially the things that are most dangerous, like the person in the woods.

"We'll talk to Jason tomorrow," Oliver says, catching me off guard. "It's a good place to start. But tonight, let's just keep our heads down, eat some mediocre pizza, and keep Jeff off our backs, okay?"

I nod, even though I have full intentions of doing the exact opposite of what Oliver wants. Well, I do plan on making the most of that mediocre pizza. But not just for eating. Dinner is an opportunity to sit down with Jeff for the first time, without suitcases and coffee shipments and woodsy paths between us. It's the perfect chance to get to know him—Jeff the business owner, the loner, the potential suspect—and figure out what keeps him in Stone Creek, surrounded by Meggie's case.

Whether Oliver likes it or not, there's no pressing pause on this adventure. And an investigation over pizza is the perfect place for Greatest Female Adventurer Number One Hundred One to start tonight.

GREATEST FEMALE ADVENTURER NUMBER FIVE:

JOAN OF ARC,

FRENCH MILITARY STRATEGIST WHO DEFIED THE EXPECTATIONS OF HER YOUTH AND GENDER TO END THE SIEGE OF ORLEANS WITHIN DAYS.

Downstairs, Jeff and Griffin sit at a circular table smooshed in the corner of the kitchen, paper plates stationed before each mismatched chair, with the greasy cardboard pizza box in the table's center. Griffin shifts onto his knees and peers into the box, hands pressed on the edge of the table so it teeters beneath his weight.

Interrogating an estranged relative over pizza isn't the first image that pops into my mind when I imagine completing a mission, but a good adventurer sees opportunity in all scenarios. Even this—Jeff, wedged between the table and the wall with his head bent over a droopy slice of pizza—is a moment ripe with opportunity, with secrets and truths and clues to mine.

"Finley, help me decide," Griffin calls, not lifting his eyes from the box. "This slice has more cheese, but only one pepperoni. But this one with the pepperonis has half its cheese sliding off."

Jeff scratches the side of his head, glancing sheepishly at the lopsided, Picasso-like pizza. But a grin sweeps across my face. I love when Griffin asks for my help instead of Oliver's, even if it's just for something silly, like a piece of pizza.

"Here's what you do," I say, plopping onto the stool beside him. "Pick the pepperonis off that piece, put them on yours, and give the cheese-less, pepperoni-less, sauce slice to Oliver."

Griffin's on the task before I'm finished giving it. "Done and done."

Oliver slumps into the seat beside Jeff and doesn't object as Griffin plops the sorry excuse for a slice onto his plate. A teeny, tiny, atom-sized part of me feels bad that he's so dejected after our fight. But the soon-to-be-famous adventurer inside me knows that with Oliver out of commission, this is the perfect time to strike. I shimmy my chair closer to the table, eyes fixed on Jeff. "Melted pizza, grumpy customers: you don't speak highly of Stone Creek, so why do you stay here?"

Jeff rips off a piece of his crust. "I promise it tastes better than it looks."

"Agreed," Griffin says, voice muffled by a mouthful of stringy cheese.

It's a tough balance, trying not to come on too serious but also be taken seriously. I drum my fingers on the edge of the table. "But why Stone Creek? I mean . . . what brought you here to begin with?"

He answers through a disgustingly full mouth, making me wonder if I'm really related to him and Griffin after all. "My parents. Born and raised, never left."

Griffin slaps his hands on the table, shaking it so hard, water spills over the tops of all four of our cups. "A-ha! So you were here on the night of Meggie's disappearance!"

Jeff stops midbite. His muscles go stiff, like he's petrified in place. I swear the house holds its breath, all the crickets pausing their songs, all the creaks and squeaks of the old radiators coming to a halt. Even Malt lifts his head from his bowl, one ear raised as though waiting for a response.

I grasp Griffin's shoulders and shove him back into his seat. "He doesn't mean that!" I say, because if he did, that would totally blow our cover. My nails dig into his shoulder blades. "He's just caught up in the story. It's all those murder movies he watches."

"That you put on for me!" Griffin pouts.

Right now, I wish I could go click on Jeff's TV and plop Griffin in front of it with his dinner. My loudmouthed little brother is going to blow this before I've even started.

"Sure, I knew her," Jeff admits. I sit upright in my seat. His tone remains light, matter-of-fact. "Everyone here did. It's a small town."

His attention turns to his dinner, but my mind snags on his words like a loose thread. Jeff knew Meggie. He was here before she vanished, back when she was a local girl, running through the woods and climbing trees. Like me.

"Were you friends?" I ask, voice bubbling with excitement. "Is that why you dedicated the café to her?"

Jeff lets out a gruff cough, sending a few crumbs flying my way. "Never knew her personally," he says. "We ran in different circles, so to speak. She helped manage her father's businesses, and I was working at your great-uncle's auto shop, which was one of the few places either the Rileys or Mr. Phillips didn't own at the time. But whether you work for them or not, everyone here knows the Rileys. And she was their oldest."

Griffin wiggles his fingers together maniacally. "The heir to the estate. Perfect ransom material."

I stomp on his foot under the table.

Jeff shrugs. "Some of the richest folks in Stone Creek, that's for sure."

Ransom would make sense—if someone had actually tried to make the swap. But the Rileys have offered their money for years, and no one has come forward.

The only way that would make sense is if the kidnappers had lost Meggie somehow. I smile to myself, imagining her valiantly escaping from her captors and, rather than heading back home, taking the chance to start a new life of adventure. Far away from her overbearing father and his rigid, boring business.

Speaking of boring businesses: "When we were at the diner earlier, someone mentioned that the twenty-year anniversary of her disappearance was coming up this month. And that it's a big deal." I shimmy forward, chair legs scratching against the wooden floorboards. "Are you going to throw a big event at Meggie's Cup to draw in tourists? If you are, we can totally help"—Oliver rolls his eyes, but I press on—"and you can even start early this year, to draw in extra customers!"

My pulse flutters at the thought of herding new customers into the shop. I imagine myself surrounded by a couple dozen caffeinated guests as they study the newspapers and point out new clues and theories just for me.

Jeff reaches for a second slice. "The local businesses set up vendor booths downtown for the festival each year. But I'm not too into that stuff."

I frown. That stuff is plastered all over the walls of his shop. It's in the literal name. If he's not interested in helping to solve Meggie's case, then why has he centered his life around it?

The more I get to know about Jeff, the less that makes sense.

"So, what are you into?" I ask. "Because Stone Creek is all about Meggie, who doesn't interest you. And it's obvious you used to leave Stone Creek a lot to see family." I gesture toward the photo wall. "But it doesn't look like you've gone anywhere in years."

"Finley," Oliver says, voice sharp and low. "Just eat your pizza and—"

I shoot him a personalized version of the look Mom

uses to quiet me. Because the only possible end to that sentence is a continuation of our fight upstairs, and there's enough going on at this table without that added drama.

Jeff leans back then, the cap of his hat brushing the clock hung too low on the kitchen wall. He scratches the back of his neck, eyes fixed on the scattering of crumbs left on his plate.

"I dunno, kid," he says in a voice that sounds more directed at him than me. "I guess I stopped going when I ran out of things to say."

The table goes quiet. It's just about the strangest answer he could have given. And I was even prepared for him to admit that real Jeff had been dead for years and he's a secret government agent sent to take on his identity and investigate Stone Creek.

Curiosity and frustration wane, replaced by something else—something that settles deep and heavy in my bones, because as strange as his words were, I know that feeling too. Standing on the outskirts of Sophie, Veronica, and Chloe's huddle, racking my mind for the perfect quip to capture their attention, to let me in—but even when I do, never letting the words pass my lips, just in case I'll say it wrong. Or that strange disappointment I get when we're scheduled to visit Dad, like each time I go, I'm reliving scenes from a play that stopped touring years ago.

Maybe Jeff doesn't know what to say because he's afraid he'll say the wrong thing about Meggie. About some involvement he had in her disappearance. But either way, that feeling is the same. Which makes Jeff and me the same too.

The thought sends a chill up my spine.

I jump when Oliver's phone goes off, ringtone blaring through the tiny kitchen. He scrambles to pull it from his pocket, knocking elbows with Jeff as he does.

"It's Mom," he says. "I forgot she was calling."

Despite myself, I perk up in my seat as he answers. He mutters for her to hold on and shimmies around the table, toward the living room.

Griffin pushes back his plate. "Thanks for dinner, Uncle Cousin Jeff! Now, about that Xbox . . ."

Griffin may not be the keenest investigator, but he's a better distraction than anyone I know. I leap from my chair and follow Oliver, eager to hear what he says to Mom.

He sits on the edge of Jeff's plump leather couch, knees pressed against the coffee table. I linger by the closed door to Jeff's bedroom, not so subtly eavesdropping.

But he's just listing what we've eaten and confirming we've all applied sunscreen. Like he's giving a report to his commanding officer.

Griffin never forgets to eat, and I never forget sunscreen. Asking Oliver to check on us about those things is like admitting she doesn't know a thing about us at all.

I inch forward, resisting the urge to yank the phone from his hand. I want to prove Mom wrong—to tell her about how, today, I found a brand-new discovery in a twenty-year-old cold case. How I'm so hot on the trail of Meggie's kidnapper that someone is keeping track of me in the woods. How I'm going to be Greatest Female Adventurer Number One Hundred One, and soon it'll be my name all over the papers of Stone Creek, unforgettable at last.

"Finley wants to talk to you," Oliver says, then extends his phone to me. "Just use the call. Don't look at anything else."

I snatch the phone. Its screen is still warm from his cheek as I hold it to mine.

"Finley, hon?"

I imagine her voice soaring from Chicago to Stone Creek, braving mountains and valleys to reach me.

"What did you kids do all day? Did you help Jeff out at the shop?"

I beam, ready to run full force into my story. But from the corner of my eye, a photo captures my attention on the wall. Suddenly they're all I can see: those smiling, distant faces, memories from another Jeff. Another time, back when we had a big, smiling family too, before the stress—of work, of us—swallowed Mom whole.

In my mind, the edges of each story are sharp. There was extended family, frequent visits. Then there wasn't. There was Mom and Dad, a family of five. Then there wasn't. There was me and Sophie. And then there's now.

But maybe there's another time I'm forgetting. An in-between, nestled in the crevices of my memory. That first time Mom got a call from a distant cousin but didn't answer. The first time Dad worked too late to come to Oliver's soccer game or to pick me up from school.

Sophie, giggling at a comment Veronica made in class. Deciding it was funnier than anything I'd ever said, or ever will say, so quick, I didn't see the moment pass.

"Yes." I tighten my grip, the phone slipping against my clammy palm. "We helped stack the chairs at the end of the day. I squished some spiders in the back room too."

I squeeze my eyes shut. The photographs vanish. Jeff vanishes. Meggie too. They're all my secrets—no, secret weapons, ones I'll deploy at the last minute before finishing my mission in a blaze of glory. Before proving myself to Mom, once and for all.

After this trip, she'll call me first. Not Oliver.

"That's great, hon," she says, words accented by a yawn. "I'm glad you're having a good time. I knew you would."

My stomach growls. It's like my body throwing me a rope to safety. "Well . . . we're still having dinner," I say. "Have a good night, Mom."

"Oh—okay, hon. I love you. Oh, and Finley?" I nod, though she can't see. "Make sure Griffin doesn't stay up too late."

"Yeah," I say, flat. "Okay."

Another goodbye, then the call ends like a sigh of relief. I walk back to the kitchen and toss Oliver's phone back to him.

Griffin looks up with puppy-dog eyes that could put

Malt to shame. "Wait, she hung up? I had so much to tell her!"

Griffin could have blown my cover, knowing the way he just goes and says what's on his mind. He could have told Mom all about the Walsh-Walsh-Walsh Adventure Agency, then passed the phone back to me when she was ready to tear in with her lecture.

But I wish Mom had asked. Or that I had thought of it. "She said we could stay up and watch a movie together," I lie. I'm good at coming up with things quickly to keep Griffin appeased when Mom's away. "I already downloaded Netflix onto my phone, and—"

As I sit, I tap the screen. It lights up with a new text from Sophie.

New.

Text.

From Sophie.

I grasp the phone, cradling it in my palms. There's a message with an attachment. My fingers tremble against the screen as I unlock my phone, then click on her message.

I open the photo first. It's a quick, semiblurry shot from her hotel window of the outdoor pool below. Colorful beach lounge chairs frame the water, and a bubbling hot tub is positioned behind them, guarded by tiki torches.

Look at this place! Hope Stone Creek has been fun too.

My mind rereads, rinses, repeats the words again and again. "Look at this place." Her place, with Veronica and

Chloe, not me. And meaning she's having fun. Does she really hope I am too? Or is she rubbing in that I'm alone in boring old Stone Creek while she's off on a better, fancier adventure with the other girls?

Or maybe she wants me to look at this place because it's so over-the-top, such a manufactured experience—unlike the organic adventures we'd discover, out in the wild. Maybe she wishes she was in Stone Creek, is imagining it's fun too, as though she were here with me. As though she could go back and change her decision.

Or it means nothing more than it says. That's possible too.

My finger hovers over the keyboard, never pressing down. I want to say something. I want to say everything. I never want to speak to her again.

"You'll need to start that movie soon, or it'll get late," Oliver interrupts, ever Mom's lackey. The screen fades to black, my thumb still motionless above.

When I text Sophie, it will be when I can send a photo too. One of me, arm in arm with Meggie Riley, the lights from news cameras illuminating our smiling cheeks.

"Okay, Griff. Let's clean and go," I say, starting with my plate.

We rustle around, collecting silverware, tossing greasy napkins, Jeff's head bent in silence as we move.

GREATEST FEMALE ADVENTURER NUMBER SIX:

ANNIE SMITH PECK,

FAMOUS MOUNTAINEER WHO DEFIED GENDER NORMS BY WEARING TROUSERS WHILE CLIMBING.

Each time sleep finally tugs at my eyelids, Griffin's open-mouthed snores or the distant scratch of branches against the window whip them back open. With each sound and shuffle, there's a moment between sleep and wake that I see the figure in the woods—imagine I'm there, in the sappy springtime air, with the weight of their eyes on my back.

Of course Oliver is perfectly asleep too, just like Griffin. He's sprawled out on his back, comforter dangling onto the floor. His perpetual scowl has finally lifted from his face, smoothed out like a wrinkle in fabric.

Now I'm the one wearing his turtle-faced frown. It's not fair that Oliver gets all the credit for being the most mature one. The one Mom trusts for accurate reports at the end of each day, as if Griffin and I are too immature and clueless to notice what's going on around us. Oliver didn't see the second figure in the woods. He didn't pick up on Jeff's strange behavior, or the way he dodged my questions at dinner. It's as though Oliver's living on a totally different planet, one where Meggie's disappearance and Stone Creek's creepy suspects don't exist.

Meanwhile, I'm left lying here in the dark and jumping at every creak the old house makes. Somehow fully and totally responsible for making sure we're not Stone Creek's next victims.

Sophie would say that the greatest women in history were the ones who took responsibility for their fates, even when the world told them to shut up and sit down. But Sophie's not here right now, so I'm just stewing and wishing all the great adventurers that came before me had demanded to be taken seriously so I didn't have to wait for the glory and praise until the very end of my adventure.

Griffin lets out a guttural snore, and Malt leaps off the end of his cot. His little paws patter against the floorboards. Then his head pops up by my pillow, tongue waggling and dark eyes glistening in the moonlight.

He whines, high and shaky. I pat his head like I'm snoozing an alarm. "*Shh.*"

He whimpers again. I throw back my comforter and scoop him up into my arms.

"Okay, fine. A walk. But only to the front steps, okay?"

I gather him close and tiptoe past Oliver's cot, toward

the stairs. The old steps groan beneath my weight as I move into the dark living room below. My sleepy eyes see everything as a murky sea of black, and part of me wants to sprint back upstairs and yank my comforter over my head.

But a good adventurer would never leave a full-bladdered puppy in need. So I bite my lower lip and descend into the oily black below.

I pause at the foot of the stairs, feeling like I'm standing in the center of a dark storm cloud: no up, down, or sideways visible around me. I keep still, blinking fast and willing the room to snap into focus. Slowly, my eyes adjust, the shadows of the room forming Jeff's furniture, photographs, and closed bedroom door.

That's when I notice him sprawled out on the couch, deep in a dream. Mom's fallen asleep on the couch before, cell phone on her stomach and TV playing infomercials while she dozes. But Jeff doesn't look like he fell asleep here on accident. A puffy pillow rests beneath his head, and a comforter that matches the ones upstairs is draped evenly over his waist and legs. His phone rests on the coffee table, plugged in to the wall as though he sets it up there every night.

I lean over to let Malt leap onto the ground. "Does he always sleep out here, little guy?"

Jeff's deep-sleep expression isn't like Griffin's drool-y, loose face. Or even Oliver, whose perpetual frown only smooths when he's fully and totally unconscious. His brow is pinched, lips set in a tight line, and his head sways back and forth as he sleeps. He grumbles something under his breath, but otherwise doesn't stir.

Maybe I just caught him at the wrong time. Or maybe he has nightmares frequently. It makes sense, living in a place like Stone Creek. I can barely sleep either, thinking about what happened in the woods earlier.

But maybe he's not scared. Maybe he's having nightmares because he feels guilty.

I hold a hand up to Malt, hoping that means "pause" in dog. Then I tiptoe toward Jeff's bedroom door, fingers slowly grasping the knob.

I suck in a steadying breath. "Maud West would be proud," I murmur to myself, channeling all the spiritual energy I can from Greatest Female Adventurer Number Thirteen.

To my right, Jeff flips his head again on his pillow. Then, he falls still.

I turn the handle. . . .

And nothing happens.

I try again, harder this time. Then give the door a little shake. And a final yank for good measure.

Nothing.

I feel like I've arrived at the end of a treasure quest and realized I dropped the key four towns back. Whatever's behind this door must be important, if Jeff's locking it and keeping guard outside. And if it's important to him, and he lives in Stone Creek, and he's dedicated his business and livelihood to Meggie, then it's important to my mission.

Malt whines again. Jeff stirs and I rush to lead the dog toward the front door, back turned to the bedroom. If Jeff wakes up now, it'll be all "Bedroom? What bedroom?" in the most innocent voice I can muster.

But, thankfully, he doesn't wake. I step onto the front porch with Malt, the cool night air tickling my cheeks. He skips off the porch, toward a bush. Out of my deep respect for Malt, I avert my eyes to the edge of the yard.

A breeze sweeps through and the treetops rattle. Long shadows dance across the lawn, and I realize it may not be the room Jeff's guarding. Maybe he feels someone's out there too, like I do.

Maybe he's on watch.

I wrap my arms around myself, suddenly chilly. "Come on, Malt," I whisper, and he rushes back to my side. Once he scampers in, I shut the front door quickly, as if something else could be at my heel, anxious to get inside.

I lead us through the dark room. Past the suspicious, locked door. Past Jeff's restless, sleeping form. Malt patters up the stairs past me, and I quicken my pace, eyes fixed on the sliver of moonlight trickling in from the attic window.

Once I reach the landing, I glance back down, toward the black hole below. I wish the attic had a door I could clamp shut too, the click of its lock like a promise.

Malt settles back in at Griffin's feet. I move toward my cot, then pause at the foot of Oliver's. He's a lighter sleeper than Griffin. Whenever Mom works late and I stay up late binging CW shows, he'd come out to shout at me to turn the TV down about every fifteen minutes. If I give the edge of his cot even the slightest shake, I know he'll roll over and wake like a disgruntled bear from hibernation.

My hand dangles midair, fingertips pointing to the end of his cot. I don't want to be the only one awake. I don't want to be the only one looking over my shoulder, making sure the dark doesn't close in. I want someone else to keep an eye out for the shadow figure with me. For someone else to keep watch on the door, in case Jeff isn't who he says he is.

Sophie used to be that person for me. Right now, I wish it could be Oliver.

My hand recoils. If I told Oliver I was scared, he'd just take it as an excuse to call off the mission. He'd say admitting fear was admitting I was in over my head. He'd say if I wasn't cut out for the stakes, I shouldn't take on the challenge in the first place. Or maybe he'd say I was being stupid. Making things up like a little kid playing make-believe.

He'd say anything except what I need him to.

I walk past his cot and slide onto mine. The comforter settles on me, a reassuring weight. I tuck the fabric under my chin and close my eyes. In my mind, I skip to the last pages of *100 of the World's Greatest Female Adventurers*, to entry One Hundred One. There, in color ink, a brave and triumphant Finley Walsh grins back at me. She's a Finley who isn't afraid of the dark or of secrets behind locked doors. A Finley who's tough and independent, one who doesn't wish she could turn to her big brother when she's scared.

I focus on her grin, run through the acceptance speech she gives when she receives her title. Then I drift off to sleep.

GREATEST FEMALE ADVENTURER NUMBER SEVEN: SUNITA WILLIAMS, THE FIRST ASTRONAUT TO COMPLETE A TRIATHLON IN SPACE.

The next morning we head to the café with Jeff, caught in our fresh routine. I'm still exhausted from last night, hours spent running over the scraps of intel we've collected on the mission so far. But I remain focused on the day ahead. After all, if I'm going to lead this adventure—and more important, get my brothers to trust me to—I have to do it with confidence.

The first step will be to get my brothers alone, away from Jeff. After last night, I'm less certain that Jeff is someone we can trust.

I try to keep it cool, though, so Jeff doesn't know I'm onto him, or Meggie's case in general. I fiddle on my phone to pass the time, opening and reopening Sophie's message, as he serves a grumpy Anne Thornton and a half dozen other locals.

The hum of customers shuffling in and out becomes a welcome background noise. Until one of them bursts in so loud and fast, the door slams back against the wall as he shoves it open and makes his way through.

"Top of the morning, am I right?" a balding, round man shouts as he enters.

At his table opposite mine, Oliver releases a tired groan. But I perk up: thanks to my current adventure, eccentric locals are my bread and butter. And this one looks oddly familiar, like I've seen his ruddy-cheeked face somewhere before.

The man's focus shifts from the front counter to me. He slaps his meaty palm on the surface of my table, making my phone shift against my hand. "I heard Jeff had some kids from out of town stopping by," he says, voice too big for the tiny shop. "Bit disappointed three great tourists like yourself are holed up in his place, though, when I would rather have given you the full Stone Creek experience at Motel Meggie."

Bald. Business owner. Two facts are enough for me to piece together that the man in front of me is Bryan Phillips, the owner of the diner—and one of the suspects in Meggie's disappearance. My eyes go wide as saucers as I stare up at him, a thousand questions brimming on my tongue.

"They're kids, Bryan," Jeff grunts from behind the counter. "They don't exactly have disposable income. And my house is bug free, unlike—"

Mr. Phillips holds up a hand. "I know Stone Creek is all about keeping history alive, but let's let some chapters rest, okay?" He surveys the room, eyes drifting over me and my brothers. "So how are you kids liking Stone Creek? Taken a crack at the case yet?"

He nudges his elbow to the side, as though he's bumping it into my rib cage. But there's nothing but an empty seat beside him.

Great adventurers know better than to let a great moment pass, though. That's what Greatest Female Adventurer Number Forty-Nine, Shi Xianggu, must have thought when she wooed a pirate captain just to take over his ship. "What's your take on the case, Mr. Phillips?" I ask. As if I'm not fully aware that he's a suspect (thanks to his own diner's receipts, no less).

He grins, round cheeks rising as though he's been waiting for this question his whole life. "My favorite piece of evidence is that ransom letter." He juts his neck toward Jeff. "You got a copy of that here, don't you?"

Jeff gestures halfheartedly at a frame by Oliver's table. I squint to read the print.

"Multiple handwriting experts have confirmed that Meggie herself wrote it," Mr. Phillips says, voice booming with pride as though he were one of those experts. "But Riley still insists that I forged it, and kidnapped his daughter to sabotage his business."

The café was already a bit empty and dull, but right now it feels pin-drop quiet, like we're all holding our breaths.

But Mr. Phillips barrels on. "But any good businessman knows the risk involved in pulling off something like that is not worth it in the long run. And a good businessman is always in it for the long run."

He grins to himself, and my stomach does a nauseating backflip. Considering the economic boom Stone Creek had after Meggie's disappearance, and catering to the tourists obsessed with it, the long-term is looking pretty good for Mr. Phillips, guilty or not.

"But that's just my ten million cents," he says. Being more adventurer than math whiz, it takes me a moment to realize he's referencing the reward money. "Coffee, four sugars, Jeff."

Jeff rolls his eyes and gets to work. I squint across the room, reading the framed image of the runaway note.

> Dad,
>
> I'm sorry.
>
> But I can't take on the family business. I'm so glad that my first discovery was able to help you achieve your dreams and build your company. But my dream has never been to work in Stone Creek. There's so much more world for me to explore—so many more treasures for me to uncover, and so many more wonderful wildernesses for me to adventure across.
>
> I wish this could have been a conversation rather than a letter, and I wish you could have been waving me off on my journey instead of me leaving without a real goodbye. But I've

started and you've stopped this talk for years, and now I know I have to go.

I love you. That is the one thing that will never change.

Meggie

I know nothing about handwriting, or forgery, or how to determine if Meggie's note is real or fake. But reading it right now, across the sleepy café, I feel more drawn to Meggie than ever.

It reads like it was printed in *100 of the World's Greatest Female Adventurers*, nothing but letters and ink. But Meggie is closer than any of those women have ever been—and if I'll be able to find her . . .

I'll finally be face-to-face with a real, live female adventurer.

Mr. Phillips saunters toward the door with his coffee in hand. He pauses, reading the note over my shoulders. "You know, Meggie's Mechanics is launching a new initiative for the twentieth anniversary that I think you might like."

I perk up. A new Meggie initiative could mean a fresh set of discoveries about her story, or a way for me to get first dibs at a new angle to her disappearance.

Seeing the way my eyes go wide, Mr. Phillips grins triumphantly. Jeff watches him pensively from behind the counter. "We're doing a soft launch of a new Meggie-themed tour bus," he says. "It will lead visitors through the greatest things our town has to offer—specifically related to Meggie, and her legacy in Stone Creek."

Already, I'm nodding. Jeff lets out a grunt. "Strange service for an auto shop to offer."

Mr. Phillips's head snaps around, eyes going ice cold. "Why don't you stick to coffee, hm?"

Jeff smiles tightly. "Well, I hope you go enjoy that coffee, then." He flicks his knuckles toward the door, as if to silently add *somewhere far away from here.*

I blink, glancing back and forth between Jeff and Mr. Phillips. The whole exchange is a bit dramatic for talking about coffee, which makes me wonder if there's something I'm missing.

"I'll come get you kids tomorrow morning," Mr. Phillips says, still looking at Jeff instead of me. "You can be the test riders for our tour."

I want to shout an enthusiastic "Yes!" but something about the crumpled look on Jeff's face makes me settle for a silent nod. Mr. Phillips finally makes his way out, door jingling shut behind him.

After a final rush of customers, the last of the morning crowd thins out. Jeff releases a tired sigh from behind the counter. "I don't know how many times I have to tell Peter Donnelly that a mocha without expresso is just a chocolate milk," he grumbles, mostly to himself. He leans against the counter, peering over toward me. "Nice photo."

I drop my phone with a less-than-subtle clatter on the

table. "N-not really," I stammer. "I'd take Stone Creek over Busch Gardens any day."

Jeff shrugs. "Suit yourself."

"Don't mind if I do," Griffin says, purposefully misinterpreting as he wedges his hand into the front pastry case.

Jeff takes up his broom and circles around the counter, leaving Griffin digging through the display box while Oliver tries to wrestle a cinnamon bun from his hand. "Is a friend of yours at the amusement park? Because I won't be hurt if you admit you'd rather be there."

I drum my nails against the table, glaring holes into my phone case rather than meeting Jeff's eye. "I don't want to be there. And she's not a friend." I swallow. "Not anymore."

I don't look, but I sense Jeff pausing behind me. I envision the broom suspended in the air, bristles pointed toward the dusty floor. "Well, if she's texting you, she probably still wants to be your friend."

I bristle, spinning around in my seat. But Jeff starts sweeping, eyes focused on the floor.

"If I hadn't responded to your mom, you wouldn't have made it here," he says, quiet, almost to himself. "So don't underestimate someone's intentions when they reach out. Even if it's been a long time."

He moves on from my table, collecting a cluster of dust in his wake. I flip my phone over again so the screen faces up, illuminated with the image of Sophie's hotel pool. I don't click the message, but I don't turn the screen off, either. I wait until it fades, the backlight dim. Then flicks to black.

I clear my throat and leap from the chair. "Walk! We should go on a nice, brisk morning walk."

I must be scream-talking, because everyone, including Malt, snaps their attention toward me. My distraction—I mean escape, definitely escape—is now or never, and given our limited time in Stone Creek, I can't waste precious time sitting in the café when I could be on my hunt for Meggie's kidnapper.

Or—if Mr. Phillips is right—Meggie herself, an adventurer who refused to be held back and someone I definitely, absolutely need to meet.

Jeff runs a hand over his stubbled chin, bleary eyes scanning us tiredly. But he doesn't object as I drag my confused brothers out onto the café's front steps.

Today there's a cool mountain mist hovering over Stone Creek. The dewy, chilled air gives me a feeling like a thousand tiny ice cubes sliding down the back of my shirt as I turn toward the diner, excited and terrified for what comes next.

Last night was just a warm-up—and a semiunsuccessful one at that—for the witness interrogation that's going to take place today.

I plant my hands on my hip, assuming my power pose. "All right, secret agents: assemble."

Griffin leaps in front of me, chest puffed and round chin tilted up toward the overcast sky. Oliver slumps beside him and yawns loud and wide enough for me to see his uvula.

"Yesterday we gave the locals the upper hand when we waltzed right into the diner, basically wearing a sign that said 'Tourists' right across our chests. But great adventurers know how to strategize and regain the high ground." I lean forward, head tilted toward them. "And that requires stealth."

Oliver throws his head back and laughs. I frown.

"I'm sorry, but stealth is the last thing the two of you have," he says, still laughing disproportionately hard. "Because that requires subtlety, and silence, and I'm pretty sure anyone who's ever met you two would not attest to your skill in either."

"Um, excuse me, sir," Griffin snaps, stretching his spine so he's closer to Oliver's height. I mimic his pose, ready to support his comeback. "My teachers have always told Mom that my enthusiasm and energy border on disruptive."

I stop mid–supportive nod. "Griff, that's not a good thing."

"She said they border on disruptive," he says, "but I never cross the line."

Oliver's already laughing again. I raise an eyebrow. "If you're going to bring this attitude to our mission, you might as well go back to sleep."

"I wish I could," he says, crossing his arms. "But we both know I can't do that."

Griffin's eyes go wide. He leans over to me and whispers, "Ollie snuck coffee!"

But I know it's not a secret stash of caffeine keeping

Oliver from a midmorning nap. When he was on the phone with Mom, it was nothing but quiet nods and mm-hms and okays, a soldier accepting his orders. While I'm on a self-directed mission to rescue Meggie, he's just a worker filling in for Mom while she's gone.

"So," Oliver continues, nodding his head toward the diner, "since I'm stuck tagging along, I'd love to hear your plan."

Now it's my turn to smirk. "If I told you, you'd talk me out of it. And being an adventurer is about doing, not *talking*."

I place emphasis on the last word because—regardless of whether or not I need or want Oliver along for what comes next—I haven't forgotten what he said last night.

I ignore the way Oliver's face crumples at my words. He probably just feels bad I'm upset, but not about what he said. So I start again, attention angled more toward Griffin than him. "Secret agents: follow my lead."

With that, I shove my way between them, elbows bumping elbows, and sprint across the empty lot that separates the café from the diner. Griffin releases a yelp of joy, bounding after me, and I hear Oliver's flat footsteps close behind.

I pump my arms, veering past the front entrance of the café to loop around the side of the building, toward the back. Yesterday we stood out in the open, inviting everyone to tell us what they wanted us to hear, to share the details they were comfortable with us knowing. Today we're the ones in charge, piloting our own destiny like Amelia Earhart piloted the plane she nicknamed "the Canary." Not only so we can find the truths no one wants to share directly—but also because exposing ourselves and our theories like we did yesterday left us vulnerable.

Vulnerable to people like the shadow figure to find us, and watch us, and follow us. Maybe today, if we keep quiet and stay discreet, they won't find us again.

I hate how relieved the thought makes me.

There's a sliver of fenced space between the diner and the edge of the woods. I lead my brothers up to it and peer between the fence's plastic loops. Through the tiny holes, I spot overflowing barrels and one giant green dumpster by the diner's back door. Fat flies buzz around me, bulbous green eyes watching as though wondering, *Will she really crawl into the garbage?*

I glare back because no bug nor beast should ever underestimate Finley Walsh. I coil my fingers through the fence, wedge my sneaker flat against its side, and hoist myself up in a sweeping motion.

The fence wobbles beneath my weight, but I know better than to look back or pause. When I tried to hop Sophie's fence after her dad declared four sleepovers was too many in a row, I made that mistake and ended up falling in a rosebush. And the only thing worse than having thorns sticking out of you like a human porcupine is being lectured by Mr. Higgins while he picks them out excruciatingly slow, one by one, with tweezers.

Without a second thought I lean my weight forward and

plunge into the garbage can below. It half breaks my fall, the plastic bag cradling my body while the bin topples over with a dramatic *boom*. The world spins upside down and for some reason, it's Oliver's fuming face that comes into focus first.

"Real stealthy," he sneers.

"Me next!" Griffin shrieks, voice louder than my fall. He grasps the fence and shakes. "Hoist me, hoist me, hoist me!"

"Only so you'll be quiet," Oliver says, voice strained as he leans to lift Griffin's weight. The tips of his buzzed hair appear over the edge of the fence and I leap up to help him over. Oliver follows shortly after, and while his fall is a lot softer than mine, he also had me there to steady him, so I'm counting it as my win instead of his.

"So, what are we doing now?" Griffin asks, bouncing on the heels of his sneakers. "Filtering through the trash, searching for old receipts?"

While I pride myself on never fearing a mess, the sticky residue left on my socks from the trash bin isn't exactly inviting me to look closer. "We're on a stakeout," I say, "to confront the busboy, Jason Jeffords, and find out what he knows about Meggie's secret lover, P. W."

Griffin's face falls. "Secret lover? Booooring."

My attention shifts to Oliver. He nudges a greasy napkin with the toe of his shoe.

"You okay with that?" I ask, eyebrow raised.

He crosses his arms over his chest. "Of course I'm okay. Why wouldn't I be okay?"

"I don't know why you wouldn't be okay," I say, a bit

shrill. Because while I don't know why, I have the feeling he isn't. Oliver has noticed something about Jason and even now—surrounded by flies and half-eaten meals and bags of spoiled food—he isn't willing to tell me.

The diner's back door whines and I whip around to see the knob jiggling as someone struggles to press the old door open. I gesture wildly for my brothers to follow, then leap over the tipped bin and dart behind the giant dumpster. Griffin and Oliver follow at my heels, the three of us ducking from view just as the door whips open, followed by the sound of approaching footsteps.

Noises filter out from the diner: clanging pots and pans, Sam the hostess's gruff voice shouting a new order, the sizzle of soon-to-be-burnt bacon. On the other side of the dumpster, someone inhales sharply just before a giant trash bag soars overhead, toward the dumpster. It hits the edge, its contents exploding so half of them rain down on our hiding spot. I grasp a hand over my mouth and the other over Griffin's as a half-eaten burger and sprinkling of ketchup-crusted french fries splat onto us. To my right, Oliver's face is red with rage hot enough to cook the egg that just cracked on his knee.

"Crap," someone mutters—that someone being Jason. He groans, as though debating whether or not he wants to clean the mess. Then, sluggishly, his footsteps approach around the side of the dumpster.

"Go," I whisper, shoving Griffin in the opposite direction. He scurries like a dumpster rat, vanishing around the other side. Oliver follows after me, the red heat still bright on the tips of his ears and cheekbones, though now looking more embarrassed than enraged. I rush to crawl after him, stepping over a heap of old dishrags that fell from Jason's trash haul. But just as I'm about to turn the corner, I push too fast, heel still on an oily rag. The ground gives out beneath me a second time and before I know it, I'm cheek to cheek with the concrete.

Jason's footsteps come to a halt. I've been found out, and by the son of our primary suspect, no less. My heartbeat rises in my throat at the thought that Jason could be the person who chased us in the woods yesterday and that now—with his shadow looming over me—I'm finally at his mercy.

I wiggle onto my back to face him, jaw tight. I'm already exposed, so there's no use running—at least not yet.

Jason stands a few feet back, dirt-splotched apron dangling from his slim waist, his mouth agape. His hands remain outstretched and empty, as though paused midreach before he found a human in the trash pile he'd planned to tidy up. The whites of his eyes shine like smooth marbles.

Then his face scrunches up, all huffy and puffy like Oliver gets sometimes (more accurately: all the time). "Are you spying on me?" he shouts. A few birds soar off for added dramatic effect. "Are you seriously so desperate to coin that stupid prize money that you showed up at my work, in my dumpster"—he winces a bit, as though regretting the choice of words, then quickly barrels on—"just to conspire against me in an attempt to ruin me and my dad's lives?"

I open my mouth to respond. But that's when he reaches

into his apron pocket and pulls out the Walsh-Walsh-Walsh Adventure Agency business card.

I sit upright. "You kept it," I say, voice full of awe.

He grips it between four fingers, ready to tear. I jolt to my feet.

"And here I thought you three could be different," he says, voice quivering, "but you're just another bunch of money grabbers, not caring who you hurt in the name of your payout."

"Wait, don't rip!" I shriek, at the same time Oliver appears behind me and shouts, "Wait, we can explain!"

Jason leaps back a foot, startled as trash-covered Oliver and Griffin appear by my sides. Thankfully, it's enough of a distraction to make him release one hand from the card, sparing it for now. "Of course you're all here," he grumbles. "Planning to split the prize three ways, huh?"

"No way," Griffin says, stomping forward. "I do the bulk of the work, so I get the bulk of the cash!"

I elbow him to the side. "That's not true. For many reasons." My gaze remains fixed on Jason. "We don't care about the money."

Griffin gasps.

"We care about the truth," I say. "And it seems like you do too. But if we're going to trust you—"

Jason gaffes. "If I'm going to trust you?"

"Then you have to answer some questions." I reach for my phone, pulling up the photo of the tree with trembling fingers. "Or rather, one question. But still."

Oliver fastens his hand on my upper arm. "What she's trying to say is—"

I stomp on his foot. "I think I can say what I'm trying to say best—"

"We're sorry we caught you off guard," Oliver continues, "and didn't mean to interrupt you at work. But we're not sure who to trust and wanted to make sure we could talk to you alone."

His cheeks flush again at the last part, but I'm pleasantly surprised by how solid his save was. Apparently, Oliver's ability to backtrack out of any less-than-comfortable situation isn't totally useless after all.

"Yes," I say, nodding slowly. "We have top-secret, never-before-seen intel, and while it incriminates your father"—Jason bristles—"we wanted to give you a chance to explain yourself before we go further."

Jason studies me, lanky fingers pressed to his chin. Oliver's grip tightens, his nails digging into my shoulder.

"Why should I trust you?" Jason asks—this time, his tone sincere. "You could just be using me to hurt my dad." His narrow shoulders slump. "It wouldn't be the first time someone did."

Oliver's grip loosens. I exhale steadily. "You can trust us, because . . ."

I glance up at my brother. His eyes are fixed on Jason and, for the first time, he looks like he's at a loss for words. Whatever Oliver knows about Jason, I wish he hadn't kept it from me—but that doesn't mean I should bulldoze over it. Sometimes I wasn't too sure about Sophie's intel: like the time she swore she overheard that goody-two-shoes Kip Monroe was the one stealing the answer sheets from Mr. Hickenbottom's desk. But being a good adventurer means knowing when to let someone else take the lead, even if you don't know where it's going.

I just hope that after this, Oliver can trust me enough to do the same for me.

"You can trust us because you're not the only one who has doubts about their family," I say.

Oliver releases my arm, gaze shifting from Jason to me. I swallow.

"I meant it when I told you the Walsh-Walsh-Walsh Adventure Agency was in pursuit of the truth. That means we want to uncover what happened to Meggie, even if it incriminates someone close to us."

Griffin tugs at my shirt. "Wait, we think Uncle Cousin Jeff killed her?" He leans past me, wide eyes fixed on Oliver. "Ollie, are we staying with a murderer?"

Oliver's face goes pales. "Griffin, no! She didn't mean that." He extends his arm and Griffin moves to his side. "No one's dead, remember? You don't have to be scared."

He shoots me a glare over the top of Griffin's head, but then his eyes dart to Jason. As tough as this conversation is, we both know we have to see it through if we want to know the truth about the Jeffordses.

I give Griffin's back a soft rub, then approach Jason, phone in hand. "Truce?"

He sucks in his cheeks. Then he nods.

"I want to see this solved. More than anyone." He runs a hand over the back of his neck. "I'm applying for some scholarships so I can attend the private high school. They have better STEM programs. But whenever anyone googles me, I know they'll just find old articles about my dad, and . . ."

His voice trails off. I don't know why anyone would want to go to school to take harder classes on purpose, but whether or not Devon Jeffords is guilty, Jason shouldn't pay the price for it.

I hold out the phone, screen facing toward him. "These aren't your dad's initials, but Oliver tells me that the way Meggie wrote them means she was in love with P. W." Behind me, Oliver makes a sound like a clogged drain, which I choose to ignore. "Do you know who P. W. is? Or if your father was aware Meggie may have been seeing someone else before the time of her disappearance?"

I straighten up, feeling like an important investigative journalist despite the dirt caked into my skin and general smell of vinegar and muck radiating from my trash-stained clothes. Jason considers the image seriously, thick eyebrows knit in concentration.

"I don't recognize the initials," he admits, "but I can see if there's anything in my dad's old high school stuff that alludes to it." He swallows, the skin around his throat tight. "At this point, I just want to know the truth, one way or another. But I won't let him know what I'm looking for, just in case."

Then, he looks me hard in the eye. "As long as you promise to do the same, if you find anything out about Jeff."

A woozy feeling settles over me—maybe from the trips and falls, or the stench of mold and rot. But thinking about Jeff—his awkward attempts to connect over dinner, the way he prepared new beds just for us, the collection of photographs on display, curated like sacred items—makes me hope, more desperately than expected, that he's not the one who took Meggie.

"Promise," I say, pushing the syllables out before they burn my tongue.

For the first time, Jason smiles. Then he returns the business card to his pocket, unscathed.

I muster a grin in return. But for some reason, it feels less like a victory than I would have expected.

The stakes feel higher now—not just because there's someone on our trail, ready to strike at any moment. But there's no room for me to make mistakes. If I do, lives are on the line.

Legacies are on the line. And that, to me, is even scarier.

GREATEST FEMALE ADVENTURER NUMBER EIGHT:

JOSEPHINE BAKER,

FRENCH SPY DURING WORLD WAR II WHO PASSED INTEL THROUGH INVISIBLE INK ON HER SHEET MUSIC.

As much as I want to keep exploring after that, the rest of the afternoon is spent bent over my vacation homework—and making sure Griffin does his vacation homework—at the café. Despite my strong (and public, thanks to an outburst in biology) opinions about homework over break, I push myself through readings about Mesopotamia and the first stages of evolution.

Unfortunately, proving myself to Mom means more than completing a twenty-year-old rescue mission. It also means completing my April break homework. But in my mind, I'm crafting new plans. Plans to follow up with Jason about the initials. To head downtown this week for the twenty-year-anniversary preparations. To find a way to capture my stalker before they capture me.

My head spins, the words of my textbook dancing together. Griffin breaks my focus. "Finley?" he whispers, shooting a furtive glance back at the counter. Jeff sits there, hunched over a crossword puzzle, his back a curved line.

I barely glance up from my book. "Mm?"

"I'm hungry," he whines. "Can we go get something from the diner?"

My gut clenches at the thought of the diner. "After dumpster diving this morning, that's the last place I ever want to eat," I mumble. "It took half an hour to scrub those food stains out of my clothes. I definitely don't want any of that in my stomach. And neither should you."

Griffin presses his hands against my textbook, square fingers obscuring the print. I poke his knuckle with my pencil eraser.

"Just grab something from Jeff's pastry case," I say.

Griffin leans across the table and drops his voice. "What if he poisoned them?"

I flick eraser peelings off the glossy page of my book and onto his hands. "Griffin, the best adventurers find potential in any situation. But they don't invent stories to make a situation more interesting." I tap the edge of his division workbook. "Right now, your mission is to fill this out so Mom doesn't bug me about it."

His face goes soft, like a scoop of melting ice cream. In a more serious voice, he says, "I'm not inventing things! You're the one who said Jeff was a primary suspect. So I don't want to eat his snacks." He sits up, crosses his arms. "Malt probably shouldn't either."

My pencil drops and rolls across the table. Usually

when Mom asks me to watch Griffin, she'll leave behind a list of instructions with things like, "Almond milk is fine, but no chocolate," and "Screen time ends at seven." But nothing has prepared me for recruiting him into my adventure agency just to scare him into starving himself.

I'm officially feeling like I've dragged him in over his head. "I didn't mean to scare you earlier," I start.

He puffs his chest. "I'm not scared—"

"In fact, everything I said to Jason: I didn't mean it."

His lower lip pouts out. "You never say anything you don't mean, Finley."

Usually, a comment like that from Griffin would make my head swell three sizes. But right now I can't help but see why Mom trusts Oliver more than me. Oliver would never say or do anything to scare Griffin like this. He'd know better. Do the right thing, say the right thing, smooth out the situation so no one got hurt.

If being a big sister is a mission, I'm failing.

"I have to consider all the options if I want to rescue Meggie. But that doesn't mean they're all true. Or that we should live in fear." I muster a smile. Inside, I wonder if Griffin would be better off if I downsized the Walsh-Walsh-Walsh Adventure Agency. But then it would just be me and Oliver, and I'm not ready to consider that scenario quite yet. "Being an adventurer means being brave. Can I count on you for that?"

His shoulders loosen a bit. "I think so. But not on an empty stomach."

I roll my eyes, but laugh. "Fine. I'll go get Oliver's card and grab you something to eat at the garbage diner."

Scanning the café for the first time since my last homework-dazed bathroom trip, I notice Oliver hasn't returned from his walk.

"Wait . . . how long has he been gone?"

None of us have gone out alone in Stone Creek. We've always been together, protected in numbers in a way Meggie wasn't when she disappeared. But if Oliver is alone, that means he's vulnerable. It means he could be cornered by the shadow person.

Griffin shrugs. "I dunno. Thirty minutes? An hour?" His eyes go wide. "You don't think he spent all the money on the card, do you?"

"Thankfully, that's not how credit works. I think." I slip from my high stool, feet landing on the café's chipped tile floor. "But I'll go find him. So I can get you some food," I add in a rush, not wanting to scare him more than I already have.

Griffin nods, looking a bit deflated.

"Jeff, I'm taking Malt for a walk," I announce, scooping the dog off from his nap spot by the door before anyone can object. "Be right back!"

The café door chimes as I dash outside into the cool spring air. I cradle a sleepy Malt in my arms and scan the area, feeling how wide and empty the lot is for the first time. Standing here, with nothing but the sound of the wind through the treetops and the shadows cast by the afternoon sun, I can see how people vanish in Stone Creek.

Despite the cool breeze, a sticky sweat beads at the base of my ponytail. I nuzzle Malt closer, his warmth and weight comforting in my arms. Then I cross the lot, caught in the empty space between the café and the diner, the woods stretching out like a horseshoe around me.

Being an adventurer means being brave. But for some reason, I can't think of the right hero to guide me through this one. My head is blank, as though the pages have been ripped free from its spine.

Then something shifts in the distance. I jump and spin, just to see two silhouettes through the foggy diner window.

My heart hammers in my chest. Malt licks my chin, as though sensing my fear.

"It's just tourists," I say. "Just tourists having a late lunch."

But yesterday we were the only tourists in town. So who else is here, in the middle-of-nowhere Stone Creek?

Curiosity leads me forward, and a blond mop of hair comes into focus. There, seated across from Jason Jeffords, is Oliver. Elbows on the table, fingers twisting a striped paper straw. His mouth stretched in a big, uncharacteristically toothy grin as he lets out a laugh I can't hear from the other side of the glass.

Jason and Oliver. Oliver and Jason. My eyes ping-pong between the two, until the truth finally registers in my head: Oliver is pursuing a lead without me. On purpose. During my own rescue mission.

The fear tingling through my veins quickly turns to hot, molten fury. Ever since we got here, Oliver's done nothing but dismiss and belittle my ideas and theories. But now he's gone ahead and taken the lead on my main suspect, as though saving Meggie had been his idea all along. As though it's stupid when I want to do it, but not when he wants to do it, because anything I do or say or touch is silly, or loud, or annoying and unimportant and childish, but the second he takes over, it's fixed. Better. Mature. Perfect. The way Mom and everyone else prefers it to be.

I clench my jaw, teeth grinding. He's not getting away with it. Not this time. Not when he left me with a scared Griffin, left to apologize for my theories while he goes ahead and steals all the glory.

I march up to the glass and pound my knuckles against it. Jason and Oliver jump, turning to face me.

I don't get to enjoy his expression, or surprise. Because at the corner of my peripheral vision, by the edge of the woods, something stirs.

Something human.

I whip around, and the figure vanishes behind the trees, leaving nothing but the briefest glimpse of a jeaned pant leg. I stare, blinking fast as though I'd made it up. But the sound of leaves crunching beneath feet carries from the woods, and I know for sure I'm not imagining it.

Once again, I'm being watched.

"It's a man," I say to Malt. "That's a lead."

I swallow hard, turning toward the woods.

"But not a lead enough," I add. "Let's go."

Without waiting for Malt's response, I sprint. The pavement quakes from my pounding footsteps as I run forward, squinting to catch shadowy glimpses of my stalker. The trees open up, inviting me into their shadowy refuge, and my sneakers greet loose pebbles and fallen twigs. Up ahead, shifting between two distant evergreens, I spot the man rushing from view.

"I can see you!" I shriek, voice echoing off the treetops. "Finley Walsh is on the pursuit!"

Probably shouldn't have announced my name. But the Greatest Female Adventurers didn't become legends by remaining anonymous. So I navigate the uneven ground with newfound confidence, gaze fixed on the man ahead like a bull's-eye.

I charge toward him, head spinning with theories. Jeff: stepped out of the café when I said I was on a walk. Devon Jeffords: set up by his son to keep an eye on us while he cornered Oliver. The reporter, or Bryan Phillips, Mr. Riley, or anyone else who's caught word of our interest in the case.

There's a bang up ahead. I jump before realizing the man has fallen, tripping just like I did the day before. A smug grin sweeps across my face, and I rush to close the distance between us.

I'm not sure what I plan to do when Malt and I confront him, but that's something I can figure out later. If the planning and the thinking and rethinking were really that important to being an adventurer, Sophie would have stuck around.

That's what I tell myself, at least.

Before I reach him, the man is up again, darting off between the distant trees until the sounds of his steps mix with the rustle of branches, a quiet murmur both nowhere and everywhere around me. I pause to catch my breath, releasing Malt from my arms. Hunched in defeat, I spot a speck of white standing out against the green ahead.

"He dropped something," I tell Malt. I leap over a twisted tree trunk and lean down to snatch up a small piece of paper, Malt at my heel. There, scrawled in long, slanted print, is a message:

DON'T TRUST JEFF

My stomach drops like a broken elevator. The paper trembles in my hands, words rocking up and down so my vision blurs. Theories swarm my mind like bees.

One: he dropped it on purpose, as a warning for me.

Two: he dropped it on purpose, to lead me in the wrong direction.

Three: he dropped it on accident, and it's a reminder he wrote for himself. Or an order someone else gave him.

Theory one makes my temples ache. It would mean Griffin is right to be scared. That I'm wrong to keep searching. It would give Oliver a reason to sabotage my mission, call Mom like I'm the one who needs rescuing, not Meggie.

"Finley!"

I jump at the sound of my name, then recognize Oliver's voice. He rushes from behind me, chest heaving with uneven breaths and loose blond hair jutting out around his temples.

I crumple up the sheet and stuff it into my pocket as though it never existed. I won't share it with anyone else—not until I know the shadow man's intentions for sure. Oliver thinks he's the only one who can handle this mission, but when he does things like keep me from our key witnesses, all he does is push me to deal with the dangerous parts alone.

If that's how he wants it, then I'm done resisting. My jaw goes hard and I turn to face him head-on.

"Finley," he repeats, slowing to a halt a few feet from me. "You can't just run off like that." As he catches his breath, his voice rises. "You don't know your way around these woods. Anything could happen to you out here, and if something happened, then—"

"Then what?"

My voice seems to boom, as if cascading from tree to tree like we're in a dome, the sound surrounding us loud and clear. Malt lets out a soft whine. I suck in my cheeks, feel steam rising in my veins.

"Mom would be disappointed in you?" I shout. "You'd lose brownie points as her little helper?"

He opens his mouth to object, but I bulldoze forward.

"Don't say you were worried, or that I could get hurt.

Because I know you don't care." Tears prick at the back of my eyes and I blink fast, wishing them away. "If you cared, you wouldn't have gone behind my back to meet with Jason. But you've never cared about me, or what I think, or what I feel. And I don't care if you don't care, but"—I step forward, leaves crunching beneath my feet—"you can't use that as an excuse to sabotage my mission!"

My chin wobbles and I clench my jaw tighter and tighter, as though the stronger and firmer and harder I am, I can push all the pain and fear away. Pain of being left behind, over and over again. Fear, because no matter how often I tell myself it's okay, I wish something—anything—I did could stop it.

The note feels heavy in my pocket, settled deep as though it knows I'll never share it. That I'll never tell Oliver about the strange man who follows me like a shadow. The strange man who's always one step ahead, as though he knows where I'll be next.

And Jeff, who sleeps like a guard dog in front of a locked room. Jeff, who may not be innocent after all.

With the secluded wilderness around me and a faceless watcher surveying my every move, I can't help but wish—for once—that Oliver would listen. Oliver remains still, arms hanging limply by his side. His eyes dart between me and the ground between us.

"Finley, that's not true," he says, voice quiet. "I care."

"You don't," I say, firm. "And that's fine. I don't need you to care. But don't lie to me about it."

His eyes flash up to mine, brows pinching. "I'm not—"

"Stop pretending like you don't ignore me at school!" I shout. Oliver's lips part, a silent O. We never talk about school—never acknowledge that we both even attend the same place, always catching Mom up on our days at separate times in the evening, always finishing our homework in separate rooms.

I may not be able to tell Oliver the truth about the things that scare me most. But I'm sick of lying about something as small as this, as though it's my job to protect him from his own behavior.

"I see the way you duck your head anytime we're in the same hallway," I continue. The words spill like they've been there, poised at the tip of my tongue, for months. "Like you're too embarrassed to even look at me. And the times you do look, and see me upset because of"—my mind skips over her name—"you just walk away. And now this thing behind my back, with Jason—"

The sentence snaps like a thread, my throat rattling so I can't hide how I'm shaking. The air feels too cool, too crisp, sharp and stinging in my lungs.

I tighten my arms around myself, a one-girl hug. "Don't pretend you care."

Silence settles around us: Malt hovering quietly by my heel, and the birds overhead seem to hold their breaths before resuming their song. Oliver hovers in place, like he's not sure if he should run toward me or away. His fists open and close by his sides.

When he finally speaks, his voice is quiet and wobbly, like he's unsure what words he'll say next. "I don't avoid you at school because of anything you did."

I swipe a tear from my cheek. "It's just because of who I am. How I am. Right?"

Loud. Annoying. Big enough to swallow the space around him whole. Small enough to swat away like a fly.

I close my eyes, hot tears burning against my lids. I see Mom, imagine the way her fingers are always poised to dial Oliver's number, not mine. How her eyes always turn to him when she needs something and only fix on me when she gets that strained, tired look like she's scared of whatever trouble I'll get into next. Like I'm never enough but far too much all at the same time.

"It's nothing to do with you," Oliver says, voice coarser than before. "It's me, Finley. I'm the problem. I'm trying to keep you away from me."

I look back up at him, ignoring the loose tear that dribbles down to my upper lip. "What? So I don't find out how annoying you are? Spoiler alert: you don't hide it very well."

He runs his hand through his hair, hard and fast as though trying to will the words out of his head and to his mouth. "Because as much as I hate to admit it, you're smart. At least when you're not yapping so much and actually give yourself time to think." He taps his heel against the mucky ground. "I knew if I let you hang around me, you'd figure it out."

He inhales a steadying breath—and probably one of the hundred flies currently swarming both our heads. "I wasn't hanging out with Jason because I wanted to steal your lead, or whatever. I was hanging out with Jason because I like him."

I open my mouth to speak because, yeah, I like Jason too. More than curmudgeonly Sam the hostess, or the living nightmare that is an uncaffeinated Anne Thornton. But Oliver shakes his head, silencing me before I can start.

"I like-like him." His ears light up like the red bulbs Mom hangs at Christmas. "The way I'm supposed to like girls."

My jaw drops, and I feel like the ground vanishes beneath me. Not in a scary, plummeting way. But in a weightless way, as though it was never there to begin with, as though—at least for this moment—all the heavy things in the world have been lifted from my body.

Oliver wasn't avoiding me. Oliver didn't hate me. Not as much as I thought, at least. He was just scared to share his secret—didn't want to share his secret. At least, not with me.

Until now.

All the little clues he's dropped since we arrived spin through my mind. The attention he paid to Jason that first day at the diner. The way he knew P. W. was Meggie's crush before I did.

I feel like a crummy investigator. But like, for once, not a half-bad little sister.

Oliver misinterprets my silence. He talks fast—faster than I've ever heard him—so his anxious words slur together. "I wasn't ready to talk about it because I wasn't even sure if it was true, but now I'm pretty sure—totally sure—that it is, but I'm still not ready to tell Mom, and I'm definitely not about to tell everyone at school, and I don't even know if this thing with Jason is a thing-thing, or just some weird school-break-friend thing, where we meet at the diner and he kind of touches my hand, though he could have just been reaching for the spoon, but I don't know why he'd be reaching for my spoon, especially since we were just having sodas, and—"

He pauses, gasping for breath. His eyes fix on me, wide and desperate. "Why is this the first time you don't have an opinion about something? Please say something. You're freaking me out."

I break out into a huge grin. Oliver blinks, quick, like he's not sure what he's seeing, and I take the opportunity to plunge forward and wrap my arms around his waist.

His body is stiff in my grip, muscles tense and arms hovering by my shoulders, but not committing to the embrace. He stammers, the wordless syllables an audible question mark.

I just tighten my grip. It feels good to have an excuse to hug him. An excuse not to have him pull back, just this once. "You're like Anne Bonny," I say, voice muffled by his shirt, "and Mary Read!"

Oliver squirms in my grip. "Anne who?"

I draw back to shoot him a glare. "Greatest Female Adventurer Number Two? Greatest woman pirate in all of history? Rumored to be lovers with her fellow pirate, Mary Read?" When his face remains flat, I sigh. "I kind of want to write you off the agency's business cards for this."

He runs his hand back through his hair. "Does this mean you're okay with it?"

"Okay with it?"

He shouldn't have to ask, because of course I am. But having Oliver ask, as if my opinion of him matters, makes me feel as tall as the trees around us.

"Of course I am. And you can trust me with your secret." I straighten up, hands on my hips like Griffin when I call the adventure agency to attention. "I won't tell Mom, or anyone else until you're ready. I'll prove to you that you were right in trusting me. I promise."

Oliver brushes a loose blond strand behind his ear, then finally lets his arm fall, resting, to his side. "Like it's secret intel?"

I grin. "Exactly. Except this mission is all yours."

Oliver smiles. Actually smiles, at me. All the hot anger inside me shifts into a strong flame, its orange flickers telling me I can do this, I can save Meggie, I can be great, someone memorable.

It's a feeling I haven't had in a while. Not since the last time Sophie twisted around in her chair in biology class, shooting me that wide-eyed, eager grin that meant she'd thought up a new adventure for us. A journey to share.

I still don't get why Sophie and Veronica and Chloe like to duck their heads and giggle when Patrick Munroe passes our lunch table, or why Oliver would prefer to sit indoors and maybe touch hands with Jason Jeffords than go on an adventure in the woods. But even if I don't get it yet, I'm glad he took the time to let me in.

I loop arms with Oliver, tightening my grip each time he tries to squirm away. "Let's head back," I say, "before Griffin convinces himself he's starving and cannibalizes Jeff."

Oliver releases a soft laugh, like a sigh of relief. For at least a few steps we walk like that, side by side, arms linked like we're little again, playing at one of the reunions captured on Jeff's photo wall.

As Oliver steps over a high root, his arm slips from mine and my hand brushes against my pocket. Against the letter the man left behind. My thumb loops against the fabric and dips inside, the tip of my nail brushing the paper's soft edge.

Then I pull my hand away, following Oliver through the woods as though the man—and the note—never existed at all.

Oliver may have shared his secret. But I'm not ready to share mine. Not if it could risk my chances of being great. Of proving myself.

Of making sure everyone—not just him—remembers the great Finley Walsh.

GREATEST FEMALE ADVENTURER NUMBER NINE:

EMMA "GRANDMA" GATEWOOD,

WHO ESCAPED FROM HER ABUSIVE MARRIAGE TO BECOME THE FIRST WOMAN TO HIKE THE APPALACHIAN TRAIL SOLO.

The next day, Mr. Phillips arrives in the middle of our morning routine at the café. A series of honks from outside are followed by the sound of a booming voice shouting through a crackly megaphone. "Calling all adventurers! All aboard the Meggie tour bus!"

I leap off my stool, my legs responding to the call like the pull of a magnet. "Well, that's my ride!" I say, and at the thought of touring Meggie's world, through Meggie's footsteps, I truly feel like this moment really is just for me.

"I still don't know how you talked me into doing this," Oliver grumbles as he follows me to the door. "What makes you think a tourist attraction is going to give us anything better than talking to actual locals will?"

"We have to explore more than the diner, Oliver. And talk to more people than—"

Immediately, his ears go red. "Okay, okay! I'm coming, aren't I?"

I'm not sure why Oliver's coming—if he really is interested in Meggie because of Jason's connection, or if he's still just keeping tabs on me for Mom. Part of me wants to ask, but a larger part doesn't want to know the answer. Oliver may have been avoiding me at school because he didn't want me to find out his secret. But just because he won't be avoiding me anymore doesn't mean he trusts me, or cares about the adventure agency at all.

Griffin bounds after us, giving Malt a goodbye scratch on the head. "Well, I'm excited, Finley!" My chest lifts, but then he says, "A tour bus around Stone Creek is kind of like taking a train around an amusement park. And besides, it'll be nice to be in the AC for a bit. The café can get a little—"

Jeff coughs from behind the counter. "I can still hear you, kid."

I pause at the door, shooting a dirty glance at my younger brother. "This is nothing like an amusement park ride. Furthest thing from it! Everything here is real. Places like Six Flags or Busch Gardens are all fake."

He shrugs. "Still fun, though."

I don't bother reminding Griffin that rescuing Vermont's greatest adventurer is an important and noble mission, not just a fun vacation in the woods. But I save my breath, because at least once I'm on the tour, I'll be surrounded by other Meggie enthusiasts. As odd as Mr. Phillips can be, he might have some insight into her life that I haven't learned about yet.

As I turn the doorknob, I glance back at the counter where Jeff stands. The sleepy customer shuffles away, sipping tiredly at her hot paper cup while Jeff stands, silent, his head held down and eyes averted from me and my brothers.

I bite my lower lip. Sure, Jeff may be a barista and not an adventurer like me. But sometimes it feels like he's not just disinterested in Meggie's story; it's like he's avoiding it.

Griffin gives me a shove. "Finley, let's go!"

But I pause. Because a great adventurer always pushes the limits of any situation they encounter, even if it feels uncomfortable. "Jeff, do you want to come?"

He runs a hand over his stubbly jaw, already shaking his head before he speaks. "I've got to hold down the fort," he says in that strange tone of his that sounds more like a question than a statement. "But you kids have fun."

Something squirms in my gut, and I want to push again. But Griffin is literally pushing me toward the door, so I turn the knob and lead my brothers down the café's front steps, leaving Jeff alone in the quiet shop.

An old white van runs parked on the curb. On its roof rests a giant megaphone, Mr. Phillips's voice blaring through its speakers.

"Welcome to the trial run of the first-ever Meggie Riley tour bus!" he calls. The megaphone releases a high-pitched buzz, and a swarm of birds evacuates a nearby tree. Oliver presses his palms over his ears as Mr. Phillips starts up again. “Hop aboard and follow the story of Stone Creek, up close and personal, like no other has before!” Then, in a slightly lower voice, as though reading fine print: “Brought to you by Meggie’s Mechanics, the best and only auto shop in Stone Creek, Vermont.”

Oliver crinkles his nose. “Best and only isn’t the marketing line you think it is.”

I jab my elbow in his side. “If you’re going to talk over the entire tour, you might as well stay with Jeff.”

He opens his mouth to respond just as the driver’s window rolls down. A skinny man with sunken cheekbones and a shiny, sunburned forehead peers out.

“You kids go on and hop in the back,” he says, giving the horn a honk for dramatic effect. “Passenger’s seat belongs to Mr. Phillips.”

Griffin bulldozes forward, yanking the back sliding door open and bolting inside headfirst. Oliver steps after him. “As if I’d leave you two alone with these weirdos.”

It makes me want to scream, the way he thinks I need constant supervision. But the driver gives the horn another honk, so I grit my teeth and leap in after him.

I settle into the seat behind the driver. The old cushion scratches the backs of my legs, and a weak air conditioner pumps a musty breeze into the back seat. Mr. Phillips sits up front, grasping a handheld microphone in his sweaty grip. The driver peers back at me through the rearview window, flashing a crooked set of front teeth.

"I'm Stu Hannigan," he says. "Part-time chauffeur, part-time mechanic, and full-time fan of all things Meggie Riley."

I shimmy forward, beaming at Stu through the mirror.

"I'm a new Meggie fan, but equally enthusiastic," I say, fast. I reach into my back pocket and pull out the map Oliver got from Sam at the diner on our first day in Stone Creek. Holding it up, I ask, "Are you going to show us where she found the Stone Creek treasure? Or any other places she used to explore, like in the woods?"

Stu grins, age lines gliding across his cheeks like cracks in warm soil. But before he can reply, Mr. Phillips interrupts, voice echoed by the megaphone outside the van. "There are some other important parts of Meggie's story we'll be covering today," he says. "Ones that are sure to connect you with the best Stone Creek has to offer." He lowers the microphone and waves his free hand at Stu. "Drive."

The van takes off with a clanky jolt. Griffin lets out an excited squeal, and I press the tip of my nose against the window, watching as the café fades away. We speed past the diner and down the road, small shops zooming by until we reach a small wooden sign pointing toward downtown.

"Hold on to your seats," Stu says, then spins the wheel so we topple like dominoes in the back, shoulders jabbing shoulders. A canopy of trees hover overhead, and my heartbeat rises in my throat. Here, surrounded by green and dirt and shadowed branches, I feel limitless potential.

The trees break and I sit upright, body straining against my seat belt. But instead of a scary cliff, or a racing river, or any other place ripe with adventure, we're faced with a street lined with little shops.

Mr. Phillips swats Stu's arms, and the brakes grind us to a halt.

"Welcome to Meggie Lane, the local hub for all things Meggie Riley!" he announces, chest puffed and chin tipped upward. "Look out your windows and let me guide you through the best Stone Creek has to offer."

I'm looking, but all I see are storefronts, some with cringe-worthy Meggie-themed titles like "Vanishing Stains Laundromat" and "Runaway Fitness." Other than that, it's half-empty parking lots, sidewalks littered with abandoned shopping carts, and one plump red fire hydrant.

I frown. "Are you sure you have the right place?"

Mr. Phillips snorts. "Of course." His voice is packed with his usual bravado, though there's an annoyed edge to his tone. "But let me explain what you may not be seeing, as each of these buildings is bursting with adventure—the kind Meggie herself dreamed of!"

I squint, reading the signs beyond the foggy back-seat window in the hope of seeing whatever it is he sees.

Thankfully, Oliver is already voicing my concerns.

"All I see is a bakery, a Laundromat, and an insurance agency," he says, tone flat.

A muscle twitches in Mr. Phillips's jaw. He lets out a tight laugh. "And this is why the Meggie bus comes with an experienced tour guide. Let me explain what you, as a newcomer to our great town, are not seeing." He gives the dashboard a thump. "Stu."

Stu taps the accelerator, and we roll forward, snail-speeding our way down the road. Mr. Phillips clears his throat, loud and raspy, like he's trying to get Oliver's doubt out of his body.

"What you see as a Laundromat is actually a community-based experience that transforms time spent waiting for clothes to dry into time spent chipping away at the greatest mystery in Vermont's history! Why go downtown to the wash and fold when you can sit with Stone Creek's locals and exchange theories and clues—the kind you can't buy, but can only get from really connecting with the people who were there when she disappeared?"

Oliver's brow furrows. "Can't buy? You literally own a diner where you sell clues," he says. "Besides, what you're describing isn't any different from a Laundromat anywhere else."

Mr. Phillips lowers the microphone. "Of course it's different. It's in Stone Creek!"

Griffin raises his hand like he's in class. "I'm interested in an adventure at the bakery, please."

An approving grin sweeps across Mr. Phillips's face.

"Good eye, young man. Meggie's Macaroons is a very, very special spot."

I shimmy forward, ignoring the way the fabric scratches my thighs. "Did Meggie discover a secret tunnel underneath the bakery?" Mr. Phillips begins to shake his head, but before he can speak, I guess again. "Oh! There's a creepy basement, where the baker keeps extra supplies in the freezers. But there are clues showing that Meggie was held captive there shortly after her disappearance, and—"

"It's actually the last place she ever ate," he interrupts, holding up the mic again.

Goose bumps erupt on my arms. Finally, that magnetic pull returns to my atoms, like adventure is calling me from just beyond my seat belt. "As in, the second-to-last place she was ever seen, before the woods?"

Stu chuckles softly. "It's not even really the last place she ate," he says. "It's just the last place she ate out."

Mr. Phillips glares, round cheeks puffing like overfilled balloons. "Bank records show the last purchase she ever made was a croissant at what was then called Baked by Steph. I recommend visitors to Stone Creek drop by what is now called Meggie's Macaroons and indulge in the last meal she ever ate—"

"Ate out," Stu corrects softly.

"—in order to get in her mindset, and walk in the same steps the world's greatest adventurer did before her sudden and suspicious disappearance," Mr. Phillips finishes.

"So, who's Steph?" I ask, voice higher than I'd like. "And why name it Meggie's Macaroons instead of Meggie's Croissants?"

"Steph?" Mr. Phillips asks. "Oh, the original owner? She sold shop when rent went up. She's unrelated."

I swallow hard, as if trying to hold on to the last scrap of the excitement I felt at the start of the tour, even as it dissolves inside me. "And the croissants?"

Mr. Phillips's upper lip curls, as though he's offended by the question. "My chef makes better macaroons than croissants. And the alliteration is catchy." He lowers the mic once more, leaning toward the back seat so his stale breath washes over me. "Listen to me when it comes to business, kid. I own everything you see on this block, and that's not luck. It's entrepreneurial genius. The kind Riley never had, and why even with Meggie's big treasure"—he spits the word off his tongue, and the sound makes my muscles clench—"he failed to make an empire in Stone Creek, unlike me."

Looking outside the window now, I can't see any trace of Meggie. Sure, her name is shoved into every storefront, her face plastered on the windows and the signs. But the Meggie at the Laundromat and the bakery isn't Meggie at all: It's all Mr. Phillips, all about him and his money and how he twisted her story to make it about himself. More and more, until he swallowed her whole.

Stu clears his throat with just as much subtlety as anything else I've seen today. But it snaps Mr. Phillips back into focus, his usual carefree grin returning to his face.

"But that's just my ten million cents," he says with a barking laugh. "And the tour bus is just a prototype. Stu didn't get around to fixing the AC before we left—"

"You said to leave it until after—" Stu clamors.

"So, I can understand that the heat may be getting to us all," Mr. Phillips says. "Why don't we head on back to the auto shop, and you can finish your job, Stu, before taking these kids home."

Griffin slumps. "So . . . no croissants?"

Mr. Phillips smiles. "I think I have something at the auto shop that you'll find a bit more interesting than the bakery."

Oliver crinkles his nose. "Really? Because, so far, it's all been a lot of the same."

Mr. Phillips responds by slapping his palm on the dashboard. Stu revs the engine, and the van sputters off down the street, passing more of the same Meggie-themed shops and businesses on its way.

As Stu drives, Mr. Phillips's phone rings, high and shrill. He yanks a smartphone the size of a brick from his pocket and starts shouting into the receiver about inventory for the hardware store.

With Mr. Phillips's attention diverted, Oliver slumps back in his seat and releases a quiet groan. "Good riddance."

For once, I agree with my grump of a brother. "Meggie would have hated all this," I say, steady and certain. I imagine reaching into the front seat and snatching the microphone, shouting into it loud and clear so it's heard by every person on Meggie Lane: *"She was an adventurer, and everything she did was for adventure's sake. Not for fame, or recognition, or money."*

Griffin leans forward, peering at me past Oliver from the other side of the back seat. "I thought all adventurers wanted to be famous. Isn't that what your book is about?"

My jaw drops and I jolt toward him, so fast that Oliver snaps back against his seat. "The women in my book are famous because they did great things, like climbing the world's highest peaks and braving its most treacherous terrains! That's nothing like what Mr. Phillips—"

"Shh," Oliver hisses, eyes darting toward the front seat.

But Mr. Phillips is still shouting into his phone. "I don't want to hear excuses, Todd. I want to hear results!"

I clear my throat. "What someone has done here . . ." I lower my voice as I add, "He's just using someone else's story to make himself look better."

"And his air conditioner's as broke as Uncle Cousin Jeff's, too," Griffin adds, crossing his arms like he's made a grand point.

As usual, Griffin's missing the point by a mile. I close my eyes and count back from five, trying to conjure Sophie in the seat beside me instead of my brothers.

"Finley, are we seriously staying with this guy right now?" Oliver whispers, snapping me out of my daydream. "Can we just head back to the café and call it a day?"

His doubt weighs heavy around me, and I know the only thing that will lift it away is for me to redirect this. To prove that I'm not wrong for wanting to find her.

I wonder if Griffin's right about me and the other adventurers after all. If I'm trying to become World's Greatest Female Adventurer Number One Hundred One to earn Oliver's and Sophie's attention, that would mean I have more in common with Mr. Phillips than I'd ever like to think I could.

The thought makes my stomach lurch. I shake my head as if jostling it out of my brain. Then I dig in my back pocket and yank out the Meggie map from the diner. Sure, it was technically made by Mr. Phillips. But if this tour has shown anything, it's that he can't see the adventure right in front of him. Meggie found adventure in Stone Creek, and so can I.

"We need to find a way to get here," I say, tapping the northeast corner of the map. There, beneath my fingertip, is the spot where Meggie had her first big adventure and found the treasure of Stone Creek. It makes my skin buzz, knowing that what I'm touching isn't just a picture like the ones in my book. "We wait until we get Stu alone," I whisper. "He'll bring us here and we can start our real mission. You'll see."

Oliver cocks an eyebrow, but I turn away, ignoring his doubt. With the map here, in my lap, I know that the path to proving myself to him is within reach.

Before the day ends, he'll see that I was right all along.

GREATEST FEMALE ADVENTURER NUMBER TEN:

JULIE D'AUBIGNY,

OPERA SINGER WITH A REPUTATION FOR CHALLENGING MEN TO DUELS AND CAUSING CHAOS ON HER WORLDLY TRAVELS.

The auto shop is at the end of the street, at the cross of Meggie Lane and a narrow street leading toward a patch of houses. Stu veers the van up the driveway through a series of poorly parked cars with dangling bumpers and missing headlights. Then, finally, we park.

I doubt there's anything at the auto shop that will help on our hunt for Meggie. But there's an unsettling slant to Mr. Phillips's smirk that makes me think that even if I don't find anything out about Meggie here, I may uncover something about him. And if today's proven anything, it's that Mr. Phillips is high on the suspect list for Meggie's potential kidnapping.

And besides, the sooner we get rid of Mr. Phillips, the sooner I can enact my next plan.

"Follow me," Mr. Phillips says, leaping out of the van with a thud. I scamper out of the back seat, ignoring Oliver's quiet "Finley, do we have to?" as I follow Mr. Phillips to the shop.

Inside is a lot of what you'd expect from an auto shop: a wall lined with tires, shelves stacked with coolant and oil, a waiting area with beaten-down chairs vomiting stuffing from their cushions. But like everything in Stone Creek, there's a twist: instead of playing the Weather Channel or *Friends* reruns, the dozens of television screens lining the back wall of the waiting area are playing old news clippings about Meggie's disappearance. It's like the decorations at the café come to life, voices reading the headlines I've become familiar with since arriving in Stone Creek.

The televisions run the same program in sync, each screen lighting up with a zoom-in of Meggie's runaway note. A female reporter speaks over the footage.

". . . experts are still accessing the note," she says, "but the missing girl's father insists that they will confirm it is a forgery left by a kidnapper."

The image of the note switches to a video of a man surrounded by reporters. He stands outside a giant black gate, a long driveway, wide green lawn, and white house barely visible in the distance. While the reporters all wear loose button-ups and bright dresses, he wears a thick, black coat and a crisp tie, collar ironed perfectly against his long neck. He stands with his head upright, thin nose held high and balding head bright beneath the morning sun. But despite the firm line of his lips and tight line of his brow, I spot a quiver in his chin. A tremble, whether from anxiety or hurt. At the bottom of the screen, the news ticker reads: "Missing girl's father, Robert Riley, speaks out against runaway note."

"There's no way Meggie would write something like that," he says, voice clear through the dozen microphones thrust beneath his chin. "Meggie always had drive and ambition, and she channeled that into the family business. Stone Creek was her home, her pride, and her greatest achievement. She would never leave."

"That makes no sense," I say to the TV. "Meggie wasn't a driven and ambitious businesswoman. She was an adventurer. Of course she could want to leave Stone Creek, especially if she was stuck in an office working!"

"He can't hear you," Oliver says, slow, like I actually think TVs can listen. I square my jaw.

"I'm saying it to you, obviously." Though, part of me wishes Mr. Riley could hear. If Meggie were here now, she'd be shouting at the TV too. She'd be right beside me, making her father listen when she says who she is. Making him read the note she wrote and believe her, maybe for the first time.

The Meggie map crinkles, folded in my hand. I know that on the paper, there's a cartoon house marking the Riley residence. Watching Mr. Riley now, I decide to add one more stop to my expedition.

Mr. Phillips's voice cuts through my thoughts. I groan. We need to shake him off and get on with our mission, and fast.

"Do you know what this store used to be called?" Mr. Phillips asks, his voice drowning out the televisions.

Oliver shoots me a tired look, and Griffin's eyes glaze over. I'm losing them. I need to get rid of Mr. Phillips ASAP, before the other two-thirds of the Walsh-Walsh-Walsh Adventure Agency drop out of today's mission entirely.

"No, what?" I prompt, like I'm waiting for the end of a knock-knock joke.

"Hank and Son's."

He wiggles his eyebrows expectantly, but I must be looking foggy eyed like Griffin at this point, because somehow the answer was even more boring than I'd learned to expect from Mr. Phillips.

But that strange, unsettling glint is still in his eyes. A chill creeps up my spine. Whatever the punch line is, he hasn't shared it yet.

"'Hank' as in Hank Walsh, your great-uncle," he says, smiling. "And 'son' as in your cousin Jeff. He basically grew up here. Or, rather, what here used to be."

A squirmy feeling rushes through my veins. When I asked Jeff about our family the other night at dinner, he didn't mention anything about his parents owning a business in Stone Creek.

"What happened?" I ask, voice softer than I'd like. Oliver shoots me a curious glance, but I keep my focus on Mr. Phillips.

He smiles eagerly. "Oh, what happened to most

people on this block. They failed to adapt to the times and got bought out by someone who did. Someone who gave the tourists what they wanted." He taps his chest with his thumb. "Me, I mean. I'm referring to me."

"Yeah, we got that," Oliver says flatly.

But my mind is snagged on another detail. "What do you mean, failed to adapt? As in, they didn't rebrand the business?"

He shrugs his broad shoulders. "Hank Walsh wasn't interested in Meggie or her story. Never was, even before she disappeared." I run my hand up my arm, that same itchy feeling I had this morning in the coffee shop rushing over me again. "But a good businessman knows that it doesn't matter what interests you; it's what interests the people. Which is why I'm still here, and he's not."

Earlier, Jeff seemed to shrink behind the counter once Mr. Phillips arrived. His disinterest in Meggie keeps seeping through—in our conversations at dinner, the way he shrugs indifferently at my questions, how he weaves his way around the topic like a snake slithering through tall grass. Was that because of something that happened with his parents before they had to sell the shop, or because of something related to Meggie herself?

That last thought makes me queasy. Not only because it means Jeff could be connected to her disappearance. But because if he isn't, it means that despite her great achievements and her even greater story, someone still managed to look away from her like she wasn't there at all.

For the first time I wonder if it's possible that—even when I do rescue Meggie—it won't change how Sophie feels about me or the adventure agency.

The shop door jingles and a mechanic in oil-stained overalls walks in. Mr. Phillips's attention diverts, his chest rising as he prepares to bark an order. I speak up again, fast. "But where did they go?" I ask. "Jeff's family, I mean."

"Sold out and left Stone Creek with their tails between their legs," he says, eyes still on the mechanic. "A lot of folks came and went during that time. Not everyone is adaptable, kid. Survival of the fittest."

Griffin scans the auto shop and shrugs. "I like the café better. It has pastries. And Malt."

Mr. Phillips waves him off and stomps toward the mechanic, already shouting something about time cards. I follow Griffin's gaze, eyes trailing around the room. There's a squeaky ceiling fan overhead, cracked tile floors, and oil-stained carpet beneath my feet. A vintage car calendar hangs by the back office, stuck on January.

I wonder how much of this is Mr. Phillips and how much was left behind by Jeff's parents when they owned the place.

I hadn't thought about what Stone Creek was like before Meggie. But inhaling the stuffy, gasoline-scented air now, I wonder what other stories Stone Creek holds. And how I might be a part of them.

Griffin looks up at me and Oliver. "Do you think

Jeff's parents were kidnapped too?" he asks in a hushed voice. "Maybe they're being held captive in Stone Creek, just like Meggie."

As usual, Griffin's theories are way off base. But the wide-eyed look on his face reminds me of our conversation at the café yesterday. His theory may be off, but the fear behind it—of Jeff's silences and secrets—is similar to my own.

"I'm sure they're fine," I say. "But we can ask Jeff when we get back to the café. Okay?"

I basically have unlimited access to Jeff during my time in Stone Creek. Mr. Phillips's van and a free driver, not so much. So, I stick a mental bookmark in my stack of Jeff-related questions and usher my brothers toward the door.

"It's time for part two of today's plan," I announce. "Operation Reroute the Tour Bus. It's time to go to the other side of Stone Creek Woods and explore the place where Meggie found the Stone Creek treasure."

The woods near the café have been the most vital to our mission—it's where Meggie was last seen, and where her phone was discovered. It's also where I've crossed paths with the shadow twice, which could mean there's something still there that they don't want me to find.

But even if the woods on the other side of town aren't connected to Meggie's disappearance, they may still hold clues about who she was, clues that will help me understand what led to her disappearance and who might be responsible. The wild no-man's-land marked on the upper right corner of my map is where Meggie found the Stone Creek treasure. Whether or not she went back there after her discovery, it holds a central piece of who she is—more than anything on Meggie Lane ever could.

Griffin nods along eagerly, but Oliver shakes his head, as if on cue. "We can't just head off with Stu," he objects. "Jeff approved of us going on the tour with Mr. Phillips. But we don't even know this guy—"

I roll my eyes. "Nothing is truly safe in Stone Creek. Everyone is a suspect." *Even Jeff,* I think. And by the way Oliver's expression falters, I know he's thinking it too. "If you don't want to come, you can head back to the café. But Griffin and I have another mission to complete before the day's over."

I spin on my heel and walk, gaze fixed on the exit sign as though I'm not totally focused on listening for the sound of Oliver's footsteps behind me. Sure enough, I hear a soft groan followed by the reluctant stomp of his sneakers against tile as he crosses the room after me.

I hate that he's probably just coming along as a chaperone. If I go off with someone who ends up being the kidnapper and Mom found out I went off with him on my own, she'd blame Oliver for not watching me, as if it's up to him to herd me safely through Stone Creek like a wayward sheep.

Still, part of me is relieved that Oliver is still tagging along. It means there's still a chance I can prove I'm worth following as a leader, as an adventurer—not just as a child who needs to be kept in line.

Outside, Stu sits in the front seat of the van, driver's door open as he tests the air-conditioning. I march up and puff my chest like Mr. Phillips does, all businesslike and official. He stirs to attention and I resist a smug grin. Sometimes, to be a great female adventurer, you've got to use the boys' stupid rules against them to get what you want.

"Mr. Phillips said he wanted to test a new location for the tour," I say, projecting my voice as if to send it through the megaphone. I pull out my map and tap the woodsy no-man's-land on the northeast side of town where Meggie went on her big adventure.. "He's busy with calls, but said you could take us down there."

The door to the auto shop swings opens and I jump. But it's just a customer in faded jeans, sighing with his head bent over an itemized receipt.

But the next person out the door could be Mr. Phillips. And I doubt he'd be okay with us taking his van and his driver on an impromptu mission into the woods.

In fact, there may be a reason why he didn't include the places Meggie actually went on the tour. There could be something he's trying to hide. Something he doesn't want me to find.

Which, of course, means I have to go.

"He said we should leave now," I tell Stu, low and fast. "Like, now-now."

Stu bites his lower lip and runs his hand over his neck. "Mr. Phillips said that, huh?"

Griffin nods like a bobblehead beside me. "I heard it too, Mr. Stu!"

I wince, feeling like a mouse right as it realizes the trapdoor is about to snap shut behind it. But after glancing between me and Griffin once more, Stu breaks out in a wide grin.

"It's tricky terrain for a big van like this," he says, a giddiness bubbling in his voice, "which means Mr. Phillips must really trust that I'm the man for the job! Let's be sure to make him proud, huh, kids?"

Oliver gives me a weary look. But I ignore it, give Griffin's arm a grateful squeeze, and nod. Finally, I'm headed to where Meggie's story started, the spot where she pulled off her first adventure and won the hearts of everyone—or, at least, almost everyone—in this town.

GREATEST FEMALE ADVENTURER NUMBER ELEVEN: SOPHIA DANENBERG, FIRST BLACK WOMAN TO REACH THE SUMMIT OF MOUNT EVEREST.

A tricky terrain is the best kind of terrain. It's the kind only the bravest and boldest will trek across, that only true explorers are able to survive. And that's what we're pulling up to now, the van bobbing over uneven patches of dirt, long branches scratching the windows like nails clawing their way inside.

I strain against my seat belt, face so close to the window that my breath fogs the glass. With each jolt forward, the van is leading me to the place where Meggie completed her first real expedition.

The front bumper thuds against a tree stump, rocking the van backward. Stu pulls the emergency brake and drags his palm over his cheeks and down over his chin.

"I reckon this is about as far as we can go." He gives the dashboard a reassuring pat, like Diane Crump probably did to her horse before and after a big race. "Nothing but woods and overgrowth past here."

I'm already reaching for my seat belt. "Well, woods and overgrowth happen to be my specialty."

Oliver scoffs. "The most nature I've ever seen you in at home is the green lawn at Sycamore Park."

I shove the door open and leap out. Soggy dirt sucks in the heels of my shoes, and I hear the hum of running water in the distance. "Because that's all our boring old town has," I snap. "But being an adventurer is as much about practice as it is about determination. And I'm determined to make this"—I gesture to the mangle of overgrown trees ahead, the ones Meggie charged through on her greatest adventure—"my specialty."

Fists balled by my sides, I channel the great wilderness explorers like Sophia Danenberg and Louise Arner Boyd and march forward. Griffin scurries at my heels, and I'm about to bulldoze through a branchy bush when Stu calls from the van.

"You kids are old enough to be out on your own, right?"

I freeze. Adventure is so close, I can literally smell it on the dewy leaves and in the soggy dirt. But if I'm going to get on with my mission, I'm going to have to shake off Stu like I did Mr. Phillips. I slowly turn, trying to recapture that businesslike expression that worked on Stu the first time.

One of his arms dangles on the window, fingers

drumming the side of the van. "I mean, you kids are at least sixteen, right?"

Griffin and I exchange a glance. "Yep, sixteen," I say as he nods along. Oliver gawks, eyes flooded with disbelief as Stu nods agreeably. But thankfully, he keeps quiet for once.

"I'll be here, then." Stu reaches into the car and yanks something beneath his seat. The chair falls back and his body goes with it, settling in for a nap. A grin sweeps across my lips. I chose the perfect adult to bring along on this mission.

If Sophie were here, she'd be proud of me for pulling this off. Back at school, she'd always be the one to sweep the schoolyard to check who was on recess duty, then develop a plan to evade them.

"Ms. Wilson always circles the yard counterclockwise," she'd say, forehead tilted toward mine and voice dropped to a whisper like we were two spies about to set out on a government mission. "Mr. Rodriguez always sticks by the boys playing football, 'cause he can't turn his coaching off. And Mrs. Domitrovich's rounds never make it past the flagpole because she's always wearing those heels that are too small for her."

We'd map out our recess adventures like that, heads bent together while our classmates ran and gossiped around us in a foggy haze. It was like Chloe and Veronica didn't exist back then, like it was just me and Sophie in our little bubble. The way it should be.

"What are we even looking for out here?" Oliver asks. A branch snags at his sleeve, and he swats it away like it's a bug. "I doubt Meggie's out here playing a twenty-year-long game of hide-and-seek."

Griffin's eyes go wide at the thought. "Oo, can we—"

"No," Oliver and I say in unison. Griffin's shoulders slump.

I suck in my stomach and wiggle sideways between two cramped bushes. "I don't expect her to hop out from behind a tree," I say, though I kind of love the mental image of it. "This isn't where she was last seen, but it's by where she found the Stone Creek treasure. She may have left something behind—some clue about herself that will tell us where she went, in case she really is a runaway."

"Maybe as a kid, but probably not as an adult," Oliver argues. "I'm not going to let you run off into the woods alone, but I highly doubt we're going to find anything out here other than a whole lot of mosquitoes."

"Well, I doubt we're going to find anything useful by sitting at the diner, talking all day," I snap, storming across a pile of leaves back toward him. "But if you'd prefer to go back, then don't let me stop—"

The earth vanishes from beneath my feet. Within a second there's nothing but air, my heels flailing against the few tangled vines beneath my sneakers as I fall into nothingness. The sky recedes overhead, like I'm zooming out of an image until it's nothing but a tiny pixel.

My stomach rises uncomfortably into my throat, and I collide with a hard surface.

I lie, shocked and frozen in a mess at the bottom of a hole. Rolling onto my back, I see a sliver of light in the distance, partially obscured by Oliver's blond head. A quiet sob rises in my throat, but I swallow it back. Whatever Oliver's about to say next will be some variation of "I told you so," and I can't let him be right.

So, despite the way my muscles ache and the throbbing pain between my temples, I don't call out for Oliver.

"Finley?" Griffin shouts, round head bursting into view above. "Are you dead?"

I bend my knees, heels scraping against the rough, dirt-crusted ground beneath. I push up to a seated position, breathing sharply. "Not dead!"

"Okay!" Griffin calls. Then, half a second later: "So, did you find Meggie yet?"

"Obviously not," I groan, though I take this moment to adjust my eyes to the inky dark around me. Wherever I am now would be a perfect spot for someone to hide a kidnapped adventurer—or, for a valiant runaway to hide out whenever she wanted to return to Stone Creek. There could be clues down here that were missed during the initial investigation.

I, Finley Walsh, could be the first person to discover this nook in the woods.

"Forget about that," I hear Oliver snap at Griffin. "We need to figure out how to get her out of there."

"No way!" I reach for the dirt wall beside me, grasping at the uneven rock to tug myself up on unsteady feet. "You two can stay up there, but now that I'm down here, I have to find out what here is. Otherwise, this entire trip was for nothing."

I mean the trip into the woods with Stu, of course. But right now, with Oliver blocking the light overhead, I can't help but feel like my entire time in Stone Creek is at risk too.

"Finley, we don't know what's down there," Oliver says. "It could be—"

"Dangerous, I know." I keep one hand against the edge of the pit, the area around me slowly coming into focus. There's a small hole in the opposite wall, leading into a dark crevice—maybe the edge of a cave or tunnel, or a nook perfect for hiding clues. My pulse quickens and I'm barely able to conceal the giddiness in my tone. "Which is exactly why I have to stay."

Overhead, Oliver releases a loud, disgruntled groan. "You're impossible!" he shouts. "Fine, you stay there, try for once not to get yourself killed. Griffin and I are going to go get Stu, and when we get back, you're getting out of there, whether you like it or not."

I clench my jaw and listen to the sound of twigs snapping under their shoes as Oliver leads them away. Meggie's friends must have said something like that to her, too, before leaving her to discover the Stone Creek treasure all by herself. Their doubt and fear probably fueled her to go farther into the woods, to discover what no one else had before.

But as the sound of my brothers' footsteps fade overhead, I wish that being a great adventurer didn't always mean doing things on my own. That Oliver and Griffin—as annoying on missions as they can be—would have crawled down here and joined me, like Sophie used to.

It's dark down here, lit only by the slivers of light extending from the hole above. I blink fast, begging my eyes to adjust faster so I can take in my discovery. My fingers trace the cool rock on either side of the cave, and I move forward in cautious steps.

My eyes adjust to the darkness, and the back of the cave comes into view. Well, maybe it's a bit much to call where I am a cave—it's more like a hole underground, enclosing me in a shadowy orb of rock and dirt. For a moment I wonder if my hunch to head into this side of the woods was wrong after all—but then my fingertips scratch against something alongside the right wall of the cave.

I know that feeling from the tree back where Meggie disappeared. Something is carved in the rock.

My phone may not have service down here, but the flashlight app still works. I pull my phone out of my pocket and flick the light on, illuminating the pale gray rock in front of me. There, etched in thin, jagged lines, is the name "Meggie Riley."

I flick my wrist, sending the light dancing over the rest of the cave. There's nothing else down here but her signature. So maybe this cave doesn't hold any grand mysteries like the spot in the woods where she found the Stone Creek treasure. But it was good enough for Meggie Riley to carve her name into the wall to make sure all of history knew that she was here, somewhere no one else in Stone Creek was brave enough to explore.

Unlike the carving on the tree, there's only one signature here, as if she carved this after her friends stopped going on adventures with her. It makes my heart sink to think of Meggie exploring this side of the woods alone, etching her name to prove she still mattered—even if her friends wouldn't join her anymore, and even if her dad made her discovery about the prize rather than the journey.

When I think about it like that, it almost feels like Meggie left this note for me to find. Like she knew, all these decades later, that I'd be here, following in her footsteps, relying on her legacy to cheer me on.

The mental image of Meggie by my side snaps me back to focus. I'm here on a rescue mission, after all. I lean forward, studying the carving. It's too sloppy for me to make judgments about the handwriting (it must have taken ages for her to carve in this rock). But it is interesting that her name is spelled out here, each letter wide and proud. It's nothing like the tiny initials carved into the tree I found on my first day in Stone Creek.

Almost as if the initials were carved by someone else.

I may be overthinking, but great adventurers never overlook the details. Adventurers rely on them to survive on expeditions—like remembering the width and height of bushes and trees to ensure you're not walking in circles through the woods. Maybe Meggie didn't write either of the markings—maybe they're both meant to deter me from where she really is. But right now, it's looking like P. W. may be more involved than I'd originally thought.

A heavy thud shakes the rocky walls around me. Loose pebbles rain onto the top of my head, and I whip around so fast my ponytail smacks my jaw. I'm sure the entire cave is about to fall in when I hear a low cough from the entrance, back where I originally fell into the pit.

I freeze. Part of me wants to call out, to make sure it's Oliver or Griffin. But there's nothing but silence on the other end of the tunnel, and I know my brothers well enough to know they never shut up for that long. Which means there's someone else here—someone I don't know.

Or someone I know but haven't met yet: the shadow man.

I flick off the flashlight app, allowing the dark to swallow me up. I take a step back, the heel of my sneaker pressed against the back wall of the cave. There's nothing but rock on every side: left, right, and up. The only way out is in the direction of the footsteps, their echo slowly growing in volume as they approach. I run my palms up and down the rocky walls, searching for a crack, a divot, a magical trapdoor that will lead me to the perfect hiding spot.

But it's just rock. Cool, damp, sturdy old rock.

Holding my breath, I listen to the shuffle of pant legs brushing together as someone walks toward me. There's no way to run other than straight into him—so no point in hiding or sinking back. Even though my limbs feel tingly and a cool sweat breaks across my forehead, I square my shoulders and step forward to face the shadow man. Once I hear his breath, I know he's close enough to see. So, inhaling softly, I flick the flashlight app back on, illuminating the tiny cave in bright white light.

A man stands, blocking the edge of the cave. He's got short, choppy black hair and a shadow of a beard along the edge of his jaw. He wears patched-up jeans and a thick button-up shirt.

All in all, he looks pretty normal. Other than the fact that he's cornering me in a cave, that is.

"Stay back!" I shout, brandishing my phone like it's a sword. For what it's worth, the light does make him raise a hand protectively over his face.

"Hey, hey, it's okay," the man says in a frantic, rushed voice. "I work for the parks department."

I cock an eyebrow. "That's a perfect line for a killer woodsman," I say.

He catches me off guard with a soft laugh. "I thought I heard voices and was scared that someone might have fallen," he explains. "It's not often people come out this far, but when they do, this"—he gestures around the enclosed space—"tends to happen."

He taps the worn fabric name tag that's sewn on to his chest pocket. Beneath the logo for the parks department, his name is woven in dirt-caked threads.

"You're Devon Jeffords?" I blurt.

His face crumbles. I clasp a hand over my mouth, as if I could shove the words back in. Now one of the prime suspects in Meggie's disappearance knows that I'm on his trail. And worse than that, he doesn't look happy about it.

Which could mean he really is the shadow man, and I'm in danger. After all, he found me pretty quickly—almost as if he'd been following me through the woods. And he hasn't moved from his spot by the cave entrance, body blocking my only way out.

But it could also mean he's innocent, and just plain hurt by the way I reacted to meeting him. If Mr. Jeffords really wasn't involved in Meggie's disappearance, then I'm just another person who's purposefully misunderstood his role in Meggie's story. It would also mean that I've assumed the worst of the kind of person who would jump down a hole in the woods just to save a stranger.

I think of Jason, the way he marched up to our table at the diner that first day to defend his dad. My stomach sinks thinking of how he'd look at me if he were here right now.

"It's okay," he says, as though reading my thoughts. "I get that more often than you'd think."

I have about a million questions for Mr. Jeffords, but looking up at him right now—seeing the tired marks beneath his eyes, the weary slant to his lips—my tongue feels too heavy to form a single one.

"Hey!"

Oliver appears at the entrance of the cave, arm in front of Griffin as he stands behind him. His chest rises and falls with heavy breaths, like he'd been running, and Griffin's face is smeared with dirt. "I thought I heard someone, and—Finley, who is this guy? Are you okay?"

I wince, knowing this is probably not the introduction Oliver wanted to one of his crush-in-laws. From the way sweat sticks his hair to his forehead and his uneven breaths, I know he's been running all over to find an adult to offer me some (unwanted) help, so he's probably already grumpy. So, I put on my most innocent grin.

"Oliver, this is Devon Jeffords," I say, slow and sweet. "You know . . . Jason's dad?"

Also known as a prime suspect. But I don't say that part. Seeing the blood rush to Oliver's cheeks and thinking of Jason's pained expression when I confronted him behind the diner, I don't like thinking that part either.

Mr. Jeffords runs his hand over the back of his neck. "You're friends of Jason's?"

Oliver stands, jaw hanging. I roll my eyes; considering that the only reason he cares about this adventure is because his crush is involved, he sure is managing to blow this encounter.

"Jason's one of our favorite people in Stone Creek," I say—which is true, considering the other options. But I say it mostly because if Mr. Jeffords thinks we're on his side, he's more likely to open up about Meggie's disappearance.

Mr. Jeffords smiles softly. "Well, I'm glad to hear that. I'm happy to help any friends of Jason's. Especially when they find themselves trapped in mucky old holes like this one."

"Finley's not trapped," Griffin says. "She's exploring."

Great—now what little shreds of cover I had left have been peeled away. Heat rises to my cheeks, making me look as disheveled as Oliver.

But Mr. Jeffords's smile grows. "Ah, you're a Meggie fan," he says with a laugh. "Well, you came to the right place. Most folks stick to Meggie Lane or downtown, but this is a lot more authentic to the Meggie Riley experience, isn't it?"

I shoot Oliver an *I told you so* glare, then snap my attention back to Mr. Jeffords. For a moment I was so focused on his potential guilt that I totally forget that he used to date Meggie. The real, live, present Meggie who was once right here, in Stone Creek. He probably knows all sorts of things about her that no one else does.

Oliver bites his lower lip. "But why stay in Stone Creek, considering . . . ?"

His voice trails off and he averts his eyes to the ground. Mr. Jeffords smiles sympathetically.

"I love Stone Creek. It's where I grew up, and where my parents grew up, and where their parents grew up too," he says.

The warm way he talks about his family history makes me wonder even more about what drew Jeff's family away from the town—and what led him to stay here, alone, in that empty little house. Back at the diner, Jason promised us he'd share anything he found out about his dad if we did the same about Jeff. I swallow, wondering if I'll be able to get the answers I need from Jeff about his family and the auto shop—and what the answers will mean for Meggie's story, and my place in it.

"I always knew I wanted to stay," Mr. Jeffords continues, "and Meggie always knew she wanted to go. It's what we were fighting about that night when she . . ."

His voice trails off, and a strained, tired look settles over his features. He must have told this story a thousand times before. The exact words are probably in one of the news clippings hanging at Jeff's shop right now. Maybe they're rehearsed, a tired speech meant to fight off guilt. Or maybe it's just the truth, one that he's forced to relive again and again, stuck in that one day, that one argument, unable to move on.

"I loved how much she appreciated Stone Creek," he says, voice gaining certainty. "We loved the same things about the town, but in different ways, ways that made me want to stay and keep caring for these woods, and ways that made her want to go out and find bigger, greater versions of what these woods have to offer." He shrugs and rubs the back of his neck again. "I like to believe she did run away, like she said she would. That she's out on her greatest adventure yet, far, far away from Stone Creek and the Rileys."

He spits the "Rileys" part out, like it leaves a bitter taste on his tongue. Mr. Phillips talked about Mr. Riley the same way too—like he could have something to do with Meggie's disappearance and orchestrated it as a last-ditch effort to regain control of Stone Creek. Everything Mr. Riley said in his TV interview showed he didn't know the real Meggie at all. That could be motive to hide her here, to save the Riley business before she could run away.

My hand rises to my pocket, where the diner map is tucked away. Hopefully, I'll be able to rope Stu or someone else into bringing us to the Riley residence next on our adventure.

"Some people say that she was killed, or kidnapped," Mr. Jeffords says. His voice is a bit breezy given the subject matter, but I've come to learn that's typical for residents of Stone Creek. Living in a grand adventure will do that to you, I suppose. "I really do think she's still out there, though. Hopefully on her own terms."

Griffin runs a hand over his chin and cocks an eyebrow, looking like a caricature of a character from the black-and-white detective movies Mom loves. "Hmm," he muses, loud and without an ounce of subtlety, "and what makes you say that?"

Mr. Jeffords chuckles softly at Griffin's persona. For some reason, the gentle way he looks at Griffin makes my muscles loosen. "I was telling the truth when I said we were drifting apart in those last months of our relationship," he says, calm and certain. I wonder if he's either a really, really good liar, or if he's really comfortable with the truth. Both seem strange, and it makes me want to hear everything he has to say. "She was starting to hang out with some other people in town—there were a lot more people back then, during Stone Creek's boom. People who moved for the Riley businesses, people who moved because of Meggie and her discovery . . ."

His voice trails off. I think of what Mr. Phillips said back at the shop: that a lot of people came and went from Stone Creek around the time of Meggie's disappearance. My head spins at the thought that all the people I've met in Stone Creek could be innocent—that the person responsible for Meggie's disappearance could have left decades before I ever knew of Stone Creek at all.

One of those people could be P. W.—someone who moved to Stone Creek for Meggie and her story, or who moved for another reason and became obsessed with her when they arrived. Someone so obsessed with her, they wanted to own her legacy themselves.

The thought makes my stomach churn—especially considering that whoever this is could be my shadow man. And if I'm going to follow in Meggie's legacy and become a great rescuer-slash-adventurer too, I could be putting a giant target on my back.

"I'm sure you've heard this part," Mr. Jeffords continues, which makes me perk up, because there's so much to Meggie's story, I feel like I haven't actually heard any of it at all. "But that night, when she called me before she left, I heard two people in the background with her. I know I didn't imagine it, because they were talking to each other while she was on with me." He lets out a bitter laugh and looks off above my head. "How could one person be having a conversation with himself?"

Mr. Jeffords could be planting a false clue to get us off his trail. But if he's telling the truth, it means there was a duo responsible for Meggie's disappearance. Mr. Riley and his wife. Maybe Mr. Phillips and an accomplice, like Stu.

Or maybe—if I were to believe the note the shadow man left me—it could have been Jeff and his dad.

All the possibilities make me squirm, like my skin suddenly doesn't fit quite right.

Across the small cave, Oliver studies me with a furrowed brow. I hate how grateful I feel when he forces a change to the conversation. "Mr. Jeffords, you said you loved living in Stone Creek, and that your family has lived here for generations. But Jason"—a muscle in his jaw tightens and for a moment, his gaze drops—"said that he planned on leaving Stone Creek for a STEM program. Are you okay with that?"

Oliver's probably asking for his crush's sake. But as much as I hate to admit it, it's a good question for our mission, too. Mr. Jeffords has a script about how Meggie's runaway note made him feel. But asking about Jason's plans to leave Stone Creek will catch him off guard. And his reaction could end up saying more about Meggie than Jason.

Mr. Jeffords shrugs his broad shoulders. "I'm proud of him," he says. Oliver's posture visibly lifts. "He's brilliant with the stuff he does. Been disassembling and rebuilding computers since he was in grade school. There was one time he made this robot for the science fair." He laughs, loud and boisterous in a way that bounces off the walls of the cave. "Its body was a plastic water bottle, but it had all these wires and cords inside, and two little metal legs that made it walk. He lost the fair prize to some kid who made a poster board on the science of farts." Rightfully, he rolls his eyes. "But I knew, right then, he was destined for great things."

Mr. Jeffords studies Oliver for a moment; then his eyes soften. "I love Stone Creek, sure. But I want him to love wherever he ends up too."

Oliver squirms a bit under his gaze, but beneath his usual scowl I can tell he's resisting a smile. I can't help but feel a fuzzy warmth in my chest, seeing Oliver settling into his real self—the one he told me about in the woods.

Mr. Jeffords turns back to me. "And I hope that wherever Meggie is now, she loves it too." He wags his finger in the air, as though grasping onto a small memory as he speaks it aloud. "You know, she used to talk about going to the Sahara, and then Antarctica, just to feel the extremes, to know she could survive them both. I hope she went on to do that and more. Far from all the commercial noise of Stone Creek."

Compared to where we live in Massachusetts, it's hard to consider Stone Creek noisy. But more important is the image of Meggie in the Antarctic, bundled against the deadly cold as she trudges in heavy boots over the ice. When the city refused to call snow days and still made us go to school, Sophie and I could challenge each other to get on the bus stop after our usual one. We'd bundle up in puffy coats, our sleeves swishing against our sides as we trekked across budding snowbanks to make it to the bus. The snowflakes stung my cheeks, and I almost forgot I had toes, they went so numb. But Sophie was there, giggling beside me and egging me on. And I knew that we'd make it and board the bus steps triumphant, hands balled victoriously over our heads as we waddled in our snow boots to our seats.

Meggie probably would have loved that. I'll have to tell her about it when I find her. Then—maybe someday—we can go to the Antarctic together, all three of us.

I want to focus on that daydream, but something about Mr. Jeffords's speech makes me feel all tangled inside, like the spiderwebs dangling overhead. He understands Meggie, who she really is, in a way no one else I've met in Stone Creek so far has. He understands Jason, too—what matters to him, what makes him tick.

But as much as he's the person who understands them the most, he's ready to let them go without a fight. Happy to imagine Meggie left without a word, dashing off to her next great adventure alone. Happy to think of Jason leaving Stone Creek, casting his family's legacy to the side.

More than ever, I know I need to talk to Jeff when I get home. Not only to understand how his family leaving Stone Creek relates to Meggie's disappearance, but how, knowing he was staying behind, his family could choose to leave at all.

A strange chill comes over me, and I run my hands up and down my arms. Oliver clears his throat.

"We should probably get going," he says. I hate that he thinks he has to take care of me, but right now I'm grateful that at the very least I don't have to be the one to announce the end to this adventure. "Do you know a way out of here?"

"Of course," Mr. Jeffords says, reaching for his belt. "I've got a rope. I'll climb on up and toss it down for you kids, okay?"

One by one, we climb out of the pit: me first, so I can hoist up Griffin, and Oliver last, so he can catch Griffin if he falls. Mr. Jeffords grips the rope tight. A bead of sweat forms on his forehead, but he doesn't let go.

I wonder what, in comparison, makes it easy for him to let go of Meggie or Jason. And, more important, if, whatever it is, Sophie has it too.

GREATEST FEMALE ADVENTURER NUMBER TWELVE:

VALENTINA TERESHKOVA,

FIRST WOMAN IN SPACE AND ONLY WOMAN TO HAVE BEEN ON A SOLO SPACE MISSION.

By the time we return to the van, a bleary-eyed Stu is getting an earful from Mr. Phillips over the phone. From the look on his face, it's clear we're not welcome to a free ride back, so Mr. Jeffords gives Jeff a call to come pick us up. Oliver keeps running his hands together, either feeling embarrassed he had to be saved by his crush's dad or embarrassed we interrupted Jeff's workday—or both. But as Jeff's car rumbles up to meet us at the edge of the woods, all I can think about are the questions I've been waiting to ask him since my conversation with Mr. Phillips back at the auto shop.

The ride back to Jeff's house is dominated by Griffin's account of the day's events, which mainly consists of his heroic search in the woods for a way to rescue me from the cave. I sit in the back seat, opening and closing my mouth like a guppy as I wait for the perfect moment to interject and ask about the auto shop. But Griffin rattles on until we pull up to Jeff's house, and by then we've all spotted Malt gnawing on the edge of the garden hose, and that's the next distraction to derail my plans.

Jeff runs across the lawn to wrestle Malt off the hose, and I go to follow. But Oliver grabs my shoulder and tugs me back.

"You've caused him enough trouble today," he says. "Give it a break, okay?"

I shrug him off, hard so his hand whips off my shoulder. But when he leads Griffin inside, I decide to follow. The questions are piled up like a house of cards in my head, but I'm not quite sure which to pull out first, so they all remain, stuck and cramped in my mind.

Upstairs in the attic, Oliver and Griffin flop onto their respective beds. Oliver whips out his phone and begins dialing a number. I figure he's about to do some crush-related damage control after our run-in with Mr. Jeffords until he says, "Mom sent a few texts today, so I'm going to give her a call."

I grit my teeth. As usual, everything's being filtered through Oliver. Meanwhile, my messages are empty—other than one unanswered text from Sophie, of course.

I listen to the faint hum of the line ringing through Oliver's phone speakers, wishing I didn't care as much as I did.

"Hello?" I hear her answer, voice distant as Oliver cups the phone to his cheek.

"Hey, Mom," he answers, already walking toward the other side of the room.

I want to grab the phone from his hand, tell Mom my version of events from the day. But there's no way I can twist me lying to one of Mr. Phillips's employees to get a free ride, running into the woods and falling into a ditch, and having to be rescued by a park-employee-slash-potential-kidnapper from an underground cave.

"Mostly hung out at the café," I hear Oliver saying. "Helped Jeff with some customers."

A big fat lie from Mom's perfect son. Though I know it's not to have my back, but so he doesn't get in trouble, since Mom's more likely to blame him than me. As if everything I do or don't do is his fault, not mine, because she expects so much more of him and absolutely nothing from me.

Then Oliver turns, blue eyes fixing on me. I brace myself for a recap of some lecture Mom's recited to him on the other end of the line, when he extends his arm, phone in hand. "Your turn," he says.

I beam, almost skipping over. The other night I practically had to grab the phone from Oliver to get a chance to talk to Mom. But today she's asking for me. It's as if she can sense my progress, knows how close I am to a legendary discovery. Knows that soon I'll be worth listening to too.

I take the phone and cup it to my face, the screen still warm from Oliver's cheek. "Hi Mom," I say, barely able to hide the giddiness in my tone.

"Hey, sweetie. Having fun at Jeff's place?"

Like Oliver, I'm going to have to find a way to navigate this without giving away too much. I wish I could tell her about Meggie Lane and my discovery in the northeastern woods but know that when it comes to Mom, it's better to tell her about the grand finale than stress her with the uncertain, murky parts in between. "Other than helping Griffin with his math packets," I say.

She laughs softly. "Nice try, Finley. But neither of you are off the hook for that." She's quiet for a moment, and I hear the sound of her nails drumming through the hotel's landline. "I was in between meetings today and was thinking about Jeff's shop."

My skin goes hot and clammy, and I'm sure I'm not hearing her right. But from the sound of it, Mom's been looking into Meggie's story too. I suck in a steadying breath, trying to keep my voice even as I say, "How so?"

"When I saw how excited you got about those newspaper clippings at Jeff's café, I did some more reading about the town," she says.

I turn away from Oliver so he can't see my budding grin. Already, I'm imagining a rebranded business card with a fourth Walsh adventure agent tapped onto the title.

"I always knew a woman had gone missing there, but I didn't know the part about her finding some expensive antiques in the woods or whatnot," she continues. Her tone is hesitant, guarded. My heartbeat drums anxiously in my temples. "It reminded me of those things you used to do with Sophie—"

Used to. The words land like darts against my chest. I try to make a sound to show I'm still listening, but my mouth remains clamped in a tight line.

"It made me a little nervous," she admits. "I know how much you enjoy those things, but I want to make sure you don't get too carried away. It's not that I don't trust Jeff—of course I do, or I wouldn't have let you stay with him. But Stone Creek seems a little strange, and I don't want you to get into any trouble."

Your strange is my adventure. I want to say that, but again, the words are clogged up inside me. All I can hear is "don't get too carried away" and "don't want you to get into any trouble." As if I'm a loose piece of driftwood being carried in a wave rather than an adventure-bound captain steering the ship. As if I'm someone who causes trouble rather than solves it, like I plan to by rescuing Meggie.

I want to tell her about the shadow man Oliver failed to notice, about the strange conflicting stories I've heard about Jeff that she didn't look into before dropping us off, to tell her that I'm the one who's fixing all of this and that ignoring things just to pretend we're fine is just another way of getting stuck.

But all I say is, "You don't have to worry about me, Mom," which is true. She doesn't. Because I can handle Stone Creek on my own. And I'm going to prove it. "And

Griffin's fine too. A little tuckered out after running around at the shop all day. He's playing on the Switch, but I'll make sure he doesn't stay up too late."

I tell her what she wants to hear, like an explorer scattering treats on the opposite path to keep bears and coyotes from following theirs. But it works; Mom lets out a tired yet relaxed yawn, satisfied with what I've said or not wanting to know what would happen if she pushed further. I say good night and hand (okay, shove) the phone back to Oliver before heading back toward my cot.

Griffin is still hunched over his Switch, but a small pout forms on his lips. "Oliver, have you seen the charger?" he asks, high and singsong.

Oliver cups a hand over the phone's speaker. "You left it on the floor, so I put it in the closet," he says. And just as Griffin starts to speak, he quickly adds, "Go get it yourself."

"But I'm so comfy," Griffin whines. Inevitably, his eyes fix on me. "Finley, since you're already up—"

I groan, stomping my way toward the closet. Tasks like this are not what make great adventurers, but all the anxious, restless energy surging through me right now has nowhere else to go. So I make my way toward the closet, thrusting the creaky old doors open in search of the charger.

I'm greeted by the smell of lint and mothballs. A small chain dangles from the ceiling, and I give it a yank. Overhead, a tiny yellow bulb flickers to light. A clothing rod holds several dozen hangers, most of them vacant except the few Oliver used to hang his clothes. His suitcase is tucked into the far-right corner, beside Griffin's charger and a pair of shorts I forgot to put in the hamper last night. The other side of the closet is occupied by a series of boxes resting side by side, overflowing with yellowing papers, the cardboard sagging beneath the weight of its contents.

I snatch Griffin's charger off the ground, then step toward the tallest tower of boxes. A thick layer of dust coats the flap of the top box, but it's puckered open, revealing the contents inside. It looks like a pile of photographs, stuffed in a box rather than carefully arranged in an album, like the ones Mom has at home.

I stand on the tips of my toes, peering into the box without disturbing the dust. Then, behind me, comes the ringing sound of Malt's bark.

I jump out of the closet, quickly closing the door shut behind me. Jeff appears at the top of the attic stairs, Malt cradled in his arms.

Griffin bounces on his mattress. "You brought a friend!"

Jeff leans down and lowers Malt to the floor. As soon as his paws touch the floorboards, he's dashing straight toward Griffin, who greets him with a wide smile and open arms.

"I wasn't expecting a call from Devon Jeffords today," Jeff muses, as though talking to himself.

I perk up. Stone Creek is like an onion, but each layer is just more and more drama. "Why? Do you not like each other?"

Jeff straightens up and tucks his hands in his oversized pockets. "I like him plenty," he says, "but anytime some coyote or raccoon comes wandering out of the woods by the café, I always call him instead of the idiots who work down at Animal Control. At this point, sometimes he plain doesn't answer my calls. I thought he'd blocked my number until I got his call today."

His words paint a different picture of Stone Creek than the one I've grown used to. The way Jeff talks, it's like Stone Creek is just another small town, full of small events like raccoons wiggling their way into restaurant trash cans.

It's almost as if he can't see the literal writing on the walls of his café—what makes Stone Creek so special, so unique. Maybe that's because there's something he wants to avoid about Meggie's story. Or maybe he's like Devon Jeffords, drawn to this place for a different reason entirely.

Either way, I want to find out.

"Well, thank you, kids, for taking Malt off my hands for a bit," he says, already heading toward the stairs. "Call me up if he gets to be too much."

Griffin beams as Malt plants slobbery kisses over his cheeks. Oliver's upper lip curls in disgust. "He could never be too much."

Jeff smiles to himself, then turns and heads down the

creaky old stairs. I abandon the closet and rush after him.

Downstairs, Jeff heads toward his usual spot on the couch. The coffee table is littered with receipts from the café, and a clunky old laptop rests to the side. He settles onto the couch with a quiet sigh, the old springs echoing the sound beneath him.

I should think of some clever way to get the truth out of him—like how I talked Stu into driving us into the woods. But as I leap down the last steps, all I manage is to blurt, "Mr. Phillips told us your parents used to own the auto shop."

Jeff looks up. The whites of his eyes flash bright, but his mouth remains in a tight, drawn line. A silence settles in around us, interrupted only by the tired creaks of the heater and Malt's distant barks. My words hang heavy in the air, like a hovering thundercloud.

"They did." He speaks slowly, as though uncertain of his memory, of our roots in Stone Creek. "I basically grew up down there."

His gaze drops, and he picks a receipt off the table. But instead of reading it or reaching for his laptop, he just tugs at the corner of the crinkly paper, as though unsure what to do next.

Unable to will my legs forward, I remain fixed at the foot of the stairs, gripping the railing as though if I let go, I'd topple right over. The note the shadow man left me said not to trust Jeff. But right now I need to know what he has to say.

Not only for Meggie's sake, but for mine, too. Maybe if I understand what drew his parents away from Stone Creek, leaving him alone here, I'll understand what I need to do to make sure I'm not left behind too.

"Mr. Phillips said that they didn't like the new Stone Creek. You know . . ." I swallow, throat rough like sandpaper. "Meggie."

Jeff continues to run his fingertips over the corner of the receipt, eyes looking anywhere but right at me. Behind him, the family photos hang on the wall. But I don't know which—if any—are of him and his parents.

"That's kind of true," he says, shoulders rising in a tired shrug. "But Phillips's version of things is never quite right, as I'm sure you've noticed."

I find myself nodding along. Because I have noticed—how Meggie Lane and the tour bus were all wrong. I want to smile, knowing that Jeff sees through it all too.

But I keep quiet, listening for what he'll say next.

"The shop had been struggling long before Meggie went missing," Jeff goes on, "but up until then we were able to keep our heads above water. Then Stone Creek became the one you've come to know—"

"Meggie obsessed," I say, as if I'm not guilty of it too.

"Mr. Phillips kept scooping up properties around town and rebranding them for the tourist boom," he says. "My dad refused to rebrand. And I think he got tired of fighting for a place in Stone Creek. So, he and my mom left."

I wait for more, but he falls silent. Listening to him now is like googling Amelia Earhart and getting a one-line description of all she'd done. But there's way more to her story—books' worth. And right now it feels like there are a few chapters missing from Jeff's, too.

"But you stayed," I say, voice growing firmer. "And you opened a Meggie-themed shop."

Jeff lifts his baseball cap and scratches the back of his head. "Yeah, your great-uncle probably wouldn't have loved Meggie's Cup."

I blink. "Wait, he doesn't know you opened the café?" My throat squeezes as I add, "Did you stop talking after he left Stone Creek?"

He shakes his head. "We still talked, and I tried to come by for holidays when I could. But he wasn't thrilled I stayed. He never said it outright, but I got the feeling he saw it as me giving in to the new Stone Creek, the one he felt chewed him up and spit him out, leaving him and your great-aunt with less than they started with."

I clench my jaw to keep it from trembling. "And he never forgave you for staying? To the point you kept Meggie's Cup a secret for all these years?" Jeff winces, as though bracing himself to share bad news. "Oh," he murmurs. "He's long since passed." Then, as if I were the one who lost a parent, "I'm sorry, kid."

Questions buzz in my head like a swarm of angry bees. But Jeff's gentle "I'm sorry" is in there too. For a moment all I see is the current scene: Jeff watching me cautiously from the couch, and me, feeling comforted from a hurt that isn't even mine.

I finally take a step into the room, away from the attic stairs. I imagine I'm an Arctic explorer, trudging through the ice around me.

"My dad left too," I say. In my mind, the Arctic sun rises higher in the sky, melting the snow at my heels. My cautious steps transform into a steady walk across the worn living room carpet. "He still calls, and we still visit. But in between all that, it's like he doesn't really exist."

Jeff looks up. I'm so used to him glancing away, the weight of his gaze is heavy, unfamiliar. But it feels steadying, too, and I lean into that feeling as I add, "Like we don't really exist. To him, at least."

Jeff's dad got tired of fighting for a place in Stone Creek—but he shouldn't have gotten tired of fighting for a place in Jeff's life, even if he stayed here, in this town. My dad never fought for us, either—like we weren't worth fighting for, like he'd never even thought we could be.

Over the years that hurt faded like an old scar. We settled into our new routine, patched the holes Dad had left. I know why Mom didn't call Dad when she found out about the work trip—that she didn't want to hear the list of projects and deadlines he rattled off the top of his head like excuses. I was fine with it too, and happy he didn't have the chance to explain the things that were more important than we were. And not staying with Dad was a relief to all of us. Griffin didn't have to pretend to want the attentions of a stranger. Oliver didn't have to fill in the gaps for a parent who didn't see the gaps in the first place. And I didn't have to feel like I should be trying for someone who'd never tried for me.

I knew we'd never end up at Dad's, but I had no idea we'd end up here, in Stone Creek. It makes sense now, why Jeff would answer the phone when Mom called, would let three strangers fill his empty house for a week.

My phone rests idle in my back pocket. I hope that by the end of this trip, I find the right way to respond to Sophie, that I'll prove to her that the adventure agency is worth fighting for.

Jeff must think Stone Creek's worth fighting for, considering that he stayed. His version of Stone Creek's a bit different from the one I see; mine's just like the map in my pocket, every corner of the woods and every street in town a landmark in Meggie's story. But Jeff's map would probably show a version of Stone Creek I don't recognize. One where Devon Jeffords was the most reliable local government employee rather than a prime kidnapping suspect. One where the woods aren't a hub of mystery and adventure, but the home to the neighborhood's peskiest pests, like raccoons and coyotes and bears.

Maybe Jeff's just content with that version of Stone Creek. Or maybe he really loves those parts of his town for what they are—even though, to me, they seem like the least thrilling or important or worthy.

When Jeff agreed to let us stay with him, he didn't

know I was an adventurer myself. He didn't know that, by the end of this trip, he'd be famous for housing the girl who went on to rescue Meggie Riley. He answered Mom's call and took us in because it's what he wanted to do—and probably because he wishes he could have reconnected with his dad, too, before it was too late for them.

Crossing the room to him now, I realize that Jeff might be the only one—even if I don't prove myself and save the Walsh-Higgins Adventure Agency by the end of this week—who won't look at me any different.

It makes me feel queasy, like there's little gaps inside me that I need to fill with the usual buzzwords—with bravado and bravery and whatever else it takes to be the World's Greatest Female Adventurer One Hundred One.

But it also makes me wonder what else I would be, if I didn't have to be the best. If I didn't have to prove myself to make Sophie or Mom or my brothers care enough to listen to what I have to say.

"I'm sorry about your father, kid," Jeff says. "It's up to you, whether you try to mend that bridge." He returns his cap to his head, tugging it down so the rim aligns with his brow. "I stayed at the auto shop for years, thinking that's what he needed from me. What the business needed to be successful."

He shrugs, shoulders loose and easy like he's come to terms with whatever he's going to say next. I'm hyperaware of the tension in my shoulders, the knots in my muscles that I thought were from tree climbing or free-falling into secret caves, but might be from something else entirely.

"But he just got angrier and angrier at the Rileys, and I got angrier and angrier too. At the Rileys, I thought. But when he sold out to Phillips just to spite them, all I felt was relief. For him, or for me, I don't know."

I blink fast, experiencing mental whiplash. Angry at the Rileys? I figured it was Mr. Phillips that Jeff's dad would have hated, for buying up all the properties around town and rebranding them based on Meggie.

I'd almost forgotten that Jeff and his family were here before she went missing—back when she was an adventurer and local hero, when the Rileys were as powerful and influential as Mr. Phillips. The treasure Meggie found helped make the Rileys the richest family in the area. Before Mr. Phillips became a powerful adversary to the Rileys, they owned most of the businesses in Stone Creek.

The map in my pocket has a mark for the Riley residence. I'm not sure how I'm going to get there, since Stu has permanently (and understandably) quit as my chauffeur. But transportation is just an obstacle I'll have to overcome, because Mr. Riley's house has to be the next stop on my expedition around Stone Creek.

Jeff clears his throat, the sound marking the end to his story. I'm still brimming with questions—about his dad's feelings about the Rileys, and why Jeff opened a

Meggie-themed shop after his dad left, and why the shadow man dropped that note in the woods, warning me not to trust a thing Jeff says.

I open my mouth, ready to fire a hundred more questions his way. But Jeff speaks first. "I'm just gonna be balancing the books," he says, reaching for the bulky laptop, "but you're welcome to stay down here for a bit, if you'd like. I don't have any siblings myself, but I figure you could use a break every now and then."

As though on cue, Oliver's voice carries down the stairs, shouting something at Griffin about "letting Malt's mucky paws on the sheets." Griffin responds with boisterous laughter, and as Oliver starts to shout back, I take the last step down the attic stairs.

Oliver and Griffin have been reluctant participants along the way—Oliver doubting the importance of Meggie's story, and Griffin always looking around like he'd run off to the next best thing if Oliver pointed in its direction. But at times, it's almost felt like they really were on the mission alongside me.

I wonder how long that feeling will last, or if they're just letting themselves be dragged along, the way Jeff went along with his father to appease him.

Tomorrow, I'll have to convince someone to drive me to the Riley residence, and I'll have to convince Oliver and Griffin to come with me. While we're there, I'll have to convince Mr. Riley to talk to me about Meggie, have to convince my brothers all over again that the conversation is worth having, that I'm someone worth following into the woods.

But right now I cross the room toward the couch, letting their voices fade into the background. I sit two cushions down from Jeff. The leathery fabric embraces my body, and a soft, faded quilt brushes against my shoulder. Jeff flips open his laptop and pulls up a cluttered Excel spreadsheet. He remains hunched over the screen, computer in his lap, only looking up to reach for the occasional receipt. The old clock hanging on the wall ticks peacefully in the background, and outside, the hum of crickets grows as the minutes pass.

For the first time since arriving in Stone Creek, I let thoughts of my adventure slip away.

Jeff is content with my company, quiet and peaceful without any adventure or heroics. Happy to sit silently with me, even after all the nagging and invasive questions I've thrown his way.

For a moment, I'm not Finley the adventurer, or Finley with a mission. I'm just me.

And for once, that feels like it could be enough.

GREATEST FEMALE ADVENTURER NUMBER THIRTEEN:

MAUD WEST,

FAMOUS MASTER OF DISGUISE AND THOUGHT TO BE THE FIRST FEMALE UNDERCOVER DETECTIVE IN LONDON.

The next morning Jeff's half as talkative as usual (which, for him, is about two syllables away from complete silence). Other than a grumble about taking Malt out to pee before breakfast and a short rant about having to hurry down to the café for the morning rush before Anne Thornton comes for his blood, it's a pretty quiet morning. It's almost as though he used up so many words the day before, he isn't left with any for today. Part of me—the one that found the note about Jeff in the woods—is anxious, thinking that Jeff regrets something he said or thought he shared too much about his connections to Stone Creek. Another part of me doesn't mind, maybe even likes that the things we shared last night get to stay there, in that one moment, preserved in that space.

Either way, it's clear I'm not going to be able to convince Jeff to give us a drive to the Riley residence for some morning adventuring. So, the Walsh-Walsh-Walsh Adventure Agency heads over to the diner for breakfast, leaving Jeff and Malt to face the morning crowd alone.

When we arrive, Sam's buzzing around like a wasp, taking orders from the handful of customers tucked into booths and balancing a stack of menus under her wrinkled arm. Jason's behind the front counter, surrounded by towers of dirty dishes and half-empty ketchup containers, a yellowing towel over his shoulder. Despite the usual small crowd, there's a frantic energy in the air, like all the workers are about to pack up shop and run off to join Meggie wherever she disappeared to.

Oliver dodges Sam as she shoves past him with a pot of hot coffee. He waves hesitantly at Jason. "What's going on here?"

"Mr. Phillips has us working overtime in preparation for the twentieth-anniversary festival," Jason explains. "All the local businesses will begin setup tomorrow, coordinating plans for when the big—or, what they hope will be a big—rush of tourists come in three weeks, on the day itself."

I crawl up onto one of the high stools, eyes wide as the coffee saucers Jason's stacking at his station. "We'll be going tomorrow too, then!"

Sam saunters back with a menu tucked under her arm. She raises a thin eyebrow at me. "Jeff's coming? I've never known him to man a booth at the festival."

If Sam says he's not likely to come, she's probably right.

Jeff's lack of interest in the Meggie case may have been drummed into him by his dad, or it could be something else entirely—something more sinister, like the note the shadow man left me suggests. But whether Jeff comes or not, we have to be there.

"Jeff might not be coming," I admit, "but the Walsh siblings will be there."

Sam purses her lips, as though expecting what I'll say next.

"We'll come along with you and Jason," I say, beaming. She groans, thin body slumping tiredly.

"I think that sounds fun," Jason says, pressing his elbows on the edge of the counter as he buffs a soup spoon. He glances at Oliver quickly, then ducks his head. "It'll be good to have some new visitors at the festival, I mean."

I swivel in my chair, fingertips pinching the edge of the counter. "Has a tourist ever come close to finding Meggie?"

Sam rolls her eyes. I quickly remember that to her, I too am an annoying tourist. "That obnoxious reporter acts like he's going to blow the lid off everything."

Richard Connors. He was one of the people in the diner our first day here—one of my main suspects, whether my brothers know it or not, because he's one of the few people who knew we were headed into the woods. One of the few who could be my stalker.

I edge closer to the counter, as though if I sit too close to him, Oliver will hear my thoughts.

"He's exhausting," Jason moans, though there's laughter

in his words. His eyes lock with Oliver's. "He kept coming over to our table the other day and asking us questions. Couldn't take a hint no matter how many times I explained I was on break."

"It would be one thing if he tipped well," Sam seconds.

I glance between Jason and Oliver. "The reporter was in the café the same time you were the other day?"

Jason nods and gives an exasperated shrug. Behind him, the chef calls a ticket number from the window and hurls a sloppy plate of wet eggs and half-burnt hash browns onto the counter. Sam sweeps the plate quickly from the surface, sending a plastic-wrapped square of butter toppling to the floor. "That man's all but paying rent."

On cue, the reporter saunters out of the men's room, typing away on his phone as he makes his way back to his seat at the counter. Sam rolls her eyes and makes a show of walking in the opposite direction, balancing the breakfast plate in her left hand.

If the reporter was at the diner when I ran into the woods with Malt the other day, that crosses him off the shadow-man suspect list. As strange as Jeff and his place in Stone Creek can seem at times, he's off the list too, since he was back at the café with Griffin. If Jason was in the diner, it could have been his dad, Devon Jeffords. Or Bryan Phillips. Mr. Jeffords knows his way around the woods better than anyone, and even if Mr. Phillips lacks subtlety and grace, he has plenty of henchmen like Stu who would be willing to carry out his dirty work for him.

"Hey, it's the Walsh Adventure Agents!" Richard calls, spotting us just before he returns to his stool. He snatches his coffee off the other end of the counter and makes his way toward us.

Oliver lets out a soft groan. Jason grabs his dish towel off the counter and turns back toward the kitchen. "Good luck," he says, slipping off just as Richard plops into the seat next to Griffin.

"We prefer to be referred to by our full title: Walsh Adventure Agents of the Walsh-Walsh-Walsh Adventure Agency," Griffin says, impressively fast for such a tongue twister, "but because you're a friend of the agency, we'll let it slide."

"Friend of the agency," Richard murmurs to himself warmly. "That's nice of you to say. I'd love to hear what you kids have been up to since we last spoke."

Already, he's whipped out a tiny notepad from his back pocket, complete with a little golf pencil to match. Griffin puffs his chest proudly, probably ready to leap into a recap of the monologue he gave Jeff on our car ride home last night. But just because it's unlikely that Richard Connors is my shadow man doesn't mean it's impossible that he's involved in Meggie's case. Or—perhaps just as bad—that he could be planning on using our clues to beat us to her on this rescue mission.

I reach over, clasping my palm over Griffin's open mouth. I smile, despite the slobbery, gross feeling on my hand. "We've been so wrapped up in helping Jeff with the café, we've barely gotten out," I lie. "But I'm sure you've been able to get a whole bunch of great interviews in the past few days . . . right?"

He taps the pencil eraser on the coiled ring of his notebook, studying me with his dark-brown eyes. "Getting interviews in Stone Creek isn't the problem. It's weeding out fact from fiction that gets to be a bit tough."

Something falters in his gaze as he adds, "Especially since, as the years go on, people begin to actually believe the stories they've made up about Meggie."

My hand drops from Griffin's face. I hadn't thought about that: that some of the clues and accounts I've gathered over the last few days could be flat-out lies. And not just malicious lies, but ones that the liars have come to believe themselves.

When I talked to Jeff last night, it felt like there were a thousand holes in his story about his dad. But he didn't seem like he was lying; more like he wasn't ready to tell the whole truth, whatever that was. I understand that feeling, even shared it during our talk last night. But right now I can't help but wonder if that's just another form of lying.

Jason walks out of the kitchen balancing a two-foot stack of pearly-white plates. Oliver leans past me across the counter. "Have you interviewed Mr. Riley yet?" he asks Richard. "We were told he'll be at the festival this week, but not participating. So it may be better to talk to him beforehand. Catch him off guard."

I cross my arms over my chest, impressed by how smoothly Oliver slipped our agenda into our conversation with Richard. For a moment it almost feels like a real member of our adventure agency is here who's as invested in finding Meggie as I am.

But it's probably just because he wants to help Jason and his dad—especially after what happened in the cave yesterday. I'm glad he's interested in the mission at all. But part of me wishes that joining the adventure agency to hang out with me was reason enough.

Richard drums his fingers on the top of his notepad, and I can almost see the gears in his mind moving. "I've been thinking of heading over to the Riley residence," he says, voice low. "It's not going to be an easy interview—not many people have gotten Robert Riley to sit down for one after the first few years of the investigation. It seems like he has a bit of a distrust for reporters."

"Maybe a bunch of them used what he said against him in their stories," Oliver suggests, "and you just need to earn his trust."

I scoff. As if earning trust is easy. Someone as guarded as Oliver should know better than that. But, for what it's worth, he's not doing a bad job of playing a part to earn Richard's trust. It's like he's an undercover agent, infiltrating enemy lines.

"Or!" Griffin shouts, smacking his hand on the counter. "Maybe he's scared to talk to reporters because he has something to hide."

Griffin, too? I sit up a little straighter, really feeling for the first time like we are adventure agents.

"Like Meggie's corpse," he adds. I deflate a bit, because at this point he should agree that Meggie is definitely not dead, and just in need of rescue. But, still, progress from my brothers at any margin is a huge win.

"We've been thinking of talking to Mr. Riley ourselves," I say, drawing the conversation back to its main purpose. I pull out my map and point to the giant, cartoonish house that marks where Meggie's family lives. "If you're headed over there today, we can come and help."

Oliver straightens up and shoots me a look. It's the same cautioning glance he gave me when I suggested we reroute the tour bus and have Stu drive us to the location of Meggie's treasure hunt. But, thankfully, he doesn't say anything. Maybe because he's given up on trying to reel me in. Or maybe because, even if he can't care about Meggie for my sake, he can care for Jason.

Richard's fingers drum faster. "It's a risky move," he says, mostly to himself. "But I suppose that's what I came to Stone Creek for."

He nods silently, as if having a conversation in his head. Then he slaps his palms on the counter and leaps to his feet.

"We'll do it," he announces. "I have my car parked out front, and we can head over right now, catch him off guard. I'll—we'll get the answers we need."

Griffin jumps off his stool. "And can Malt come too?" I open my mouth to argue, and he quickly adds, "He is on the business cards, after all. Same as the rest of the Walsh-Walsh-Walsh adventure agents."

"I don't know who Malt is," Richard says breathlessly, jingling his keys. "But make sure this Malt is ready to go, because I sure am."

He marches toward the diner door, nearly knocking into Sam on his way out as though if he hesitates, he'll backtrack. But the important thing is that we've scored a ride to the Riley residence. I high-five Griffin and mouth a silent *Yes!* Even Oliver cracks a grin.

After Griffin wrangles Malt, we pack into Richard Connors's sedan and speed off toward the Riley residence. It's not far from where we went exploring yesterday, and I stare out the window on the ride over, scanning the woods for a glimpse of Devon Jeffords. But rather than turning onto the beaten path that leads toward the cave, we remain on the main road, where the thick clusters of trees break to reveal sprawling yards and grand, three-story houses with long, winding driveways.

It's nothing like Jeff's side of town and all the tiny ranch houses tucked into pockets of empty woods. These rustic mansions—with their sweeping front porches, gazebos, and sunrooms the size of Jeff's house—remind me of something called glamping that Chloe was going on about once at lunch after we got back from winter break. I curled my upper lip and picked idly at my turkey sandwich, bored at the idea of a wilderness experience that stripped away everything that made it, well, wild. But Sophie had nodded along, murmuring in awe and asking questions about Chloe's trip. At the time I'd hoped it was just to humor Chloe until we could laugh about it alone later. But there was no later; when the lunch bell rang, Sophie remained fixed by Chloe's side, their conversation carrying all the way along our walk to fourth period.

We drive down a road lined with mailboxes that guard long, twisty driveways that curl deeper into the woods. Richard slows and puts on his blinker as we approach a tall blue mailbox labeled RILEY. It feels like a sign waving me forward, calling, *Adventure starts here!*

Unlike the pothole-ridden, cracked roads I've come to be used to in Stone Creek, the Rileys' driveway is paved and smooth. The car slides easily over the pavement and rolls slowly along the winding road toward the Riley residence. Goose bumps rise on my arms, and a fresh wave of excitement and curiosity moves through my chest.

Richard slows the car to a stop several yards from the gate, the car angled so it's obscured by a patch of trees and bushes. He cuts the engine and leans back, releasing a breath through pursed lips.

"I need some more time to get my questions together," he says. "But you kids don't need to wait for me. You can go on ahead."

Finally, an adult who trusts I can handle this mission on my own. After my call with Mom last night, Richard's words are music to my ears. I'm already reaching for my seat belt.

Oliver, of course, tries to ruin everything by pushing the issue. "Seriously? You're going to let us walk right up to the main suspect's front door alone? I thought you were the one who wanted an interview."

I reach over him for the door handle and give him a shove. "Richard is a friend of the adventure agency, remember? He knows we can handle this on our own."

So shut up and go, I think, giving him one more push toward the door. Oliver groans but steps out, Griffin and I rushing after him and Malt staying behind, slumped as he naps in the back seat. I don't waste a second before trekking down the winding driveway, using Oliver's obsession with chaperoning me to force him to follow along.

Oliver jogs to catch up. "You have to admit that's weird, though, that he just dumped us here like this."

I shrug, eyes fixed on the road ahead. "It's no different than when Stu gave us a ride."

"Stu gave us a ride to drop us off," he argues. "Richard was supposed to come in. So why isn't he?"

"He said he needed to think of his questions," I say, continuing to march forward. The house grows larger on the horizon as we approach. "I, on the other hand, have had a list of questions for Mr. Riley since day one."

Griffin bounces next to me. "Question one," he says in a cartoonishly deep voice, as if Batman were a police detective, "what did you do to Meggie, and where are you keeping her?"

"Maybe with a bit more subtlety," I say with a gentle

wince. "But we do need to get answers. And a head start on Richard should work in our favor."

Oliver huffs and leaps in front of us, grinding Griffin and me to a reluctant halt. "Are you seriously just going to march up to his door, ring the bell and demand information on his missing kid? That's nuts, Finley—even for you." I open my mouth to object and he quickly adds, "Besides, rich people like this—especially ones who have been part of a literal missing persons case—definitely have a huge security system. So before you suggest crawling over the gate like it's a tree"—Griffin's eyes go wide as saucers, and I can't help but resist an eager grin at the thought too—"remember that the second we're near the house, they'll know we're there. And probably have an entire police squad on their way over too."

I grind my teeth and cross my arms, searching my mind for the perfect comeback. But he's got me—on the security camera part, at least. I wish he didn't, though; after my call with Mom last night, I want to prove I can do this. That I can be trusted to do this. And even if Richard didn't feel the need to supervise us, Oliver's points have proven I may need more supervision than I'd like.

Maybe if he acted like we were partners on this, it would feel more like it did with Sophie. Like these conversations were suggestions, ideas for us to work through together. But from Oliver, they just feel like orders and put-downs.

I cross my arms. "We'll just ring the doorbell, like

Richard was planning to," I declare. Oliver's upper lip curls, still doubtful. "If we show we have nothing to hide, then there's no reason we should."

The three-story home looms in the distance, obstructed by the large, black fence I recognize from the news clip at the auto shop. It looks different now, though, twenty years leaving their mark on the home. The gate is rusted at its hinges. Vines creep up the edge of the three-car garage. The shutters are closed, the drapes are drawn, and the small fountain in the yard is still, the water idle and hued green. According to what I've been told, the Rileys used to be as rich and powerful as Mr. Phillips. It's obvious that compared to Jeff and the rest of Stone Creek, they're still doing pretty well. But it's as though Meggie's disappearance left an imprint, something dark and eerie looming over the house.

I roll my shoulders and reach up to the gate. There's a small keypad on its left side, and I press my finger down against the thick black button at its top. Its speakers buzz faintly, signaling that a bell is ringing inside the house. I hold my breath and wait for the gates to click and swing open.

I squint through the gaps in the metal gate, scanning for signs of movement: a shutter puckering open, a shadow slipping past a curtain. But there's nothing but the rustling leaves overhead and scuffle of squirrels and birds across branches.

I press the doorbell again, harder this time, as if it'll

ring louder inside the Riley residence. Still, nothing.

"Well, they definitely know we're here now, at least." Oliver gestures to the cars in the driveway. "Because it's clear someone is here, and just not answering. Which means they probably don't want to talk to us." He scans the quiet woods around us before his gaze returns to the house. Remembering that the cars mean someone likely is home, the home's windows suddenly seem like giant, watchful eyes. "And, honestly, it is sort of creepy."

I swallow. Creepy is right, but unlike Oliver, I don't think it means it's time to turn back. "It could also mean they're in there and plan on answering, but are trying to hide something—or someone—inside before they let us in." A tired look crosses Oliver's features, but Griffin's drifting attention snaps back to focus, so I hurry on. "We have to take a different approach," I say, because the best explorers need to know when it's time to test a different trail than the one they've set out on. "The Walsh-Walsh-Walsh Adventure Agency is about making discoveries. We don't need to talk to Mr. Riley to get answers. We can find them ourselves."

Oliver raises an eyebrow, but Griffin nods eagerly. A surge of warmth floods my chest, and I wish Mom could see this side of me, the way Griffin seems to in this moment, rather than just the version of me Oliver recites to her over the phone.

"In case someone is in there, and they're trying to hide something before letting us in, we have to move fast so we can catch them in the act," I say, pointing to the Riley residence. "We can use the cover of the trees to sneak around to the back of the house and see if we can spot anything suspicious. Anything that implies this is where Meggie is being held hostage."

Griffin salutes me with dramatic rigor. As usual, Oliver's expression is as flat as an old bottle of soda, but I charge forward nonetheless.

I trek alongside the driveway, a few feet off to the left so the woods obscure us from view. The trees are a bit farther apart here than they are in the woods we've explored so far, but the shade from the branches high overhead provides a shadowy protection from the road.

I lead my brothers around the side of the house, past a rolled-up hose, a garden that's mostly dried-up dirt, and a picnic table stained from seasons left outside. The gate is tighter to the house here, but there's not much to see on the left side of the house: just a few closed windows, curtains dangling to block the view inside.

Disappointment starts to settle in like a rock on my chest. If one of the Rileys really is inside, rushing to hide something suspicious before answering the door, it's impossible to see it from here.

Or so it seems. But that's when I turn the corner toward the back of the house and spot it: a tiny, curtainless window close to the ground.

"They have a basement!" I say, soft though I'm excited enough to shout. A basement is a perfect place to keep a captive adventurer, or evidence you don't want found. "This is it," I announce with certainty, ignoring how Oliver rolls his eyes. "Follow me."

I head over to the edge of the gate, tiptoeing carefully across the tall grass. The closer I get to the house, the easier it would be for a motion detector to notice us and alert the Rileys that we've made our way around the back of the house. I lower myself to the ground, imagining I'm in a heist movie and have to avoid invisible lasers to steal a valuable piece of artwork. I shimmy forward in the dirt, not caring how it scrapes against my knees or cakes on my T-shirt.

With my elbows on the ground, I'm almost eye level with the small basement window a few feet ahead. It's too far for me to see in, though, and dark inside, its contents lit only by the stream of morning light trickling through the glass window. I shimmy forward until my nose touches the cool metal gate, but no matter how hard I squint, I can't see inside.

In second grade, Mr. Higgins bought Sophie a pair of binoculars for her birthday. I'd always relied on her to have them with her, tucked at the bottom of her purple backpack. I never thought I'd be on an adventure without her, but for the first time, I consider that I might need a pair of my own. I lean my forehead against the gate and close my eyes, racking my brain for a solution.

"I've got it!" I interject, reaching into my back pocket for my phone. I hold it up to one of the gaps between the gate's bars and open the camera app. Then, focused on the basement window, I swipe the screen with two fingers to zoom in.

"Creepy," Oliver murmurs, and I can't tell if he's horrified or impressed.

The images still aren't perfectly sharp, but the contents of the room are visible on my phone screen. It looks like a normal storage basement. Framed photos line the walls. In the corner, boxes are stacked and sealed with shipping tape. There's a cabinet displaying old trophies, thick-spined hardcovers filling the gaps on the shelves. But like all things in Stone Creek, when you look closer, there's a Meggie twist.

"It's all hers," I say, pointing to the phone screen. "Photos of her, boxes of her stuff. Her awards and books about explorers." I grin proudly and say, "The books' spines are too far away to read, but I recognize a few of them from my collection."

Saying that out loud gives me a bubbly feeling in my chest, like Meggie and I really are connected. I bet if she was still here in Stone Creek, she'd turn off the security system and invite me in. We could go through the books together, plan out our next adventure based on the brave explorers who inspire us most.

"It's just a bunch of her old stuff?" Griffin asks, sounding deflated. "What about her? Do you see her in there?"

I shake my head. "If they're holding her hostage, they wouldn't do it by an open window."

"Open window?" Oliver scoffs. "We're literally sneaking through the grass to spy on them. They could still be guilty."

Seeing the basement, I'm starting to feel the opposite. No one has pulled the shades or is rushing to hide her belongings, even though they must know we're here and heard us ringing the bell. Preserving her things like this seems more like a way of honoring Meggie—not a way to keep her hostage.

And it makes sense that they would keep her things down here. Seeing her things around the house, as if she were still in Stone Creek—would be too painful. When Dad left, Mom must have removed his things from the house pretty quickly, because I never remember finding little bits of him around the house. And as hard as it is to see everything with my phone camera, I prefer it to using a pair of my own binoculars, because doing that alone would be like admitting Sophie's left me behind for good.

The sound of crunching leaves and grass comes from the distance, toward the left side of the gate. I prop myself up onto my knees, searching in the direction of the approaching footsteps.

It's probably just Richard, finally ready to come join us. But whenever I hear someone before I see them, my first thought is of the shadow man.

My stomach rises in my throat, a queasy feeling rushing through me. I leap up, shoving my phone in my back pocket and placing a steadying hand on the gate. "Someone's here."

Griffin rises beside me. "Time to confront the kidnapper, once and for all!"

"Shh," Oliver says, waving his hand. "Considering what happened to Meggie, and that whoever's inside wouldn't meet us at the front door, this could be dangerous. We have to go. Now."

I know he's just saying it because Mom would want him to. But once again, I reluctantly agree with Oliver. "We have to get out of sight, or else we'll blow the whole mission," I say, taking hold of Griffin's hand. "But," I add, shooting Oliver a sharp glance, "we can't be so far we don't see who it is."

I'm tired of being the one chased through the woods, powerless as the shadow man creeps in closer and closer. Whoever this is, I'm going to find out, once and for all.

I rush in the opposite direction of the footsteps, pulling Griffin along with me. The woods are a few feet away from the gate, and I weave between the first few trees, searching for a trunk thick enough to hide behind. There's a plump, green bush off to the side, which I direct Griffin behind. Then I sneak around the side of a tree trunk a few feet away, nodding with approval as Oliver does the same.

The sound of footsteps comes closer. I remain fixed behind my tree, allowing myself only the tiniest of peeks around its trunk. Ahead of me, Griffin kneels behind the bush. He tucks his fingers into its branches and pulls them apart for a bigger view.

I want to shout but know my voice will give us away just as much as what's about to happen. One of the branches snaps beneath his hand, loud and obvious and totally giving us away. I suck in my cheeks, bracing myself for confrontation.

The footsteps pause. At the edge of the woods, by the gate, stands a tall and thin older man. His hair is wispy and gray across his forehead, and he wears a button-up shirt that hands loosely on his narrow frame. He's different from the Mr. Riley I saw on the news, a version softened with age. But it's definitely him.

And he's about to catch us trespassing on his property.

To my right, Oliver presses his forehead against his tree's trunk, hand over his mouth as he searches for a way out of this situation. Griffin remains hunched behind the bush, hands over his head as though that will hide him from view.

Mr. Riley looks out into the woods, straight toward where we're hiding. I duck behind my trunk, hoping that if I can't see him, he can't see me.

Then, he calls out, voice faint and uncertain.

"Meggie?"

My heart stops in my chest. Why would Mr. Riley be calling out for Meggie? Was she still here in Stone Creek? But if Mr. Phillips was right, and he had forged the run-away note and was holding her hostage to stop her from leaving the family business, wouldn't she be inside the house rather than out here, in the woods?

There are no frantic footsteps, no rush to secure a loose captive. He's still standing there, waiting, at the edge of the woods. Watching, hoping that this time she'll be there to answer his call. Hoping she's finally returned.

My fingers tremble against the ragged bark. I want to be like Meggie, but if I'm not careful, I could end up like her father instead. Alone and left behind, hoping that the people who moved on from me will come back someday, so long as I hold on to their memories tight enough.

The next few seconds feel like hours: Mr. Riley hovering there and me holding my breath, fighting every urge to swat away the mosquito that's making a game of buzzing around my head. But eventually the footsteps retreat, slow and dejected.

My body feels stuck in place, but I can't let the moment swallow me whole. I wave for my brothers and we sprint off through the woods, around the opposite side of the house and back toward Richard's car.

GREATEST FEMALE ADVENTURER NUMBER FOURTEEN: ELIZABETH BLACKWELL, WHO WAS ADMITTED TO MEDICAL SCHOOL AS A JOKE, BUT STILL ATTENDED, GRADUATED, AND WENT ON TO BE THE FIRST-EVER FEMALE PHYSICIAN, WORKING IN BOTH THE UNITED STATES AND BRITAIN, AND AS A NURSE IN THE CIVIL WAR.

We run through the woods, following the twisting driveway a few yards to our left. I don't slow until Richard's car is in view, right where we left it at the end of the road. Gasping for breath, we all freeze, recovering from the almost confrontation with Meggie's father.

Oliver's the first to speak. "So, he's totally guilty."

I gawk up at him. It's great to have Oliver invested enough in Meggie's legacy to have his own theory, but this? This isn't what I got out of our discoveries at the Riley residence. "How can you say that? He's keeping all her things together for when she returns. He knows she's out there, and he's waiting for her, no matter how long it takes." I fight to keep my voice even as I say, "And why else would he call out for her, unless he was still hoping she'd come back?"

The sound of Mr. Riley's voice, wavering and hopeful, echoes in my mind. The memory of it makes my heart clench like a fist.

Oliver's eyebrows pinch together. "It's clear now that he was at home and not answering the door because he was afraid to let us in—afraid we'd find something. And he was probably calling out to her because he was afraid she escaped whatever kidnapper's den he keeps her in." I shake my head, but he rattles on. "And keeping all her things? More like hoarding them like creepy serial killer trophies."

Griffin bounces on his heels. "Oo, are we going to capture a serial killer? That would make an awesome movie!"

Maybe Mom's right and I do let him watch too many scary movies. But that's not the point right now. "Mr. Riley's not a serial killer. He probably didn't hear us ring the bell because he was outside already, on a walk. Oliver's just being a jerk because he can't imagine what it's like to miss someone the way Mr. Riley misses Meggie."

My tone is biting, but part of me wishes Oliver would argue with that instead of his theory about Mr. Riley. That would prove that he does care about me and Griffin, and not just because Mom expects him to.

He shrugs, the back of his shirt brushing against the

tree's bark. "I'm just saying that it makes a lot more sense than anything else we've heard so far. Meggie's runaway note gives him a motive—and if the Rileys used to be just like Mr. Phillips is now, I'd bet he'd do anything to keep his business afloat. Even if it meant trapping his daughter in Stone Creek forever."

His voice picks up speed. "And maybe something happened, and their confrontation went sour. So now he's gone a bit"—he circles his fingertip around his ear—"with grief, and keeps up this act like she's going to come home, with that one-hundred-thousand-dollar reward and the festival and everything. Because he can't live with what he did, so he can't take responsibility or move on."

"That's far-fetched," I snap. "Or at least not sure enough that we can just stop our search now. She could still be alive, and if we just assume she's dead, then we're no better than anyone else who's given up on finding her!"

Earlier today I let myself believe Oliver finally appreciated Meggie's story for what it was, that he was interested in finding her for the right reasons. But all he wants is to find the easiest way to put an end to her story so he and Jason and everyone else can comfortably move on to the next chapter in their lives.

"And even if you are right, that doesn't mean the rescue mission is over," I say, voice wobbling at the end. "If Meggie really is"—I inhale softly—"dead, then we still need to find her and uncover the truth. No one—including Mr. Riley—should control the ending to her story."

No matter what happened to Meggie or where she is now, she matters. And I won't let anyone—especially Oliver—take that away.

Oliver shakes his head, exasperated. "And what, you're the one who can tell her story? You've never even met her, Finley."

The words fall hard, like a slap. After all we've done, Oliver still doesn't get it.

Doesn't get me.

"Guys, where's Malt?"

Griffin pushes past us, pointing toward Richard's car. The front seat is empty, with no sign of either the reporter or the dog. My stomach drops in my gut, and Oliver and I exchange a glance over Griffin's head.

"They probably went for a walk, or got bored waiting for us." Griffin remains still, chin wobbling. I give his shoulder a squeeze. "We'll find them. Okay, Griff?"

"But Ollie just said we're on a serial killer's property," he says, gaze still fixed on the empty car. "What if that's why Richard never made it to the house for his interview? And what if we're next?"

I shoot Oliver a dirty glance, stealing the *I told you so* look he usually gets to use on me. "Mr. Riley is not a serial killer," I say, sure and certain. "Oliver's just throwing out dumb theories because there're other things he'd rather be doing than looking for Meggie."

His nostrils flare and he straightens up. Then, to Griffin, he says, "Let's go look for them, okay?"

I imagine Oliver's version of today's events in a text chain with Mom, framing him as some puppy rescuer while I lagged behind, head in the clouds. I can't let him get away with that—with always reframing things so he's in the center, so Mom and Griffin and everyone else see him as the hero.

"We'll find them faster if we split up," I say. Before Oliver can object, I stomp off into the woods, as fast and as far from my brothers as I can get.

Without my brothers' constant chatter, I realize how quiet this part of Stone Creek is. Tucked far away from the bustle of downtown or foot traffic by the diner and café, the woods are still. They feel less alive than the woods by the café; here, the trees are farther apart and the usual murmur of birds and frogs is replaced by the distant hum of the creek.

Up ahead, a figure sits nestled at the foot of a tree. I pause, ducking behind a thorny bush. It could be Richard—but it could also be Mr. Riley, waiting to catch us venturing around his property.

Or it could be the shadow man, finally about to capture me alone.

I take a cautious step forward. Immediately, a branch snaps loudly beneath my shoe. The man beneath the tree stirs, rising to his feet.

Crap. I was so rushed to prove Oliver and Griffin wrong, I mucked up my mission right from the get-go. Oliver probably would have pointed out a safer route so

I could have sneaked up on the man—just like Sophie used to map out our schoolyard adventures to avoid the chaperones. But for him to do that, Oliver would have to care enough about this mission to follow me, even if I led us into danger. Considering I haven't even had the chance to tell him about the shadow man yet, it's unlikely that will ever happen.

I straighten up, chin held high as the man approaches. But it's just Richard, staring at me with red, puffy eyes as he grips the end of Malt's leash.

Which isn't as scary as the other alternatives I'd imagined. But it is kind of weird, and a little suspicious.

"Did you find something?" I ask, cautious but intrigued.

He stares, eyes dull and dazed. "Oh, you kids are back already," he murmurs, mostly to himself. "I lost track of time. Sorry if I scared you, leaving with Malt like that . . ."

Why did he leave with Malt? I glance down at the dog, who's panting happily, his tail wagging high behind him.

I step forward, dried old leaves crunching beneath my heel. "Is Malt okay?"

Richard lets out a rough laugh. "That's kind of you to ask, when it's clear I'm the one who's not okay."

All of Oliver's talk about serial killers spins around in my head, and part of me wants to step away and call for backup. But Richard's eyes are gentle, and he extends his hand so the leash is held out for me to take. I swallow back my doubts, imagining Malt is Meggie and this is a brave rescue. I step forward and take the end of the leash from Richard, who releases it without any fight.

"I did take him for a walk," he says, rushed and a bit sheepish. "But it was mostly for my sake. I wanted to get some fresh air, hoping that if I was really here, standing on the Riley grounds, I'd get the courage to go and ask for an interview."

He runs a hand over his face. It lingers, cupped over his mouth to guard his expression. After a moment of thoughtful silence, he shakes his head sadly.

"I couldn't do it," he says. "Interviewing folks at the diner or around town—that's what I'm used to. Highly local, low-stakes coverage. But asking a father about his lost daughter, when he's been grieving for so long . . ." He shakes his head faster, looking like the bobblehead my bus driver keeps on her dashboard. "I'm not the person to cover this story."

Malt settles at my feet, warm body pressed against my ankles. I resist a smile when Richard refers to Mr. Riley as grieving.

"I knew I wouldn't be up for interviewing him before I even left Burlington," Richard goes on, "but my brother told me it was the chance of the lifetime, that he knew I could do it, and . . ." He trails off, eyes focusing. For the first time, he looks at me directly, as if just noticing I'm there. "I had a bit of a panic, thinking about all of it," he admits. "Malt helped calm me down. Is he an emotional support animal, or . . . ?"

"He provides plenty of emotional support to Griffin," I say. "And probably Jeff, though I can't quite get a read on him."

That sharp, professional-reporter flicker returns to Richard's eyes. I've said a bit too much about the wrong thing. I quickly redirect, like an explorer changing course to avoid a storm. "That's nice that your brother believed you could do it, though. Oliver disagrees with me on principle. And Griffin's too busy agreeing with everything Oliver says to listen long enough to see if he agrees with me."

Richard smiles, though there's a pained look in his gaze. "Sometimes unconditional support isn't ideal either. It's easy to get stuck in the wrong spot that way, isn't it?"

Wrong spot? Richard is a reporter, so of course his brother would believe he was a great one. And I'm an adventurer, which means my brothers should, theoretically, trust me to lead a mission like this. No one else can tell us if our goals are the wrong thing to pursue.

Malt straightens up, suddenly alert. Griffin must be nearby, still searching for him. No matter how frustrated I am with my brothers right now, I can't leave them out in the woods alone, scared for Malt. No member of the Walsh-Walsh-Walsh Adventure Agency left behind and all that.

"You can interview Mr. Riley tomorrow, at the festival

setup," I say. Richard grits his teeth, so I add, "I'll be interviewing him then, if that helps."

I wish we could have talked with Mr. Riley today, but jumping out from my hiding spot by the basement window and demanding answers from the man whose property I'd sneaked onto didn't seem like the right move. Sometimes, even for an adventurer, the bravest move can also be the dumbest one.

But at the festival, we'll both have a reason to be there. Richard will too—and maybe if I interview Mr. Riley first, it will give him the courage to talk to him.

The kind of courage and reassurance his brother gave him. That I wish mine gave me.

Malt lets out a booming woof, and I call for Griffin in its echo. Sure enough, the sound of snapping branches comes from up ahead as they break beneath my brothers' feet.

Tomorrow, with all of Stone Creek gathering to discuss and celebrate Meggie, anything can happen to change the course of this rescue mission. Hopefully, whatever happens next, it will give me the chance to prove myself to my brothers, once and for all.

GREATEST FEMALE ADVENTURER NUMBER FIFTEEN:

BESSIE STRINGFIELD,

THE FIRST AFRICAN AMERICAN WOMAN TO RIDE ACROSS THE UNITED STATES SOLO, AND A MOTORCYCLE DISPATCH RIDER FOR THE US ARMY DURING WORLD WAR II.

The next morning Jeff sits on the front steps of Meggie's Cup while I hover on the curb, squinting down the winding street for a glimpse of Sam's car. Today is the soft launch for the anniversary festivities, and since Jeff doesn't plan on going, I've arranged for us to carpool downtown with Sam when she goes to set up the booth for the diner.

We're leaving in four days, so we'll have to rescue Meggie and uncover the truth long before the actual date of her disappearance and the thick of the anniversary festivities. But great adventurers see opportunity in adversity, so I've decided that being three weeks too early means I get a head start no one else does.

While Oliver paces behind me, Griffin plops down

next to Jeff and takes over scratching behind Malt's ear. Jeff rises to his feet with a low grunt and stalks toward us, tired eyes fixed on the road.

"I'm glad you kids have taken an interest in Stone Creek's history," he says, running a hand down his unshaven chin. "When your mom asked to have you come, I was worried this place would be a bit too . . . eclectic for your tastes."

He has no idea how perfect Stone Creek is to me. How I'd rather be here than anywhere for April break.

But Jeff is still one of my top suspects, even if moments like this make that feel a bit funny. So I keep my mouth clamped shut, swallowing down the giddy excitement that bubbles in my chest.

"Will Jeffords's kid be joining you too?" he asks, gaze grazing over me and Oliver. "You seem to have taken a liking to him."

Oliver stops midpace, ears going fire-truck red. "Finley! You said you wouldn't tell anyone!"

I speak through clenched teeth. "I didn't, you idiot. But you just did."

The red spreads from his ears to his cheeks like spilled hot sauce. Jeff blinks a few times, his pre-coffee brain slowly registering our exchange.

And then he smiles.

"Well," he says, giving Oliver a quick pat on the shoulder as he turns back toward the café, "I'm glad everyone's getting along."

With that, he heads toward the front steps, where Malt pants eagerly as he approaches. I brace myself for part two of Oliver's blowup. But he just stands, watching Jeff's back as he walks away, the slightest edge of a smile forming on the corner of his mouth.

A rusty old sedan peels onto the curb in front of Meggie's Cup, close enough that I leap off the sidewalk. The driver's-seat window rolls down in slow motion, and Sam begins shouting before it's halfway down.

"Hey, this isn't a game for all of us!" she yells. "Some of us have to actually work today. And Mr. Phillips does not condone tardiness."

Sam honks her horn as though we're not huddled on the curb, already saying our goodbyes to Jeff and Malt. As Griffin gives the dog a final head scratch, another car drives past and pulls over by the diner. Jason leaps out of the passenger seat, long limbs unfolding as he stretches to full, awkward height. I edge forward, squinting at the side mirror, hoping to catch a glimpse of his dad.

Then Sam honks again, making me jump. "Today, kids!"

Spotting Jason, Griffin sprints around the front of Sam's card. "Dibs on shotgun!"

Across the lot, Jason's eyes lock with Oliver's, who rolls his eyes and shrugs, drawing a white-toothed grin from Jason.

As Oliver and Jason climb into the back seat of Sam's car, I turn to Jeff. He's staring pensively into the distance, as though waiting for a grumpy Anne Thornton to leap out of the bushes and demand her morning cup.

"You sure you don't want to come?" I ask, because I still don't get why he wouldn't want to.

He tucks his hands in his pockets, shakes his head slow and soft so his whole upper body sways. "I'll leave it to you kids." The horn blares, long and unrelenting. "And Sam."

I feel like I'm being picked up by Mr. Higgins, ready to ride with Sophie to school. My arms dangle awkwardly by my sides, muscles twitching as though expecting a hug.

But Jeff isn't Mom, and he still doesn't feel like family. Not when I have all these doubts storming in my head about him and Meggie.

I squeeze into the back seat and Sam peels off, accelerating past the diner so the car soars over bumpy pavement. Woods spin past in blurs of green, broken by a sliver of brownish water and an old stone bridge. The car rocks over cobblestone as we drive over the town's mucky namesake, passing into the opposite side of town.

"This is my favorite time of year," Sam muses.

Oliver shifts, knee bonking mine. "Spring?"

"The start of anniversary season," she says. "The days I'm not stuck in that grease pit of a diner, but before the tourist rush."

Oliver crinkles his nose. I want to ask about the Rileys—how they rarely come out in public but may visit the festival today. But considering Jason only told Oliver the truth after I named Jeff as a suspect, I decide to keep that nugget of info close to my chest. I'm grateful for the ride from Sam, but that doesn't mean she's impartial. She works for one of the town's main suspects, after all.

The suspect I'm still not sure about is Mr. Riley—especially after our visit to the Riley residence yesterday. But hopefully today, downtown, I'll find out more about their true motives.

Summoned by my thoughts, the cloud of trees breaks to reveal a quaint downtown area. Sam slows as we drive onto a wide street lined with shops on both sides, the sidewalks crowded with booths and stands as local businesses prep for the festivities. A few pedestrians wave as we pass, but Sam remains furrow-browed in pursuit of parking.

That's when I see it: In the distance, where the main road turns off toward the east residential area. A giant, peeling billboard with Meggie's smiling photo blown up so her head stands higher than the trees. Thick red lettering shares the Rileys' tip line, and the promise of the $100,000 reward upon her safe return.

I strain against my seat belt, head blocking Oliver's as I lean forward to take in the view. Meggie, hovering over the town, the biggest, boldest thing for miles. Imprinted there, in the minds of all locals and all visitors, forever.

I wonder if, wherever she is—whether she's waiting for her rescue, whether she's a victorious runaway—she's proud to know the footprint she left on Stone Creek.

I wonder what it's like to know, with certainty, that you'll never be forgotten.

Sam attempts to parallel park, then stops in the middle of the road and cuts the engine. We file out and into the sticky, humid air, surrounded by the sounds of excited voices and shuffling employees putting booths together.

Sam pops her trunk, reaching for the 24/7-ish Diner special anniversary sign inside. "Jeff asked me to drive you, not babysit you. So go off and entertain yourselves so I can do my job." Already, Griffin is gunning for a half-formed stand for Meggie's Macaroons. "Jason, you're with me."

Jason leans toward Oliver and me and whispers, "I'm going to look into my dad's old boxes tonight. Let me know if you find anything too."

"Oh," I say, voice packed with gusto, "we plan to."

Jason grins, and then his eyes flicker toward Oliver's. My brother swallows, trying not to look nervous but coming across as five thousand times more nervous because of it.

"I'll text you tonight about what I find." The way Jason says it, it sounds more like a question than a statement.

Oliver musters his best serious look. "Yeah. Sounds good."

I glance back and forth between them, still not getting why Sophie and everyone else are so obsessed with their crushes. For a thrill-seeking adventurer like me, all these awkward smiles and cautious conversations are more exhausting than a climb up Mount Everest or trek across the Sahara could be.

To add to my struggle, Mr. Phillips is sauntering across the street. He waves to each booth as he passes, calling out "Good to see you, Johnny" and "Keep up the good work, Priya" as he wanders our way.

Mr. Phillips may be the epitome of exhausting small talk. But his name's still on my suspect board, so as much as I want to run after Griffin and stress-eat some macaroons, I offer a sugar-sweet smile as he approaches.

"Jason! You guys made it," he calls, arms extended as though he's embracing us all in his mind. "The staff from Motel Meggie beat you here by so long, I thought you might have gotten the time incorrect."

Jason gives a courteous smile, though Oliver scowls beside him. I can't pretend to be interested in how he runs his business—I'm an adventurer, not an entrepreneur—so I redirect the conversation.

"Are you excited for the festival, Mr. Phillips?" I ask, blinking my eyes all wide and innocent.

He tucks his thumbs through his empty belt loops and smiles. "Of course! A fifth of the year's revenue comes from this month alone."

I maintain my smile through a grimace. Sometimes the way he tacks a dollar sign onto all things Meggie is so suspicious that it almost isn't suspicious.

"Besides . . ." He nods to his right. I follow his gaze to a giant, glossy blowup of the runaway note. It stands on display, propped up against a white folding table by an unmarked and unfinished stand. "I love seeing the money and effort Riley puts into crap like this each year. It's sad, honestly, how obsessed with blaming me he is."

I stare at the note, twice as tall as me so the handwriting is blown up, each stroke several inches. Imagining how many people have pored over this note the past twenty years—detectives, handwriting experts, truth-seeking tourists like me—makes me doubt that somehow, despite all odds, I can be the one to dig up the truth.

Mr. Phillips shrugs his small shoulders. "Maybe if he wasn't so obsessed with proving the note was fake, Meggie would feel comfortable enough to come back and make amends."

Jason releases a strained laugh. "Mr. Phillips . . ."

He throws back his head and laughs. "That's just my ten million cents!" He snaps back to focus, attention zeroing in on the supplies Sam's pulling from her trunk. "Now, let's get started on this booth, shall we?"

Oliver and I step to the side as Mr. Phillips ushers Jason to Sam's car. I cast one last glance at the runaway note, imagining that Mr. Phillips's theory is true. Maybe Meggie is out there, a runaway waiting, still, after all these years, for her dad to see her truth. To stop trying so hard to morph the world around what he wanted her to be, that he's finally able to see her for who she is.

Griffin hobbles back toward us from Meggie's Macaroons, body slumped as though bent by the weight of the world.

"They're just setting up the booth today," he grumbles when we reach him. "No macaroons until closer to the actual anniversary. So, basically, the day's a bust."

Oliver frowns. "Jeff just gave you breakfast."

I wince. Remembering Jeff's charcoal toast and runny eggs has me leaning toward Griffin's side. But if Juliane Koepcke could survive over a week alone after her plane crashed in the Amazon—with nothing to eat but some candy she found in fallen luggage—soggy eggs will do me just fine.

"This isn't a buffet, Griffin." I wave my arm with a flourish, gesturing to the half-formed displays down Main Street. "Think of it as a treasure hunt."

His eyes light up, and he gestures up toward the billboard. "Yeah, there is a whole lotta treasure at the end!" He cups a hand over his eyes like a visor and whips his head back and forth sharply, surveying the crowd. "One of these people is the murderer," he announces with certainty.

"You don't know that!" Oliver snaps, but my attention is hooked on a stand to the left. It's one of the few displays that's already complete, with three enormous, framed photos propped up on wooden easels around a small table where the shop owner sits. In front of him, a paper banner dangles from the edge of the table, its print rippling in the wind.

"'Memories by Meggie,'" I read.

Griffin spins on his heel and points. "Aha! They kidnapped Meggie, regretted it, and erased her memory so she'd never tell! All along, Meggie has wandered the earth, haunted by the faintest recollections of a past long forgotten—"

I yank his arm down from the sleeve. "Reel it in! You're veering out of adventurer territory and into fiction. Remember: the best adventurers are driven by facts and truth. That's why so many explorers were scientists."

Griffin pouts. "But you got a C in science class!"

I bristle. "Well, I got a C in English lit, too. But that's not the point. Being an adventurer isn't about studying, it's about doing."

Before, I had Sophie for that part: the thinking, the planning. But so far I've done just fine without her. And obviously—considering she hasn't texted again since the other night—she's doing just fine without me, too.

I'll wait to reply, to share all this with her. I'll wait until I'm right up there on the billboard with Meggie, the two us standing side by side, beaming because she's finally been found. Because I was the one to find her.

I return my focus to the photographs. "It looks like a frame store. But I recognize one of those photos from the café clippings. They're the last pictures Meggie took on her phone before she dropped it in the woods and disappeared."

The three frames depict blurry shots of the woods.

Light from the flash creates an abrupt glow on thick trunks and ragged bushes, casting thick, inky shadows across the edges of the photo. And there, at the corner of each one, is the briefest glimpse of another figure—rumored to be the person who took Meggie.

"We need a closer look." I usher my brothers closer. "Secret agents—"

"Attack!" Griffin shouts, interrupting my more nuanced command. With that, he sprints across the street, straight toward the frame store. Oliver and I exchange a quick glance before I shrug and jog after him.

As Griffin approaches, the man at the table startles as though woken from a nap, uncrossing his legs and smoothing his shirt. "Welcome to Memories by Meggie. What brings you three here so far before the festivities?"

"Our mom," Griffin answers. "Oh, and Uncle Cousin Jeff. But technically, I guess, Sam drove us."

The man blinks as though digesting his words one letter at a time. I clear my throat and step forward, business card in hand.

"We're the founders of the Walsh-Walsh-Walsh Adventure Agency," I say, pushing through the tongue-tie as fast as I can. "We're interested in your prints."

A grin sweeps across the man's face. "Wonderful! Here at Memories by Meggie, we're honored to showcase what we believe to be the best evidence found to date." He stands and positions himself between two of the easels, like he's Mr. Hickenbottom presenting a PowerPoint.

"We believe that the best evidence, when framed correctly, can be seen in a brand-new light. With custom sizing and antiglare protective glass, your eyes can focus on the details of the photo while we"—he pauses, stepping forward in a choreographed step—"focus on the details of your frame."

Oliver's face contorts like he's tasted something bad. But all I can see are the photos, blown up to half my height. "And these are all the photos she took that day she vanished?"

The man nods. "But these aren't all the frames offered by Memories by Meggie. We have a full-service storefront just back three doors on Forty-Second and Main Street—"

Griffin clears his throat. "That will do, sir."

Usually I'd apologize for that, but when the man turns to me expectantly, I offer a noncommittal shrug. It does the trick, and he slinks back to his table, making room for me to get closer to the photos.

I'm nose to nose with the glass, the faintest shimmer of my reflection projected onto the blurred image of the woods. It's a mess of green and black, with a blur of blue jeans at the corner of the frame where someone is walking—either leading Meggie forward, or leaving her behind.

My stomach twists to think it could be the latter. That she really was whisked away in that one moment, never to be seen again. The jeans are a smudge of blue, but seeing them against the shadows of the woods jogs my memory. I think of the man yesterday—the small glimpse I captured before he vanished from my view and Oliver found me.

I clench my hands into fists by my sides to hide the way they tremble. But it's not just the creeping feeling of fear that settles over me. Looking at the photo and realizing how similar it is to what I saw last night, I feel closer to Meggie than ever.

In my hazy reflection, a smile buds across my lips.

"This gives us nothing," Oliver huffs. "Everyone up here wears those old, worn-down jeans. Including Jeff."

My stomach lurches. I still haven't shared the shadow man's note with Oliver, but looking at the photo now, all I'm seeing is another excuse to keep Jeff dead center in the suspect pool.

Oliver taps his finger against the glass. "And we don't know who this guy is. Her boyfriend? P. W.? The kidnapper? And any of those people could be the same person too. And Mr. Jeffords said he heard two voices on the phone with her, so it either means he's lying or someone in this frame is missing." He leans his head back, head tilted up to the cloudy sky. "This is beginning to feel like a waste of time."

I start to object, but someone says the words before I do. "When you feel like that, it's your mind telling you it's time to push further."

Stepping up from the edge of the sidewalk is

Richard Connors, wearing a name tag that reads, THE BURLINGTON BIWEEKLY. Against the background of flannel-clad locals, he stands out like a sore thumb in his tight-fitting button-up and ironed slacks.

If my brothers and I stick out like that too, then it's no wonder the shadow man is always one step ahead.

"What, have you actually discovered something?" Oliver asks, crossing his arms as Richard approaches. "Other than every single menu item at the diner, that is?"

Despite Oliver's tone, Richard offers a generous smile. "Long-form journalism isn't always about finding the answers. Sometimes it's just about diving deeper into the questions."

"Or diving deeper into the woods with our cousin's dog," Oliver grumbles. Which is kind of fair.

"So," I say, arms crossed, "you've got nothing so far?"

Richard pulls out his phone, snaps a photo of the framed prints. "But don't you wonder why we have nothing?" Oliver sucks in his cheeks, looking frustrated enough to blow steam from his ears. I'm dreading some response about how it's because Richard is a bad reporter, or investigating a stupid case, or anything that would be exactly what I wouldn't want to hear if I were him—especially after the breakdown in the woods yesterday.

Thankfully, Richard says something semi-useful next. "In such a small town, with so few suspects and so much evidence, you have to wonder why nothing's been discovered in over twenty years." He straightens up, lowers his voice, and says, "It's almost as if someone doesn't want visitors to find anything."

"Well, duh!" Griffin says. "The culprit is that someone."

"Right," Richard agrees. "So, what culprit has enough influence to silence leads over so many years?"

Crap. Now I kind of get what he means about useful questions. I'm not a fan of quizzes, but, thankfully, a hundred answers leap right into my mind.

"Bryan Phillips," I blurt, raising my hand like I'm in class. "Or even Mr. Riley. I heard they both own a ton of stuff in town, and they're the only people rich enough to bribe everyone into keeping quiet."

Richard nods. "The Rileys have kept a stronghold on this town, even with everything else they've had to deal with. But the prize for Meggie has never been raised over the years—not by one dollar." His gaze shifts to the billboard in the distance, looming over Main Street. "Some say it's because they didn't want to tempt people to share false leads. Or make themselves victim to another crime, like a robbery."

I nod along, digesting my next theory with each of his words. "Or, they may not have any extra cash, because they've been using the rest of their earnings to pay off anyone who gets too close to the truth."

Richard grins. "Exactly."

Pride swells in my chest. It's been a while since anyone

validated one of my ideas without picking it—or me—apart first.

Oliver's nodding along—probably not in agreement with me, but because Richard thinks Mr. Riley is guilty. Which has, for some reason, become Oliver's hill to die on too. But thinking of our almost encounter with Mr. Riley yesterday, something still feels like it doesn't quite add up. "But why would her own parents want to do that to her?"

The words come out softer, syllables more fragmented than I intended. Why would Meggie's parents hide her from the world while building an entire town in her memory?

With her big, smiling face stationed above us like the top of a shrine, I can't help but wonder what's worse: having your family keep you so close that you can't belong to anyone but them, or having them cast you so far it's as though the tie never existed.

"Because of what her runaway note said," Oliver answers. "She was going to leave the family business and he wanted to stop her."

"So, what?" I demand. "He kidnapped her and has her working, trapped at the family estate? It makes no sense."

"That's assuming she survived whatever confrontation she had," he grumbles, bringing up my least favorite theory again.

"Egos run big in Stone Creek," Richard muses,

tucking his hands in his pockets. "I was just able to get an interview with the other two Riley sisters, and they both still live at the Riley residence, and work for the business too. The family takes it all very seriously, so one of them leaving would be seen as a blow to the business and their brand."

My eyes go wide. "Her sisters are here?"

Richard points down the road, toward the booth for Riley Realty. Two women in their forties stand, one in a dress and oversized necklace and the other in a crisp pantsuit. The one in the dress is stacking flyers while the other pins up photos of Vermont houses on a tackboard behind the booth.

"And it doesn't seem like Meggie's disappearance was terrible for their business, either," Oliver says. "Sure, it sounds like Mr. Phillips was able to gain some power in town after the Meggie fiasco, given how much money the Rileys pumped into the search. But the Rileys still aren't doing bad, by any means. I mean, advertising their businesses at their sister's missing persons event? That's almost worse than some of the stuff Mr. Phillips pulls."

"But all of this is for her," I argue. "The fact that the whole family stayed in Stone Creek, as if they're waiting for her to come home, is proof of it."

"Or proof that they're remaining here to keep control of the story—to hide something." I shoot Richard a dirty glance and he shrugs. "I know some people never leave home, but as someone who's never lived in the same town for more than a few years at a time, I can't say it makes much sense to me."

"Of course you move more," I say. "You're a reporter, and the Riley sisters are local businesswomen."

"But Jeff's dad was a businessperson in Stone Creek too, and he left," Griffin says. "And right after Meggie disappeared. That's what makes Jeff one of the suspects, right?"

My mouth opens and closes like a revolving door. Suddenly, I'm hyperaware of the note in my pocket.

Richard perks up. "What about Jeff?"

I stammer, hoping that if I say enough words and fast, it'll cover up anything Griffin said. "It's nothing. Not important. The Rileys are what's important. They're the ones making money off of all this. Right?"

Richard studies me for a moment. Then he pulls out his phone, edges toward the owner of the frame shop. "I still need a few more quotes to fill out the section I'm working on. But you have my card—ring me if you find anything."

With that, he shuffles off. Oliver shakes his head as he goes. Before he can yell at me, I yell at Griffin. "You can't share our leads with suspects!"

"I thought Jeff was your suspect."

I press my hands into my pockets, cupping my fingers around the note as though I could contain it—and my suspicions.

"I have a lot of suspects."

I sigh. Between Griffin's cold feet, big mouth, and closed ears, I'm beginning to seriously doubt if he's professional-adventurer material. I need space to explore, to think. And I can't do that with him buzzing around me like an anxious fly.

"I have a mission for you, but you have to act fast and not linger at any table"—as in, not talk to anyone—"for too long."

His smile goes wide and a surge of guilt floods my chest. Sure, I need the evidence he's gathering. But it doesn't change the motivations behind my request.

"Go collect business cards from every booth on the street," I say. "Then we'll study the results and see if anyone has the initials P. W."

Griffin salutes and darts off toward the next stand. Oliver moves to chase after him, and just as I reach for his sleeve, I spot someone familiar in the distance.

I grab Oliver's arm with both hands and yank it like the rope to a church bell. He shouts.

"What is wrong with you?"

"Mr. Riley," I whisper, low and quick. "There, at the end of the street."

Oliver follows my gaze, off toward the opposite end of the street where Sam parked. There, walking with his head ducked and hands in his pockets, is the silver-haired man from the café photos.

Suddenly, my throat feels like a clogged drain. I thought I'd be excited to see Mr. Riley, and potentially confront him like I'm warrior Queen Boudicca riding into battle. But right now, as I watch the way he stands hunched over—shoulders sunken by age and face creased with deep lines—he suddenly feels too real.

I sink my nails into Oliver's arm. "Maybe this isn't a good idea," I say, mostly to myself.

The brave and great Finley Walsh can take on a kidnapper headfirst. She can outrun the shadow man, climb any evergreen tree or restaurant dumpster, and crawl through any underground cave she needs to in order to complete her mission. But right now the thought of facing Mr. Riley and seeing all his saggy-eyed grief veers just a bit too far out of my comfort zone.

"I've been saying that all along," Oliver snaps, but it's too late. My owl-eyed staring has earned me some awkward, unbreaking eye contact with Mr. Riley. He stands, yards away, attention locked on me as though the rest of the festival faded around us.

Then he takes a step forward.

"Good idea or not, we're too far in to back out." I grimace. "Mr. Riley is headed straight for us."

GREATEST FEMALE ADVENTURER NUMBER SIXTEEN: LOUISE ARNER BOYD, THE FIRST WOMAN TO LEAD AN ARCTIC EXPEDITION.

He hobbles across the pavement, closing the distance between us. Seeing him up close, stature crunched like an accordion, I'm reminded how long twenty years really is. His features are marked by the years, and not good years at that.

Oliver stands upright, a soldier at attention. I roll my shoulders and brace my jaw as Mr. Riley stops in front of us. This close, I can smell the musty scent of his old coat. See the way his tired eyelids droop when he smiles. He's more than a photograph brought to life. Right now, he feels like the realest thing in all of Stone Creek: an exposed, beating heart.

My mind keeps screaming over with silly, childish questions that have nothing to do with finding Meggie. Things like what was she like and what did she like?

If she was here now, do you think she'd like me?

Do you think she's like me?

Mr. Riley smiles, extends his weathered hand. "You must be Jeff's."

I stammer, prepared for just about any introduction but that.

It's not that he knows who we are. Gossip travels so fast here, half the town probably knew I was coming before I did.

It's the way he says it. Like we belong to Jeff. Like we're a part of him.

It's hard enough to make a name as a famous adventurer without being associated with a maybe-kidnapper. If Jeff and I are the same, that just about brings the ceiling in on my plans for greatness.

But, on the other hand, the thought spreads a warm, comfy feeling through my chest. Like Mr. Riley couldn't finish the sentence, because family isn't just one thing. Like you can just belong to one another, be part of one another, and that could be enough.

But Oliver fills in the blank. "He's our mom's cousin," he explains, whittling the relationship down to the barest bones.

I nod. It would be naive to think it could be anything more—that the ties between us go any deeper than the simple lines on a family tree. Still, looking at Mr. Riley now, I wonder what it was like for Meggie to be part of his family. Maybe the runaway note was fake, and he always loved her this deeply, like she was a part of him, a thread from the same fabric. Or maybe he changed after she left—maybe it took losing her to find her in everything he was and wanted to be, to discover how she'd been there, a part of him, all along.

When I rescue Meggie, he'll be complete again. And—having proven myself in a blaze of glory—I can be too.

Mr. Riley smiles, the wrinkles on his face lifting like heavy wings. "I heard you'd be coming to town. Nice to think of some young folk keeping Jeff on his toes."

On instinct, I look toward Griffin, who's currently thumbing through a handful of Stone Creek Insurance business cards like he's about to deal a hand of poker. Griffin certainly has me on high alert the past few days, but thanks to my big mouth, he's more stressed about Jeff than Jeff is about him.

"Jeff's a good guy," Mr. Riley says, running a hand over his chin. "Stone Creek wouldn't be the same without his contributions."

Oliver and I exchange a glance, which Mr. Riley thankfully misses as he turns to point toward the enormous print of the runaway note.

"He donated that for our tenth-anniversary festival," Mr. Riley explains. "Jeff has always been great about cutting through the"—he pauses—"junk that people spew to get a headline. Always focused on the facts. He's been a great support for us in Stone Creek."

I clench my jaw with all my might to keep it from

snapping wide open. Jeff as a support to the Rileys? Jeff as dedicated to the facts of the case? Jeff donated to the festival?

The way Jeff acts, it's like he doesn't want anyone to know he cares or is interested. But apparently he's just as involved as the rest of the town—he just doesn't advertise it. Maybe because he has something to hide.

The shadow man's note rests heavy in my pocket. Right now I wish I could tear it to shreds.

"Speaking of junky headlines," I say, crossing my arms. "I heard from a reporter that . . ."

Mr. Riley cocks his head. I'm sure he's heard a thousand tourists start a sentence just like this before. But watching him brace himself, I wish I could backpedal my way full out of this conversation.

Great investigators like Nellie Bly would never let fear veer them from the truth, though. I have to ask. "There's a theory that you stayed in Stone Creek after she vanished to profit off of her story. And that's why you hold this festival every year."

I leave out the part about them making Meggie disappear, or any of the other parts Oliver and Richard theorized about. But the words still leave a sour taste on my tongue. Oliver glares at me, aghast, but then glances at Mr. Riley with a twinge of curiosity. The older man sighs softly.

"I've heard that more times than you can imagine," he says, a sad chuckle escaping his throat. "But I'd trade every last penny we have to get our Meggie back."

I squirm a bit beneath his sad gaze but have to ask, "I saw an interview about her runaway note, though. All you talked about was how great of a businesswoman Meggie was, as if that's all that mattered."

"And she was," he says. "She was brilliant. Always making brave choices, and paying attention to detail. That note was fake, and that's how I know." His eyes go a bit cool as he adds, "You can't believe anything anyone says about her wanting to leave Stone Creek behind. People like Devon Jeffords have reasons to lie about who Meggie really was. But Meggie was a part of our family, first and foremost. We loved her more than anything and she, the same."

Mr. Riley's still looking at me as he speaks, but as he continues, it's almost as if he's not here at all. It's as if he's on a stage, reciting a familiar monologue. As if he's standing with a thousand other Finleys that he's given this speech to before, eyes pleading for someone to listen, to believe each word he speaks. "We hold this festival every year, whether we know it'll bring in revenue or not. We keep all our businesses running in her name, to make sure no one ever forgets that she's still out there, waiting to be found. And we'll always stay in Stone Creek, so we're here when she comes back."

Oliver touches my arm, a silent *Leave it, Finley*. And as much as I feel like I should question and push more, when I look into Mr. Riley's distant eyes, all I see is the basement at the Riley residence, packed to the brim with all of Meggie's old things. All I hear is his voice, cracked and unsteady, as he called her name out into the empty woods.

All I see is someone stuck, and sad. Defending himself on cue. Grasping onto what's left of someone long gone. Terrified that if he lets anything about him or Stone Creek change, he'll finally lose Meggie for good.

When I saw the basement yesterday, I thought it was the perfect celebration of Meggie, a way to preserve her legacy and keep it alive. But speaking to Mr. Riley now, the basement looks like an anchor in my mind, holding the Rileys down as it sinks them deeper and deeper into the ground.

When Dad left, he washed his hands of us completely. Agreed only to the weekends he had to take, as if being our father was a hobby rather than a part of who he was. I'd always thought that meant I was easy to leave. But if Meggie came back today, I wonder if she'd be happy to see how her father ended up. Or if she'd wish he'd been able to let go, to lean into whatever his life could have become after she left.

It makes me wonder what would come after Sophie, if I decided not to reply to her text. If I threw out the Walsh-Higgins Adventure Agency cards and replaced them with the Walsh-Walsh-Walsh versions instead. Or if I retired the cards entirely, as if I didn't need a brand or a title in order to matter.

Who would I be then? If I loosened my grip on the people around me, would I find I was the only one holding on after all? And if I did, what would happen to me next?

Mr. Riley scratches the back of his balding head, eyes slowly returning to focus. "Why don't you go take a look at your cousin's contribution, then?" He nods toward the enormous print. "The note was certainly forged," he says easily, as though it's a fact, "but that doesn't make it any less valuable. I still maintain to this day that it's the best clue we have. Jeff says that too."

I want to tell him not to worry—that I'm an adventurer, just like Meggie was, and I'm going to be the one to rescue her once and for all. She'll be home soon, and I'll be standing with her, the two greatest adventurers Stone Creek has ever seen.

The words fall limp on my tongue. For the first time, they don't feel quite right, like spoiled food that's been left out too long. But I don't know what else I'm supposed to say. So, even as my chest feels so full it could burst, I say nothing. "It was nice meeting you kids," Mr. Riley says. "I hope you enjoy your time in Stone Creek."

Oliver nods and with that, Mr. Riley walks off, arms swaying by his sides like loose ropes. I look up at my brother, shaking my head slowly.

"He's innocent," I determine.

He raises an eyebrow. "This again? Seriously, Finley, how can you possibly know that?"

Griffin sprints across the street, nearly bulldozing Mr. Riley, who veers to the side, chuckling warmly as Griffin runs on without a second glance.

I shrug. "I don't know. He just is."

Griffin reaches us, waving a wad of business cards in the air. "I'm rich with contacts! The networking king of Stone Creek!"

Oliver rolls his eyes. I snatch at the stack greedily. "Good job, Griff." I thumb through, scanning the first letter of each name as fast as I can. "Find anything good?"

"Nope," he admits, loud and proud. "But I did meet just about everyone in town. Even the trash man gave me a card. He didn't put his name down, though."

Oliver shoots back some quip, but suddenly I'm digging through the cards in search of that one. There, in the center of the stack, is a torn scrap of paper with a phone number scrawled in quick black ink, no name, business, or address.

I focus on keeping my voice light. "What did he look like?"

He frowns. "I said he was a trash man. So, he looked like a trash man. Do you even listen, Finley?"

I have a thousand follow-up questions because, with Griffin, you never know if that means the man was wearing a Stone Creek Sanitation uniform, or if he just happened to run into him by a recycling bin. But the more I push, the more suspicious he—and Oliver, especially Oliver—will get. And if my theory about this phone number is right, then I'm not ready to share it with them yet.

I slip the sheet out of the stack, then hand the rest to Oliver. As his attention locks on the cards, I shove the number into my pocket with the shadow man's note, filed together as though by the same author.

Which I think they are.

"There's no P. W.," I say as Oliver reads through. "It was a dead end."

I keep my hand in my pocket, my palm crinkling the papers inside.

Oliver groans, slapping the cards back into Griffin's hands. "This is useless. We're stuck here for the rest of the day, and pretending we're going to find something at the center of a tourist trap was stupid to begin with." He runs a hand through his hair and glances past me, over my shoulder. "I'm going to go see if anyone at the diner needs help setting up." I raise my eyebrows, so he quickly adds, "So we can get this done and leave sooner!"

I don't object. If Oliver's crush keeps him distracted, that gives me time to sneak off and call the mystery number. "You take Griffin. I'm going to go brave one of the Porta-Potties."

Griffin grabs my elbows and gives me a serious, furrow-browed look. "Remember: our dumpster mission prepared you for this."

I lock my hands on his elbows in return. "I won't fail."

Oliver yanks Griffin by the sleeve, tugging toward

Sam and Jason. I give them a hearty wave, then make my way in the opposite direction, toward the orange Porta-Potties. They stand at the edge of the woods, lined up like parking cones, as though their presence is the only thing keeping the woods from swallowing downtown whole.

I pass between the booths for Stone Creek Pizza and Riley Realty. Pavement turns to grass beneath my feet. With a quick glance over my shoulder, I duck between the Porta-Potties to the other side, hidden in the shadow of the trees. The warm spring sun vanishes, the cool settling on my shoulders like a chilling mist. Sewage and mud fill the air and I resist a gag.

I take out my phone with trembling hands. Maybe I'm about to reach the sanitation department after all—and I do have a few words to say about these Porta-Potties—but that's not what I'm expecting.

I close my eyes, inhale a nauseating but steadying breath. If my hunch is right, Griffin was face-to-face with the shadow man. Which means the shadow man is here, walking around in plain sight, noticed by no one.

Not even me.

I open my eyes to the light of my screen. My thumb presses the call button, and my list of recent contacts pops up. Mom and Sophie, again and again on repeat. Griffin and Oliver, scattered here and there when I scroll. Almost never Dad.

I press the keyboard and reach for the crumpled paper. I don't remember anyone in *100 of the World's Greatest*

Female Adventurers saving the world by making a phone call next to a toilet. But there's a first time—and a first female trailblazer—for everything.

With an unsteady hand, I dial.

The phone rings, each beep staticky and distorted. I clutch the phone to my face, the glass screen cool against my cheek.

The receiver clicks. Then, a male voice.

"Finley?"

My name in an unfamiliar voice. I grasp the phone closer, as though somewhere in the static I'll hear his name too.

"I know who you are," I say. Which is only half-true. Or maybe less than that, but I've never bragged about my math skills. What I know is that this is the man who followed me in the woods—twice. Someone who knew I was investigating at the diner that first day. Someone who wants me to doubt Jeff, either to mislead me, or to protect me.

"That doesn't matter," he says, though to me, it's all that matters. It's all I think about when the tall trees sway around Jeff's house at night. All I think about when I walk through the woods, glancing into the dark wilderness and wondering if, somewhere, he's looking back. "Just listen."

I lean back against the Porta-Potty to steady myself. Thankfully, my sense of smell is gone. Everything is gone but the way my blood beats through my body, angry and wild, so my temples and wrists throb.

Just listen. I imagine those as some of the last words Meggie heard. Climbing down from her tree, a note for her secret lover left tucked in its branches. Walking through the cool April dark, grateful for time away from her dad and all his expectations. Hearing the crunch of footsteps behind her, followed by the command: "Just listen. Just listen, and I won't hurt you."

This is where Sophie would say we'd officially gone too far. That I needed to hang up and call for help. But girls like me don't get help. Not before we've earned it. Sophie has the ability to say the right things, to be the right things. To draw people to her like magnets to metal. But Meggie and me? We're the kind of girls who make history before we make friends. The kind that people meet in the headlines, not the cafeteria.

Who would I call? Jeff, one of my main suspects? Oliver, who would use my fear as proof that I can't handle anything? Mom, who would swoop in and pick me up like returning a baby to its crib?

The treetops close in above me, like the space is shrinking in.

"I'm listening," I say.

The man doesn't respond. I hear rustling, and I am sure he's about to emerge from the trees and whisk me away in plain sight. But then something crackles on the other end of the line, followed by the muffled sound of an audio recording.

I hear a girl's voice, tense, with a twinge of annoyance.

"Hey. Just wanted to let you know I'm on my way." Her shoes crunch against twigs and leaves in the background. I close my eyes and see myself walking through Stone Creek Woods. "I ran into that guy who works at the auto shop, and . . . well, it doesn't matter. I'll be there soon."

The audio cuts. My eyes shoot open, and the shadow man's voice returns to the other end of the line.

"Jeff—"

"That proves nothing," I say, sharp. "How do I even know that's Meggie's voice? And how do I know you didn't force her to say that, on a recording, before kidnapping her? And how do I—"

The man interrupts, and his voice is tense, but tired. Worn thin like the paper crinkled in my hand. "If I was the kidnapper and I'd made her say it, wouldn't I have turned this in years ago? Because the only reason I can think to fake something like this would be to frame Jeff for something I did. And if that were true, he'd be in jail and I wouldn't have to be here, calling you for help."

I suck in my cheeks. "Who are you? Devon Jeffords? P. W.?"

"I'm a coward," he says without missing a beat. "And you don't have to believe me, one way or another. But I was too scared of being . . . misunderstood to come forward. But you're closer to him than anyone's ever been. You can find some real evidence . . . finally set this right."

I open my mouth to respond but am met with a click. I hold up the phone and sure enough: call ended.

My fingers shake, nearly missing the buttons as I redial. It rings for one moment, then cuts into a high-pitched series of beeps.

"The caller you have dialed is not in service . . ."

I click end and resist the urge to fling my phone into the rooftops. I should have recorded the call. If Sophie were here, she would have let me put him on speaker while she recorded on her phone.

I'm not good enough to be a great adventurer on my own. I can't be One Hundred One without my One Hundred Two.

I clutch the phone in both hands and press it to my chest. There's a fair chance I'm being set up—that someone's derailing me and my rescue mission. But there's another, equally real chance Jeff isn't who he says he is. And only one way to determine which is true.

Tonight, when we get home, I'm going to find out what he's guarding in the locked room.

GREATEST FEMALE ADVENTURER NUMBER SEVENTEEN: BARBARA HILLARY, CLIMATE CHANGE ACTIVIST AND FIRST BLACK WOMAN TO REACH BOTH THE NORTH AND SOUTH POLES.

That evening, back at Jeff's, the hours pass excruciatingly slowly, and I wish I could fill them by talking to my brothers, sharing the explanations, theories, and stories about the days I've had when they weren't paying attention. Instead, *Legend of Korra* reruns play loud through my phone's speakers, Griffin laughing at every joke like it's his job and Oliver resting peacefully beside him, texting Jason. And I lie, phone-less and partnerless, stretched out on my cot as I stare at a lonely spider on the ceiling.

Oliver chuckles to himself. Griffin smiles, thinking he's finally appreciating the cartoon, but I know Oliver better than that. I wish I could yank my pillow over my head, but I don't want Oliver to think I'm being rude about him having a crush on a boy, because I'm annoyed by all crushes equally.

He catches me staring at him. His ears turn red and he starts stammering. "Jason wants to meet tomorrow," he says, quick like a distraction. "Not just me, I mean. Not like that. He found some stuff at his dad's house he wants us to look at."

He holds up his phone as proof. I skim past all the flirty nonsense until I see mention of his dad.

I found his prom photos, yearbook, transcripts, and a bunch of other junk from high school. I can't make any sense of it, but you might notice something I don't.

It should say Finley might notice something he won't. But I let it slide this one time, for Oliver's sake.

Guilt settles over me as I think of Jason rummaging through his dad's things to help our mission. When we'd made the agreement to work together, I'd shared my doubts in Jeff to even things out. But at the time, I didn't think Jeff could really be guilty. Not the way I do tonight, at least.

I hear the sound of footsteps approaching up the stairs. Every muscle in my body clenches and I'm paralyzed, eyes locked on the ceiling.

"Hey, kids," Jeff's voice comes, before he's reached the final step. He stands at the top of the stairs, half in and half out of the attic. One hand rests on the railing, and the other is pressed against the side of his head, midscratch. "I'm taking Malt out for a short walk; then I'll be calling it a night. Need anything before I conk out?"

Oliver clamps his hand over Griffin's mouth before he can beg for dessert. "We're good, thanks."

Jeff nods. I figure that'll be it, but then he looks to me. "Finley?"

His voice is sheepish as ever, unexpectant. But all I can do is blink at him.

I'm not used to being asked separately from my brothers. Not after Oliver's given his final word, at least.

Warmth floods my chest, like I've won something even though I haven't finished my mission yet. Even though I don't deserve to feel like I do.

I bite the inside of my mouth as though I can swallow back my grin. "I'm good. Thanks, Jeff."

He nods, eyes always fixed above my head rather than right on me. When I first met him, I figured he was just a bit shy after living out here, alone with just Malt, for so long. But after my call with the shadow man today, I wonder if there's another reason he never looks right at me.

"Okay, then. Have a good night, kids."

I just smile, scared of what will happen if I open my mouth. There's too much spinning inside my mind for me to trust my words right now—not in front of him, or my brothers. He finishes that head scratch, drops his arm to his side, and treks back downstairs, where he's greeted by Malt's excited yelps.

Oliver and Griffin return to their screens. But I focus on the sound of Jeff's footsteps crossing the living room through the thin floorboards below my cot. At last, the room shakes as the door opens downstairs. From the window I hear Malt yapping in the yard.

The coast is finally, finally clear. With everyone in the house distracted, I can finally do some on-the-ground exploring.

Starting with the attic closet. The other day, when I went in to grab Griffin's charger, I found a huge stack of old boxes. They could be nothing, but that feeling I got when Jeff entered the room again—like I had to hide and lie about what I'd seen—tells me my explorer senses are working, and I was on the verge of a great discovery. Besides, if Jason's going to show up tomorrow with some of his dad's things, it's only fair that I do some proper exploring at Jeff's house.

I leap off the mattress, a bit surprised by how unsteady my legs are beneath me as I cross the room toward the closet. Part of me doesn't want to look—some small part of me I barely recognize, who hesitates at the edge of a great discovery.

The easy calm that surrounds Jeff could be a distraction. Something to lull me into a false sense of security, to get me off his trail. But as I open the closet and step toward the tall dusty line of old boxes, I hope I don't find anything, and that the Jeff I think I know is the only one that exists.

If Sophie were here, she'd remind me that Meggie was ready to run away from her family to pursue greatness.

And if I want to be like Meggie, I have to face the truth about Jeff—whether I like it or not.

I reach for the first box. Searching old boxes in an attic feels huge, but I can't imagine what it would sound like in *100 of the World's Greatest Female Adventurers*, so I imagine the dust is soot from a volcano and I'm climbing to the top despite the threat of lava from above.

I fall to my knees and flip the cardboard flaps apart. The contents bulge from inside, papers stacked haphazardly one over the other. I rifle through, squinting to read with the little light trickling in from the lamp near Oliver's bed.

It's a whole lot of boring old documents, mostly about insurance for the café or property taxes. And all from the last couple of years too.

Which means I need to dig deeper. The other boxes probably have older things in them—maybe even from back when the auto shop was run by our family. When Meggie was still around.

One by one, I unpack and repack the boxes. One is full of photos like the ones out on the walls in the living room, including some from family reunions. I spot Mom in the background of a few photos, laughing at something another cousin said or reaching for a second corn on the cob while no one's looking. I wonder if she has copies of these photos too that she looks back at, wishing her life had taken a different turn.

Another box is filled with old cards Jeff received over

the years, and I wonder if he receives birthday cards like these anymore. Or if after he stopped attending the family reunions, it was as if he no longer existed at all. He always sent us birthday cards, though. Usually bland with just his name as the signature. But now that I know him, I know that's just how Jeff is. That he might want to say more but can't find the words, even when Hallmark writes them out for him.

Once I reach the final box, I kneel again, hungrily pulling the flaps apart. Inside are old newspaper clippings and photographs, much like the other boxes. But these are the oldest yet: photos of Jeff as a kid over the years, the images faded and yellow after years left in the box. Even as a kid he wore baseball caps, though back then he had oversized ears he hadn't quite grown into peeking out on either side of his head from beneath the cap. He also has a big, open smile. A bit goofy in a photo or two where he's missing a front tooth. But, still, a happy, confident Jeff I don't know.

My fingers shake as I peel back the layers. I watch the photos slip through my fingers, waiting for the moment that smile fades, transforms into that quiet, reserved look I've learned to expect from him.

It's like walking back in time, tracing the steps he took to become who he is now. It's how I want to get to know Meggie, to understand her, how to be like her. But for Jeff, I feel like it's the opposite, like I'm tracking his path on a map so I know where not to step.

The swarming thoughts in my head scatter when I find a photo of Jeff about my age. Not because of the hideous tie-dye shirt he's wearing, or the smear of dirt on his and the other kids' cheeks in the photo. But because one of those kids is Meggie.

He stands with his arm looped around her shoulders, even though she's a bit taller than him. She has a wide, loose grin and leans into his side, a similar pattern of dirt over her arms and cheeks. It's like they'd just come back from a hike or from crawling through a cave like the one I found the other day. There are other kids with them too—ones I don't recognize. But that's not the point.

The point is that Jeff knew Meggie. Was even friends with her.

And he lied about it.

I rummage through the books, scouring for any more photos of Meggie. Just as disappointment rushes over me like an ocean wave, I notice an unusually shiny spot of hardwood floor to my right. In the yellowish glow of the overhead light, I can make out a clear square of clean floor, its edges rimmed with dust.

Meaning there was another box here, and recently. One that Jeff must have moved.

"Finley, did you get locked in the closet?"

Griffin's voice is full of more laughter than concern. I can almost picture Oliver's face as I hear him say, "She's probably hiding from you, loudmouth."

I grab the photo of Jeff and Meggie and stuff it in

my back pocket, next to the one that holds the shadow man's note. I feel armed, the way Meggie must have the day she climbed out of the woods with the Stone Creek treasure—her, doing so defiantly despite her friends leaving her behind. Me, knowing that holding on to what I've found probably means pushing someone else away.

I need to get out of this closet. I need to get downstairs, before Jeff comes back from his walk. I need to find out if the final box is in the locked room.

I burst out of the closet. "I need to pee."

Oliver groans. "No one cares."

Griffin laughs, and I don't know if it's at his show or Oliver's comment. But it doesn't matter. I bend over, as though looking for my shoes, but instead lock eyes with Oliver's jeans—the ones he wore until he switched into pajamas for a cartoon binge. I slip them toward me and reach into the right pocket, withdrawing Mom's credit card.

Then, as subtly as possible, I straighten up and rush to the stairs.

GREATEST FEMALE ADVENTURER NUMBER EIGHTEEN: LIV ARNESEN, FIRST WOMAN TO SKI SOLO TO THE SOUTH POLE.

My socks pad against the wooden slats as I make my way down to the living room. Sure enough, it's empty, the porch light streaming a yellow glow by the doormat. Malt's leash and Jeff's coat are gone from the hanger, and I have less than five minutes before he's back.

I make a beeline for his bedroom door, passing the couch as I go. It's bare, except for Jeff's smooshed throw pillows. If it wasn't for the fact I'd caught him the other night, I'd never know he slept on the couch. He must set up his makeshift bed night after night.

I'm not sure what waits behind his bedroom door. But it pulls my stomachs in knots, thinking of him living like a guest in his own house. I imagine that the bedroom will be empty—that he sleeps out here, beneath the photographs, to feel connected to his lost family. It makes me think of Mom—of all the nights she fell asleep clutching her phone, open Messenger tabs with distant family she'd lost touch with after we came along.

If I don't rescue Meggie, I may end up alone too. So I march past the couch and toward the bedroom door, determined to uncover the truth, no matter what it is—or what it means for me.

I grasp the handle, lifting so it's as up-and-out as I can pull. Then I slide the card where the lock meets the door.

I'm met with resistance. I turn the knob, opening it as far as I can before the thick lock resists. Then I push at an angle, wedging the card against the square lock to slide it between. It presses against the edge of the lock and I sway the card up and down, steadily inserting it between the lock and the door.

By the time I'm done, the card may be scratched beyond recognition. But Mom will probably forgive me once we cash in on the Rileys' reward money, so I push harder, shifting and shaking the card until the knob turns open in my hand.

The door creaks open. I pause, shooting a last glance at the front door. I can't hear Jeff or Malt, which means they're probably at the end of the driveway. Time is running out, but I use what I have and step into the room.

I lean against the door, clasping it shut behind me. Then I reach, palm patting the wall until I find the switch. A blinking bulb flickers overhead, and the room illuminates in an orangey glow.

I brace myself for the truth that lives between the pieces I've collected along the way. My eyes adjust and I see the bare bedroom: mattress stripped of its bedding. Light-blocking curtains with age stains dangling over two windows. A squeaky old radiator, uneven floorboards, and a door-less closet with flannels and faded jeans dangling from its hangers.

And, tucked in the corner of the bedroom closet like it used to be in the attic closet upstairs, is the final cardboard box.

I rush to the closet and whip open the cardboard flaps, heartbeat rising up my throat. I asked Jeff if he knew Meggie on our first night here, at dinner. And again, when I tried to learn more about why his dad sold the auto shop after Meggie went missing. And he never mentioned this: another photo, this one of him running across a soccer field with Meggie and a few other kids. Or this photo too, with him posing in a small group in front of a cake and HAPPY BIRTHDAY banner in the background.

Beneath the photos is a newspaper clipping with Meggie's image in color. It's similar to a few others I've seen before, the headline **LOCAL GIRL DISCOVERS MYSTERIOUS TREASURE**. It's the only one about her discovery that he's kept, though, so I lift it up and skim the vertical text down the page.

It's most of the same thing I've read before: the tale of Meggie Riley, a brave and driven young girl who set out into the woods in search of adventure. When the terrain got tough, her friends decided to go back, trickling off one by one until she was the only one left. The only one who pushed forward and discovered the stash of buried antiques underground.

But this version of the story shares the names of the kids who she'd gone exploring with. The ones who had turned back.

Including Jeff Walsh.

Jeff didn't just know Meggie. He went on an adventure with her. Like Sophie used to go on adventures with me.

But he turned away, left her to complete her greatest expedition alone. And when she did, Meggie became a hero. Her family became rich and powerful in Stone Creek.

And the whole time, the auto shop was failing. And Jeff's dad blamed the Rileys. And then he sold out to Mr. Phillips, but Jeff stayed behind. Opened a Meggie-themed shop.

But he pretends he's not interested in her story. Avoids the festival and the tourists and my theories.

And most of all, he lied about knowing her. Which means the shadow man was right: I can't trust Jeff.

There are gaps in the story, ones the photos and news clippings can't piece together. What happened between Jeff and Meggie after she found the treasure? Why did his parents really leave Stone Creek? And why did he stay?

The possible answers make my skin go hot and

clammy. Suddenly, the walls around me feel too small, like I'm about to be swallowed by the dark.

I turn on my heel, pacing toward the door. I have to go back upstairs. Show the photos and newspaper to my brothers, then force Jeff to admit the rest. With Mom's card slipped into my pocket alongside the shadow man's notes and the photos and newspaper clipping in hand, I turn the knob and step into the living room.

Just as Jeff does too, boots brushed against the doormat. He and Malt turn in unison, eyes locking on me.

I stretch my arm to the right and slap the light switch off, as though turning the room dark could make me disappear. But from the look in Jeff's eyes—and a dash of common sense—I know it's too late.

I've been caught.

He opens his mouth, and I don't know what's at the tip of his tongue. Lies, excuses, confessions, threats. All I know is I have to get ahead of it, before he wriggles into my head.

I pretend I'm Catherine II, overthrowing my enemy before they have the chance to put up a defense. "You lied," I say, firm and confident. Because whatever happened to Meggie, this is true. He lied about his involvement in her case. And with the Rileys. He lied about his interest, and why he lives in Stone Creek. Why he opened Meggie's Cup to begin with.

He lies, just like Mom does every time she tells me "You don't need to worry," and "I believe you can do anything." He lies like Sophie, pretending she still cares.

Jeff's mouth clamps shut. He bends over, releases Malt from his leash. The dog scurries off, bounding up the stairs to escape the scene.

Only Jeff and I remain.

"You said you weren't interested in Meggie's case," I say. "But I met Mr. Riley, and he couldn't stop talking about how supportive and helpful you were. He had this giant print you'd donated on center stage. And then I found this." I reach into my back pocket and pull out the photos and newspaper clipping. I don't understand what I'm holding or what it means. But it sits bad at the base of my stomach, like spoiled food. "You said you never knew Meggie, but you were friends with her. You were there when she found the Stone Creek treasure—a treasure that could have been yours, too, if you'd followed after her."

My chin wobbles. The house is dim, but I feel like a hot spotlight rests above my head. In the shadows I see Sophie and Veronica and Chloe and Mom and Dad and Oliver and Griffin. I see all of Stone Creek, and all of history, watching and waiting to see if my next words earn me a spot in the books.

"You were involved in her disappearance, and you're trying to hide it," I say. "You were the last person to see her alive, and you're guilty."

I fall silent and the house creaks, like it's releasing a heavy breath. Jeff stands, still and staring.

He kind of looks like Mr. Riley in this moment. Like the world is so heavy, he could snap right in half.

"You're a smart kid," he says. The words could lead up to a super-villain speech, but his tone is sad and wet. I brace myself, trying to remember that guilty is guilty, whether or not he feels bad about it now. "You're right, Finley. About part of it, at least. We were friends, once, long ago. And I was the last person to see her alive. I'm sorry you had to find out this way."

I bite my lower lip, shift my weight hip to hip as though I'm a goalie blocking the door to the room.

But he remains fixed by the door, like he's afraid of taking up too much space. Like he's not sure where he belongs, even in his home. "I've never told anyone this. Never thought to, or had to. People don't really come out here, you know. I didn't even think your mom would go through with it. People always talk about visiting, but they never do. Life gets in the way . . ."

His voice trails off. It's the same explanation Mom gave for why we stopped seeing family. She was too busy with us, with Dad. She was too busy until it all fell apart, and suddenly there was so much space that we couldn't begin to fill it.

"We were friends, you could say. It was a long, long time ago, and we were very young." He scratches his head in that same awkward way he always does, like he's trying to pluck the right words from his mind. "Meggie was always talking about lost treasures and deep-wilderness survival and all that. I wasn't as into it as she was, but it was something fun to do with good friends. And in a little town like Stone Creek, you don't take either of those for granted."

"So you never really liked her?" I ask. "You were just pretending to be her friend and care about her interests because you were bored?"

When I look up at him, waiting for an answer, all I can see is Sophie.

My muscles tremble, bracing for the impact the truth might carry.

Jeff shrugs. "I considered her a friend at the time."

"So what happened?" I demand. "Why didn't you want to hang out with her anymore? What did she do wrong?"

All this time I thought that if I did everything exactly how I thought Meggie would, people would want to keep me around them too. But even Meggie was left behind by her friend.

My phone weighs heavy in my hand, arm swaying a bit under its weight. If that's true, there's no point in ever replying to Sophie. There's nothing I can say or do to save our friendship, to convince her I'm worthy. She was probably just like Jeff: bored and tagging along on my adventures until someone better came along.

"She did nothing wrong," Jeff says. That just makes me feel even worse, because even when Meggie did everything right, she still lost so much. "I just was too chicken to follow her into the woods that day she found the treasure. And because of that . . ."

I want to fill in the blanks, speed up the confession. The answers are right there, and I can picture them in my mind, predict what he'll say next.

But despite everything, I can tell Jeff is trying to tell the truth. Tell his story, in his own way. And even if he's guilty, I know I need to let him tell it himself.

"As proud as Mr. Riley was of Meggie, my father was disappointed I didn't go after her that day," Jeff says. "That I didn't find the treasure, or at least find it with her, so we could split the rewards. He never said that," he adds, tucking his hands in his pockets and shrugging his shoulders, "but it was clear that's how he felt. It's why he blamed the Rileys when things went south with the auto shop. As if their success was taking away ours, because Meggie was the one to find all that money for her parents."

Whenever I thought of the kids who missed out on the Stone Creek treasure, I thought of it as a way to prove a point—to show Oliver and Sophie and anyone else who doubted me what happened to the people who didn't trust adventurers like me or Meggie. But I never thought about the real impact it could have on them: how it would feel knowing they'd just missed greatness by a quarter mile or so.

But thinking about it now, with Jeff standing in front of me, I realize that I've started to feel more like those kids than I do like Meggie.

"I didn't talk to her much over the years after that," Jeff says. "Like I told you the other night, I let my dad's thoughts become mine. Until he left Stone Creek, at least."

It makes me sad to think of Jeff and his father drifting apart, one staying and one going, with nothing to keep them connected. Everything about Jeff feels like it could be packed away into the boxes upstairs, like there's a distinct before and after in his life. The before: family photos and cards and adventures with friends. The after: the blank walls and empty corners of this bedroom.

But that's not what matters now, I remind myself. I suck in a deep breath and ask, "What does Meggie's disappearance have to do with you and your dad? It seems strange he left Stone Creek so shortly after she vanished."

Meggie, the girl Mr. Walsh wished Jeff had followed into the woods and discovered the treasure with that fateful day. Meggie, whose father bought up chunks of Stone Creek, whose success made Mr. Walsh jealous and spiteful. Meggie, who they saw to blame for their failures.

Jeff's eyes soften beneath their heavy lids. "I did see Meggie in the woods that night. And it's haunted me ever since. I've never come clean, not with anyone."

I hold my breath. If only Sophie were here. If only she could feel it too: the way the ground shifts beneath your feet when you're standing on the edge of answers.

Jeff continues. "Not even the cops knew who I was when I called in," he says. "I was too scared of being misunderstood, or falsely accused. Because if they blamed me, they'd be right."

I blink, thoughts and theories scattering in my mind like roaches under a light. Somehow, I'm more confused than ever.

"I was on my break from the shop. Needed to get away from my dad for a bit. I took a lot of breaks back then, escaping for some peace in the woods. That's when I ran into Meggie." He shrugs again, though his face is hard, square chin wobbling. "She looked a bit frenzied, sure. But it was a look I used to know. The one she got before she ran into the woods when we were kids, even as the rest of us turned back." His face softens a bit, though his eyes remain clouded, dark. "She was trying to get away from her dad, too. So when she saw me, she kind of laughed, like it was fate."

I try to picture it in my mind: a young Jeff in his work overalls from the auto shop, trudging through the woods. His head bent down, eyes narrowed as though if he squinted hard enough, the rest of Stone Creek—his dad, the auto shop, the Rileys—would fade away.

And a young Meggie. Thick blond hair wild around her head. Eyes piercing and determined, cheeks flushed from her sprint through the woods, all the way from the Riley estate up to the northern end of Stone Creek, where the diner and café now stand.

It's a different version of the photos in my hand. A different version of how things could have gone, if the money and the rivalry and all the differences between them hadn't stopped them from being friends over the years. Hadn't soured their relationships with their families and with Stone Creek.

"She essentially told me what was in her letter to Mr. Riley," Jeff says. I remember what Mr. Riley said at the festival about the runaway letter being a donation from Jeff. Maybe her note was real, and Jeff knew it. Maybe he donated to the Rileys' cause so the best piece of real evidence out there would keep the town off him and his dad's trail.

But something still doesn't seem quite right. So I remind myself it's Jeff's story to tell, not mine to imagine, and nod along so he knows I'm listening.

"She knew I was unhappy at my family's business, too. Asked if I wanted to come along, for old time's sake." He shakes his head sadly. "I think we both knew I'd say no. That the old times were too far gone and my dad had twisted me up too tight for me to unwind for a Riley that fast. I told her I'd never leave my dad or Stone Creek. So I left her there, and now she's . . ."

The sentence dangles, unfinished. Jeff doesn't know what she is. Where she is. Because he wasn't the kidnapper.

"I should have told someone I'd seen her. Should have shared what she said. But with each day, and each month, and each year that passed, I knew it would just look worse and worse. So I did this instead." He gestures around the room, toward the door and the house beyond. "I've tried to crack her case, in my own way. Stayed here in Stone Creek, even after my dad sold shop and left. To make up for what I did, or didn't do."

His voice breaks. He doesn't cry, but I feel it in my chest: that deep, dark empty that's worse than tears.

"And you sleep on the couch because . . . ?"

"Not used to having people here. And I didn't want to worry you kids with what was in that box." He inhales softly. "I understand if you want to leave," he says, voice serious. "I can call your mom now, and I'll explain it all. You don't deserve to feel unsafe, and—"

I glance at the photographs hanging over the sofa. Smiling, distant faces, Jeff speckled in among them. "Is that why you stopped seeing family?" I ask, voice smaller than I'd hoped. "Because you felt guilty?"

He runs a hand over his face. His fingers pause at his jaw, shielding his mouth from view.

Something hot and damp bubbles in my chest, wriggles its way up my throat. I try my best to swallow it down. "So it's just you and Malt? Because of Meggie?"

Once, Jeff had a big family, just like I used to. Jeff had a future, like I want to. Then he crossed paths with Meggie, just like I did. And he took a wrong turn, and it changed everything forever. Just like it could for me.

All I've thought about since starting this is how impressed everyone will be when I rescue Meggie. I hadn't considered what would happen if—somehow—I made things worse.

"I enjoy Stone Creek, kid," he says, and I hope it's true—that it's not something he's saying for my sake, or for his. "But like I said before, being around all them, I just ran out of things to say."

"Because all you thought about was Meggie. And she was the one thing you couldn't talk about."

Jeff crosses the room. He slumps onto the couch, like he can no longer face gravity alone.

It should hit me like a ton of bricks, thinking of him out here alone, swallowed by his guilt. It should terrify me to think of someone who took one wrong step and spent the rest of his life on the couch, tangled in nightmares about what could have been, what should have been, what is, because of that one mistake.

But right now—seeing him slumped on the sofa, the room coming into focus around us—all I can think about is that he told me the truth. That he trusted me with his identity as the anonymous source, even after years of keeping it secret from everyone, including the rest of our family.

Me, a kid.

Me, a silly girl.

Me, Finley Walsh, amateur adventurer.

Me. The one everyone thinks is good for nothing but make-believe.

Jeff trusted me.

Oliver avoided me at school to keep me from learning his secret. Mom still doesn't trust me with anything since the divorce, as though I'm young enough to survive our family changing but not to really be a part of it. Sophie turns to Veronica and Chloe like they have all the answers, never thinking of me, Finley Walsh, because I'm someone you outgrow, not someone you grow with.

But Jeff trusted me with the biggest secret of his life. He didn't dodge or sugarcoat. He just told me, face-to-face, as though I earned it.

Or maybe—just maybe—as if I didn't have to.

I cross the room, floorboard creaking beneath my weight. Edging around the coffee table, I settle into the sunken seat cushion beside him. I grab a throw pillow and cradle it my lap like a security blanket.

"I'm sorry I looked in your room. And the closet," I say. "That was wrong of me. But you see, I'm a semi-amateur adventurer, and—"

He shakes his head. "It's fine. I'm glad you did. It was wrong of me to ever hide it."

I think of my conversation with Richard. "I get it. People prefer answers to questions. When all you do is ask questions, they assume you have nothing to say."

And then, as though on command, you run out of words.

"I guess I figured you kids could find it, if you actually came," he says, mostly to himself. "But either way, you've been good company. Malt likes you all, at least."

I smile. Because now is the time the lecture would usually come on what's safe or not, or how I should pick up a less messy hobby if I want to keep my friends, or how I've gone too far and I need to step back, backing myself away and away until there's nothing of me left. But Jeff doesn't say any of that. He just stares ahead, into the distance, looking the closest to content I've ever seen him.

"I'll come clean. I promise I will," he says, eyes fixed on a distant wall. "I'll make it right."

The couch creaks beneath our weight. It's baffling that this is all it took—me discovering his boxes, confronting him until he came clean—but at the same time, it's not. I can't imagine all the things I'd say if Mom asked. If Sophie added a question mark to her texts, or Oliver looked at me long enough to see my secret fears.

Maybe I, too, would come clean if given the chance.

I adjust myself, legs tucked beneath my thighs. "You won't send us home, though, right?" He tilts his head toward me, though his eyes still don't meet mine. "I want to stay here a bit longer. You know . . . with Malt."

Jeff smiles, the tired lines of his face rising. "You're welcome as long as you'd like. Whenever you'd like."

I pull my legs closer together, fingers against my ankles. I never thought I'd get new family—not after we lost touch with everyone, and certainly not after Dad left. I figured that from that point forward, the numbers would dwindle until it was just me, standing alone, hoping I earned my place as One Hundred One to win everyone back.

Upstairs, my phone rests in Griffin's hands, no new messages from Sophie. But maybe it's okay if Sophie isn't my forever friend. Maybe I'll find a new friend too, just like I found new family. Like how Jeff found a new home in Stone Creek after his dad left. After he found his own way to move on.

The thought scares me. But fear feels similar to excitement, the way it quakes my bones.

"I'll make some calls tomorrow. I promise," Jeff says. "But it's not your responsibility to lose sleep over that."

I nod and leap to my feet. The couch breathes a sigh of relief as my weight leaves its old springs.

Malt is already at the foot of the stairs, ready to take my place beside Jeff. Just like this morning, my arms dangle awkwardly as though unsure if they should initiate a hug. Just like this morning, I ignore the feeling and walk away.

But this time, my gait feels steady, assured. Tomorrow I'll begin my mission to uncover the truth about the shadow man and why he tried to frame Jeff. But, for now, all that matters is Jeff's innocence—and that he was willing to share the truth with me, dark spots and all.

GREATEST FEMALE ADVENTURER NUMBER NINETEEN:

PREMLATA AGRAWAL,

THE FIRST INDIAN WOMAN TO CLIMB ALL SEVEN SUMMITS, AND THE OLDEST TO SCALE MOUNT EVEREST.

The next morning is like any other, the four of us—and Malt—set up in Meggie's Cup, serving Anne Thornton and other locals who trickle in for their morning caffeine. I pretend to revisit my homework, but what I'm really doing is counting down the minutes until Jason's break. Oliver arranged plans for us to meet today to look through the box of high school memorabilia he found in his dad's room, and now that I've crossed Jeff off my suspect list, Devon Jeffords and Meggie's secret lover, P. W., are higher on my suspect list than ever. I'm hoping that I'll spot something in the clues that Jason overlooked and be able to identify Meggie's kidnapper once and for all.

Jeff's stationed behind the counter, diligently scrubbing a stained coffee pot. With the morning crowd thinning out, now's my perfect chance to get my brothers away and fill them in on what I've learned—and our next steps for the mission.

"Malt needs to pee," I announce, because apparently spontaneous bathroom breaks are the only excuse I can ever think of to get privacy. "Oliver and Griffin, will you help me walk him?"

Oliver's focus remains on his phone. "It doesn't take three people to walk a dog."

I bite my lower lip. "Well, he, um, drank a lot of water."

He looks up long enough to shoot me a glare. "What does that even mean?"

Thankfully, Griffin is ready for any opportunity to abandon his workbooks. "Come on, Ollie. Take me and Malt for a walk!"

Oliver groans. "Fine, if it means you'll burn off some of this muffin-fueled sugar rush."

Our chairs scrape in unison as we leap to our feet. Jeff glances up from his task, giving me a disinterested glance that suggests he probably knows what I'm actually doing, but doesn't object. After our talk last night, he said he was ready to come clean to the rest of Stone Creek, so me telling my brothers the truth is just a small step in the right direction.

I guide Malt and my brothers around to the side of the café, by the edge of the parking lot. While Malt busies himself sniffing a dandelion, I usher Oliver and Griffin in for a huddle.

"I went on a solo mission last night," I announce, "and it was a major success."

Oliver's eyes go wide. "What do you mean, a solo mission? Where did you go?"

"Just downstairs," I say. Griffin's eyes glaze over, losing interest, so I quickly add, "After discovering a box full of new Meggie clues in Jeff's closet."

That gets both of their attention. I quickly explain how I caught him sleeping on the couch, then developed a plan to search the closet and locked room while he took Malt on a walk.

"So we're not staying with the bad guy?" Griffin asks. He looks up at me with big, hopeful eyes, and all I want to feel is relief. But murky guilt settles in my gut as I realize how much I scared him by voicing my suspicions about Jeff.

When I started this adventure, I wanted Griffin to see that I could be as brave and clever as Oliver—more so, even. But instead I did the opposite, scaring him to the point he didn't feel safe in his own home.

"That's right," I say, placing a soft hand on his shoulder. "You're safe, Griff."

Oliver holds up a hand. "I wouldn't go that far," he says, sharp gaze fixed on me. "We still need to be cautious. I've said it a thousand times, but you're anything but subtle. If the kidnapper's still in Stone Creek, they can see you coming from a mile away."

I glance down at my sneakers. Now would be the

perfect time to tell Oliver about the shadow man. But I can't do that with Griffin right here. Especially when he's smiling—really smiling—for the first time in days.

"No one wins by playing it safe," Griffin says, puffing out his chest. "We'll face the kidnapper head-on. Won't we, Finley?"

My mouth opens and closes, caught between two answers. At the beginning of this trip, all I wanted was to get Oliver and Griffin on my side, to buy into the mission. But now that we're actually getting closer to the truth, I can't help but wonder if this would have been a better mission done solo: without Oliver's snarky chaperoning, or Griffin's way of teetering between determined and terrified.

I've never been known for being the level-headed one, but right now I feel like I'm the only one seeing the mission for what it is rather than one extreme or the other.

An electronic wailing cuts through the quiet morning scene. Behind Oliver, from the direction of downtown, a police cruiser zooms over the road, toward the café. Red and blue lights flicker as it approaches, slowing to a halt a few yards from where we stand.

Malt abandons his dandelion and patters toward my ankles. As the officers step out of the front seat, the dog lets out a threatening yelp. The men don't cast us a glance, their focus fixed on the front door of the café as they stalk forward. Across the lot, a small crowd of nosy patrons forms outside the diner.

"Jeff said he was going to come clean about what happened," I say. But the words fall apart on my tongue, not adding up when placed together. If the cops knew the truth about Jeff's innocence, why would they be showing up with lights and sirens to hear the rest of his story?

Heat rises to my cheeks and—before my brothers can object—I rush after the cops.

The café door chimes as Malt and I storm inside. The officers stand at the counter, talking to Jeff in gruff voices.

". . . down to the station with us," one is saying. "We have a few questions you'll need to answer."

Jeff runs his hands over his dishrag. Maybe to hide the way he's shaking. "It's funny you say that, because I was going to make a call to you this morning."

My stomach drops. Jeff didn't call the cops. Which means this isn't about his confession. Something else must have happened.

A heavy silence hangs in the air. When the cops don't respond, Jeff speaks again. "Can I ask what this is about?"

The door jingles. Griffin rushes in so fast he slams into my back. Oliver enters behind him and steps to the center of the room, suspended between us and the adults.

"We received new evidence in the Meggie Riley case and have reason to believe you were involved in her disappearance," the first cop says.

Jeff stammers. "Y-yes—I mean, I was there, but—" His eyes flicker between the cops and the framed clippings, as though searching for the right words to say. "I wasn't involved, you see. I was actually going to call and explain this today," he adds with an awkward chuckle, "but—"

The cop holds up a square hand. "It's best you save this. We'll want anything you say on the record."

Griffin digs his nails into my elbow. "I thought you said he wasn't guilty?" he whispers.

I watch as Jeff drops the rag and steps around the counter. "He's not."

The cops stand on either side of Jeff as though herding him toward the door. Oliver shoots a glance back at me and Griffin, then steps forward. "You can't just take him without any reason!"

Griffin peers around my arm. "Yeah! I've watched a lot of crime shows when my mom's not home, and Uncle Cousin Jeff has the right to remain silent! He doesn't have to tell you anything."

"Not that he has anything to tell," I quickly add. "I mean, he does have some things to tell. But he can explain—"

"He will explain," the cop says, face hard, "with us, down at the station."

The other cop steps forward. "Do you kids have anyone to stay with?"

The café door chimes again. I spin around to see Sam in the doorway, the lines by her mouth sloped like angry exclamation points.

"They'll be staying with me," she announces. "This shouldn't take you long, anyway, since whatever new evidence you've got is definitely fake. Jeff's good people. Ask the Rileys yourself."

The officers start walking toward the door again, as though ready to bulldoze us over. I can't see Jeff as he passes, the second cop's body blocking him from view. They slip through the café door and—with one last chime—they're gone, as though none of them had ever been here.

Including Jeff.

Malt rushes toward the door and barks as though begging it to reopen. I stand, stiff and frozen, my arms clutching onto Griffin like he's a buoy in rough waters. His body trembles beneath my grip, and he stares up at Oliver expectantly, as though waiting for him to say it will all be all right.

Which, right now, feels like an impossible statement.

Sam glances between the dog and us, a thousand frantic thoughts visible in the whites of her eyes. "I . . . I have to make some phone calls," she says, holding up her hands. "Everyone who's anyone in Stone Creek knows this isn't right. We'll get Jeff out of this."

Then she points at us. "You three: stay right here. Lock up the shop, and if anyone else comes by, you come get me. Don't talk to anyone, including the police. You hear me?"

We nod in unison, like we're being scolded by a stern teacher. She remains still, finger pointed, as though unsure if we'll scatter like loose marbles the moment she lowers it. Then, in a frantic rush, she pushes out the door and runs back toward the diner.

The door slams shut behind her with a ding. Malt releases a high whine. Oliver steps over him and quickly bolts the door.

Griffin spins out from under my arm. "Do you think they found the secret box? Did they break into the house? Because that's illegal. I know that from TV too."

Oliver leans his back against the door. "There's nothing incriminating about keeping old photos or news clippings about Meggie. Especially in a town like this." He shakes his head. "No, they have to have found something else."

Griffin blinks. "Doesn't that mean he could be guilty?"

"No!"

My voice comes out loud—too loud. As though I'm using volume to try to make up for the way it trembles.

But Jeff's not guilty. I know he isn't.

Oliver's right: there's no way what I found in the bedroom is enough to incriminate him. And even then, they couldn't have searched the house without a warrant.

The only other evidence that could incriminate Jeff is the shadow man's voice mail from Meggie.

All the doubts the shadow man put in my mind—all the evidence he stacked against Jeff—wasn't to help me find the truth about him. It was to frame him for a crime he never committed.

A crime the shadow man is responsible for.

"It's Devon Jeffords," I say. Oliver's mouth drops. "Or P. W. One of them is guilty."

Oliver's eyebrows narrow. "How do you know that?"

I press my hands over my eyes and draw in a steadying breath. Even behind the dark of my palms, I feel the whole world spinning.

"Meggie left one of them a voice mail saying she saw Jeff in the woods before she disappeared," I explain, hands still cupped over my face. "Which meant Jeff was either the kidnapper or the anonymous source. And since he's not the kidnapper, that means whoever Meggie left the voice mail for was. Otherwise, they'd have no reason not to submit it to the cops to try and frame Jeff. She sounded in the voice mail like she had planned to meet up with the person, like it was her boyfriend, Devon Jeffords, or secret lover, P. W. I know I can't rule him out completely, but it really didn't sound like she was talking to Mr. Phillips."

I lower my hands. Oliver's expression twists with confusion and frustration.

"What voice mail?" His eyes go hard. "You didn't go on just one solo mission, did you?"

I bite my lower lip. "I've had some contact with a suspect—"

Immediately, Oliver blows up. "What do you mean you've had contact with a suspect? You can't just run around, talking to whoever like that! These people are dangerous. Anyone could be dangerous in this town!" His nostrils flare, arms waving as he speaks. "You can't trust anyone! And you can't face them alone."

The last part hits me like a slap. I ball my fists. "I did

face him alone. And nothing happened to me. I'm fine." I straighten my shoulders. "I don't need you to supervise everything I do. If I let you, we'd never rescue Meggie!"

"You're fine?" He waves his arm toward the empty counter. "Glad to hear you're fine, Finley, because whatever you've been messing with has Jeff in serious, life-ruining trouble."

His words hit me, heavy, like gravity is collapsing on my body. Jeff being arrested isn't my fault, it's the shadow man's. But I did let the shadow man distract me. Let him set me on the wrong trail, digging up evidence against the wrong man.

And now Jeff has to pay for it.

"How was I supposed to tell you?" My voice comes out wobbly, my throat tight as I choke back tears. "You never listen. Even now, you're not listening."

This is exactly how I expected Oliver to react, whether I told him about the shadow man days ago or waited. No matter what I said, or how close I was to the truth. No matter how brave I'd been on my mission. No matter what, Oliver always finds some way to blame me. Belittle me. To do anything but what I need him to.

I swipe at my eye, careful not to let a tear leak down my cheek. The other day, out in the woods, it felt like Oliver was seeing me for the first time as someone dependable, someone he needed. But with him, everything feels like one step forward, five miles back.

Griffin raises his hand. "I'm confused," he says.

"Me too," Oliver grumbles, dark eyes boring into me.

Griffin keeps his arm raised, making it clear it's his turn to talk. "If you've met this other suspect, how do you not know whether they're Devon Jeffords or P. W.?"

I suck in my cheeks. What I'm about to say next is going to blow Oliver's fuse all over again.

"Because I never saw him," I say, keeping my tone matter-of-fact. I hope the calm in my voice encourages my brothers to respond the same. "He followed me in the woods and dropped a note about Jeff. Then I called him from that anonymous number you found, and he played me the voice mail he received before Meggie disappeared."

Oliver presses his hands over his face.

"You're being followed?" he asks, voice low.

"You can't be mad at me," I snap. "You didn't even notice anything was going on."

He runs his hands up his face and through his hair. His eyes stare past me, at the wall. "I need to call Mom," he says.

That was the last thing I was expecting. And somehow worse.

He reaches into his pocket, withdraws his phone. I storm forward. "No! She'll come pick us up. She won't let us stay if Jeff's gone."

He turns so the phone's out of my reach. "Good."

I stretch my arm past his shoulder, grasping for the phone. "What about Jeff? We still need to prove he's innocent. And Meggie still needs to be rescued. We can't just abandon them!"

And I still need to finish this mission. If I back out now, in the eleventh hour, I'll never make it into *100 of the World's Greatest Female Adventurers*. And I'll never be able to reply to Sophie, either, because I'll have nothing to say.

"This place is a death trap," he says, shooting me a glare over his shoulder. "The sooner we're out of here, the better."

He walks to the other side of the room, one hand holding the phone and the other pressed to his ear to block me out. I stand, muscles all clenched like a fist, and glare holes into his back.

I can't leave now. Not when I'm so close. And not because Oliver tells me to.

Griffin leans over to pet a sniffling Malt. "We're not really going to abandon Uncle Cousin Jeff, right?"

"Of course not." I kneel beside him. Malt stares up at me with his black doggy eyes. My plan clicks into place in my mind. "I'm still going to meet Jason to look through his dad's stuff. He has his dad's yearbook, and P. W. could be in it too. I'll figure out which is guilty, clear Jeff's name, and rescue Meggie in no time."

Saying it now, it sounds like an insurmountable task. But Junko Tabei didn't stand at the bottom of Mount Everest and think, *This is nothing.* She must have felt small in its shadow, had a flicker of doubt: *Can I really do this?* But the important thing is she pushed on anyway, confident in all the prep she'd done, confident that there would be challenges and she could face them.

Everything I've done since arriving in Stone Creek led to this moment. No—every mission I'd ever completed with Sophie led to this moment too. While she and everyone else thought I was playing make-believe, I was gaining the skills I needed for this adventure. So if anyone can rescue Jeff and Meggie, it's me: Finley Walsh, World's Greatest Female Adventurer One Hundred One.

"You need to stay here, though," I say. Griffin's face drops. "The shadow man is following me closer than ever. And if he really is Devon Jeffords, I could be walking into a trap. You'll be safer in the café."

The words are a bit sour on my tongue. Right now I'm not treating Griffin any different from how Oliver treats me. But the shadow man is my mess, not Griffin's, and I can't let him get hurt like Jeff did. I need to set things straight before I let the kidnapper hurt anyone else I care about.

Oliver walks back toward us, phone returned to his pocket. Griffin and I leap up so fast, we nearly bonk heads.

"She's booking the first flight back from Chicago," he says. My chest falls. "But she won't get here until tomorrow morning at the earliest."

All that heavy gravity lifts back up and suddenly, I'm weightless. My cheeks lift into an impossible-to-hide grin. "That means we have one more night in Stone Creek," I say. Oliver's lips part, ready to comment, and I quickly add, "And as long as we're here, we might as well do everything we can to rescue Jeff. Right?"

We can't let him be blamed. Not when he's spent his life doing everything he can to make up for what he did—or didn't—do. There needs to be a next chapter for him. A life where he can take new photos with people he cares about.

Jeff was the first person to put his trust in me. I can't let him down.

And if his reputation can't be saved, then that means mine can't be either.

"Fine," Oliver concedes, and I feel light enough to leap off the ground. "But nothing crazy. We'll just start by seeing Jason, and take it from there."

Hope floods my chest. The odds are stacked against us, but that's to be expected in the final stretch of a deadly, high-stakes adventure. If I can come out on the other side of this victorious, than no one—my brothers, Mom, Sophie—can doubt me ever again.

I smile. "Then let's go."

GREATEST FEMALE ADVENTURER NUMBER TWENTY: SYLVIA EARLE, OCEANOGRAPHER WHO LED OVER A HUNDRED UNDERWATER EXPEDITIONS.

Oliver leads the way out of the café, glancing intermittently at his phone as though half expecting Jason to cancel on us. Malt hovers by the door, tiny tail wagging as I prepare to push it shut behind me.

"Make sure to lock it," I remind Griffin. "We'll be back real soon."

He gives a silent nod. For a moment I consider pushing the door wide open and waving my arm for him to follow. But I know he's safer in here, tucked away from the things that follow me. I press the door shut and listen for the click of the lock before following Oliver to the parking lot.

As we step onto the pavement, Jason rushes out of the diner, a backpack looped over his shoulder. He jogs across the empty lot, gesturing toward the edge of the woods.

I gulp. "We have to meet out of view," I explain,

mostly to myself. "Otherwise, the kidnapper will know we're onto them."

Oliver frowns. I'm sure if we were meeting anyone but Jason, he'd drag me back to the café. I'm glad he's not forcing me to stay in and wait for Mom to come get us, but it still hurts to know he's not here because he trusts me or my plan.

Jason's lanky form vanishes between the thick evergreens that guard the entrance to the woods. Almost every time I've run into the shadow man, it's been out there, in Stone Creek Woods, where Meggie disappeared. If Jason's dad is guilty, he could know we're onto him and be out there, waiting. I trust Jason not to sabotage us—especially after all that's happened with Jeff—but that doesn't mean he's a savvy enough adventurer to have kept off his dad's radar while going through his things.

Even if Jason didn't set a trap, this could still be a trap.

As we trek across the empty lot, I feel exposed, as though every treetop is filled with watchful eyes. I cross through the woodsy barrier, entering into the cool, shadowy woods. Jason stands a few yards ahead, shifting his weight leg to leg. His eyes are wide, his chest heaving as though he'd just run a mile. He starts talking the moment we're within earshot.

"Sam's been calling just about everyone in town," he says, breathless. "She's already convinced the Rileys to head down to the station, and she got Mr. Phillips to call his big-city lawyer for us."

Jeff, Mr. Riley, Bryan Phillips. It's like crossing names off a long list in my head as he says them. Which would usually feel good if it weren't for the frantic look in Jason's eyes. Because with each name off the list, we get closer and closer to finding his dad guilty.

But he's still here, digging in his bag to pull out his dad's yearbook. It makes my chest clench to think we could find something in there that could hurt him, after all he's done to help us. Oliver must feel it too, because his eyes remain fixed on Jason, unblinking.

The book slides out of his bag, a heavy, gray hardcover with CONGRATULATIONS, STONE CREEK SENIORS written in shiny letters. "I wasn't able to find anything interesting in here," he admits, wrist bending beneath the volume's weight, "but maybe you'll see something I didn't notice." He swallows. "Or something I didn't want to notice."

Oliver's hand shifts by his side, like he's not sure if he should pat Jason's shoulder, or whatever people like him and Sophie should do when their crush is upset. Thinking of Jeff locked up for something he didn't do, I wish I hadn't searched for reasons he could be guilty. That, like Jason, I had looked for the best in my family, even if it meant overlooking the tiny red flags along the way.

I extend my hands, fingers wiggling. Jason chuckles softly, and the tension in the air cracks just enough for me to smile back. He passes the book to me. My arms bob beneath its weight and I settle, cross-legged, into the grass. I cradle the book in my lap, and the boys sit down beside me on either side.

I open the book and finger through the table of contents. It's followed by a series of ads from local sponsors. As I reach to turn the page, my fingers brush over an ad for Hank and Son's Auto Shop.

I pause, fingertips pressed against the glossy page. When I arrived in Stone Creek, all I cared about was Meggie and that first great adventure she went on when she was my age. I understood why the town honored her the way it did, why every shop and storefront was named in her memory. There was nothing more I wanted than to rescue her and meet her. To pick her brain and learn how I, too, could be great. Could be the kind of girl that people think is important.

But because she's the only person Stone Creek considers great, so many other stories and legacies were lost along the way. It makes me wonder how things might have been different for my family if that treasure had never been found, and who Jeff would be today if he and Meggie had never crossed paths.

If I fail my mission, I don't want to become just another person who couldn't live up to Meggie's legacy. I don't want to leave Stone Creek like Uncle Hank Walsh did, bitter and angry, never looking back for the people he'd left behind.

I'm not sure what that would look like for me, or how I would face the noise without the shield of success. But I know that, no matter what, I have to promise myself that I won't let my story end here, in Stone Creek. Not like that.

I take a handful of pages and flip, landing in the middle of the senior photos. I flip to *J*, scanning for Jason's dad. I see his big, white teeth first—just like Jason's when he smiles. The photo was taken years before Meggie's disappearance, and he looks nothing like the version of himself I saw in Jeff's newspaper clippings or met in the cave. That Devon Jeffords walked with his head down, trying to avoid the snapping lights of photos. His face was drawn, tight lines marking the skin around his mouth, and his shoulders had the same sloped look Mr. Riley's did, like gravity hit them just a bit harder than everyone else.

My gaze flickers up to Jason. He remains focused on the book, expression hard, though his chin wobbles a bit. After the initial pain and press around Meggie's disappearance, Mr. Jeffords moved on—got married, had kids, raised a family in Stone Creek. But after meeting him the other day, I know things like this never really go away. They can fade like old photos, but they stay, dull colors still visible on the surface.

If I can't rescue Meggie and Jeff, Stone Creek will mark me, too.

"Turn to *W*," Oliver says through clenched teeth.

"I know," I snap, though I'm relieved, too, to turn away from Devon Jeffords's photo.

I flip anxiously through the pages, the alphabet spinning past me. I land on *Z*, backtrack a page, and scan for *W*.

Oliver reaches over me, jabbing his pointer finger against the page. "Paul Willoughby!"

I slap his hand away so I can see. There, grinning an awkward, lopsided grin, is a dark-haired, pale-skinned boy, the only P. W. in the yearbook. Which, arguably, is not incriminating on its own. But my heart rises, fluttering like a butterfly in my throat, because I know this P. W. is my P. W. immediately.

"It's Richard Connors," I say, realizing it as the words escape my mouth. I tap my finger against his face in the photo, silently begging Oliver and Jason to see what I see. "It's the reporter from the *Burlington Biweekly*. He lied about his name—or changed his name—and he lied about not being from here, about just coming for an article. He was Meggie's secret lover."

Every interaction I've had with Richard zooms through my head like scenes from a movie reel, from that first moment he zeroed in on us at the diner to Oliver complaining that he kept hovering over him and Jason during their secret meeting. One moment snags, trapped on replay: our conversation with Richard at the festival, when Griffin blurted out that Jeff was my main suspect. Hearing that, he must have realized the note he dropped me had worked—that he'd succeeded in making me doubt Jeff. From there, all he had to do was find a way to talk to me alone, to play that voice mail and fully frame Jeff in my mind.

I tighten my grip on the book, fingers crinkling the edge of the glossy pages. Thinking about the voice mail reminds me that I put Griffin right in the shadow man's path when

I sent him to collect the business cards at the festival. I'd just wanted a break from his overactive imagination, some time to pursue suspects without him blurting out all my theories and leads. But in doing so, I'd led him right into the culprit's path.

Overhead, the trees rustle in the wind. I hear the patter of distant footsteps—probably squirrels, or raccoons, or birds. But each crunching leaf and trembling branch sends a chill up my spine and makes me grateful I left Griffin back at the café, out of harm's way.

I brush my thumb over Richard's—P. W.'s—photo. Something tugs at the back of my mind: reasons it can't be Richard. Conflicting times and accounts. Alibis. But the proof rests in front of me, and the truth about the details will come with my next steps.

"This means he's also the man who's been following me all this time," I say, voice small as though he's right here, listening.

Jason's jaw drops. "Wait, Finley—what do you mean, man who's been following you?"

Oliver goes tense beside me. "I only just found out too," he says, like an explanation.

I clench my jaw. I know Oliver's not feeling guilty that I was facing danger alone, he's just embarrassed he didn't notice.

But how would he, when he only looks at me when he needs something to critique? To micromanage, so he can feel smarter and more mature?

"None of that matters now," I say, slamming the book shut with finality. "What matters is that we know P. W.—Richard—was the kidnapper, and he's the one framing Jeff. We need to gather our evidence, and then get down to the station."

Oliver and Jason exchange a look. Jason holds up a hand. "But wouldn't someone have recognized him, if he was from Stone Creek? He was at the festival, and I even saw him interview Meggie's sisters. If he were from here, someone would have noticed."

I drum my fingers on the page in concentration, listening to the soft echoing sound the thick volume makes beneath my nails. Everyone knows everyone here—or so I thought. But somehow Richard walked around in plain sight, unnoticed. And as proudly as he wears that *Burlington Biweekly* badge with his pseudonym, it's unlikely that would convince anyone who knew him as Paul before.

The echo continues beneath my fingers, and I'm suddenly aware of how big the yearbook is for a small town. I imagine a lightbulb flickering on above my head as I say, "Your dad told me a lot of people moved in and out of Stone Creek when he was younger. The Rileys' businesses were booming, and people were interested in Meggie's story and their success. Mr. Phillips said the same thing."

I nod to myself as I add, "When Richard was talking about the Rileys, he made a comment about how he thought it was strange her sisters stayed in Stone Creek their whole lives. He said he's always moved every few years and never stayed in the same place. So, theoretically, Richard could have lived in Stone Creek, briefly, if his family moved here during the business boom. And he could have left shortly after. He wouldn't have been here very long, and he would have been one of many temporary residents. So it makes sense people wouldn't recognize him."

My heartbeat quickens. I imagine it's a similar, but more intense version of what Sophie feels at the amusement park, riding a roller coaster as it's about to dip to its hundred-foot drop. I'm on the edge of saving Jeff, of finding Meggie. Of timeless glory. Of being the World's Greatest Female Adventurer One Hundred One.

Richard Connors came to town to manage the story, not report on it. I'm not sure why he chose the twenty-year anniversary after being away so long, but either way, he must be here to skew the facts and make sure he isn't caught, that no one cracks the case during the anniversary celebrations.

But Richard Connors doesn't stand a chance against the great Finley Walsh. And I'm going to prove that, once and for all, by capturing him and setting Meggie free.

"This means my dad's innocent," Jason says. He blinks down at the book, eyes glossy. "In the end, both of our families were innocent."

Oliver reaches out and places his hand over Jason's. "I'm glad it worked out."

Jason intertwines his fingers with Oliver's and gives a squeeze. His shoulders loosen, and I imagine all the weight that's been stacked on his family lifting for the first time.

"You helped save him, Jason," I say with a proud smile. "We didn't know what we'd find out, but you looked for the truth anyway. That's what makes a great adventurer."

A twig snaps in the distance. Footsteps echo through the woods, moving our way. Reality crashes back down on me. Jason's part of this mission may have just come to a happy ending, but the shadow man is still out there, waiting for his chance to strike. To get me off his trail, once and for all.

I leap to my feet so fast the book flies out of my lap and smacks against a mossy rock. "He's here." I wave my arm at Oliver and Jason, snapping them back to attention. "Don't you hear that? He's here."

They sit, blinking as though their minds are still buffering. But I don't have time to wait. So far, the shadow man has always been a step ahead. But right now I have proof—incriminating proof—about his identity. Just enough to convince the police to look into a new suspect, to reconsider their interpretation of the voice mail.

I lean down and snatch the yearbook, shoving it back into Jason's bag. Then, slinging it over my right shoulder, I bolt off in the direction of the footsteps.

Blurs of green stretch out on either side of me as I run. Twisted roots and bramble tug at my ankles as I dash forward, the backpack bobbing against my spine. Up ahead, I see a form making its way toward me, into the woods. I suck in my cheeks and aim right for it.

If Meggie was kidnapped by her secret lover—Richard, P. W., Paul—she must not have known what was coming. She must have come here to meet him, thinking they'd talk through the breakup, talk through how she chose Devon, how they'd just be friends. But now, armed with the truth, I sprint toward the danger head-on. I pretend I'm Meggie, blond hair waving behind me as I run, ready to rewrite history, to fix everything in Stone Creek that ever went wrong.

To reclaim my legacy.

The trees break and I skid to a halt before I slam headfirst into Sam. She's panting, out of breath from running and what looks like a full morning of yelling on the phone. Pink splotches dot her wrinkled cheeks, and squiggly red lines decorate the whites of her eyes.

The boys catch up behind me. Her attention lasers in on Jason.

"Your break ended ten minutes ago!" she shouts. Overhead, a family of birds abandon their tree. "I need your help in there. I'm expecting a call from Bryan's lawyer and need you to take over the front for me."

Then she turns her focus to me and Oliver. Her face scrunches up like a balled fist.

"And you two!" she yells, each syllable like a slap. "I told you to wait in the café! I'm busy over here trying to help your cousin, and all I've asked is that you stay put, eat some muffins, and keep out of the way."

She takes a step forward. My heartbeat rises in my throat.

"Can you do that for me? Or is that too hard?"

Oliver and I nod frantically, crying out "Yes, ma'am" and "Sorry, Sam."

She gives us a stiff yet satisfied nod. Jason moves to follow her, pausing by me as he walks past. "Keep me updated, okay? And Finley"—he pats his bag, still slung over my shoulder—"You keep this for now."

I adjust the heavy bag on my back, its weight both reassuring and a reminder of how much is still at stake. "I'm going to do it, you know. Rescue Meggie."

He smiles. "I know you will. And my dad will be relieved."

As Jason rushes after Sam, and Oliver leads the way back to the café, I cast a final glance at the woods, imagine Richard looking back. He's followed me this whole time, but I've still managed to be one step ahead—to be the great adventurer that would defeat him, once and for all.

Whatever Richard was preparing to print in the *Burlington Biweekly* will never run. The reality he's created—the lies he's spread over the years—are finally coming to an end. Soon, after gathering all my evidence for the police, I'll be the one to cast a light on what happened in those woods. The one to save Meggie, giving her a chance to rewrite her story.

Staring into the shadows of the woods, I imagine that instead of Richard, it's her looking back, waiting for me to find her.

GREATEST FEMALE ADVENTURER NUMBER TWENTY-ONE: FREYA STARK, EXPLORER AND TRAVEL WRITER KNOWN FOR TRAVELING THROUGH THE ARABIAN DESERT.

I lead the way back to the café, shoes pounding against the concrete. The grass is still smooshed, soft and flat beneath my feet, where the police cruiser pulled onto the curb. Hot rage bubbles in my chest as I think of Jeff being taken away from the store, held for a crime he didn't commit. I tighten my grip on the backpack strap, hoping that the evidence I've gathered against Richard will be enough to clear his name.

I step up to the café and give the door a rough series of knocks.

"Griffin!" I shout, pounding to each syllable. "Let me in! I have a lot to tell you."

Overhead, the sun is casting an orange glow over the treetops. I slam my fist again.

"And we're running out of time!"

Malt's barks carry through the wooden door. I let out an impatient huff and turn to Oliver.

"Did we agree to a code word I'm forgetting?"

Oliver crinkles his nose. "Finley, this isn't a game."

I turn back to the door and pound even harder this time, all my pent-up rage slamming against its old wooden surface. After everything I've accomplished, it should be obvious that this isn't a game to me. That I'm not just playing make-believe, the way everyone thinks I have ever since I started the adventure agency.

I reach for the doorknob. I don't have time to keep arguing with Oliver. If he doesn't trust me at this point, the only thing that will win him over is rescuing Meggie once and for all. I just need some time to go over my evidence and next steps, and then he'll see I was right all along. About everything.

I give the knob a jiggle, ready to shout again. But it turns easily in my hand, door swinging open to the café. An embarrassed flush rises to my cheeks. I could have sworn I told him to lock the door. But now, apparently, I just did one more thing wrong. One little thing that will give Oliver an excuse to lecture me for the rest of the afternoon.

Malt bounds up to my feet and raises his head to release an excruciatingly loud bark. I groan and step past him.

"Yes, yes, we'll go for a walk now," I say, because not only did I forget to lock the door, I forgot that locking Griffin up with the dog probably wasn't as kind to the dog as it was to Griffin.

Malt scurries after me as I step into the café. He leaps with each yelp, tiny body shaking from the volume of his barks. The sound echoes off the walls, the space empty of anyone other than me and the dog.

"Griffin?" I call, shrugging the backpack off onto my usual table. The room is still, no sign of Griffin. He must be in the back room, stuffing his face with Jeff's storage of snacks. "We're back!"

I pause, listening for the sound of his footsteps, for the rustle of his pant legs as he runs to meet me. But other than Malt's cries, I'm met with silence.

Oliver fastens the café door shut behind him with a clack. "Did you just break this thing open?"

Whatever I say, Oliver will be mad. So I scoot past him and head toward the counter. Malt follows at my heels, still barking hysterically. I shove the swinging door that leads to the back room.

"Griffin?"

The narrow space is empty, storage cabinets untouched. Malt barks again, shriller this time, as though calling me to finally see what he does.

My chest feels tight, like the air's slowly being squeezed out from my lungs. I press my hand against the cool metal surface of the utility sink, steadying myself. Malt hovers below me, staring up with expectant eyes.

I tighten my grip on the edge of the sink until the tips of my nails bend against its hard edge. The walls narrow around me and, before I use what little air's left in the room, I rush back into the café.

The door swings so hard and fast it slaps my ankles. I press my weight against the front counter, finding my balance. Then I reach into my pocket for my phone.

There's one new message from Mom, keywords like "flight back" and "sorry this happened" scattered across the lengthy paragraph. But nothing from Griffin.

I close my eyes, letting the café fade to black around me. Griffin must have sneaked off to find some clues on his own. Of course he did—it's what I would have done if Oliver had told me to wait while he went on an adventure without me. Griffin took to Jeff faster than either of us did. Maybe that's why he was so scared that Jeff could be guilty. Why he's now so determined to clear Jeff's name.

I open my eyes, reluctantly turning to Oliver. As much as I hate to admit it, there's a good chance Griffin did tell us where he went, but didn't think to go to me first—even after everything I've accomplished on this trip. I swallow my pride down like a horse pill. "Did Griffin send you a text?"

Oliver responds by holding up his cell phone. No—not his cell phone. Griffin's, with its race-car-red case.

I run my hands over my temples, tugging loose strands from my ponytail. Only an amateur would leave their phone behind before going on a solo adventure. Sure, I may have left my phone upstairs with him the other day when I sneaked into Jeff's room—but at least I was still inside the building. And with my years of experience, I'm far from being an amateur, so a risk every now and then isn't a big deal.

A sudden off-tune ringing makes me jump. The café phone blinks beside the cashier, its flashes reminding me of the cop car.

Maybe it is the cops. Maybe they caught Griffin out alone, brought him back to the station. Hand shaking, I snatch the phone off the receiver.

"Hello?"

There's quiet breathing on the other end of the line. Goose bumps erupt on my arms like tiny volcanoes.

I've been here before. Clutching a phone to my ear, listening to those steady, eerie breaths. A caller that pauses before he speaks, never wanting to say too much, to give himself away.

I pull the phone from my ear, quickly jabbing the speaker button. Soon, his quiet breaths are the only sound in the café.

Then, his voice.

"Listen carefully," he says.

It's just like before: that feeling that I'm standing exactly where Meggie did, following his instructions as though—if I'm good, if I behave—he can't hurt me.

Oliver rushes around the counter. His eyes are wide, a thousand questions racing across his pupils. But I remain silent, focused on the caller as though my life depends on it.

Which it probably does.

"You will meet me at the place this began," he says, voice low and steady, "and you will hand over everything you have on Paul."

My gaze flickers from the phone to the backpack, laid out on my table. In my pocket, the shadow man's notes are folded away like tiny secrets. These little things aren't much, but they're all I have to save Jeff. To rescue Meggie. There's no way I could ever turn them over. That I'll just stay quiet and give up.

Not a semiprofessional adventurer like me.

"If you don't . . . ," the man continues, voice rising. My throat goes tight, and I feel reality closing in around me, feel the false bravado and confidence slipping away like a waning tide. "Your little brother will join Meggie. For good."

The line clicks. A dull dial tone rings through the café, like the phone is releasing a long, final breath.

The phone slips through my fingers, clattering onto the counter. The sounds of the room fade, the dial tone and Malt's barking nothing more than a buzz in my ears. I inhale a breath, but it's like my lungs are shaking too, unable to accommodate the air inside them.

My vision is fuzzy around the edges, but details of the café come into sharp focus around me. Chairs pushed out from the table, one lying lopsided on the ground. Frames askew. One of the windows only half-shut, its edges scraped like they'd been clawed open with a tool.

Signs of a struggle. All the details I'd missed when I'd walked into the café, proudly toting the backpack on my shoulder as though I'd already won.

Maybe the reason Sophie stopped going on adventures with me wasn't just because she'd outgrown them. Maybe she knew if we tackled anything real—anything riskier than snooping in Mr. Morrison's yard—that we'd be in over our heads.

Like I am now.

When I speak, it sounds like another girl's voice. Like I'm hearing someone else from across the room. "He took Griffin."

The words come out slow and cautious, reality setting in with each syllable. It didn't make sense. The shadow man was mine. He followed me, because this was my mission. Because he saw me as a threat. He was supposed to be my shadow, no one else's. Griffin should have been safe in the locked café, away from me and the things that followed in my wake.

But the shadow man is always a step ahead. It's how he's kept Meggie for all these years, undetected. I'm not the first person to come to Stone Creek, convinced I'd be the one to finally uncover the truth, to finally save the day.

He's been guarding his secret for years. And I'm just a girl pretending to be something she's not, caught in his rigged game.

"It was supposed to be me," I say, choking on the

words. "Griffin wasn't supposed to get hurt. I thought he was after me."

My gaze settles on Oliver's shoes. I can't bring myself to look up at him, to hear his I-told-you-so's and all the blame that comes with them. Because this time I know he's right. That I led us in over our heads, and it's my fault Griffin's hurt.

The edge of the counter goes blurry. Hot tears bud at the back of my eyes and I blink hard and fast, begging them to go away. I can't stand to look any weaker than I already do—especially with the shadow man watching, Griffin in his grasp.

"I'll fix this." I nod along to the words, as though I'm trying to convince myself. "It's my fault if he gets hurt, so I'm going to fix this."

I thought making Griffin stay at the café was a way to protect him. But, really, it was just me pushing him away—out of my way—as though lying to him could keep him safe. I'm no better than Mom, or Oliver. I did to Griffin exactly what they do to me.

And it's up to me to make it right.

I give the edge of the counter one last squeeze, feeling the balance return to my wobbly knees. Then I push past Oliver, gaze fixed on the backpack.

"Finley?"

I zone him out, his voice melting together with Malt's barks in my mind. I can't listen to his lecture right now. I can't listen to him list all the ways this is my fault, all the ways I'm not cut out for this adventure, all the ways I've failed him and Griffin and all of Stone Creek.

Right now, it needs to just be me. Just me, World's Greatest Female Adventurer One Hundred One, off to prove herself on her final mission.

Because if I fail this time, there's no coming back.

I sling the backpack over my shoulder, its weight reassuring against my back. I tighten the straps, imagining I'm carrying a precious antidote to save Griffin's life from the shadow man.

"Hey, wait!"

A hand grasped hard around my forearm. Oliver spins me around to face him.

"What are you doing?" he shouts, eyes wide and flashing. "Are you seriously about to go confront this guy alone? In the woods?"

I wriggle in his grip, but his hand just tightens. "What else am I supposed to do? We can't exactly call the police—not after how they're treating Jeff. Sam and the other adults are busy helping him, and if you call Mom, she'll just—"

I swallow, and my throat feels like it's full of tiny rocks. Mom will hold on to this for the rest of my life. She'll dangle it over my head as just another reason why she can't trust me with anything, not even Griffin. Why she has to turn to Oliver. Why I'll never be enough.

I twist my arm, and Oliver's fingers slip. "I know you

don't think I can do it. I know that you've never thought I could handle any of this."

He's said it enough times: that I'm just playing make-believe like a kid, the kind that girls like Sophie outgrow. But right now I don't care what he thinks—what anyone thinks—anymore. Not when Griffin's in danger because of me.

I just need to get out of this café, into the woods. I just need to confront the shadow man by myself, once and for all, and finish what I've started. "For once . . . just leave me alone, and let me do this."

The old floorboards groan beneath my weight as I charge toward the café door. My eyes fix on its chipped-paint surface, and my heartbeat rises in my throat. As I get closer—ready to step out into the cool spring air and into the shadow man's view—I rack my mind for an adventurer to inspire the next stretch of my mission. But as I turn the pages in my mind, all I see is Griffin: looking up at me, eyes sad and hopeful as I close the door, locking him alone in the café.

The edges of the door go fuzzy, tears threatening their way back up. I walk faster, as though if I move quickly enough, I'll reach Griffin before all the bad, murky feelings catch up to me.

Just as I reach for the door, Oliver leaps in front of it, arms spread out to block its surface. I skid to a halt inches from the door. My fingers twitch by my side, stretching toward the door, but he clasps his hand on its handle, holding it shut in place.

"Oliver, I don't have time!" I shout. "Just get out of my way!"

He stands with his shoulders back, shaking his head. "I can't let you do this alone."

I clench my teeth, nostrils flaring. I'm ready to charge into him like a bull, smash him over as I fly out the door. "Every second we stand here arguing, Griffin's in more danger! I don't know what happened to Meggie, but I can't let it happen to Griffin. Not because I . . ."

Because I left him. Because I messed up. Because I made the same mistakes about him that Oliver makes about me.

"Just put being Mom's lackey on pause for one second," I plead. "Trust me to fix this. I'll get Griffin back, and you won't even have to tell her what happened, okay? But right now I don't need your supervision."

I reach for the knob, ready to peel his fingers from it like pesky strips of tape. He shifts to the right, angling his body so it blocks the handle from my view and reach.

I start to shake. With each second wasted, the walls of the room are closing in around me. The headlines scream in bold, bright letters, the words "missing" and "kidnapped" and "deadly" spinning around me like seats on a Ferris wheel. If I'm not fast enough, Griffin's name will be on these walls too. But still Oliver stands in my way, like he always does. Glaring up at him now, all I see is Mom pulling him aside before she left, whispering as though I'm too dumb to hear. All I see is Mom texting him, and calling him, and booking a flight back for him, because I've never, ever been enough.

If he doesn't let me fix this, I never will be.

"Oliver, please." I grasp at his arm, shoving him with all my might. "Just move—"

"Why don't you think I can help you?"

The whiplash of his words steals my balance. My grip slips from his arm. "What?"

I glare up at him, already forming my next retort in my mind. But Oliver's expression shifts, teeth biting into his lower lip and chin wobbling. It's nothing like the cool-eyed glare I was expecting, with his too-well-rehearsed lecture poised at the tip of his tongue.

I want to reach for the door again, give him one last shove. But for some reason, looking at him now, my muscles start trembling like loose Jell-O.

He inhales a sharp breath, his eyebrows scrunched up as though he's gathering the confidence to speak. "Look, I know I'm not as good at these adventure things as you are. All those things you did with Sophie . . . I haven't done anything like that in years. But . . ."

His words drift off, tangled and unsure. I'd never thought of myself as better at those things than Oliver—and I definitely didn't think he thought that either. We used to do them together as little kids, before he left me behind like a toy he'd outgrown. I figured it was because he thought adventures were for children, something you can't be good at, something that just makes you silly, immature.

But right now, seeing the embarrassed blush rising to his ears, I realize he may not have outgrown them because he wanted to. Oliver stopped spending time with me after Dad left, and I figured it was because Mom chose him. Because Oliver was smarter, more responsible. Better than me. But I never thought about how that must have been for him.

I've spent so much time hating him for being that person for Mom instead of me, I never thought about the pressure that must have come with it too.

He remains fixed in front of the door, though his arms fall to his sides. Now would be the perfect moment to push past him, run out into the open air, escape his judgment and his rules. But I remain fixed in place, attention locked on him, watching as his fingers tremble by his sides.

He follows my gaze and quickly curls his hands into fists, hiding the shaking. "I know I'm not as good at this stuff, but do you really trust me that little? Because this guy has been following you this entire time, and you didn't even think to tell me. It's like . . . you don't trust me at all. Like you don't think I can do anything."

My mouth opens, a thousand conflicting thoughts battling on my tongue. I figured when he found out, he added it to a list of reasons why he can't trust me. Not the other way around.

"And maybe you're right," he says in a rush. "Maybe you don't need me. But if you're going to confront this guy, and if it's to save Griffin, then please . . . let me come." He runs a hand through his hair, sending tousled strands sticking upright by his temple. "Because if I didn't, and something happened, I . . ."

Would have to report back to Mom.

Would have to take the blame.

Would have to explain why I let you do this in the first place.

That's where I usually think that sentence would go, at least. But I'm reminded of when he chased me through the woods—the first time I had a close run-in with the shadow man. When he'd found me, eyes wide and out of breath, I figured he was just trying to herd me back home like a wayward sheep. But seeing a similar look on his face now, I realize he wasn't just upset. He was scared.

For me.

In my mind, I've lumped Mom and Oliver together like they're one and the same. But Mom tries to protect me because she doesn't think I can handle things. Oliver does it because he's scared of things going wrong. Of getting hurt. It's why he avoided me at school, afraid I'd discover his secret before he was ready. It's why he pushed back on my rescue mission, afraid we'd get in trouble. That something bad could happen to us.

Something like this.

"I didn't think you'd want to come for the rest of the

adventure," I say. My voice sounds small, unfamiliar. Nothing like it does when I'm calling down to my brothers from the rooftops or calling for them to follow as I sprint far ahead, unafraid of what I'll find. "I figured you only came out into the woods to see Jason, not because you wanted to help me."

He shakes his head. "I like Jason, but I went because I didn't want anything to happen to you. I knew you wouldn't listen if I told you not to go, and after you said you were being followed . . ."

It fills me with a mix of relief and sadness to know that he came along not to keep tabs on me, but because he was worried. But now, with Griffin in the kidnapper's hands, all I've done is prove his fears right.

"I'm sorry," I blurt. "I wanted to prove to everyone that I could do something great, but all I did was make things worse."

Keeping the shadow man a secret for so long was supposed to show how brave and independent I was. That I didn't need partners like Sophie to finish my adventures. But no matter what I did on my own, it still impacted the people around me. Oliver, harboring his own guilt and insecurities. Griffin, pushed to the side and directly into harm's way.

I wasn't brave or tough by ignoring the people around me. I was just another person in Stone Creek, using Meggie's story to get what I wanted without care for how it impacted the people closest to me.

"You were just trying to protect him by having him stay here," Oliver says. He inhales steadily. "I was too."

It sends a rush of relief through my chest, knowing I'm not alone—either on the adventure, or with the blame. But watching the guilt settle on Oliver's shoulders, I know that when Mom finds out, she'll only blame Oliver. Because he's the one she asked to look after me and Griffin, as though he could be an extension of herself.

"It was both of our faults, then," I say. "So when Mom finds out, I'll make sure she knows what really happened. Okay?"

If Oliver and I are going to really, truly be partners on this adventure, that doesn't just mean him helping me finish my quests. It means I have to pay attention to what he needs too: everything I overlooked because I was too busy being jealous of exactly what was hurting him most.

"But we can't tell her yet," I say, a desperate twinge to my voice. "We have to find Griffin first."

My words falter. The task seems insurmountable now that I've come this far and messed things up so royally. Even with the shadow man's notes in my pocket and identity tucked in my bag, I feel like the least-suited person for this mission.

"Hey." Oliver grips my arms, firm and secure as though he knows I'm slipping. "You can do this. You're the only one who Jeff told the truth to. You've cleared

Devon Jeffords's name. And you're closer than anyone's been to finding out who the real kidnapper is."

Said back to me by Oliver, everything I've done so far seems realer than ever. I imagine the words lining up on page 101 of my book, followed by ellipses. It blinks, waiting for what comes next.

"We'll find Griffin," he says, low and certain. "He'll be okay. We all will. I promise."

Before I can rethink it, I reach out and wrap my arms around his middle. I squeeze as tight as I can, ignoring the sharp yelp he releases as I do.

"I'm sorry I didn't tell you the truth sooner," I say, voice muffled against his shoulder. "It wasn't that I didn't trust you. I was just scared you wouldn't want to help. That's all."

Cautiously, Oliver returns the embrace, still a bit stiff but grip as steadying as ever. "In my defense, this is all a bit crazy. But . . . you don't have to do it alone."

I close my eyes and pretend Griffin's here too: wedged between us like he was when Mom hugged us goodbye on our first day in Stone Creek.

Ever since Sophie left the Walsh-Higgins Adventure Agency, I figured that the only way to be a real adventurer was to do everything on my own. To prove my independence and that I was fully capable without her or anyone else. But even though I slowly pushed Oliver and Griffin out of my new agency—convinced they'd just hold me back, take away from my glory—I needed them too.

More important, I wanted them. And that didn't make me less brave, or independent, or worthy.

Sophie may have moved on, but that didn't mean I deserved to be left behind. That I had to change who I was because of her. Oliver and Griffin may not be the perfect adventure partners, but they're mine. And I'm not going to give up until the Walsh-Walsh-Walsh Adventure Agency has all its members back together, no matter what it takes.

I'm not sure what will be waiting for us in the woods. I'm not sure whether I'll be brave or strong enough to face it—to save Meggie, and Jeff, and Griffin, and every corner of Stone Creek that's been hurt by Richard and his plans. But right now—having Oliver beside me, finally believing in me—I know that I can at least try.

GREATEST FEMALE ADVENTURER NUMBER TWENTY-TWO:

BHAKTI SHARMA,

THE FIRST ASIAN WOMAN AND YOUNGEST PERSON TO SET A RECORD IN OPEN SWIMMING IN ANTARCTIC WATERS.

This time, I don't have a moment to think as I enter the woods. Sam could step out of the diner at any second for a smoke and spot us out of the café—and then she definitely wouldn't let us out of her sight again until Mom arrives. So without a second thought, I chase across the empty stretch of pavement leading to the woods. I cut through the trees so fast, it's like flicking channels on a television as I land into the new scene.

I know my way by now, following the diner map in my mind. Each step is familiar, but with the added context of the original scene coming together: Meggie, rushing through the woods to go meet up with her secret lover. Jeff, out on a walk after a tough day working with his dad at the auto shop. Richard Connors—aka Paul Willoughby—preparing to meet her, a more sinister plan in the works.

I feel closer to that history with each step. Closer to Meggie, the truth about what happened. It's not fair that Paul got to take her story away from her. That he disappeared her away and became a reporter, misrepresenting facts and rewriting history to suit his needs.

Meggie was just as real as him. She deserved a chance to tell her own story.

As green speeds by me on my run, Oliver close at my heels, I wonder what Sophie would think if she saw me now. If she'd think I was cut out for this, like Oliver insisted I was back at the café. If she'd be impressed at how easily I run across the wild landscape, so unlike our suburban hometown.

Maybe I'd just misunderstood her somehow, like I did Oliver. Maybe, behind her giggles about boys and her selfies with the prettier, more popular girls, she secretly wanted to be here with me too.

We're still a ways out from the tree when I spot a figure walking in the opposite direction. I skid to a halt, Oliver nearly colliding with me as he catches up.

"There he is!" As I point, leading Oliver to see, a warm surge of relief floods my chest. Finally, I'm not the only one looking for the shadow man in these woods. "But why is he going that way?"

I can't let him get away. Not with Griffin. Whether or not the original deal-slash-blackmail stands, I'm confronting the shadow man. Right. Now.

I peel off, gunning toward him. It's like zooming in on

my phone's camera, the way the scenery slips away around me and he comes closer into view, sharp and focused in the center of my vision. Meggie must have run toward him like this too. But she had no idea what he was capable of. Not like I do.

I've come prepared.

Before he's within arm's reach, I lunge. The earth vanishes from beneath my soles and we collide, my weight toppling him over into the crumbly soil below. I push myself up by my hands, still pinning him down with my legs.

Richard Connors lies, flat on his back, chest heaving with heavy breaths. Unkempt stubble lines his chin, and his black hair juts out awkwardly around his pale face. He looks transformed in a way, as though me uncovering his true identity stripped his fake one away.

The woods are quiet around us, empty expanses of trees guarding our scene. It feels good to know, for once, that I'm not being watched. That this time I'm the one in control.

"Where's Griffin?" I shout, voice booming off the rooftops. "You said you'd bring him if I met you. So, where is he?"

Behind me, Oliver catches up, heavy breaths audible as he speaks. "If you've hurt him, I swear—"

"He's n-not with me!" Richard—Paul—stammers. His arms rest, spread out on either side of him, but he makes no move to shove me off him.

Which is strange. Because, admittedly, my tackle needs some finesse (it is my first time body-slamming a kidnapper, after all). But he just lies there, arms up by his head as though he's experiencing a horizontal arrest.

Oliver hovers over me. "What do you mean he's not with you? Where is he?"

A damp sweat trickles down my neck. Griffin was supposed to be here. I was supposed to see him, know he was safe. Know I could still save him.

"Is he with Meggie?" I ask, voice shakier than I'd like it to sound.

Paul's eyes go soft. For some reason, it makes me more scared than any answer could have. "He's with my brother," he says, "and if you'll let me sit up, I'll explain everything."

I don't budge. "What do you mean, with your brother?" I remember him mentioning his brother when we visited the Riley residence, but I never suspected he had an accomplice—meaning two people we needed to face to save Griffin. "And how do I know you won't run off the second I let you up?"

"Because I want to get him back too," he blurts, an edge of desperation to his voice. "All of this has gone too far, and I want to bring an end to it before anyone else gets hurt."

None of this was what I expected to hear during my climactic confrontation with the kidnapper. My head's spinning, trying to catch up to what he's saying. I glance up at Oliver, debating my next move.

He blows a long breath out his nose. "She'll let you up. But if you're lying, you'll have both of us to answer to."

Paul cringes as though imagining what that impact would be like. Satisfied, I take Oliver's hand and pull myself up onto my unsteady feet.

Paul sits up slowly, brushing dirt from his jeans as he stands. But he doesn't make a run for it, which I'm taking as a win for now.

"We know who you are," I start.

"Obviously," Oliver interjects.

"And I know your real name is Paul," I say, crossing my arms triumphantly. "And that you used to date Meggie."

His eyes go wide at that last part. I smile, glad that there was at least one thing I was able to keep from his watchful gaze.

He shakes his head. "I never dated Meggie."

I clench my jaw. "I don't have time for any more lies! Not when Griffin—" I stop, not wanting to show him my fear. I can't let him have the upper hand—not now, not ever. "I found your initials with hers in the tree. And you played me the voice mail she left you. I know that she was cheating on Devon Jeffords with you, and that it's probably why you kidnapped her. So she couldn't leave you. So no one else could have her."

Not even her family. Not even Meggie herself.

Paul holds his hands up by his head, just like he did when lying on the ground. "She didn't put our initials in the tree. I did." My crossed arms slip a bit. I can feel myself losing my footing in this moment, bit by bit. "And that has nothing to do with what happened to her. It was just something stupid I did back in high school, because I . . ."

He gets that same pink-cheeked mushy look that Oliver got when he opened up about Jason. My stomach does an uncomfortable somersault as realization settles over me. "You weren't dating her, but you had a secret crush on her?"

"It was a long time ago," he says, voice half-defensive, half-wistful. It's a weird sound that makes him seem very, very old, and makes me feel very, very young. "My father got a job managing the Rileys' general store, so we lived here for about five years, starting with my senior year of high school. From my very first year in Stone Creek, I loved Meggie. I loved how carefree she was. How brave she was. That she was determined to do everything her own way, no matter what the world—or her family—told her. And despite all that, she was kind. And you don't take that for granted in a small town like Stone Creek."

I imagine the Meggie he's describing, another tiny piece of a larger puzzle. One I can snap into place with the things I've read in the newspaper, the things I've heard from Jeff and Mr. Riley and the other locals.

"Even after we graduated and I outgrew things like initials in a tree"—he laughs roughly at the last part, though there's a fond edge to his words—"I would have done anything to get her to like me back, or even consider it. That's why I helped her run away."

Oliver and I exchange a glance. That was not what I was expecting—even though I'd fantasized about it, that she was someone who sneaked off to go on wild adventures, just like I want to. But with all the conflicting theories about her runaway note, I'd almost forgotten that this was a true possibility.

"That means she's still out there," I murmur, mostly to myself. "But if all you did was help her run away, why are you threatening us?" My lower lip quivers as I ask, "Why did you take Griffin?"

He didn't want to run away. He just wanted to be with me, with Oliver. To be included in our family.

Griffin is the last person who would ever run away. And once I get him back, I'll make sure he never feels like he has to.

Paul's face sinks. The lines left by age deepen their creases, and it's as though, in a blink, the years between his love for Meggie and this confession now piled on all at once.

"Things . . . didn't go as planned."

The woods go silent, the crickets and birds holding their breaths, waiting with me for what comes next. My hands clench and unclench by my sides.

"The runaway note was real," he says. His words are slow and uncertain, and I can tell how unfamiliar they are on his lips—that he hasn't spoken them in years, perhaps ever. It makes my chest swell with pride to think that I, Finley Walsh, brought him to this unprecedented moment. But it also fills me with dread for whatever deep, dark secret comes next. "She was going to meet me in the woods, by my tree."

The one with the initials. I imagine a young Paul—torn from the pages of the yearbook—waiting beneath its thick branches. Imagine Meggie meeting him there, oblivious to their names carved into the bark far above.

"We didn't have much time. And she was running late as it was. She had had a fight with Devon, her boyfriend at the time." My heart clenches, thinking of everyone who blamed Jason's dad for her disappearance. "And then she ran into your cousin, Jeff, on her way to meet me. We had to get her out of Stone Creek before her parents got back from this charity event they were holding downtown. So when she left me that voice mail saying she was late, well . . . it made me a bit nervous."

He says that part like it's the confession. And maybe it is: maybe that fear accounts for whatever scary, awful thing he's about to say next. I imagine a young, awkward Paul waiting for larger-than-life Meggie, nerves piling up on top of nerves until the pressure got to be too much. Until everything around him was so much bigger and better that he fell apart in their shadows.

I know that feeling. But I keep my mouth clamped shut, nodding silently for him to continue.

"We started to rush after that." His eyes fix on the ground, locked on a loose leaf by my sneaker. Acid rises in my throat as I realize I'm on the verge of the truth about

Meggie—about all of Stone Creek. "It was dark at that point, and we knew we were running late—real late. The flashlight on her phone wasn't working, so Meggie kept taking photos so the flash would go off, just so we could see. That's how late we were."

"The photos," I murmur, mostly to myself. Paul was the man in the photos, but he wasn't leading Meggie through the dark. He was the one being led. And each time she snapped that camera, light illuminating the woods, they felt time closing in on them, pushing them further from their endgame.

"My brother agreed to help us get out of Stone Creek. He picked us up, but we were worried we would get caught. That we were cutting it too close."

I remember Mr. Jeffords saying he heard two people on the phone that night. That he wasn't surprised Meggie was with someone else, that she'd begun spending time with some of the newer people in town. The pieces click together in my mind, though too late.

Paul presses his fingers to his temples. I imagine the memory inside him, flickering like a dull flame, threatening to fall to smoke. Wanting to fall to smoke, to lose its form, to be anything but what it is. Anything but the truth.

With that, I know what he's going to say before he says it. He says the words like he's reading from my mind instead of his.

"I kept telling Mark to go faster, faster. And Meggie

was so rushed too, she never put her seat belt on. She kept leaning forward to the front seat so she was between us, watching the speedometer, yelling with me to go faster, faster, before her dad or Devon found the note and caught up to us."

He falls silent, as though that's it. As though he doesn't need to say anything more.

But I need to hear this. After all this time—after all my dreams about her, all my hopes for her—I need to hear it.

"Meggie, she . . ." I swallow and it feels like my throat is full of needles. "She's dead?"

His hands cave in from his temples, fingers cupped over his eyes. "We should have come clean then. But the Rileys—they're not like us. They're rich, and powerful. You've seen it—how they run this town! How they got everyone searching for Meggie like it was their lives that depended on it."

His hands drop from his face, streams of tears exposed on his hollow cheeks. "She dropped her phone in the woods, but all the messages I'd sent her, all our calls—she'd erased them as they came in. It made it easier to hide, but . . . it made it harder to think I could convince anyone of the truth."

His voice changes, gaining volume like he needs us to hear, to understand. Like he's telling this to himself, too, as he probably has a thousand times over the years, recited like a poem. "There was no way anyone would believe me. They'd just want someone to blame and . . . and they wouldn't be wrong to blame me, or Mark. I was only twenty-three. I didn't want to spend the rest of my life in prison for something I never meant to do. We only had seconds to decide what we should do. And even though the car's hood was dented and the windshield was shattered, the engine still started, so"—the confident tone lapses for a moment, his voice wavering—"we followed the back roads out of Stone Creek, down to some woods at the base of a mountain, and . . ."

Paul pauses, swallows, but doesn't finish the sentence. But I can still see its ending clearly: the great Meggie Riley buried in an unmarked grave, surrounded by a vast wilderness she never had the chance to explore. "We didn't tell anyone," he continues. "I moved away shortly after. A lot of people did around then—Stone Creek was changing, and as much as tourists loved the new version of Meggie's story, the families who moved here for stories of treasure and business success weren't as keen to stay. Without much of anyone noticing, I changed my name, started over. And we made sure no one ever, ever found out."

His hands fall to his sides, a silent *That's that*. And it's all laid out in front of me, the full story, its ugly colors gleaming before me in the evening light.

Hearing it, I feel Meggie slipping from me. Feel the daring runaway that guided me through these woods rise from my body. Feel my dreams of meeting her, of rescuing her, of becoming the hero of Stone Creek fading like old news clippings.

Suddenly, it's just me without her. Me, Finley Walsh, the last standing female adventurer in Stone Creek. I was too late to save her. Too late to give her a second chance. Too late to rewrite her legacy.

I shake my head, ponytail bobbing. "That's not fair."

Oliver places a hand on my shoulder. "Finley—"

I shrug him off. "No!" I shout. My voice feels big, powerful, as though it could send the branches trembling overhead. I let it fill the woods, let it ring across the landscape where Meggie was last seen, where she was last real before Paul and Mark and all the years in between stole her away. "That's not fair that you got to just lie about that for all these years! That you took her away from her friends, and family."

People who actually wanted her. Who wanted to keep her. Who, given the chance, wouldn't have cared if she was different from them. People who would have wanted her for all she was rather than not have her at all.

The kind of friends and family I want, more than anything.

"She wasn't just some idea of a person, someone you could try on for a day before deciding it wasn't a fit," I say, taking a step toward him. "She was a real, whole human being. And she deserved better."

Better than to be left behind, as though she'd never existed. Better than for one person to cast her aside, to determine her fate through theirs.

Tears bud at the back of my eyes because I know that

feeling, what it's like to wake up one day and realize you're not wanted anymore.

Oliver places his hand back on my shoulder, gentler this time. I let him tug me back a step, away from Paul. I see the damp shimmer on Paul's cheeks, then realize I'm crying too, silent tears leaking from my eyes.

It's not just Meggie. It's him, too. A young man that, in his fear, made a choice that changed the rest of history. A choice that led to Jeff staying in Stone Creek, and his parents leaving. A choice that led to the Rileys spending their fortune on billboards, and flyers, and giant rewards in the hopes of finding their daughter. A choice that tarred Devon Jeffords's reputation to the point his son was afraid to try at anything, or risk having it all dredged back up again.

Losing Meggie scares me. But Paul's fate does too. Because as much as I want to imagine I'm more like her than him, I'm not as great as the women in my book. And with one wrong move, I could change history too.

I run my palm across my cheek, shooing away the tears. "What does your brother want with Griffin? Because I won't let—" My voice breaks. Oliver's grip tightens, fingers pinching my shoulder. "I can't let something like this happen to him."

Paul swallows, Adam's apple bobbing in his throat. "I didn't lie about why I came back to Stone Creek. I was here to report on the twenty-year anniversary—but the reason I took on the story was to get up-to-date on any leads. Make sure that no one was on my trail."

His eyes settle on me. I can't help but squirm.

"I wanted to leave well enough alone," he says, as though anything about Stone Creek is well enough since Meggie died. "But my brother had a different idea."

The tears dry, leaving sticky trails on my cheeks. At the mention of his brother's plans, my muscles firm up again and I stand, posture upright, in place. If his brother has Griffin, then that's all that matters now.

Meggie may be gone, but my mission isn't over. My adventure doesn't need to be about glory, or making the books. If I get Griffin back, that's more than enough.

"He wanted to take it a step further," Paul explains. "He figured: Why stop here, when we could use what we know to get the Rileys' reward?"

Oliver's jaw drops. "You're after the reward for the girl whose death you've covered up?"

"I'm not," Paul says, shaking his hands in front of his face, "but I couldn't talk Mark out of it. He feels like this whole thing has set us up for failure. That starting over, scared of being caught, we never stood a chance at becoming anything. So, he went after the reward money."

When we spoke at the Riley residence, I thought Richard was lucky to have a brother who encouraged him to write a story that was out of his comfort zone. To come to Stone Creek and talk to the Rileys, even if it scared him. Now it's like seeing the memory through a tinted film: different colors highlighted, and others dimmed to dark. Mark wasn't cheering Paul on or supporting his career. He was pushing him back to the scene of their crime, mapping out a way to both cover their trail and claim the reward.

Oliver's still bristling beside me, but in my mind, the evidence is stacking up, coming together in a neat little pile. "Your brother is the shadow man," I say. "He's the one who dropped the note about Jeff, and who gave Griffin the number for me to call before playing the voice mail."

Jason and Sam said Richard—Paul—was at the diner at the same time the shadow man dropped the note for me in the woods. And I'd just spoken with him when Griffin reappeared, saying a man by the trash had handed him an untitled business card. Both those times, it hadn't been Paul reaching out to me. It had been his brother, Mark.

Oliver's nostrils flare. "So your brother's the one who kidnapped Griffin? Who's been stalking my sister?"

"I want this to end as much as you," Paul insists. "I came out here to help find him and put a stop to this, before anyone else gets hurt."

And by that, he means Griffin. And Jeff, the person his brother's determined to frame for a crime that never occurred.

"I never wanted Meggie to get hurt, or for my brother to take things this far to keep our secret." Paul's eyes are wide, pleading. "I never wanted any of this to happen. Any of it."

The sentence hangs there, suspended in the air with the spring mist and the scent of fallen pinecones. I imagine, for a moment, that Paul's wish was heard by the woods, that a gentle spell is being cast around us, setting the clock back to that night. Instead of hiding her body, Paul and his brother come forward, tell the truth. Spare Stone Creek and its residents years of wondering, of speculation and pain. Or perhaps the spell reaches further: back to the moment Meggie trekked out into the woods, off to meet Paul. Or further: when she picked up the pen, ready to write her note to her father. Instead, she drops the paper and ink and leaps up from her table. Instead, she rushes downtown to meet them outside the event. Instead, she tells them right there—shrill and loud and confident so all of Stone Creek hears—that she doesn't want to take over the business, that's she going to go on adventures like she always wanted, like she was always supposed to do.

The clock sets back, and Meggie tells the truth. I tell the truth—tell Mom how I feel when she turns to Oliver and not me. How I feel when she tells me not to worry as though my own world is too much for me to bear and she needs to protect me from it. From me. The clock sets back and I never had to save Meggie to get her attention, or Oliver's, or anyone else's.

I pretend, for a moment, that all I had to do was ask. All I had to do was speak when everyone else was silent. When telling the truth hurt. As if there are smaller, yet scarier ways to be a hero. To be brave.

"We'll confront him. Together," Paul says, like a promise. "We're going to set this right."

I exchange a glance with Oliver. Then I nod. Because

maybe it's not too late to set this right—the lies that have tarnished Stone Creek for nearly two decades. And if we can fix this, maybe it's not too late for me, either. Maybe—once this is over—I can tell my truths too.

GREATEST FEMALE ADVENTURER NUMBER TWENTY-THREE:

EDITH "JACKIE" RONNE,

KNOWN AS "ANTARCTICA'S FIRST LADY," WHO WAS THE FIRST WOMAN TO SET FOOT ON THE CONTINENT DURING A WINTER EXPEDITION.

Paul leads us through the woods, and I'm fully aware this could be a trap. But if there's even the smallest chance that he's bringing us to Griffin, I have to follow. Oliver walks a few steps ahead of me, tight on Paul's trail, and I'm relieved again that I don't have to face this alone.

Whatever comes next—whatever new history we create in these woods—it won't bring me the glory that saving Meggie would have. But everything I've done has led up to this point. Every adventure I invented to have fun with Sophie. Every lead I've pursued since arriving in Stone Creek. Every tree I've climbed, every suspect I've confronted, every close call I've survived. It's all prepared me for this, so I can be the one to save Griffin.

Paul stops abruptly, then rushes forward at double speed. "Mark!"

Oliver and I rush behind him. Up ahead, the tree—Paul's tree, my tree—comes into view. And with it, Mark and Griffin.

Mark—the real shadow man—stands a few feet from the tree. Griffin sits with his back against its trunk, its thick roots and bramble erupting from the earth around his bound legs. His arms are fastened behind his back, and a slap of duct tape covers his mouth.

But he's here, in one piece. Here, waiting for me.

I lunge forward, arms pumping by my sides as I race toward him.

Oliver grasps my elbow, tugging me to a halt. Dirt puffs up in tiny clouds around my sneakers as I regain my balance. He pulls me back to his side.

"We need to be smart about this," he says, eyes fixed on the brothers.

Every atom in my body is buzzing, straining toward Griffin. But, for once, I join Oliver on the side of caution. Right now the stakes are too high for me to make a mistake.

I inhale a steadying breath and take in the scene around me. Griffin, squirming where he sits with eyes fixed on me and Oliver. Paul, a few yards ahead, taking steady steps toward Mark. And then Mark, standing in full view for the first time since our paths first crossed here in these woods.

Somehow, it's more unsettling to see him like this

rather than as a blur at the edge of my vision, a silhouette at the edge of the woods. The shadow man felt like something mystical, but seeing Mark—a square-faced man with bushy brown hair, wearing dirt-stained denim and a moth-munched flannel—makes him almost too real.

His eyes lock on me, swelling with recognition.

"Finley," he says, his voice like Paul's, but somehow also distinctly his: the shadow man's. "You came. And I see you brought what I asked for."

Instinctively, I clasp my hands around the straps of my bag, where the only evidence I have to clear Jeff's name is tucked safely inside.

Mark moves toward me, hand extended expectantly before him. Oliver steps between us, arm extended by his side. "You're not getting anything until you untie our brother."

"Mark, come on," Paul calls. "You have to know this has gone too far. Please, just let the kid go and we can all forget about this."

My nose crinkles. I'm not sure I'll ever forget about this, but right now, I'm not about to object. Whatever it takes to get Griffin back, I'm here for it.

But Mark's attention remains fixed on me and my bag. "This is why we came back, Paul. To find the evidence and make sure no one else ever did. I've already scraped off that stupid mark you forgot you left in that tree. Now I just need the rest of it."

He continues to approach, the only sounds in the woods the crinkle of leaves beneath his boots. Oliver steps back, pushing me with him.

"If any of this gets out, it's over for us. The Rileys will make sure of it." He swallows. A vein in his neck twitches. "And I'm not letting that happen. Not because of one stupid mistake, and not after all the years I've spent paying for it."

I lean forward, pressing against Oliver's arm. "The years you've been paying for it? You're the one who actually did it. Not Jeff, or Devon Jeffords, or anyone else who's been suffering because of your lies for all these years!"

Oliver shoves me back. "Finley, shh."

But I agreed to be cautious, not quiet. "You don't know how the Rileys will react. You've never known! You just went ahead and made that choice for them."

Beneath the tree, Griffin shifts against his binds. Every second he spends there, scared and alone, my stomach sinks further and further into the ground.

"So forget about the reward money," I plead, "or framing someone else. Just tell the truth and give them the chance to make it right!"

"Finley," Oliver whispers again, low and serious. His eyes dart to the Willoughby brothers. Catching my breath, I realize how Paul positions himself in front of Mark, forcing him to a halt. They're caught there, in the center of our clearing, their focus only on each other.

I nod, slowly understanding. If Paul is here to confront

Mark, we don't have to. We can focus on Griffin and leave the rest to him.

The path between us and Griffin is clear. But if I make sudden movements, Mark may be distracted long enough to come after me. So I edge slowly to the right, taking cautious moves around and forward, Griffin in my peripheral vision.

I wait to take steps until Paul speaks, aligning the crunch of earth beneath my shoes with the sound of his voice. "What happened to Meggie was a mistake. But this?" Paul gestures wildly around the scene. "There's no coming back from this."

Mark scoffs, and the sound vibrates in my chest. "It doesn't make a difference anymore, Paul. So long as they're still looking for someone to blame, there's a chance they'll find us."

Griffin's eyes remain locked on me, wide and desperate. I take another cautious step in his direction, Oliver tight by my side. I imagine I'm the great Artemisia, using my wits to distract my enemies in order to complete my mission.

Paul shrugs, shoulders sloped with exhaustion. "Then let them. I can't keep this up anymore. I never meant for Meggie to get hurt, and I don't want to keep lying like what happened was my fault." His voice breaks like a twig beneath my shoe. "I just want this to be over."

I step past a patch of bramble and over a mossy rock. The giant tree's roots are steps away, their winding limbs leading to Griffin.

"That doesn't matter," Mark sneers, "because I'm not going to spend the rest of my life in prison for something you made me do. And you don't get to make that choice. Not by yourself."

Paul straightens. "Yes, I do. And I'm not going to let someone else take the blame for what we did. Whether or not you get the evidence these kids have on you, I'm going forward. I'll tell the truth. So you have to let them go."

Something shifts in the air as he says it, and I know, instinctively, that the scene is about to break. Mark's face scrunches, red heat blotching his cheeks. Then he lunges at Paul, just like I did earlier, but with what looks like three times as much force. They stumble to the ground, wrapped in a struggle just about a yard from where I stand.

Oliver gives me a push. "Now!"

It's like a gun going off before a race. I soar over the roots, the sticks, and the rocks, straight toward Griffin. My shoelace snags on the edge of a bush and I tumble, knees scraping against the dirt. Pebbles and soil sting the scratches on my shin, but I edge forward, arms outreached so my hands clasp around Griffin's shoulders.

"I'm here," I say, breathless. "I'm here."

I pick at the edge of the duct tape and yank it from his mouth. He lets out a high-pitched yelp as it tears, leaving a pink mark in its wake. Then he looks up at me, eyes bloodshot and watery.

"Finley," he gasps, voice coarse, "it's the trash man! The trash man is the killer."

I cup my hands on either side of his face, fingers brushing dirt from his short blond hair. Right now I can't imagine ever thinking of him as a distraction, or an annoyance, or someone who could get in the way of my adventures. Right now—even with scraped-up skin and dirt-crusted knees and musty breath—I never want to let him out of my sight ever again.

"Your trash man, my shadow man. He's not a killer"—*yet*, I think, hearing the sounds of struggle behind me—"but he's definitely guilty." I reach behind Griffin and tug at the tape by his wrists. "And we're going to get you far, far away from him. Okay?"

Griffin bites his lower lip and nods.

Oliver kneels in front of Griffin. He grasps at the bindings on his ankles, fingers searching for a breaking point. "Hey, buddy. Are you okay? Did they hurt you?"

His last question is interrupted by a howl of pain. I jump, casting an anxious glance over my shoulder. A few yards off, Paul continues to struggle with his brother, buying us precious time. But though I missed what happened, I can see a trickle of dark-red blood streaming down Paul's chin.

I pick at the edge of the tape, the sticky adhesive slowly peeling off. But there's too much of it, one layer over another so his wrists are cupped in a sticky blob.

"It's not coming off," I murmur. At this rate, Paul will be overpowered before I get Griffin out of here. And I can't let that happen—not after we've come this far. I survey the ground, searching for something to break it with.

My eyes catch a pointed rock, and I snag it from its spot beneath a root.

Griffin squirms against the binds. I reach behind him and begin jabbing the sharp edge of the rock against the tape, steadily poking it thin enough to rip.

"You guys gave me the easy part of the mission, and I still messed it up," he says. His lower lip trembles, and kneeling so close, I can feel how his body shakes as he fights back tears. "If I get out of this—"

Oliver shoots him a serious stare. "We'll get you out."

"Then I don't blame you if you kick me out of the adventure agency. You can replace me with Malt, because at least he didn't get taken for ransom. Because if Uncle Cousin Jeff ends up in jail forever, it's my fault."

I open my mouth to object just as a resounding thud echoes through the woods. From the corner of my eye, I see a form slump to the ground, unconscious.

The tape continues to peel back beneath the rock's pressure. I keep pushing and tugging, pretending in my mind that it's Mark who's fallen. Though somehow, without looking, I know it's not.

"Great adventurers are successful under even the worst time crunch," I think aloud. It doesn't matter if my brothers hear me and think I'm dorky for pretending to be like the girls in a book. Right now I need all the inspiration I can get, unfiltered and unashamed.

The tape breaks free, exposing Griffin's wrists. Heavy

indents mar his skin, along with straggly strips of adhesive. But his body seems to sigh with relief as his arms fall naturally to his sides, no longer bound behind him. He rubs the angry skin with his palms, circulation steadily returning to his arms.

"Glad to see you've got your brother back."

Mark bounds toward us, fists hanging by his sides. Blood marks his knuckles, and his face is twisted with rage and something else indefinable, deep and wounded by the years of lies and fear and hiding.

Right now, staggering toward us with that dark, threatening look in his eyes, he's exactly how I pictured Meggie's murderer to be. But that's not who he is—or who Paul is either. Still, the lies kept twisting in around them until they were suffocated, until they exploded. Which is somehow scarier than even the wickedest of villains could be.

Because a heroic adventurer like me could never hurt anyone—not on purpose, at least. But the things that have happened with Jeff, and Oliver, and Griffin, and everyone else—all the people who I've misunderstood, or hid myself from, or pushed aside—all those things, if left to fester too long, could make me no different from Mark.

"Now you'll need to finish your half of the deal," he says, gesturing toward my bag. "Hand over whatever you have on me and my brother."

I tighten my hand on the rock, tucking it close to my side. "You can still come clean. You can still make this right."

He shakes his head, takes another step forward. As the inches close between us, the air seems to shift, pulled thinner and thinner around my lips.

"I've spent my whole life hiding from the Rileys," he says. "I won't let you ruin this for me now."

He lunges, arms grasping the straps of my bag. They pull from my shoulders and I bend my arms, the crooks of my elbows the only thing keeping the bag from sliding right off me and into his grasp. The force of his pull drags me across the ground, gravel scraping the skin of my knees.

The rock slips from my hand as I grip the straps to keep him from sliding the bag off me. The photo of the initials he's since scratched off the tree, the matching name in the yearbook, the secret notes left behind: it's not much, but it's all I have to prove the truth. To save Jeff, and my family.

I grit my teeth, sneakers skidding against the ground. My palms burn against the bag's scratchy fabric. Mark gives another hard tug, shouting something about the Rileys and what's owed to him. I feel like a rag doll in his grip, wiggling helplessly against his pull. My arms ache as I resist, and his hard knuckles knock against my shoulders with each pull.

He gives me a violent shake, and my arms feel like thin branches ready to snap off their trunk. I let out a yelp of pain, and the bag slips from my grip.

This is it. He's going to take the bag. He's going to take away the only thing standing between Jeff and a life in prison for a crime he didn't commit.

And it's going to be my fault.

"Get away from her!"

A resounding thud echoes through the woods, and the pressure lifts from my back. Around me, the woods return to focus. I twist around to see Mark toppled onto the ground, running a hand over his shoulder. Oliver stands behind him, the rock I dropped now in his hands.

The color of his cheeks matches the wide whites of his eyes. "Finley, are you okay? Did he hurt you?"

"Those are two different questions," I say, voice ragged and scratchy. "But I'll be fine."

Already, Mark is recovering from the shock of the rock's impact. We don't have much time. We need to run, now—but as I go to call to Griffin, I see him with his knees tight to his chest, struggling with the remaining tape on his ankles.

"I-I'm sorry," he stammers. "It's not coming off."

I snatch another rock and crawl toward him. "It's okay, it's okay," I say, hoping to convince us both. "I've got it."

There's movement behind me. I wish I could fight back against Mark in a one-girl duel as if I'm pirate captain Shi Xianggu, but I keep my focus on Griffin, trusting that Oliver will fend him off long enough for me to rip his binds.

Griffin's gaze darts back and forth between me and the scene over my shoulder. "Ollie—"

"He'll be okay," I say, scraping at the tape. "He's scrappier than he looks."

Griffin's lower lip puckers. "But you're always saying that you're better at this adventure stuff than he is, so—"

"I am better," I assert, "but that doesn't mean Oliver's

bad at it. And I was wrong to ever tell you that he was."

I jab at the tape, fast, so the edge of the rock scrapes Griffin's skin. He swallows back a yelp.

"And you're not bad at it either," I say.

With my head bent down, I pick the rock at the last of the duct tape. Griffin tugs at the edges, helping to peel it free. My pulse beats in my temples, like a clock counting down the seconds we have left. Its rhythmic thumping dulls the scene behind me. Right now there's nothing in the world but this tape, stripped apart between my jittery fingers.

Then, with a final pull, the tape falls to expose bright-red skin beneath. Griffin's ankles drift apart and he stares at them with big eyes, like he's a baby deer about to learn to walk.

"All right, Griff," I say, helping him to his feet. "We have to run—"

A strangled cry rings out through the woods. I drop my hands from Griffin and turn to see Oliver bent over, grasping an angry wound in his shin. He's splayed out with the pointed rock rolled from his grip.

"Oliver!"

He grits his teeth against the pain, unresponsive to my call. I glare at Mark, something hot and angry boiling in my gut. "What did you—"

"He's the one who came running at me with a weapon," Mark snarls, standing a few feet back from Oliver. He holds his hands up like Paul did before, as though shaking off any guilt, or responsibility. "No one has to get hurt. You're the ones making this messy."

My stomach lurches. It makes me wonder how far he's distanced himself from what happened to Meggie. How much he blames on her—or on her parents, her boyfriend, this town. On Paul, or anyone beside himself.

"Just hand over the bag," he says, taking a step toward me, "and we can end this."

Seeing Oliver curled up on the ground—jaw clenched as he bites back the pain—I hate myself for ever pursuing this mission. For thinking I was strong enough, or brave enough, to chase away the dark, scary things that haunt Stone Creek. I want to tear off my backpack and toss it to Mark, surrendering the little bit of evidence I have to prove Jeff's innocence. I want to raise my white flag and tear myself out of the revised edition of *100 of the World's Greatest Female Adventurers* in my mind, page 101 crumpled in my palm.

But even though Oliver never wanted to go on this mission, scared we'd get hurt, he did it anyway. For Griffin's sake, and for mine. His eyes meet mine, bleary, as he squints through the pain. I'm reminded of everything he said back at the café, after we realized Griffin was missing. All the people whose histories have been warped by Mark and Paul's stories—all the people whose truths I'm fighting to bring to light.

I don't have to be great, or perfect, or legendary, like the girls in the books. I don't have to earn anyone's approval—not Mom, Sophie's, or anyone else's. But I want to be someone I'm proud of. Someone who—even when the universe turns against her, doesn't trust her, doesn't want her anymore—refuses to step down, or fade into the white noise.

Running is out of the question now, and I know from my first trip in the woods that Stone Creek's spotty-at-best phone service is nonexistent in these woods. Which means that whatever we need to do to get out of this situation, it's going to take longer than the two seconds I have before Mark lunges at me again.

I scan the space and imagine all my adventures with Sophie and all my adventures with Oliver and Griffin make up the pages of a new, fresh Greatest Adventurers book, dedicated just to me. I flip through all the hijinks I pulled off, every fence or tree I've climbed, all the times I eavesdropped for intel and sneaked into places unexplored.

All those things—all those silly games Sophie outgrew, that Mom saw as proof that I was too young, too childish, too immature—all those things prepared me for this moment. And now no one is better suited for it than me.

The pile of duct tape rests by Griffin's feet. By the tree's fat roots. By the patch of bramble.

My plan forms in my mind at the same time it rolls off my tongue. "Griffin, pass me the old tape! Oliver—"

He's one step ahead—literally. As Mark moves forward, fists clenched by his sides and eyes set on me, Oliver pushes himself up from the ground, a strained hiss escaping his lips. His legs wobble beneath him, and pale sweat breaks across his forehead. But he's able to stand long enough to thrust his body into Mark, sending him off-balance and tumbling against the roots.

I have nothing more than seconds to work with. But it will have to be enough.

I rush to the bottom of the tree and dig my fingers into the patch of bramble at its base. Small thorns prick my skin as I tug, twigs snapping against my pull. Their limbs snap free, the sound like corn popping. Tiny dots of blood speck my fingers as I tug, tug, tug, imagining I'm pulling apart a clump of rope.

Griffin hovers beside me, the used clump of tape in his hands. "What do I do with it?"

"Hold on to it," I say, rising with my armful of tangled bramble, "and stick as much on his limbs as you can when I say when."

The first semblance of a smile buds at the corner of his lips. "A reverse kidnapping!"

Not exactly my point, but I'm not about to argue with Griffin right now. I rush to where Oliver struggles to pin Mark against the ground. The bramble and tape won't hold him for good, but it will be enough to hold Mark in place until I can get somewhere—climb somewhere—to make a call for help.

Oliver presses his weight down against Mark as I work on his hands, wrapping the bramble around his wrist as tight as I can before it snaps. Mark struggles, limbs lashing.

My muscles strain as I press his wrists together, ignoring his threats and shouts.

I call to Griffin and he passes tape, which I slap in its crumpled clumps to clamp the bramble in place. Within moments, Mark is tied in the hodgepodge of materials, limbs straining against their hold and threatening to break through at any moment.

"You can't do this to me!" he snarls, writhing against the restraints. "I never meant to hurt that girl—I never wanted any of this. So just let me go, and let me be!"

He lurches in violent motions, the binds struggling to keep hold of him. I leap back, pulling Griffin with me.

"We have to get up," I say in a rush. "I got service when I first climbed the tree. We can call for help, if we're fast."

I glance at Oliver's hands, pressed against the cut on his shin. He looks up at me, eyebrows furrowed and serious. "I'll be fine," he says, "so take Griffin and go. I'll hold him back if he gets out of this."

A lump settles in my throat. It's not easy for an adventurer like me to let someone else take over such a dangerous part of a mission. Especially when it means turning my back and blindly trusting that my partner won't leave. That they won't vanish, even though I know they can. That at any moment, anyone in my life can make that choice. Like Dad or Sophie did.

It takes a whole lot more bravery than a one-on-one duel with Mark would have. But I nod and, tugging Griffin behind me, rush to the trunk of the tree, ready to climb.

I prop my heel against the lowest branch, following the path I did my first afternoon in Stone Creek.

The first time I climbed this tree, I envisioned Meggie with me: a girl starved for adventure, determined to claw her way out of the small town and her family's expectations. That version of Meggie ended up being realer than I imagined—but it was Paul's footsteps I'd actually followed up this tree. The man so desperate to be seen, to be appreciated, to be loved, that he took the risk no one else was brave enough to take for Meggie, and helped her run away.

As I push up, my feet leave the earth and I rise, the shadow man and his brother vanishing behind me. For a moment it's just me and the branches, the same steps but a different path.

Something tickles at the back of my head. I glance down and see Griffin fixed at the base of the tree, staring up at me with big, uncertain eyes.

"I don't know how to climb, remember?" He balls his fists by his sides, grinds his sneaker in the dirt. "Dad never taught me, and Ollie never taught me, and when you tried to show me, you went too far ahead and I couldn't catch up."

I'm suspended in the air, one leg dangling and the other propped against a branch. The path below me looks obvious: right arm, left arm, big push with the right foot to get to the perfect spot for the left foot. The steps race through my head faster than I can speak them. So I call out, "It's okay, Griffin! It's not as scary as it looks. Just pull yourself up from the first branch, and follow me."

I press my loose foot against the trunk and hoist myself up to the next branch. Once situated, I look back down to see Griffin hasn't budged an inch. He stands there, neck craned up at me and shaking his head.

"I don't know how, Finley!" His voice is caught somewhere between a yell and a whine. "I can't do it."

A few feet to his left, a piece of bramble snaps off Mark's legs. Oliver hovers beside him, on alert and ready to pin him back down, though I know he's too weak to do it alone. We're running out of time—out of the precious moments the bramble and tape bought us, the precious moments to make our call and return to Stone Creek, the truth in our hands.

I don't have time to teach him how to climb a tree. I don't have time for him to be scared, for him to complain, for him to make mistakes.

He just needs to climb.

He just needs to be faster.

Faster, faster, faster.

Those are my first thoughts. The ones I always have when it comes to Griffin. Whether I'm back at home, wishing I could binge *Riverdale* and text Sophie rather than play soccer with him outside. Whether I'm in Stone Creek, wishing he wasn't so scared of Jeff, so I didn't have to watch my words. Wishing he wasn't dropping clues to my suspects, so I didn't have to micromanage where he was and who I let him speak to. Wishing he wouldn't notice if I hung up before Mom could talk to him, scared he'd say the wrong thing, do the wrong thing, be the wrong thing, and send her on my case.

Those are my first thoughts, even now, after everything that's happened. They kick me in the gut like an instinct, quick and easy and familiar. And this is the moment I could call down for him to run, to leave Oliver and me to handle the rest. That getting away is in his best interest, even though, secretly, I just think it's easier for him to be away.

Those are my first thoughts. But I ignore them. One limb after another, I descend from the tree until I'm close enough to leap onto solid ground, acorns crunching beneath my heels. I shrug off the backpack and hold it out for Griffin to take.

"You go ahead of me," I say. "I'll be down here in case you fall. And once you're up on that big, thick branch, you should have enough bars to call the police."

I push the bag forward, forcing it into his arms.

"That's the mission now. Okay?"

Griffin blinks up at me, eyes bloodshot and watery. "Finley, I can't—"

"You can."

I wish I could scrunch my brow to get that serious look Oliver does, or snap my words the way Mom does to call us to attention. But all I can do is look at him, lower lip trembling and eyes brimming at the edges, and hope he knows—sees—how serious I am. That despite all my instincts and fears and doubts, I know he's just as cut out for a Walsh-Walsh-Walsh adventure as I am.

"And I was wrong to ever make you think you couldn't."

Wrong to make him feel like he had to be the loudest, had to be the funniest, had to be the brashest to get my attention—to earn it, like it's something he had to work for. Wrong to push back every time he reached out, to make him smaller so I could feel bigger.

To make him feel how Sophie made me feel. How Mom does too.

Right now is the worst possible time to pause and make things right. But that's what Meggie thought too—and Paul, and Mark. That's why they pressed that accelerator. That's why they hid her, and what happened. That's why we're here now, twenty years later, replaying the same mistakes on repeat again and again.

But I won't let that happen anymore. Not when Griffin is involved.

"You're the bravest adventure partner I could have asked for," I say, hands still on the bag as I wait for his arms to raise, for him to take it in his grip. "The moment I suggested we look into all of this, you were right there, supporting me. You were ready to run into the woods and face anything that came your way. And even when you were scared because of our doubts about Jeff"—his chin wobbles, eyes dart to the ground—"you were kind to him. To Malt. And no matter what crazy idea I came up with, from garbage crawling to business card collection, you went in full force."

His arms raise and I release the bag into his hands. I

grip his shoulders hard as though I could transfer the frantic, beating thump of my heart into him.

"And when the shadow man came for you, when I left you all alone"—I inhale, my throat rattling like a loose pipe—"you faced that on your own and braved through it until we showed up."

Guilt swells in my chest like a rising wave, but I force myself to look straight into his eyes, to keep my mouth a firm line, to keep my words from breaking with sobs. No one made it into my book for giving her little brother a pep talk, but I don't care. I don't care what I'm supposed to do, or supposed to be. I don't care if I never get the glory for solving Meggie's case, if I never earn Mom's trust, if I never win back Sophie's friendship.

I only care that I don't make him feel the way I do. That he never feels how Meggie did that night she left her note and ran away, fading to nothing but a story.

"Griffin, you can do this," I say. "And whatever happens, I'll be here, at the base." I press my palm against the tree, fingers spread. "I'll be here in case you fall."

He bites his lower lip, then throws his arms around me. His fingers curl into fists against the back of my shirt, gripping me close. I let my eyes drift shut, inhale the scent of the sun and dirt caught in his hair.

It feels good to have him here, wrapped in my arms. To have him secure, safe, a thing I can wrap together in one place and hold on to like nothing bad could ever, ever happen to him.

But I have to let go. Even if it scares me. Even if I'm more scared than he is.

So I do. I let go. "I'll give you a boost, but the rest is you, Griff. You've got this, okay?"

Griffin swings the backpack onto his back, tightens the straps. Then he plants his heel against the bark—just like I did, when I didn't know he was watching—and with my hands propped against his waist, he reaches for the first branch and pushes up.

He slips from my fingers, rising one branch to another. I plant my hands against the base of the tree and watch like Sophie used to, my head back and neck bent as he soars up, up above.

"You've got this, Griffin!" I call as the shadow man wrestles against his binds, and as Oliver holds him back through his pain. As the sun sets over Stone Creek Woods and Jeff sits at the precinct and Mom soars through the clouds to claim us.

As Meggie rests somewhere far away, hidden from the world, ready to rise and reclaim her legacy.

"Just keep going!" I call. "I'm right behind you, okay? You've got this."

True to my word, I wedge my heel against the tree. Stretch my arms above my head.

Grasping a branch, I feel the ground vanish beneath my feet.

GREATEST FEMALE ADVENTURER NUMBER TWENTY-FOUR:

CINDY LEE VAN DOVER,

DEEP-SEA EXPLORER AND FIRST WOMAN TO PILOT A DEEP-DIVING SUBMERSIBLE.

Griffin almost drops my phone from where he sits on the branch, but thankfully catches it at the last minute and dials 911. I sit a few branches below and watch as Mark snaps free from his binds, his eyes planning his route up the tree. We shake the branches with as much force as we can, sending a drizzle of acorns and twigs raining over his head. It's not the glorious moment I pictured my final showdown with Meggie's kidnapper to be, but it does the trick until the officers and paramedics come rushing through the woods, finally ending the terrible scene below.

Things are a blur from there, bodies moving so fast it's like watching a scene change in a play, one set tucked away to make room for a new one. The paramedics loading Paul onto a stretcher, coaxing him back to consciousness. The cops replacing our bramble with metal handcuffs. An EMT applying pressure to Oliver's leg while Griffin and I scurry back down the tree—him doing so like he's suddenly a tree monkey.

Within minutes, we're being guided out of Stone Creek Woods. My head spins, processing everything that's happened so I can explain to the cops as succinctly as I want my entry in *100 of the World's Greatest Female Adventurers* to read. But as I cast one last look over my shoulder, hoping to catch a glimpse of the tree, I'm suddenly out of the woods, standing in the diner's parking lot, which is the fullest I've ever seen it.

I don't have a chance to digest all that's happened until I'm watching it reported on the news through the TV in Oliver's hospital room. He's wearing about four hospital gowns draped one over the other and has his bandaged leg propped up so he looks like a ballerina midstep. Griffin sits on the edge of his bed, his elbow accidentally knocking Oliver's shin each time he scoops a bite of the Jell-O he stole from Oliver's tray. I sit in a chair beside them, legs pulled up to my chest and eyes locked on the TV.

A clip caught on someone's phone plays again and again behind the news anchor's voice, showing Mark being led out of the woods by the cops. It almost makes them look like the heroes who took him down, but I'm trying not to get too hung up on who gets the glory. The people who matter know what happened out there—or will, soon, when Mom arrives and inevitably comes barreling in here demanding answers.

". . . brother, Paul Willoughby, has confessed to burying Meggie Riley's body after a fatal accident twenty years prior," the anchor is saying. "Officials are still confirming his statement and report that they may be releasing a separate, former suspect from questioning soon."

I smile, tightening my grip around my legs. Knowing Jeff will be free from this—free from Meggie, too—makes everything feel worth it.

"Thank goodness," Griffin mumbles through an overflowing mouthful of Jell-O. "Poor Malt's been stuck with Sam all night, and the diner's muffins are not as good as Jeff's."

Oliver frowns. "You better not have been feeding muffins to the dog."

A knock comes at the door. Before we can respond, Jason steps in, tired bags under his eyes but smile as bright as ever. Seeing Oliver, he stops in the doorway, eyes wide and a smirk brimming on his lips. "Whoa! Did the nurse's closet throw up on you?"

A satisfied grins tears across my cheeks. Oliver's ears go bright pink. "It's thin material, okay?"

Griffin scooches over as Jason settles onto the edge of the bed, shoulders turned toward Oliver. I drag my chair closer to him. "Tell us news of the outside world," I beg. "You've got to know more than the loop they're playing on the local channel."

"I think you know more than anyone does right

now," Jason says with a chuckle, "but my dad asked me to thank you, even though I think he's a little hurt I went through his things."

My stomach squeezes, thinking of the night Jeff caught me in his room. "I get it," I say. "But it's hard, sometimes . . . to fully trust someone without having proof you can."

I tug at a loose thread on the edge of Oliver's sheet. It was scary to hand Griffin the bag, knowing he might not make it up the tree. To turn my back on Mark and just hope Oliver could hold him back long enough for us to make a call. And right now I'm having trouble trusting me—that I'll be able to say what I need to when Mom comes. I have no proof that I can—no precedent to point to and say, *Aha, there: it's possible.* I have nothing but the blind hope that when she's the one who comes rushing through the hospital room door, I won't let myself lose my words.

"Speaking of people this town's never trusted"—Jason skillfully pivots, smile returning to his cheeks—"Mr. Phillips said that Meggie's Motel already has more bookings than it's had in months, and he's expecting the biggest surge in tourists yet!"

He taps a finger to his chin as though debating his next words. Then shrugs.

"He also said he's a little peeved you uncovered the truth, because after the current rush, people will likely lose interest in Meggie and he'll probably have to rebrand all his businesses."

I crinkle my nose. He may not be guilty, but that doesn't mean I have to like him.

"Won't matter for you," Oliver says, giving the end of Jason's sleeve a gentle tug. "You'll be out of that diner in no time, spending all your time in your fancy STEM program."

I still don't get how Jason considers school to be a reward, but I keep my mouth clamped shut when I notice the way his eyes meet my brother's. Jason nibbles at his bottom lip, eyes shifting to his lap.

"You'll probably be super busy with school," Oliver says, "so we won't have time to keep in touch."

Jason's eyes dart up quick, like he's about to object. But then he nods, slow and steady. "But maybe we'll see each other again, when you guys come back for the twenty-five-year anniversary festivities, right?"

I want to snatch the Jell-O cup from Griffin and toss it at my brother's head. I don't know much about crushes, but I'm pretty sure you don't press pause on them for five years if you're serious about getting a boyfriend.

But Oliver and Jason seem a lot calmer than I am inside. There's a sad glint in their eyes, but they're smiling, too. Maybe they're not ready to keep in touch yet—kind of like how I haven't been ready to text back Sophie.

When I first arrived in Stone Creek, I admired how the Rileys held on to Meggie's memory, dedicated their lives to celebrate hers. But sometimes, holding on too tight to something doesn't mean you get to keep the things most important to you. Sometimes it means you stay too stuck to see all the other things you can be and can love. I hope that now that Meggie's story has an ending—not one that's been invented for her, but one that is really, truly hers—the Rileys can move forward and help Stone Creek evolve into whatever it will become next, after Meggie's chapter.

I wonder, for a moment, what this realization will mean if I ever do reply to Sophie. "They only allow so many people in here at a time," Jason says, "and I don't want to hog your one visitor spot. So . . ."

Oliver swallows. "Yeah, so . . ."

The silence dangles between them. Then Jason leans down and plants the quickest, smallest, gentlest peck on Oliver's lips before making a mad dash for the door. Oliver's still blinking, shocked, by the time the hospital room door slams shut.

Griffin's jaw drops. "Ollie has a boyfrieeeend!"

Oliver's cheeks go redder than the Jell-O. "I don't—no, that wasn't—I mean—"

I cross my arms and grin, big and smug. "First crush, first kiss, first breakup. And don't forget, first time solving a twenty-year-old cold case."

Griffin nods seriously. "Yep, that too."

"Oliver Walsh is growing up." I shimmy onto the bed, stealing Jason's vacant spot. I press my hand against Oliver's forearm and tug Griffin to my side with my other. "And it's nice, being back together again like this.

For a moment there I was worried that . . ."

On the TV, the image of Mark being led from the woods plays again. I close my eyes and inhale a steadying breath.

"That I'd wrecked the Walsh-Walsh-Walsh Adventure Agency," I say. "But I don't want to lead it on my own. I think I might need you two goons after all."

Griffin drops his spoon with a plop, sending red spatters of gelatin in all directions. "Ew, Finley's being mushy!" He crinkles his nose and turns to Oliver. "You're both mushy today."

I swipe a napkin off Oliver's tray and slap Griffin's arm. "Oh, shut up. We've earned it."

The phrase sticks in my mind, just like the red Jell-O is currently sticking to the hideous abstract painting hanging over Oliver's head. Mom will be here any second now. I wonder if I've earned the ability to tell her the story as I see it, or for her to listen.

As the news anchor teases an upcoming appearance from the Rileys, the hospital room door swings open without warning. Summoned by my thoughts, Mom comes bursting inside, hair pulled into a collapsed bun and dark-gray rings under her eyes.

My stomach drops and I imagine I'm falling from the top of Paul's tree, except there's no ground beneath to break the fall. Everything that's happened—everything I've done—races through my mind. I want to apologize. I want to boast. I want to shrink up in a ball and hide beneath Oliver's bed.

Griffin leaps to his feet and pummels right into Mom's stomach, sending her staggering backward on her heels as she catches her balance. He wraps his arms around her middle, so tight the color returns to her hollowed cheeks.

"Mom, we're gonna be rich!" he sings. "Say goodbye to work trips and hotel breakfast, because we're about to cash in on the biggest reward in history!"

Mom looks over the top of his head to meet Oliver's gaze. He groans. "Griffin, we've gone over this already. There's no prize money for finding a girl that was never even kidnapped."

"She was body-napped," Griffin argues, voice muffled by Mom's coat.

Her eyes go wide at the mention of Meggie's body. I wince, remembering that Mom doesn't approve of all the scary movies I've let Griffin watch while she's away.

The way she's looking at Oliver—lips parted and wordless as she draws her thoughts together—I know that she's mentally drafting the biggest lecture of his life. If I sat back and said nothing, he'd probably take it too. As exhausting as Oliver's micromanagement can be, I know he puts too much pressure on himself, too, as though everything really is his responsibility, just because Mom said so.

But we made a promise to each other before we went to save Griffin. He held up his side of the deal and had my back during the final stretch of my mission. Now it's my turn to keep my end of the promise.

I stand up so fast, my chair topples over behind me. "It wasn't Oliver's fault!" I blurt before Mom even has the chance to speak. "All of this was my idea, and I know you told him to watch us"—her chin drops a bit—"but he couldn't stop me, so he went along with it to make sure me and Griffin didn't die." I gesture around the room. "Which we didn't. So."

Whatever relief Mom had at seeing us, it's faded from her face by now. There's a storm brewing behind her eyes, and the too-loud news footage of Stone Creek Woods probably isn't helping.

I can hear her putting on that voice—the one that shuts me up real fast—before she even speaks. "I do not understand how any of this could have happened," she starts. Her fingertips press against her temple, as though fending off an impending headache. "I knew about the history of this place, but nothing had happened in years. Jeff said it was safe—"

"It *was* safe!" I object. Despite how my doubts helped the Willoughbys frame Jeff, he was actually the safest thing about Stone Creek. He's dedicated his life and business to making it that way, after all: a place better than the one it was that fateful night he met Meggie in the woods.

Mom releases Griffin, crosses her arms. "Then how did this happen?"

Her eyes scan the room, lingering again on Oliver. He opens his mouth, inhaling softly as he gets ready to explain.

"Why do you keep looking at Oliver?" My voice booms off the room's tiled floors, its plain white walls. I imagine all the neighboring patients' heartbeats spiking, their machines beating in unison. But it's like all the words I've been swallowing back over the years come tumbling out at once, a clogged drain bursting open.

"I'm the one telling the story," I say, "because I'm the one who wanted to rescue Meggie. It was my idea, and there's nothing Oliver could have done to talk me out of it."

Mom runs her hands over her face, smudging what's left of her eyeliner into the bags beneath her lids. "I don't understand," she says again. "Stone Creek has been safe for years, and it sounds like you purposefully went out of your way to change that."

Tears glint at the corners of her eyes. Despite the storm raging in my stomach, it makes my heart clench.

"I know you like to make up games like this when you're playing with Sophie," she says, voice softer, "but this is real, Finley. This is what I was scared about when I called you the other day." She says that part slowly, purposefully, as if this is what she'd expected from me all along. Something wrong, something messy. Something so disappointing only I could manage it. "You could have gotten yourself—or your brothers—seriously hurt."

Of course it's not a game, I think. Because the great Finley Walsh doesn't play games, or make-believe. She goes on real adventures, like the women in her book.

Finley Walsh didn't take on the biggest adventure in Stone Creek because she thought it would be fun. She did it because she knew she could, because she's the bravest and strongest and most triumphant adventurer of all time.

That's what I planned on saying, at least, from the moment I first learned about Meggie. When I saw the news clippings, when I talked to Jeff and Sam and Stu and all the other locals, I knew this was it. This was my chance to prove myself, to show how great and unforgettable and important I could be. Even before that, as we drove into Stone Creek, I was looking for it: neck craned to stare out the window, scanning for an adventure that would let me show Mom what I was worth. No, before that too—when we'd first planned for April break, when I asked Sophie to join me, hoping I could remind her what we had, who we were. Of our greatness.

Everything I did, I did so I could give that speech. But right now the words feel tired, faded like the clippings on the café walls. Jeff told me that he stopped seeing family because he'd run out of things to say. I never run out of words. But all this time I've been using the wrong ones.

"I did all this because I wanted you to look at me, not him," I say. "I thought that if I could find Meggie, that you would trust me more. That you wouldn't keep hiding things from me, and asking Oliver to supervise me, and—"

"Finley, I never mean to hide things from you," she says, a soft shake in her voice, "but you have to realize that when you do things like this—"

"Oliver did it too," I say, waving toward him. "So did Griffin. There's a lot we do when you're not around—"

Her face falls like she's been hit in the gut. I quickly backtrack.

"Which I know isn't your fault," I add in a rush, because as annoying as it is to have her pin Oliver on me, and me on Griffin in a strange circle of supervision, I know she wishes she could be with us on evenings and weekends. I know she wants us, still, even when things aren't perfect. That she chooses to stay even though she doesn't have to.

There was a time I thought parents had to. But I've known that's not true for some time. After Dad left—when he stopped answering calls and stopped holding up to his selected weekends—and now, knowing how things ended between Jeff and his parents all those years ago.

Being a family means showing up again and again and again, especially when it's inconvenient or uncomfortable or hard. It's why Mom reached out to Jeff. It's why he replied. And thinking about it now, I can't help but wonder—for the briefest moment—if by ignoring Sophie's text, I'm making the opposite choice.

"But I want you to take me seriously, like you do Oliver. I know this looks bad"—I gesture weakly around the room: Oliver's injured leg, the bind marks on Griffin's wrists, the scratches all along my limbs—"but we pulled it off. And I needed to do all this because . . ."

The easy words: *Because I'm going to be the World's Greatest Female Adventurer One Hundred One.*

The real words, the ones that rattle in my throat and sting on my tongue and draw salty tears to my eyes: "Because I wanted you to be proud of me for once. For you to look at me."

I duck my head as more tears spill from my eyes. Her heels clack against the tiles as she moves toward me, but I can't see her through the blur of tears.

"It didn't work, anyway," I say, words soggy and unsteady, "because all I've done is prove that I can't be trusted alone. But I still wanted to tell you—"

Her arms wrap around me, tugging me tight to her wool coat. Its fabric scratches my cheeks, but I lean in, grasping on so I'm surrounded by her and the smell of her lavender perfume.

"I never want you to feel like you have to do something like this to get my attention," she says, voice breaking.

"I wanted you to turn to me, like you do for Oliver ever since"—I swallow, searching for the words we never really say out loud—"ever since Dad left." Her grip tightens around me. "He and Griffin can tell you everything I pulled off this week—but that's not the point. The point is . . . I don't want to have to prove myself anymore."

I sink into her arms, like I'm too tired to keep standing upright on my own. And despite all I've said, and all I've done, she grips me close. Tired as she is—from the flight, from the news, from me—she holds on with all her might, ready to support my weight.

I close my eyes and remember I'm safe. That I can say these things—the truth—and not risk losing her. That she, at least, is staying. Here, with me.

I wonder how different everything would be if Meggie had read her note to Mr. Riley instead of leaving it in her wake, a final remnant of herself. They probably would have argued. He probably would have pushed back, told her what was best for her as if he knew better. He denied she wrote the letter for all this time because he refused to believe she'd think that—that any Meggie existed other than the one that lived in his head.

It probably would have been hard for them both. But at least she'd still be here. At least they'd have a chance to fix things.

"I'm not gonna cry," Griffin speaks up, voice slicing through the tension in the room, "but can I have a hug too? Because I also proved I'm pretty tough, and learned how to climb a tree all by myself."

That last part is a big fat lie, but I let it slide. Mom plants a kiss onto the top of my mess of hair, holding me close before we let Griffin in.

"You don't have to prove anything, Finley," she whispers so only I hear. "I'm sorry I ever made you feel like you had to. It's not that I trust your brother more than you, I just—"

She pulls back and cups her hands on my cheeks. It makes me feel like I'm little again, small enough to be held in her hands. But I don't pull back.

"I still see you as my little girl." She smiles softly. "Which you still are. But you're a lot of other things too. I promise to pay more attention to that. Okay?"

As I start to respond, Griffin wedges himself between us. "Stop being a hug hog, okay, Finley?" He nuzzles beneath Mom's arm. "I'm having Malt withdrawals."

I let Griffin hijack my moment. I said all I needed to—and all I'm probably able to—for now, at least. But that's okay, because I know that it doesn't have to end here. Because Mom's not going anywhere, and neither am I.

As I wrap my arms around Griffin and Mom, Oliver waving his arms in objection as they turn to glance at him, I wonder if maybe, after all this is over, I might respond to Sophie's text.

GREATEST FEMALE ADVENTURER NUMBER TWENTY-FIVE: LIZZIE CARR, PADDLEBOARDER, ENVIRONMENTAL ACTIVIST, AND BELIEVER THAT "ADVENTURE ISN'T ALWAYS ABOUT CROSSING REMOTE JUNGLES OR DESERTS, OR SCALING THE HIGHEST MOUNTAINS. IT'S ABOUT RECONNECTING . . . WITH OURSELVES."

Mom pulls the car up to the curb in front of Meggie's Cup, loaded with our bags from Jeff's house. She holds the keys to his home, ready to drop them off before we head out on the long ride back to Massachusetts. The parking lot between the café and the diner is fuller than I've ever seen it. News vehicles are still parked outside the woods, and tourists are trickling back into town to listen to the updates directly from the locals. Bryan Phillips has already updated the diner receipts, so Sam and Jason have their hands full with an influx of customers.

Griffin leaps out of the back seat, running to greet Malt as he bounds down the café's front steps. Jeff follows closely behind, squinting against the morning sun like emerging from a deep sleep.

It's my first time seeing him since he was taken in for questioning. Part of me wants to fly right out of the car and start exchanging stories. Another part of me feels like I weigh a thousand tons, like I'll never be able to lift myself from the comfort of my seat.

Mom steps out, jingling the house keys in the air. "Welp, we're headed out, then."

She extends her arm and Jeff flips his palm, lets her drop the keys into his hand. They just stand, squinting, like they're not sure what comes next. Usually, this would be the part where Mom says how thankful she is for his hospitality, and Jeff would say what a pleasure it was to have us. But none of that quite fits the moment, so they just stand, half grinning in silence.

Thankfully, witnessing this is the final push I need to crawl out from the car. "So what are you going to do with the café now?" I ask. One, because compared to everything else we're probably thinking, it's an easy question. Two, because with Meggie's disappearance explained, I'm not sure where his branding stands.

Jeff tucks his hands into the pockets of his weathered jeans and shrugs his big shoulders. "Guess I'll just keep at it, for now. There're a lot of people in this town I'd be scared to see without their coffee." His eyes dart to the side, toward the diner and beyond, where the street leads to the creek and downtown. "And considering the other options in town, I'm the one thing standing between this place and chaos."

A smile spreads across my cheeks. It feels good to hear Jeff say something positive about himself. It gives me hope that all the guilt that's swallowed him up over the past twenty years has started to lift its hold on him, inch by inch.

"The Rileys' donation is sure to help if you do choose to change things up," Mom says, poking her chin as she speaks. "I thought that was such a kind gesture. Gives you a safety net for when the current rush dies down."

Griffin crinkles his nose. We won't be seeing any of that reward money. The story about two men hiding a car accident, and three kids tackling the truth out of them in the woods, didn't seem to hold the $100,000 glory that the Rileys were expecting. I picture that, in their minds, a young detective—handsome, but haunted by his complicated past—would march into town and, after a muscle-y duel with a sinister kidnapper, return from Stone Creek Woods with Meggie cradled in his arms, gorgeous and brilliant as ever despite literal years locked in an underground bunker. Needless to say, we didn't fit the bill. But the Rileys didn't hoard their cash; they put it back into Stone Creek as a thank-you for everyone who helped to find the truth about Meggie. All the small and independently owned Meggie-themed businesses got a cut, and though Bryan Phillips publicly called it a "macabre marketing ploy," I don't see Jeff complaining.

"Well," Mom says with finality, "I think my kids have

put you through enough. And we have a bit of a drive ahead of us, so . . ."

Jeff glances our way. The three of us stand, shoulder to shoulder, the width of the sidewalk suddenly feeling infinite between us.

Jeff scratches the back of his head, tipping his baseball cap askew. "Malt will miss you all," he says, making eye contact with my sneakers. "He got spoiled with those long walks you'd take him on."

Griffin scratches behind Malt's ear, bouncing him in his arms. "I'll miss him too." As he lowers Malt back down, he turns to Mom. "Can we get a dog when we get home—"

Mom responds through a tight grin. "Nope, no. Sorry. Absolutely not."

She looks pre-tired at the thought. But from the way Griffin's smirking, I know it won't be the end of the conversation.

"You've been a good friend to him, kid," Jeff says, nodding to Griffin. "Why don't you go grab some pastries for the road, huh?"

Mom's eyes go wide and I, too, have horrible flashes of the locked-car sugar rush that's to come. But Griffin runs past him and into the café before we can object.

Oliver crosses his arms tight over his chest and sways on his heels. "I know we weren't easy guests, but . . . thanks for putting up with us, I guess."

Jeff smiles. He leaps down the last steps, closing the

distance between us. Then he pats a hand on Oliver's shoulder.

"Your siblings are lucky to have you," he says. "And I know you'll be missed in Stone Creek."

His gaze flickers toward the diner, fast, so only we notice. Oliver bites his lower lip, resisting a smile.

Then Jeff turns his head toward me. As always, his eyes are never looking quite at me, and I wonder if it's force of habit—if over the years he's been scared they'd tell a truth he wasn't ready for. He was scared he'd meet the wrong person at the wrong time, say and do the wrong thing, not know how to find his way back.

But I look right at him, face bright and smiling. Jeff was the first person to trust me—really trust me—before anyone else. He didn't get mad when I asked questions, didn't shut down when I got too close to the truth. And despite all the ways I messed up—royally, enormously, astronomically messed up—he never blamed me.

And I don't think that's because he's better than the others, or kinder, or more generous. I think it's because we share that part of ourselves, that tiny, silent part that knows the boldest thing we can give one another is forgiveness.

"Next time, we should take a group picture," I say. "Then you can hang it on your wall."

Mom reaches for her purse. "I can take one now if you—"

I shake my head, eyes locked on Jeff. "No. Next time."

Mom smiles, lets her purse drop to her side. I know she wants it too—a second chance at building a family. At choosing people who will choose us back.

Griffin returns with a plastic bag full of sticky cinnamon rolls, and everyone moves toward the car. Just as I go to follow, I run back at the last minute and toss my arms around Jeff, like I've thought about doing so many times before. He's even stiffer than Oliver, like a machine that hasn't been oiled in decades. But I just close my eyes and squeeze tighter, feeling the soft fabric of his flannel against my cheek and inhaling the scent of pine and woods.

"We'll be back," I say. "I promise."

In my grip, I feel his muscles loosen—enough to almost miss, but enough to know they did.

We pile into the car and wave as Mom pulls off in the opposite direction of downtown. We'll be on this road for miles before the next highway—Griffin inhaling his sugar buns, Oliver fiddling with the radio, Mom drumming her fingers on the wheel as we roll over potholes. I settle into the back seat, its gentle cushions embracing me like I'm being welcomed home. My phone rests on my thigh, screen black as we drive.

I tap it. Light illuminates the homepage. I don't have service yet, but I could draft a message if I wanted.

I open my last text from Sophie, then click. The cursor hovers, blinking, waiting for my next move.

Nothing I say will change what's happened. Nothing

I've done here in Stone Creek will reignite the Walsh-Higgins Adventure Agency, or convince Sophie to leave Chloe and Veronica, to be friends with me and only me. Things have changed. We've changed.

But maybe we could still choose each other, even if it is different. Maybe we can still be friends—even if it's not the same. Even if we've kept quiet this long, resentments building and misunderstandings bubbling, pushing and pulling apart as we drift away.

Maybe, still, we can be something new.

The trees blur past, Stone Creek vanishing behind us. I begin to type.